MURDERS IN

STRANGMOOR BOG

A number of very wonderful people helped me prepare this book for publication. Each contributed significantly. Thank you Evie, Andy, Steve, Dave, Jack, Jim, Bette, John, Charity, George, and Gay.

MURDERS

IN

STRANGMOOR BOG

MICHAEL CARRIER

GREENWICH VILLAGE INK

AN IMPRINT OF ALISTAIR RAPIDS PUBLISHING

GRAND RAPIDS, MICHIGAN

Copyright

MURDERS IN STRANGMOOR BOG

Published in 2015 by Greenwich Village Ink, an imprint of Alistair Rapids Publishing, Grand Rapids, MI.

Author can be emailed at mike.jon.carrier@gmail.com. You can follow Michael's tweets at @MikeCarrier999.

ISBN: 978-1-936092-88-8 (trade pbk)
Printed in the United States of America

Library of Congress Cataloging-in-Publication Data

Carrier, Michael.
MURDERS IN STRANGMOOR BOG / by Michael Carrier. 1st ed.
ISBN: 978-1-936092-88-8 (trade pbk. : alk. paper)
1. Hard Boiled Thriller 2. Mystery 3. Thriller 4. Novel 5. Murder 6. Burglary 7. New York. 8. Michigan's Upper Peninsula.

Contents

What people are saying about the "Getting to Know Jack" series

Top Shelf Murder Mystery—Riveting. Being a Murder-Mystery "JUNKIE" this book is definitely a keeper ... can't put it down ... read it again type of book... and it is very precise to the lifestyles in Upper Michigan. Very well researched. I am a resident of this area. His attention to detail is great. I have to rate this book in the same class or better than authors Michael Connelly, James Patterson, and Steve Hamilton. — Shelldrakeshores

Being a Michigan native, I was immediately drawn to this book. Michael Carrier is right in step with his contemporaries James Patterson and David Baldacci. I am anxious to read more of his work. I highly recommend this one! — J. Henningsen

A fast and interesting read. Michael ends each chapter with a hook that makes you want to keep reading. The relationship between father and daughter is compelling. Good book for those who like a quick moving detective story where the characters often break the "rules" for the greater good! I'm looking forward to reading the author's next book. — Flower Lady

Move over Patterson, I now have a new favorite author, Jack and his daughter make a great tag team, great intrigue, and diversions. I have a cabin on Sugar Island and enjoyed the references to the locations. I met the author at Joey's (the real live Joey) coffee shop up on the hill, great writer, good stuff. I don't usually finish a book in the course of a week, but read this one in two sittings so it definitely had my attention. I am looking forward to the next installment. Bravo. — Northland Press

My husband is not a reader— he probably hasn't read a book since his last elementary school book report was due. But ... he took my copy of *Murder on Sugar Island* to deer camp and read the whole thing in two days. After he recommended the book to me, I read it— being the book snob that I am, I thought I had the whole plot figured out within the first few pages, but a few chapters later, I was mystified once again. After that surprise ending, we ordered the other two Getting to Know Jack books. — Erin W.

I enjoyed this book very much. It was very entertaining, and the story unfolded in a believable manner. Jack Handler is a likable character. But you would not like to be on his wrong side. Handler made that very clear in *Jack and the New York Death Mask*. This book (*Murder on Sugar Island*) was the first book in the Getting to Know Jack series that I read. After I read Death Mask, I discovered just how tough Jack Handler really was.

I heard that Carrier is about to come out with another Jack Handler book—a sequel to *Superior Peril*. I will read it the day it becomes available. And I will undoubtedly finish it before I go to bed. If he could write them faster, I would be happy. — Deborah M.

I thoroughly enjoyed this book. I could not turn the pages fast enough. I am not sure it was plausible but I love the characters. I highly recommend this book and look forward to reading more by Michael Carrier. — Amazon Reader

An intense thrill ride!! — Mario

Michael Carrier has knocked it out of the park. — John

Left on the edge of my seat after the last book, I could not wait for the next chapter to unfold and Michael Carrier did not disappoint! I truly feel I know his characters better with each novel and I especially like the can-do/will-do attitude of Jack. Keep up the fine work, Michael, and may your pen never run dry! — SW

The Handlers are at it again, with the action starting on Sugar Island, I am really starting to enjoy the way the father/daughter and now Red are working through the mind of Michael Carrier. The entire family, plus a few more are becoming the reason for the new sheriff's increased body count and antacid intake. The twists and turns we have come to expect are all there and then some. I'm looking for the next installment already. — Northland Press

Finally, there is a new author who will challenge the likes of Michael Connelly and David Baldacci. — Island Books

If you like James Patterson and Michael Connelly, you'll love Michael Carrier. Carrier has proven that he can hang with the best of them. It has all of the great, edge-of-your-seat action and suspense that you'd expect in a good thriller, and it kept me guessing to the very end. Fantastic read with an awesome detective duo—I couldn't put it down! — Katie

Don't read Carrier at the beach or you are sure to get sunburned. I did. I loved the characters. It was so descriptive you feel like you know everyone. Lots of action—always something happening. I love the surprise twists. All my friends are reading it now because I wouldn't talk to them until I finished it so they knew it was good. Carrier is my new favorite author! — Sue

Thoroughly enjoyed this read — kept me turning page after page! Good character development and captivating plot. Had theories but couldn't quite solve the mystery without reading to the end. Highly recommended for readers of all ages. — Terry

If you enjoy this book you should consider reading the other books in this series. And, I would appreciate a short five-star review on Amazon. You can do this by going to this book's page on Amazon. — http://amzn.to/1IEUPxX. It is not necessary to have purchased the book from Amazon, only to have an Amazon account. Thanks, Michael

About Strangmoor Bog

String bogs (the word "strangmoor" actually means "string") are a peculiar type of peat bog. Representing subarctic patterned bog ecosystems, which many experts believe were created by the rapid glacial melt-off, they are characterized by alternating strips of dune highlands and wetlands that run in a terraced fashion along very gradual inclines.

Located in Michigan's central Upper Peninsula, and within Seney National Wildlife Refuge, the ten thousand acres that comprise Strangmoor Bog were designated a National Natural Landmark in 1973. It represents one of the largest undisturbed string bogs in the country.

One of the most fascinating characteristics of peat bogs is that decomposition within them often takes place in slow motion. So, when a body falls into such a bog, whether it is the body of an animal or a human, it can be preserved virtually intact for long periods of time—sometimes for thousands of years.

The Pain

The pain was exponentially greater than before, and it seemed to Jack that it would never end. He could not help but groan in agony. His tormentor, face fixed in a Himmleresque smile, ground the switch vigorously with his thumb as though the added pressure might force more electrical current through Jack's body. And then, just as it seemed Jack would succumb, evil lifted its thumb and abated the torture.

Chapter 1
The squeeze play

(A brief backstory is provided in the *Cast of Characters* at the end of this book.)

Neither Jack nor Kate had actually seen anyone in the parking lot. But it did appear to Jack that what Kate had spotted was a light shining out from beneath his Tahoe, and that they needed to investigate.

Jack silently stepped out of the front door. It faced the river. He was careful not to allow it to shut loudly behind him.

Once outside he stood silently for a moment, waiting for his eyes to adjust to the dark.

Kate slipped out the back door and headed for the driveway entrance. They figured that if someone was tampering with Jack's truck, the culprit would have to escape toward the road or St. Mary's River.

From just outside the door, Jack inventoried the boats tied up at the pier. Not noting anything unexpected, he cautiously made his way toward the river. *Could be one or two men dragged an inflatable up and hid it on shore,* he reasoned, *perhaps someone is even lying in wait in the tall grass.*

But he did not have time to confirm his suspicion.

Within seconds, Jack saw the figure of a man walking rapidly toward him from the direction of the parked Tahoe.

Jack dropped to his haunches. The man had not yet spotted him, and so he was headed directly to where Jack was waiting.

When the man approached to within thirty feet, Jack raised his Glock to a ready-to-fire position and shouted, "Stop right there! I want to see both hands above your head! *Both* hands! Now!"

The man stopped in his tracks and raised his hands over his head.

While Jack did observe that both of the man's hands were empty, he could make out what appeared to be a large black bag strapped over his left shoulder.

"Stay right there!" Jack shouted. "You alone? Or you got friends? Speak up before I drop you!"

"I'm alone," the man said. He was dressed totally in black and was wearing black paint on his face.

"Why don't I believe you?" Jack replied. "Who brought you here?"

"Nobody's with me. I'm alone."

"Still don't believe you," Jack said. "Where's your buddy?"

"I'm tellin' you the truth—I'm alone," the man said, starting to put his hands down.

"Get 'em back up there!" Jack commanded. "Or I'll blow your knee off. … *Do* it!"

The man sensed Jack would do as he threatened, so he immediately thrust his hands back above his head. But as he did he gave away the location of his partner by glancing over Jack's right shoulder toward the St. Mary's River.

Unfortunately, there was no time for Jack to react. Before he could even follow the man's eyes, a loud but muted "pop" pierced the silence behind him. His hand involuntarily released his Glock, and it fell useless to the ground. He watched it tumble in front of him.

He knew immediately what had happened. Someone in the deep grass along the river had fired a round using a suppressor. The bullet caught him under his right arm, which was left exposed by his protective vest.

Jack leaped to his left to avoid additional gunfire, reaching for his calf-holstered Walther .380 as he rolled onto the ground. It was an awkward move, as he had to use his off hand to pull the smaller gun from the holster. He continued scrambling in the grass until he had fully retrieved it.

Handling the Walther with his left hand, Jack rolled to his stomach and clicked off the safety. First he pointed the gun toward the area of the shooter. Seeing nothing, he cranked his body around and surveyed the area where he had last seen the man in black. Still seeing nothing, he turned back to where he suspected the shooter had been.

A few seconds later, Jack heard the sound of an outboard motor. Writhing in pain, he re-engaged the safety on the Walther and then felt around until he found his Glock. Struggling to his feet, Jack momentarily switched the Walther to his right hand, to which some feeling had returned, while he strapped in his Glock.

When he switched the .380 back to his left hand, he saw just how much he was bleeding.

Slowly he walked toward the bank of the river, arriving just in time to see the back end of an inflatable motoring off across the river to the southeast.

Kate had not heard the suppressed shot, so she held her position at the road. Finally, Jack turned and headed toward her.

"Dad," Kate said as he approached. "You okay?"

"I'm going to make it," he said. "So I suppose I'm okay."

"What happened?"

"I had one of them pinned down, but could not determine the location of the second. I must be getting old. I had to assume that there would be a second and that he would be positioned near the river. But the guy from the parking lot came at me from a bad angle—caused me to expose my flank."

"What's wrong?" Kate asked. "What's up with your right hand?"

She had seen that he was carrying his backup pistol in his left and that he was just dangling his right arm.

"I took one. Under my right arm. Not sure how severe it is. Starting to hurt like hell when I try to move it."

"Let me take a look," Kate said as she hurried toward him.

"I don't think you can see much. It entered under my right arm," Jack said. "I'm not about to try to lift it. Need to get it to a hospital, I suppose. I'm going to sit down here. You call Mary and have her pick up the boys for the night."

The "Mary" Jack was referring to was Mary Fletcher. She and her husband Jim were caretakers at Kate's Sugar Island Resort and frequent caregivers for Robby and Red.

"Call for an ambulance?" Kate asked.

"No. Just drive up here and pick me up. It'd be quicker than waiting for the ferry twice. If my senses are not deceiving me, I feel a lot of moistness under my shoulder blade. I think it might have hit a rib and bounced backward. Otherwise, it'd have punctured a lung, and I'd have trouble breathing. At least I *think* that's what happened. Don't know—I'm no doctor. But just hurry and grab the car. *Not* the Tahoe. Who knows what's up with that?"

Kate drove around to where Jack was waiting, and started to get out to open the door for him.

"Stay there—I'm not dead," Jack said, letting himself in the passenger door. "... I'm just hoping the bullet didn't drop out of my clothes. Sure felt like it did exit. Make sure they look for it at the hospital.

"You have your key for the Tahoe?"

"Yeah."

"Well, here's mine," he said, handing her his whole keychain. "Make sure no one tries to start it. Hard telling what that painted man was doing under it."

"*Painted* man? What does that mean?"

"His face was painted black."

"Maybe he was African American."

"No reason to think that," Jack said. "He was dressed totally in black, and it looked to me like he had his face painted.

"Get a bomb squad out here as soon as possible. Those boys were up to no good. Could be something remotely activated. Or maybe it detonates when driven away from a specific location."

"Activates if driven away from a *transmitter* planted at the scene?" Kate asked.

"Could be something like that," Jack said. "And if the battery in the transmitter gets weak, might activate the explosive anyway. Relate those concerns to Sheriff Green … or the FBI. Whoever the hell does the investigation. And make sure Mary gets the boys far away from the resort, and that the sheriff gets on this right away."

"Mary is on her way to pick up the boys right now," Kate said. "I'll call the sheriff."

Just as Sheriff Green answered Kate's call, Jack laid his head back on the seat, winced, and said, "Might be bleeding a bit inside, too. I feel cold. I think I'm going to get a little sleep now."

He then shifted his weight slightly to his left side and collapsed on the center console.

Chapter 2

Several days earlier

It was one of the most naturally uninhabitable places in North America—Strangmoor Bog.

Officially, no one lived there. And, certainly, no census records listed Mr. Russell Lawrence Cox, or anyone else for that matter, as residing in Strangmoor Bog. In fact, not many people aside from the hardiest of deer hunters ever ventured out into the bog, much less attempted to live in it.

At one time in his life Cox would have been able to fit into polite society—some still alive could attest to that. But to judge by his current appearance, Cox certainly looked the part of a *bog dweller*. He paid little attention to personal hygiene, and he often wore clothes that were excessively soiled. It was obvious to anyone who might catch a glimpse of him that he had no interest in pleasing anyone other than himself.

His hair had not seen a pair of real barber shears in decades. Instead, he tied it back in a ponytail that hung well down his back. When it grew to the point that it displeased him—which was usually when it started getting in his way—he would pull it around to the side and cut off the stragglers.

When he first moved into the bog his hair was thick and dark. But as the years wore on, it grew thin and gray.

It was the fourth of August, in 1995, that he first realized he was prematurely morphing into an old man. He had broken his only mirror years earlier, so he had not been able to observe himself save for a dimly lit reflection in a cabin window. But on that memorable day, when he pulled his ponytail around for trimming, he saw that it had turned mostly gray. He was shocked. Immediately he walked outside the cabin to get a better look at it in daylight.

His shock turned to resignation.

From then on he cut his hair on the first Monday of every month. He saved the little sheaves, tied them together using a two-foot length of darning yarn, and then hung the khaki-colored strand of wool from a tack in the wall. Every month he would tie the trimmings onto the thread just below those from the previous month.

Once a year, on the first Monday of August, he would measure off and hang a fresh piece of yarn and start the process over.

Initially, the cuttings of hair were thick and long, with an ample component of dark mixed in. But month after month the gray grew more pronounced, the growth slower, and the hair, what there was of it, appeared finer and sparser.

At first he found the progression discouraging. But recognizing that he could neither stop nor slow it, he steered the whole matter into an arena he could affect—an obsession with documentation.

If a person were to ask Cox why he lived in the bog, he wouldn't answer the question directly. Instead, he would inform his inquisitor that Strangmoor was not actually a true bog. Technically it was a fen.

"Fens," he would explain, "differ from bogs in that they are fed by both groundwater and one or more streams, while bogs rely strictly on groundwater.

"While Strangmoor may have started out as a bog, a massive but failed effort to drain it during the 1890s caused it to evolve into a fen."

And that's all he would say on the topic.

Cox had not always lived in Strangmoor Bog. It was not until the mid-1970s that he, as a man in his early twenties, found, and for fifty dollars purchased, a one-room tarpaper shanty that had served as a hunting cabin for a group of deer hunters from the Lower Peninsula.

The shanty had no running water and no electricity. Cox had a single oil lamp, and it served as his only source of light during the long winter months. However, he seldom lit the wick. When it got too dark to see, he went to bed.

During the summer, he relied totally on the sun for light.

The cabin had originally been built to serve the needs of loggers during the late 1800s. But, unlike most structures built in bogs, it was fairly substantial. Those who constructed it had found one of the most desirable spots within the northeast section of the bog on which to build. Not only was this strip of dune substantial enough to support foundation stones, it rose sufficiently above its surroundings to provide root structure for a fairly large number of evergreen trees—something that did not happen in most other parts of Strangmoor Bog.

And, thanks to the heavier growth of trees and brush surrounding it, the cabin was barely visible to anyone who was not specifically looking for it. That suited Cox just fine. He relished his privacy.

Driggs River ran just north of the cabin, and it was from where that stream drains into the Manistique River that Cox obtained his water. When he first moved into the bog he boiled all of his drinking water. But eventually he built up his immune system to the point that except for times when the water level dropped, which elevated the level of microbes within it, he was able to drink straight from the river.

During the forty-plus years that he had lived there he made virtually no changes to the cabin. Fortunately, the hunters before him had insulated the walls and ceiling with fiberglass batting and had installed a one-half-inch layer of plywood to the entire inside of the cabin—walls and ceiling.

This made it much easier to heat during the long northern winters.

His home's decor was Spartan, consisting mostly of various types of wall hangings—some utilitarian, others decorative. Listed among the former were several dozen steel leg traps—Oneida Victor single and double spring. They alone occupied a sizable section of the rear wall. During trapping season, all of them would be in use. But from spring through fall, Cox just hung them on his wall. Periodically he would pull one or two of them off the wall and examine them to be certain that surface rust would not inhibit their functioning properly.

Cox didn't trap bear. He used his traps exclusively for muskrat, mink, and beaver. Of course, he occasionally ended up with a raccoon. But it was never his intent to trap raccoons because their pelts did not sell for as much as those of the other animals.

In winter, when the traps would all be in use, Cox would hang in their place on the wall dozens of hand-shaped boards containing fur pelts.

Because of the smell, described by some as "bad enough to sick a dog off a gut wagon," most trappers would hang their pelts in an outbuilding to dry. But Cox didn't mind the stench at all. To him, it smelled like money. And besides, he didn't have any other place to dry them.

Other wall hangings included the aforementioned strings of dated hair trimmings, numerous hunting knives, fishing gear, and the clothing he needed on a daily basis.

Because he had no closet, and therefore no place to store his outerwear, winter coats were hung alongside his summer jackets.

His winter hat and scarf hung on nails along with pots, pans, and various handcrafted kitchen utensils.

Just to the left of the front door Cox had tied up to dry several different types of plant leaves, which he used to make tea.

Hanging beside the drying plants were three fairly large ginseng roots.

Those he had dug from a secret location in a nearby hardwood forest. Even though federal law now prohibited the harvesting of ginseng, Cox was still known to occasionally gather and sell the rare elixir when he needed the money.

His only other wall hanging was a yellowed photograph of a young man. It was creased at the corners, suggesting that before it had been thumbtacked to the wall it might have been shuffled around in a junk drawer, or perhaps carried in a billfold. While with its deckled edges it was slightly larger than a typical high school picture, it was still small enough to fit in a wallet. It had no writing on it.

A small white teakettle was always at the ready on the wood stove.

Most of his mugs and plates were of chipped and rusted blue enamelware, all probably retrieved from the area's secluded trash piles after having been tossed away by cabin owners from the Manistique Lakes area. While Cox did not venture out of the bog very often, when he did have to replenish his cupboards he would always scour the roadsides and area dumping grounds for what he considered "golden nuggets."

A hoarder by no means, Cox did have a keen eye for discarded items that he thought might prove useful to him.

For instance, the previous year while riding his bike along River Road by M-77, on his way to Curtis, he spotted a braided rug lying a dozen feet off the road. He quickly recalled that there had been no recent rainstorms, and, therefore, the rug might not be seriously damaged from moisture. He jumped off his bike and unrolled enough of it to make a better assessment. It looked fine to him.

He realized that the only way he'd be able to transport the fifty-pound rug back to his cabin would be to cradle it on the bike seat and handlebars, and then to push the bike west on River Road. Once the going got tough, he would ditch his bike and carry the rug over his shoulder the rest of the way.

Of course, for him to return home with the rug would mean that the trip to Curtis would have to wait for another day. That was a tradeoff Cox was willing to make.

So that's what he did. He balanced the rug on his bike and wheeled it back toward his cabin. When he reached the point where he had to ford Diggs River, he hoisted the fifty-pound rug over his shoulder and walked it back through the bog.

Even though no person other than Cox himself had ever witnessed how nice that braided wool rug looked on his rough-cut pine-board floor, or how well it blocked the cold from coming through it, he could not have been prouder of his find.

This year he was looking forward to possibly picking up something to cover his bare windows and perhaps another blanket or two. His bed linens had not been replaced in the past twelve or fifteen years. He had two sets of sheets, and every few months he'd switch them out. Eventually he'd wash the dirty bedding. When he did, if it were summer he'd pin the clean laundry outside on a clothesline. But in the winter he would hang it over a clothesline he'd stretched behind the wood stove. And there it'd remain until needed—perhaps for months at a time.

He knew very well that if he were ever to have curtains or some new bedding, he would need to buy them. So he was gearing up for an ambitious trapping season over the winter. That's why he was tuning up his traps and carving new stretching boards.

Most trappers used stainless steel spring stretchers for their pelts. But Cox did not have the means to buy the expensive manufactured products. Besides, carving boards to accommodate various sized furs gave him something to do during the long summer evenings.

Every spring he would apply pine pitch to any portion of the roof that he thought needed it. Only once did he replace the tarpaper on the roof. That was in 1992. He saved up the money he'd earned trapping beavers and muskrats for the previous three years, and sold their pelts to pay for the new stone-coated roll roofing material. It was fern green. Cox was very pleased with the appearance of the cabin, largely because of its "new" green roof.

Aside from the money he needed for necessities such as major roof repairs, an occasional pair of winter boots, waders, overalls, a warm coat, and food staples, Cox did not engage in typical commercial activities. That is to say, apart from his trapping and special sale of a little clandestine ginseng from time to time, he didn't have a regular source of income.

While he didn't drink alcohol, were a person to ask him he would immediately admit that he did have one vice—he enjoyed fine cigars.

So, whenever he would have to go into town to buy food or other provisions, if he had received what he considered to be a good price for his fur pelts, he would always treat himself by buying two or three good quality cigars. To preserve their freshness, he would store the cigars in Xikar aluminum tubes.

But even though Cox did not have a regular job, he did keep busy—*very* busy. And what kept him so very occupied had little to do with his trap lines.

Every morning he would rise before the sun, don his boots and appropriate seasonal clothing, and make his way up and down the terraces of the string bog.

He carried a large hand-carved ironwood walking stick to help him keep his balance. Simply walking through Strangmoor was not an easy task all by itself. Sometimes the flow of water through the bog would rise considerably—usually the result of substantial rainfall or dams caused by beavers or accumulated brush. When this happened, and it often did, he would be forced to temporarily change his route.

But as soon as it was possible, Cox would always come back to his original walking pattern—even if it meant wearing waders.

Russell Lawrence Cox would use his walking stick to poke and prod at the spongy peat that comprised almost the entire bog. He was obviously looking for something. But only he knew what that something was.

Chapter 3
The Red and Robby expedition

It would take Red and Robby just under four hours to hike in from where Jack dropped them off on the Creighton Truck Trail to a point less than half a mile into the southern portion of Strangmoor Bog. That was the plan.

"4 hrs in," Red frequently texted Robby during the planning stage, "2 hrs there & 4 hrs back out. Easy."

Neither Jack nor Kate had prompted the boys to take on this adventure. It was totally initiated by Red.

As he anticipated, Red had found it easy to convince Robby to join him in the adventure. All he had to do was to show his friend a picture of the area, and Robby was ready.

Convincing Jack and Kate had not been so easy. When Red and Robby first presented the idea to their guardians, both Jack and Kate were skeptical.

But, as always, the boys were tenacious. They had an answer for every question.

Red and Robby had carefully selected the time and setting to broach the topic with Jack and Kate. They selected to formally present their idea right after dinner, the night before they intended to go.

The reason they chose that night was so there'd be little time for mind changing. All they had to do was to sell the idea and then get dropped off the next morning. It went almost exactly according to plan.

"Write us a proposal," Jack finally told Red, after Robby had spent several minutes articulating their intentions. "Explain to us *exactly* why you think this hike is a good idea, what you want to accomplish, and how long you anticipate it will take. And then we will consider it."

"I've heard about that section of Seney," Kate added. "Do you have any idea just how impassable that bog is? There's really no good way to penetrate it. There are no trails. Put that in the proposal as well—exactly *how* you intend to pull this off. The logistics. Do you plan to camp out for a night? What sort of equipment will you need? Can you assure me that you will be safe? Have any kids your age ever done this before? And, exactly why do you guys think you should attempt this? Is there a point—a purpose—to the whole thing?"

* * *

Red and Robby had become best friends during the past year. In fact, they were more than best friends. They were like twin brothers.

They were almost exactly the same age—fourteen years, ten months. Both had lost their parents. And both had found a loving home under the roof of the Handlers.

Kate had actually become the legal guardian for Red. That placement was a no-brainer for the county, because the boy was not only orphaned, but he turned out to be the son of Jack's brother-in-law, Alex Garos, the original owner of the Sugar Island Resort.

When Garos was murdered, Kate learned that he had left the resort to her in his will. Red, who was the love child of Garos and one of his employees, had spent most of his days at the resort after his mother was killed in a gas explosion. Child Protective Services had experienced so many run-ins with Red through the years that they were eager to sign off on any program that had a chance of working. The placement with Jack and Kate worked perfectly for all concerned.

Red and Robby had become friends at a Maritime Camp a little over a year earlier. Robby's parents were both murdered, leaving the boy without family. It just seemed natural for Robby to move in with the Handlers, which is what he did.

However, Robby's living arrangement with the Handlers was not as settled as it was for Red. But the Handlers did make the resort their permanent home—at least it was the established residence for Jack and Red. And Robby was very happy living with them at the resort. Those facts, taken together with the way things are sometimes done on Sugar Island, made the situation workable. Authorities were willing to turn a blind eye to the fact that there was no official court order authorizing the placement of Robby with the Handlers.

Of course, it helped that the school accepted Robby without question.

Kate had a way of putting it succinctly: "Sometimes things just work out for the best when civil authority simply allows good people to solve their own issues."

When Jack heard her say this the first time he laughed out loud.

"I can't believe that radical shit is coming out of your mouth," he said. "Aren't you just the perfect example of a New York City homicide detective? … I guess you really are my daughter after all."

Both boys had winning personalities. Of course, Red could not express himself verbally. So when necessary, Robby, who was gifted with extraordinary communication skills, would do the talking for both boys.

Red complemented his friend. He was the planner and project manager. And, he could fight. Together they presented a formidable "against all odds" team.

* * *

Of course, both boys knew that Jack and Kate could not be intimidated, nor would they allow the wool to be pulled over their eyes.

The boys understood that if they were going to have their plans for the Strangmoor Bog expedition approved, they would have to present a convincing case to support it. They had carefully planned their strategy and had it all laid out in a single-page Word document.

In fact, they had spent the better part of two weeks developing the plan. Completing it just the night before, they reworded it several times to make it concise and then printed four copies—one for each of them and separate copies for Jack and Kate. The boys were prepared.

Red motioned that they all sit down at the kitchen table, which they did. And then he slid the four sheets out of a file folder, gave a copy to each of them, and kept one for himself.

Chapter 4

The proposal

Task: To gather soil samples from the parallel strips of dune highland and wetland—from more than one of each, time permitting.

Purpose: To obtain the Boy Scout "Geology" Merit Badge.

Logistics: Leave Sugar Island at 5 a.m. Wednesday morning. Head west on M-28. Go through Seney to Creighton Truck Trail. Turn south about 7.5 miles to the Highwater Truck Trail. Drop us off there.

We will then hike approximately 1.5 miles along the Highwater Truck Trail to a place close to where we can ford Duck Creek. We will then hike approx. three miles northeast and enter the Strangmoor Bog, and then another two miles to the part of the bog our scout leader wants us to test. The marsh areas will present a challenge, but the aerial maps we have copied should be helpful. We have several.

Basic equipment needed: Waders, strong walking sticks, drinking water, mosquito nets (for our heads), oatmeal bars, first-aid kit, flashlights, compass (2), Garmin, various maps, knives, gloves, and cell phones. We will also bring sleeping bags—just in case.

Tools: AMS Core Sampling System, strapped storage bags to transport samples, and permanent markers.

We expect to exit the bog about 5 p.m. We will call when we reach Highwater Truck Trail, or as soon as we can access a cell tower.

Chapter 5
Adult reaction

"You mean that's *it*?" Kate inquired. "That's all you'll need for your adventure? I was thinking that a last will and testament might be in order. I've heard about Strangmoor Bog. It is rough terrain. *Very* rough."

"It is for sure," Robby agreed. "But we will have GPS. And cell phones. If we run into something, we can call you and you can rescue us."

Jack laughed. "Right! Can't you just see me wading through two feet of marsh? If anything, we'd come in with a helicopter. That is if we even *tried* to rescue you. I suggest you take food and water for a few days. Maybe a week's worth."

Kate glared at her father. "Your Uncle Jack is kidding. Of course, we'd get you out. Not sure exactly how we'd go about it. But we'd find a way. If we had to send in a chopper, it'd cost you a few thousand dollars. Probably *much* more than a few. So you'd better think this through."

"Look at the expression on those two faces," Jack added. "Do they look like they haven't thought this through?"

"Where are you going to get the tools?" Kate continued, listening but not responding to her father's question. "You're going to need some specialized tools. Right? Where are you going to find them?"

"Mr. Idestam," Robby replied, almost interrupting. "Mr. Idestam, our scout leader, he has connections with Michigan Tech, and he's already got us all the equipment we will need, and it won't cost a penny."

"Where?" Kate asked. "You already have the equipment?"

"Sure do," Robby said. "It's in our room. Plus, Mr. Idestam said his friends will analyze our findings … at no charge. They've done some work there themselves, and they do not have a problem with helping us."

"He teaches at the college, doesn't he?" Jack asked. "I *think* Harry teaches there. Or at least has some affiliation with the school."

"I think so too," Robby replied. "But I don't know for sure. His business card says he is some sort of 'consultant.'"

"And what does Harry think about this adventure of yours?" Jack asked.

"We suggested it," Robby replied. "And he had some concerns. That's what he called them—concerns. But he said if we could convince you and Kate, he'd accept the work for the merit badge. That is, if we did a good job. But he is going to need you to sign a paper—a permission sheet."

"I'm sure he does," Kate kicked in, as she accepted the one-sentence document that Harry Idestam had prepared.

She looked at it briefly and slid it over to Jack.

Jack pretended to be studying the short note, but actually he was just thinking, *I wonder how long it will take the boys to convince Kate?*

From experience Jack knew that once the boys had made up their minds to do something, it was virtually a *fait accompli,* as far as Kate was concerned. And it was totally obvious to him that they were determined.

Jack smiled as Kate continued.

"But so soon!" she said. "Why do you have to do this so soon? Don't you think it would be wise to consider it more carefully?"

"Kate," Jack said. "They've been planning this for weeks. They have made up their minds. I'll give Harry a call yet this evening and get his opinion. This is obviously not a spur-of-the-moment project. If Harry is convinced that these two characters are capable of pulling this off, then we should let them do it. I just know that I do not intend to drag my bones out into that godforsaken swamp—"

"Bog," Robby interrupted. "Technically. It is a string bog. That's different from an ordinary swamp."

"Right," Jack replied. "And Strangmoor Bog is one of the best in the world. In fact, I think it has received national recognition as such."

"It's a swamp," Kate countered. "I don't care about all that technical terminology. From what I've heard about it, it's a glorified swamp."

"The government declared it a National Natural Landmark," Robby said. "It is the best-preserved string bog in the lower forty-eight states. That makes it pretty special."

"Doesn't the federal government frown on trespassers? Particularly into one of their *special* swamps?" Kate asked, serving the conversation as the devil's advocate.

"I can answer that," Jack said. "The NNL Program is a *voluntary* agreement between a property owner and the federal government. If the Seney Wildlife Preserve does not have a problem with allowing public access to the site, the government doesn't either."

And then, turning his attention back to the boys, he asked, "I trust you have permission?"

""Mr. Idestam said it would be okay," Robby said. "He talked to some people. We'll gather two core samples—in a section he has not yet tested."

"Red," Kate said, turning to Robby's silent partner. "What do you think?"

Red keyed into his phone, "Im up 4 it."

Kate finally just leaned back in her chair and smiled.

"I can see that I'm outnumbered here," she said. "My father and I will discuss this further. And then we'll let you know what we decide. After Dad has had a chance to talk to your scout leader, of course."

The boys knew that the meeting was over and that they had prevailed.

Chapter 6

Boots on the soft, wet ground

"What do you think, Red?" Robby asked. "Is this about where we enter?"

Red checked his GPS and then shrugged his shoulders.

The coordinates were what they were looking for—46.199353,-86.182116. But the terrain leading off to the north did not look at all welcoming—certainly not as inviting as it did on Google Earth.

Red did a 360 but saw nothing that he thought matched the satellite image. Everything was overgrown. The grassy areas around him were dry and golden-colored, with a verdant mossy mat spreading beneath. For just a short moment, his mind was drawn to something he had just read about bogs: "Certain types of carnivorous plants can thrive on the peat moss that makes up a bog."

He was consumed by that thought until Robby began to talk.

"This looks like the trail we saw on the map," Robby said, pointing to the northwest.

"According to the Google Satellite image, there should be a little path leading off the Highwater Truck Trail. It should meet up with Duck Creek after about five hundred feet.

"Once we hit Duck Creek, we would follow it to a point just downstream from a substantial pool of water. That would be 46.200912,-86.180142. Google imaging looked promising for an almost dry crossing right about there. But this terrain changes all the time.

"And then, once we get across Duck Creek, we should have a relatively clear path north. And from there it's a couple miles or so until we enter the main section of the bog. And then one more water hazard ... west of Marsh Creek. Is that how you see it?"

Red nodded his agreement.

"But I have to say," Robby began, "that this is a little rougher hiking than I was expecting."

He usually knew better than to complain.

Red frowned briefly at Robby's comment and held out his Garmin like it was King Richard III's Dragon Banner.

Robby could see his friend's determination pouring from his re-energized body. For a moment, Robby simply stopped to admire.

Red's waders were too large for him. The legs were drawn up tightly to his crotch by the cinched-up shoulder straps, yet the legs still folded in several places.

With a plastic-bag-encased Garmin in one hand, a physical map (also enclosed in a plastic bag) duct-taped around his left forearm, and using a four-foot-long sturdy ironwood walking stick to help keep his balance, Red trudged through the knee-deep mush like a man on a mission.

Although always seeking out the drier terrain, still he was repeatedly forced to backtrack.

Red checked his Garmin—46.199101, -86.177095.

He stopped and looked back to make sure Robby was still following. He quickly spotted his friend, and they exchanged smiles.

But just then, over Red's shoulder, but probably a hundred feet deeper into the bog, Robby caught a brief glimpse of something moving.

"Holy sh ... cow!" Robby shouted. "Did you see that?"

Chapter 7

Time to break out the tools

When Robby reached his friend, Red gave him a wide-eyed expression that Robby had come to recognize.

"I don't know what I saw," he said, pointing in the direction of the movement. "It looked like someone was watching us—some *old* guy. I thought I saw eyes looking at us. But, I suppose it couldn't have been. It's just that I've had that feeling ever since we crossed the stream. It's like we have company out here."

Red turned to the direction his friend was pointing and then looked back at Robby and delivered his palms-up nonplussed gesture. Red then began fiddling with the straps on his backpack.

After what seemed an eternity to Robby, he noticed Red slowing. "Is this it?" he asked, standing only a few yards behind his friend. "Is this where we are going to take the first sample?"

Red, pleased that his friend had kept up with him—especially through the large stream—smiled as he slipped off his backpack, tossed it into the limbs of a small pine tree, and detached the heavy AMS Signature slide hammer. That unit alone weighed over ten pounds.

Resisting the urge to eat an energy bar, Red attached the auger device to the cross-handle tool. This would allow him to cut through the first inches of surface soil before using the driver to pierce through the portion he wanted to sample.

Robby also slid off his backpack. He hung his on a higher pine branch, as though to prevent it from being swallowed up by the bog. He removed two bottles of water, uncapped them both, and handed one to Red.

After gulping down nearly the whole bottle, Red handed his back to Robby, who re-capped it and tucked it into Red's backpack.

Red spun the auger several times, cutting to a depth of four inches. He then removed the auger and prepared the driving hammer.

The boys had already inserted the plastic soil core liner into the split soil core sampler. So, aside from screwing the collection device onto the end of the hammer, no additional preparation was necessary—at least for the first sample.

Red carefully slid the collection end into the auger hole, cautious as possible not to drag soil or debris into the hole as he did it.

Once the assembly rested on the bottom, he raised the weight on the driving hammer and brought it down with moderate force.

His first effort forced the device about one inch into the soil.

The plan devised with Harry, the scout leader, and Robby was to obtain a two-inch-by-twelve-inch core sample, beginning at a depth of four inches.

The second time he drove the hammer down, he did it with more force. This time he forced it to a depth of six inches.

The boys had wrapped the sampling device with a piece of black duct tape at sixteen inches. Using the tape as a guide, they would know to stop driving when their marker was even with the surface.

After a few more drives, Red stopped to examine the position of the tape.

Robby, dropping to his knees, also checked it out. "Two more strikes, wouldn't you say?" he suggested.

Red didn't respond audibly; he simply stood erect and landed two more blows.

Robby, still on his knees, said, "Give it one more. Maybe a little softer. Looks like we might want it just a *little* deeper."

Red raised the hammer and delivered one more firm blow.

"Perfect," Robby said. "Let's pull it out. Be careful not to lose it. Maybe drop it to the side a bit to keep the sample in the tube. Hard to tell just how wet that sample might be. It might want to just slide right back out."

Chapter 8
Sample two—moving on

Red carefully lifted the hammer assembly out of the hole, lowered the handle to horizontal, and unscrewed the split soil core sampler. He slid the transparent liner out and capped it—the red plastic cap on the shallow end and the blue on the deep end.

The sample was moist, but it held up well in the sample cylinder. They pulled one of the red permanent markers from Robby's backpack and labeled it with a number one.

"Great job!" Robby applauded. "You nailed it. Absolutely *nailed* it. Now, let's see if you can do it again."

Red smiled at Robby as he inserted a fresh plastic cylinder into the tool.

The two boys then walked down a slight incline. That brought them to the strip of wetland directly below the dune where they had obtained their first core sample.

They waded out into the moist sediment and basically repeated the process they had executed earlier.

First, they augered down about four inches. In addition to stagnant water, this time they had rotting limbs and other debris to deal with. Still, Red did his best to clear out the initial four inches.

"I don't think you're going to get it any cleaner than that," Robby advised. "I'd say give it a shot and see what we get. If we don't like it, we can move a few feet over and try it again."

Red seemed to agree with his friend's assessment, so he dropped the core sampler into the hole and pushed it downward without using the hammer.

The tool slid easily through nearly five inches of the wet soil, and then it stopped abruptly. The boys looked at each other, and Red gave it another shove, still not using the hammer. But it did not sink much deeper.

Robby checked the duct tape marker.

"We need another eight inches," he said. "Maybe you should use the hammer."

Red raised the slide hammer and rendered a sharp blow.

The sampler pushed past or through the obstruction.

Robby checked the tape again.

"We still need another two inches," he said.

This time Red just gave the tool a stiff push. It sank about an inch. He did it again and forced the tool nearly another inch.

"Just a hair more," Robby said. "Less than an inch will be perfect."

Red even more gently pushed downward.

"Perfect," Robby said. "Do you think we can pull it out without losing the sample? I'll bet it's pretty wet."

Red did not pull the tool directly out. Instead, he laid it on its side and lifted the business end upward. Sludge dripped from the tool, but the sample appeared to remain pretty much intact.

Carefully, Red unscrewed the cylinder from the tool and capped the shallow end with the red plastic cap, and then capped the deep end with the blue.

"Success again!" Robby announced. "Red, are you the rock star, or what?"

Red just smiled as he wiped the transparent cylinder with a rag.

But as he cleared off the excess moisture and mud, his jaw dropped.

Chapter 9
Surprise! Horror!

Robby could not yet see what it was that so captured Red's attention.

Red wiped the plastic liner off again and scrutinized it even more closely. And then he handed it to Robby.

"Whatcha got here?" Robby asked, examining it with keen interest. He turned it in his hands to get a better look.

Robby studied it for a long moment and then said, "I think that's a gold ring! It looks like the edge of a gold wedding ring." He stood and held it in front of Red.

"And I can guess what that sliver of brownish white next to it is," Robby continued. "Care to make a guess?"

Red already knew what his friend was talking about. Next to the ring was the jagged edge of something sharp and deeply yellowed. It did not look like a twig. Instead, both boys assumed that it was a piece of a fractured finger bone.

"We've got to call Jack and Kate right now," Robby said, hurriedly pulling out his cell. "I sure hope we've got service here."

First he had to turn his phone on. The boys knew from experience that if they kept their cell phones switched on for extended periods of time in an area with spotty coverage they would run the risk of depleting the batteries. So, in situations such as this, where an emergency might dictate the need to communicate, they would turn at least one of the cell phones off to preserve battery.

In this case, they both had shut down their cells.

"None," Robby said. "I don't have coverage right here. See if you do."

Red's smartphone was exactly like Robby's, but he went through the exercise anyway.

Robby, looking over Red's shoulder, finally said, "Neither one of us has cell right now. We should record the coordinates and leave a marker so we can come back to this exact spot. More than likely there's a whole body down there, and the cops are going to want to bring it out."

Red was already thinking the same thing. He had tied the cloth he had used to clean off the sample liner onto the end of his walking stick, and then he pushed the other end of the stick into the sample hole.

Even though they knew their Garmin would record the location of the samples they had taken, Red thought it a good idea to physically mark the exact location where they had discovered the ring as a backup.

"That'll do it," Robby said. "Here. Take my stick. You're gonna need it more than me. I'll find another one."

Red held his phone so Robby could read a message he was feigning to text: "Thnk. Garmin wll get us out. I go first."

That made sense to Robby. Because Red had led the way into the bog using GPS, both agreed that he was best suited to get them out.

It took the boys only a few minutes to pack their gear.

"Water," Robby advised. "It's a long hike back. Rough going. We don't want to dehydrate."

Both boys guzzled down the contents of their water bottles. And then Robby had an idea.

Pulling out his Swiss Army knife, he cut off the cap end of his bottle and slid the bottom of it over the end of the stick above the flag.

"That might show up even better when the cops close in."

Red nodded his approval.

It was well into the afternoon of this late summer day. The trip in, while it was uneventful, took longer than they had anticipated. The sun would soon be sliding behind the trees, so they knew they had better get moving.

Chapter 10

Finding their way back

Initially, they had planned to reach their destination, take the samples, and then start heading back—all by two p.m.

It was now after four.

The hike into the bog turned out to be more difficult than they had planned. They knew they would have good light until at least eight. So that meant they would need to hurry.

While the 2,000-point tracklog function of their Garmin made retracing their steps simple, it was anything but easy.

For one thing, they were tired—more so than they had anticipated.

They had known that the hike would be a tough one. But they had encountered more running and pooled water than they had expected.

The waders helped. But a few well-placed bridges would have been even better.

Again, the toughest fording was over the western tributary of Marsh Creek. While just as they had on the hike into the bog, they found a handy narrowing of the creek twenty yards below a beaver dam, still the task was made difficult because the water was deep and fast moving—perhaps due to recent rainfall.

Even though the water was slightly above their waists, it had not posed a problem for their equipment on their way in.

They had hoped for, and expected, the same level of success for the hike back.

However, just as Red reached the middle of the creek, his left foot broke through the rotting branches that lay at the bottom, and he was immediately thrown off balance.

The Garmin, instrumental to finding his way out of the bog, went flying.

Unable to verbally alert Robby that he had lost the Garmin, Red simply shouted as best he could.

Robby interpreted the excited cry as indicating that his friend needed help to regain his balance.

It was a very precarious situation for Red. Struggling to pull his foot out of the tangle of decaying branches, he was barely able to keep the water from running over the top of his waders by using the hiking stick to keep himself upright.

Robby took several quick steps toward his friend, put his right hand under Red's arm, and attempted to help him shift his foot to a more secure position.

All the while Red was pointing toward the Ziploc bag containing his Garmin, which was floating downstream.

When Jack originally bought the device, he also purchased the foam rubber protective cover. It was designed to help keep rain and weather out, but also to protect it from being damaged if dropped.

Kate took it a step further. She enclosed the Garmin in a one-quart Ziploc bag.

Therefore, when the Garmin went flying out of Red's hand and into the creek, it drifted downstream like a fishnet float.

Realizing that he was not going to be able to communicate the loss of the Garmin to Robby, Red turned his attention back to freeing his foot.

No matter how hard Red tried to pull his foot out of the tangled web of branches at the bottom of the creek, he could not. One of the sticks that had broken under his weight jabbed into his wader whenever he tried pulling his foot upward past it.

Robby was not aware of the extent to which Red's foot was caught. To him, it appeared that his friend's foot might be just stuck in mud, while in reality it was wedged in more like the foot of a bear in a steel trap. If he had been able to physically observe the problem, he might have been able to exert pressure on the offending branch and push it down far enough to allow Red to remove his foot.

Red recognized the problem but could not communicate effectively just how his foot was trapped. He thought there was a chance that if the boys both steadily pulled upward, perhaps the branch would snap and he could escape.

Instead, when both boys exerted maximum upward effort, the branch pierced the wader and stabbed deeply into Red's foot.

The pain was excruciating.

Red screamed as only he could scream. Robby got the message and ceased lifting under his friend's arm.

Even though he was in immense pain, Red was finally able to communicate to Robby that he had lost the Garmin.

For several moments, the two boys searched the stream with their eyes. But both knew that it was no use. They recognized as fact that even if they were able to catch a glimpse of the Garmin floating downstream, the immense overgrowth of sphagnum on both sides of the creek would totally obscure the device from their view if they attempted to approach it from the bank. Slowly it sunk in—they would not be able to retrieve it. That meant they would have to find their way out of the bog without benefit of the Garmin.

Resolving himself to the reality of the situation, Red pulled his cell phone out of his backpack and feigned another text: "Stick poked thru boot and into foot. HURTS BAD. Must leave Garmin." His hands were shaking so badly from the pain he could barely hang on to his phone.

Robby read the message over Red's shoulder as he wrote it.

"Ouch!" Robby said in sympathy. "Do you think it broke the skin?"

Red nodded.

Robby then felt around with his foot until he touched the right branch.

Red nodded and grimaced in pain, signaling that Robby had found the stick that had penetrated his waders.

The impaling branch was under nearly three feet of cold, muddy water. But Robby knew what he had to do.

He stood straight up and closed his eyes. After taking five very deep breaths, he immersed the upper part of his body into the creek. Using his right hand to grasp underwater sticks and debris, he pulled himself deep below the surface.

He ran his left hand along the outside of Red's wader until he found where the stick penetrated it. He then felt around with both hands until he located the same stick nearly two feet from Red's foot. And then, pushing downward on the stick close to Red's foot, he jerked up sharply on the other end of it, snapping it in two.

He was then able to remove it from Red's foot.

Robby popped his head out of the disgusting dark brown water, eyes still closed but proudly holding the arrow-sharp stick above his head.

He tossed it away and began wiping the mud and water from his eyes.

With the stick removed, Red was able to pull his foot out of the hole, and hobble to the other side of the creek. Limping badly, he fell forward and virtually crawled up on the bank.

From there the two boys slowly made their way to a fallen tree. Red flung off his backpack and hung it on a broken limb. He then unhooked the straps on his waders, sat down on the tree trunk, and slipped them off.

He raised the waders upside-down and poured out nearly a quart of bloody water.

Robby stood speechless.

Red then carefully stripped off his badly stained sock.

Both boys were shocked to see the severity of the injury.

The stick had penetrated the waders midway up the top of the foot. And then, sliding down Red's foot to a point just inside the large metatarsal, it not only punctured the flesh, it speared its way through his foot until it caused the skin on the sole to bulge midway down the proximal phalange. But it did not break through the skin on the bottom of his foot.

Unfortunately, at some point during the ordeal the tip of the stick had broken off inside Red's foot. The boys could see the dent it was making on the bottom of his foot, but none of it remained above the surface on the top, so there was not a way for them to pull it out.

"There's nothing to get a grip on," Robby said with a very serious expression on his face. "I'm no doctor, but I can see that we've got to get you to one. This is going to require surgery."

While there was no longer much bleeding, significant swelling was already beginning to set in. It was clear to both boys that not only did Red need medical help, but he would not be able to put any weight whatsoever on the injured foot.

So, rather than attempt to rescue the Garmin, they determined their best option would be to forge ahead without it. They did, after all, have a compass. And they knew the general direction they had to hike to make it back to Highwater Truck Trail, and then eventually to Creighton Truck Trail.

With great pain, Red eased his waders back on, while Robby pulled his waders off to empty them of the muddy water that had filled them when he went underwater to free Red's foot. Robby then put his waders back on.

They figured that somewhere along the way they would regain cell service. Not wishing to drain both cells unnecessarily, they decided to keep only one of the units on at a time. That way they could monitor tower strength without draining both batteries. Once they achieved a good connection, they would make their call to Jack.

But, if the battery became exhausted on the cell they were using, they would still have one in reserve.

They momentarily turned both cell phones on to test for tower strength. Neither cell indicated any signal reaching them.

They then compared battery strength. Because Robby's cell indicated ninety percent, and Red's only seventy, they selected to leave only Robby's cell on.

"This is how I suggest we do this," Robby said. "We take it a little at a time. As far as we can go. And then rest. As soon as we can get a few bars on a cell, we hold up and try to reach Jack. Jack's our best bet. He needs to know that we no longer have a Garmin. And that you're injured. I'm pretty sure he can track our cells. But first we're gonna have to get to a place where we have some signal. Once we can call him, we'll probably want to stay put and let him come to us."

Red nodded his approval of Robby's plan, but his face told a different story. It had grown pale, with muddied droplets of pain streaking down it. And everywhere Red had touched his face, his blood-smeared hands left a telltale sign of his condition.

Robby was not sure if his friend was sweating or crying. But he did know that Red was hurting badly.

As they started off, Red gripped the walking stick in his right hand and the compass with his left. He wrapped that same arm over Robby's shoulder. He was unable to put any weight on the ball of his left foot. At most he could use his heel to steady himself but not to carry any of his weight. For the most part, Robby's right shoulder took the place of Red's injured foot.

Under the best of conditions, the going through this rugged terrain was very slow—now it was less than sloth-like.

The two boys would proceed south ten to twelve feet, and then have to rest. More often than not, physical obstacles forced adjustments in direction. As best he could, Red tried to keep them heading south.

And with every other new position, Robby would check for a signal. After a dozen such attempts, he yelled, "I think I've got something!"

His cell was bouncing between one and two bars, and then down to none.

He led Red to a fallen tree and helped him sit down.

"This is the first signal we've had since we started back. Wait here and I'll see if I can call Jack."

It was nearly five p.m.

Chapter 11

Earlier that same day

It was nearly eight a.m. by the time Jack had dropped the boys off. He saw no point in driving all the way back to Sugar Island only to turn around and head back to Seney to pick them up.

Sure like to find a cup of hot coffee, Jack thought. So after a few miles on eastbound M-28, he turned off onto M-77 toward the main entrance to Seney Wildlife Refuge. He had remembered having several years earlier stopped at a small restaurant in Germfask—*Sally's Germfask Cafe,* he recalled.

If it were open he would stop there and buy a small second breakfast. Mostly he was just after some fresh, hot coffee.

"Hey. How are ya?" said the pleasant woman behind the counter. She was wearing a clean red bib apron over a long-sleeved white shirt and blue jeans. Her hair was short and sandy blonde, and she had friendly, sparkling blue eyes.

"Don't recall seein' you here before. My name's Sally—just like the name on the sign. And I'm gonna get you a cup of coffee, and ..." She hesitated, waiting for Jack to finish her sentence.

"Coffee sounds good," Jack replied, stopping a moment to think. "Maybe I'll think of something later. But coffee sounds good for right now. Can I just grab a stool at the counter?"

"Sit anywhere you want," she said, now in a near baritone voice—one honed by years on the job, and maybe a million menthol cigarettes.

"In fact, Clair, in the booth over there by the window, she'd probably like to have you sit with her. Or even on her lap. But wherever you choose to sit is up to you.

"By the way, my name is Sally. Did I already tell you that? Probably did. Anyway, what's yours?"

"Jack. My name is Jack Handler," he said, smiling as he took a seat on a stool.

Jack observed that when he announced his name, in the far corner a youngish forty-something with a shaved head quickly snapped his face toward Jack, but then just as quickly returned his eyes to the book that he was reading.

That's strange, Jack determined. *Must be he recognized my name. I wonder how he's heard about me.*

"Jack Handler, you say?" Sally replied. "Ever been here before? I'm sure you're not one of my regulars. At least not yet. But I do get a lot of one-timers just passin' through. You sort of look familiar."

"Pretty sure I stopped here once," Jack said, occasionally stealing a glance at the skinhead in the corner.

The man did not look over again, but Jack did notice that his eyes were fixed in a gaze over the top of his book.

"I was up in the area with some friends. We were fishing the river just up from Manistique Lake. And we stopped in here for a late breakfast."

"You fishing here again?"

"No, not this time."

"Then whatcha up to?" she asked. "If you don't mind my askin'."

Jack did mind. He was always cautious about revealing too much—especially when it involved his boys.

"I'm not fishing this time," he said. "I'm with some friends. They are spending the day at Seney, and I thought I'd just hang out at the Curtis

Library for a while. They still open at nine?"

"Hell if I know," she laughed, turning her attention to the skinhead in the corner.

"Hey, Z, what time does the Curtis Library open during the week? I figured you'd know if anyone would. You're reading all the time."

"Nine. I'm pretty sure," the man replied, looking a little uncomfortable at being called upon.

"That's what I thought," Jack said as he stood up and walked toward the man. "You frequent that library?"

"I go there from time to time."

"Is it a pretty good library?" Jack continued, trying to draw the man out. "For instance, would I be able to access information about the region? Books, documents, and stuff like that? Information specifically about the Curtis area? And Seney in particular? They have materials like that?"

"I really wouldn't know," the skinhead replied. "I like to read fiction. Primarily by local or regional authors. And the librarian there, Karin, she does a real good job at chasing them down for me. So I'd imagine she'd be very helpful to you for information like that. She seems to have a lot of knowledge about the area, and she's very accommodating."

"Oh, I'm sorry," Jack said. "I didn't introduce myself. My name is Jack Handler. And what's your name?"

The skinhead was seated alone in the far corner booth facing the entry to the restaurant. Jack had moved over and assumed a position that would have blocked any attempt to leave.

"My name is Zach—Zach Tanner."

"How do you do?" Jack asked, holding out his hand to shake.

The skinhead did not like this attention. He did, however, lean back in his seat and extend his hand toward Jack.

Just as I expected, Jack thought. *A cold, wet hand.*

Jack the detective liked to force people whom he suspected of something into an uncomfortable position. He did not know what this skinhead might be guilty of doing, but Jack was convinced that he was a shady character.

"Well, Mr. Tanner," Jack said. "I'm pleased to make your acquaintance. Now, just what is it you do besides reading? Let's see. That looks like a Zane Grey novel. It is. It's a classic, too—*Riders of the Purple Sage.* That's one of my favorites. Don't think it was written by a local author, however."

"I read a lot of different things, and I do a lot of things, Mr. Handler. I do a *lot* of things."

The skinhead was clearly displeased with being the subject of Jack's inquisition. His irritation was obvious and growing.

"Don't be so modest, Z," Sally said, trying to relieve some pressure. "Z here is a very important man in the community. He owns a lot of property in and around Seney and Curtis, and even a bunch of the area's businesses as well."

"That's just terrific," Jack said. "I like to meet people who are successful. And how is it you know me?"

"I don't know you. I know your name is Jack Handler, but only because that's what you said it was. Beyond that, I've never heard of you."

With that the skinhead stood, slammed his book closed, peeled off a twenty-dollar bill from a roll of money he carried in his front pants pocket, and slapped it on the table.

"Thanks, Sally," he said, sliding uncomfortably between the stationary Jack Handler and the next table.

"Now, if you'll excuse me, Mr. Handler, I'll be on my way. The library in Curtis opens at nine. I think you'll like it."

The skinhead continued toward the door, but before he left he turned and said loudly in Jack's direction, "And I'd try one of Sally's sweet rolls if

I were you. She bakes them herself. Very good."

Jack watched the skinhead as he left the restaurant and walked to his Basalt Black Metallic Porsche.

As he opened the car door to get in, the skinhead's eyes again met Jack's. He smiled at Jack and then rapidly drove off.

"So, you bake the rolls yourself," Jack said, turning his attention back to Sally.

"Every morning. Get a lot of compliments too."

"Then I suppose I'll have to try one. You can just bring it over here to Mr. Tanner's booth. I'll sit here."

Sally was about to set Jack's coffee on the counter where he had at first sat down. Instead, she swooped it back up and delivered it to Jack's booth in the back corner of the restaurant.

Chapter 12

News and more news

Do you have any local newspapers?" Jack asked as he sat down.

"Sure do, hon," Sally replied. "I'll bring one over. It's more regional than local though. But my customers all seem to like it."

Jack raised his coffee to his lips. "This is just great. *Amazing*, in fact. What kind of coffee is this? I've got to buy myself some of it to take home."

"Ever heard of the Dancing Crane Coffee Shop?"

"Of course," he replied. "I buy my coffee from them—they roast it, I grind it."

"Well, this is Dancing Crane coffee."

"I should have guessed," Jack chuckled. "It just makes sense. If you're going to bake your own rolls, you're not going to come up short with the coffee."

"That's how I see it. If you can't serve the best, then close the doors and move to the city. Half the residents of the area walk through my doors at least once a week. If I don't keep them happy, they'll stop comin'. Not sure exactly where they'd go, but it wouldn't be here."

"We're loyal, Sally. You know that," one of the male customers said. "No matter what happens, you'll always be our favorite."

"What's that mean?" Jack asked.

"Oh, nothin' much," Sally replied, placing her palms on Jack's table and leaning in toward him. "It's just that there's been talk about the empty gas station across the street. That fellow who was just in here, Zach Tanner, he owns it. And he's thinking about opening up another restaurant. That is, unless I sell him this one."

"Can a community this size support two restaurants?" Jack asked.

"Hell no," Sally said without hesitation. "It can't hardly support one. I barely scrape by. But with all his money, if he goes through with it, I'll have to close. And he could afford to lose money for years. It'd just be pocket change to him."

Sally feigned a broad smile and said, "Darlin', I'll get you that roll now. You're gonna love it. Everyone does."

She returned a couple minutes later with a copy of *Lake Superior Magazine* and one of her homemade frosted cinnamon caramel rolls.

"Are you serious?" Jack asked through a grin. "This is *huge*. Do people actually eat this whole thing at one sitting?"

"Some do. But we have take-home boxes for those who can't. No extra charge."

"I'll tell you right now, I'm going to need one of them when I leave. This looks just wonderful. But it's so big."

Using his fork, Jack knifed off a generous bite and prepared to put it in his mouth. Sally was now back behind the counter, but Jack noticed that she was watching for his reaction. They made eye contact. He smiled. He slid the tasty-looking morsel into his mouth, nodding his head approvingly as he chewed.

"This is really great," he said sipping his coffee. "I never expected such a treat. Dancing Crane coffee, and a phenomenal cinnamon bun. I'm for sure coming back here again."

That was the reaction Sally was used to seeing when a stranger first tried one of her specialty buns.

"Think you'd like a scoop of vanilla ice cream with your roll?" she asked.

"*Much* too early in the day," Jack chuckled. "I'll just read my magazine, drink my coffee, and work at this wonderful creation you've just handed me. But I'm sure I'll not finish it here."

After a few minutes, Sally returned to Jack's booth with a Styrofoam take-home box.

"Here ya go, darlin'. I really think you're gonna need this."

"How long have you run this place?" Jack asked.

"Oh. … It seems like forever. My husband bought it for me twenty-three years ago. We used to own a lot of property in the area. The restaurant was pretty much *my* project. And I guess you could say it stayed that. Right after he bought this, he just upped and ran away. Or disappeared. Anyway, he'd been drinking way too much, and gambling. Then one day he said he was going out fishing with a friend, and that was the last I saw of him. It's been interesting, to say the least. But I've made it this far. Lost all the rest of our land, but managed to hang onto this. Knock on wood."

Sally turned and walked back toward the counter. As she walked she turned around halfway and said, "Hope to see you back here again, Jack Handler."

It'd be a damn shame to see this place go away, Jack thought as he smiled and fingered through his copy of *Lake Superior Magazine.*

* * *

"I love those who can smile in trouble, who can gather strength from distress, and grow brave by reflection. 'Tis the business of little minds to shrink, but they whose heart is firm, and whose conscience approves their conduct, will pursue their principles unto death."
— Leonardo da Vinci

Chapter 13
Hello, Curtis

"Would you have a nice comfortable place where I could do some reading?" Jack requested as he made his presence known at the Curtis Library. "Maybe even with some sunlight?"

Karin, the head librarian, was happy to please. "Follow me," she said as she peeked into the room she designated the "reading room."

It was not an especially large room. But the Curtis branch of the Bayliss Public Library System of Michigan's Upper Peninsula was not a particularly spacious facility.

The room was about eighteen feet wide by twenty-four feet long. The walls were, of course, filled with floor-to-ceiling shelves of books. A library in a larger city would most likely adorn its walls with hangings of various sorts—perhaps paintings by local artists, or historically significant photographs.

But the librarians at the smaller libraries, such as this one in Curtis, felt constrained to utilize all available wall space for the stacking of books. "After all, it is a library, not an art gallery," Karin was fond of saying when the subject came up.

There was even an added benefit to the wall shelving. The curved spines of stacked books contributed in a marvelous way to the overall acoustics of the reading room. So, even though the room was relatively small, with patrons sometimes closer together than might seem ideal, the books tended to absorb noises that otherwise might have proved distracting.

"There," she said pointing to a full-sized wooden office desk in the corner of the room, "why don't you use that desk? It has a nice window beside it. If there's too much sun, you may close the blinds. But I don't think that the angle of the sun will be a problem this time of year."

"That will do nicely," Jack said. "And, by any chance, do you have Wi-Fi here?"

"We have Wi-Fi. And it works great at that desk. The password today is 'curtislib'. Don't tell anyone, but that's the password all the time. At first we tried changing it every day. And then every week. It was just a pain in the neck for staff. And I don't have a lot of help around here. I'm not complaining. I have all the help I need. Wonderful people. Volunteers mostly. And they do a great job. But we can be more helpful to our patrons if we don't keep switching around passwords. We switch it off at night as a safety precaution."

"Excellent," Jack said. "This desk, I mean. It will be perfect."

"If there is anything else I can help with," Karin said, "just look me up. Usually, I'm at the main desk."

"There is one thing," Jack said. "Do you have any good books—non-fiction—relating to the history of Seney? I've heard that it has a bit of a storied past."

"Do I ever," Karin said with a smile. "I'll go snatch it off the shelf for you. And you're right. The town of Seney was a real rough and tumble town back in its heyday. I've got the perfect book."

Jack seated himself behind the desk. He was pleased that the chair was nicely padded. He was planning on a fairly long day—possibly until closing. The softer the seat, the more comfortable it would be.

"Here," Karin said, handing Jack a well-worn copy of *Incredible Seney*, written by Lewis C. Reimann. "I have two copies of this book. This is the old one. It's from the early 1980s. You can tell how popular it is because many of the pages have let loose from the binding. I don't circulate this copy anymore because of its age. I do have a newer copy, but it's out right now.

"I think you will find this book useful for your study. The author cites some of his sources. Perhaps that will also help. We might not have a lot of books in this branch, but the Bayliss Library System as a whole is at our disposal. I can request books. So, just let me know if I can help in any way."

"You already have," Jack said. "I'm sure this book will be adequate for today. I actually have two boys, my nephew and his friend, hiking in the Strangmoor Bog as we speak. In the western section of the Wildlife Refuge. So I'm sort of killing some time waiting to pick them up."

"Not in the bog itself?" Karin asked.

"Afraid so. They are acquiring a sample of the peat in order to fulfill a requirement for a Geology Merit Badge. They are in the Boy Scouts."

"But in the *bog*? I didn't think it was even possible to hike in the bog. I hope they're wearing tall boots."

"They've got waders. GPS. Cell phones. Water. And me waiting in the wings."

"Some of our patrons here at the library volunteer at the Wildlife Refuge. And, according to what I've heard, Strangmoor Bog is a very difficult place to hike in. And the *mosquitoes*. They can be very bad. But there's this netting you can get. That would help, I should think. It is getting a little late in the season. I think the mosquitoes would be worse in the spring."

"But I know what you're saying. That's why I'm hanging out here—close by. And not back on Sugar Island."

"Well," Karin said. "Just let me know if you have any more questions,

I'll be right over here at my desk."

"Thanks, Karin. You've been very helpful. And I will take it easy on this Seney book."

Jack observed the quiet room sign and slid his cell phone out of his pocket and put it on silent.

Karin's comments regarding the hazards of Strangmoor Bog did not reveal anything to Jack that he did not already know. While he was optimistic that all would go as planned, he was very serious about his readiness to rescue. At some point, he anticipated a call from the boys informing him that they were all set to be picked up. Whether that call came as an emergency or not, he wanted to be prepared to act.

But, it was early yet. He did not expect to hear from them for several hours. In the meantime, he would learn more about the history of Seney.

Jack unpacked his case and opened his MacBook Pro, found a power outlet, and plugged in his cord. *No point in running my battery down,* he determined.

He then logged on to the library's Wi-Fi and activated the application that could trace the boys' cell phones.

First he tried Red's. Finding that there was nothing recorded for that cell, he then tried Robby's.

"Nothing," he said aloud but audible only to himself. "Must be their phones are still turned off."

That was just what he expected. It was the plan. Unless there was an emergency that required their getting in touch, they would leave their cell phones off.

Jack checked his watch. It was 11:50 a.m. He surmised that the boys would still be hiking back into the bog—that it would be another couple hours, perhaps more, before they would reach their destination.

He settled back into his padded chair and began reading about the incredible logging town called Seney.

Across from the title page was an illustration. It pictured a 19th century bar, obviously located in Seney. In the artwork, a bartender was smashing a bottle of liquor over the head of a man wearing a suit. In the man's hand was a short-barreled handgun.

Behind the bar was a picture of the great bare-knuckled fighter, John L. Sullivan.

The caption below the picture read: "The Dan Dunn–Harcourt Feud. Steve Harcourt's first shot ricocheted and drilled the picture of John L. Sullivan. Dunn shot Steve twice and killed him."

Jack chuckled. *Doesn't that just about tell it all?* he thought.

Karin was keeping an eye on him, and when she saw his animated grin, she said, "Isn't that just amazing? That little town of Seney. Not twenty miles from here. And so much violence. You'd think it was the Wild West. Somewhere out in Wyoming, or Arizona. Not here in Michigan. Not even in the Upper Peninsula.

"I just love reading about Seney. You know, we still have a number of families that date back to that era. Sure, a lot of it was tied up with the lumber industry. And when the war came, much of it changed. But some of those very same families stayed in the area, and they now live in places like Curtis, Munising, and Newberry. And some even stayed around Seney."

Jack did not reply. He merely smiled at her, nodded his head, and returned to reading the book.

Every twenty minutes or so, however, he would check to see if he might be able to track one of the boys' cell phones. So far there was nothing.

Jack was not used to eating a lunch. If he had anything at all, it would be salted nuts and a bottle of water.

But today, after he had eaten almost half of Sally's cinnamon roll, he was not hungry even for a handful of pecans.

At 2:15 he checked his watch, set the book down, and tried again to access the boys' cell phones. But still he had no luck.

And then he smelled something.

Chapter 14
The aroma

Jack glanced down at the page number—103. He turned the page to see how close he was to the end of a chapter.

Page 105 started chapter sixteen. He found the title intriguing—"The Murder of Tim Kaine."

He could not keep himself from reading the first paragraph: "Violent death was not an unusual occurrence in and about Seney. There are many tales of men done to death during those riotous days in the '80ties and '90ties, men secretly disposed of by gamblers to cover up their cheating, by highwaymen, who waylaid lumberjacks for their winter's stake, and by saloon keepers and bartenders who 'rolled' the men down from the woods in order to conceal their robberies."

This will just have to wait, Jack thought as he turned the book over to hold his page. *I've got to investigate the source of that smell.*

Following his nose out of the reading room, he first turned left. But then he heard a familiar sound—the last gurgles of a coffee maker as it boils through the final drops of water.

He turned toward the sound.

Could this be what I think it is? Jack wondered. *It sure smells like it.*

There standing in a small utility room he saw Karin pouring two cups of coffee. And beside the black Mr. Coffee-style coffee maker was a one-pound bag of Dancing Crane Coffee.

"Have I died and gone to heaven?" Jack asked. "What would you charge me for a cup of that coffee?"

"Actually," Karin said, "I was about to ask you what you would like in your coffee. You just looked like a coffee drinker to me."

"You've got to be kidding me—Dancing Crane Coffee. I love that stuff. And you were really pouring it for me? Karin, what a sweetheart you are. If I could have just a touch of something white in it—milk, cream, creamer. Anything. That would be great. Just no sugar."

"I've got creamer. I don't like to keep stuff in the refrigerator. It can go bad if the power goes out. Would creamer be okay?"

"Great. It would be just great. And is it okay if I have it in the reading room?"

"I generally don't encourage drinks in the reading room. But this is what I'll do. I will bring it to you on a serving tray, and we will pretend it's a special occasion."

"That doesn't sound like a good idea. I have no desire to break your rules. Where are you going to have yours?"

"At the front desk, where I work."

"How about if I have mine with you, and you can tell me a little bit about your library. And about yourself. Would that be okay?"

"That would be fine. I will pull up a chair, and we can chat. I'm really interested in your nephew's exploit. Hiking in the bog. Maybe you can tell me a little more about that. And maybe tell me about you. You seem like an interesting man."

Jack liked the librarian. She struck him as a genuinely nice person. And, he really liked her coffee.

"My first question for you is this. How is it you use Dancing Crane coffee? That coffee shop is clear over in Brimley."

"One of our patrons, Sean Bronson, maybe you know him, he gave me some here at the library. And we all liked it so much that he drops off a bag every week or two. It's quite a treat. The first bag he left was whole bean, but we don't have a grinder. So he brought one in for us to use. Very sweet of him. But it was very noisy. So I asked him if he could grind it for us. Now he has it ground at the coffee shop, and brings it to us all ready to use.

"Did I make it too strong? What do you think?"

"It's perfect. That coffee is so good it is forgiving. Strong or weak, it still tastes fine."

"Well, I'm glad you like it, Mr. … You know, I don't think you told me your name."

"I'm sorry. I must have neglected that. My name is Jack Handler. And I know your first name is Karin. But I don't think I know your last name."

"Slaughter. My last name is Slaughter. Just like the famous author but we're not related."

"Well, Mrs. Slaughter —"

"It's actually *Miss* Slaughter. I'm not married. Or at least no longer married. My husband left me years ago. But no one calls me Miss Slaughter. People just call me Karin."

"I need to get back and check on my boys in the bog. Thanks for the coffee."

After Jack had excused himself, he headed back to the desk he'd been using and checked to see if either of the cell phones had been switched on.

Still nothing.

He checked his watch. It was 3:07 p.m.

Chapter 15
Back to the story of Seney

At four p.m., Jack repeated his attempt to locate the boys' cell phones—again without success. He kept the application active as he turned back to Reimann's book about Seney.

"Let's see," Jack mumbled as he adjusted his reading glasses. "Where was I? … Page 135, I think."

"Dunn reached into his pocket for his gun. Jim Harcourt, who had drawn the short straw, saw the move and, quicker than sight, whipped out his gun and fired four shots into Dunn's body before it fell to the barroom floor. The first shot struck him through the heart. Jim turned and gave himself up to the sheriff. The officer took the gun, which Dunn still clasped in his hand."

"Hold on," Jack mumbled as he flipped back to the first pages of the book.

Yeah, just like I thought, he said to himself. *That caption reads that Dan Dunn shot Steve twice. Jim Harcourt, in exacting his revenge on Dunn for shooting his brother, shot him twice as many times. Sounds like justice to me.*

Jack hurried on in his reading. He wanted to finish the book before he received the call from the boys requesting that he pick them up, plus he knew that the library would be closing at seven p.m.

Jack continued to read.

"In its bawdiest days Seney boasted ten 'hotels' with bars, and two mammoth bawdy houses on its outskirts as well as a score of smaller ones on its back streets. There were twenty-one saloons, two general stores, six drug stores, numerous meat markets, groceries, and a jewelry store."

Jack checked the page number and closed the book. He wrote "Page 187" down on a pink Post-it Brand note he found on the desk. He then leaned back in the chair and contemplated the sort of city that Seney once was.

Earlier, another patron had entered the reading room. When he did he greeted Jack with a friendly smile and a nod.

Jack could not resist engaging the man.

"Have you ever read anything about the village of Seney, back in the 1890s?"

"Karin had me read the book you're reading right now," the man replied. "It was a real surprise to me."

"I get the twenty-one bars," Jack said. "Obviously the great pastime was drinking and gambling—"

"Don't forget the girls," the man said with a grin. "They liked their girls too."

"There were plenty of whorehouses as well," Jack agreed. "In this book they're called *bawdy houses*. I can see that too. But six drug stores. Why would they need six drug stores? Most of the significant drugs had not yet been developed."

"I know what you mean," the man said. "Six stores to buy snake oil and rubbing alcohol. Seems like they would have sold that type of product in the grocery stores anyway. That struck me too when I read the book. I'm gonna have to read it again. It's been a few years.

"One thing that *is* fresh on my mind is the final paragraph in the book," the man continued. "The part where an old lumberjack accompanied the author to the neglected original cemetery. I've tried to visit that graveyard myself but couldn't find it. I think he called it 'Boothill.'

Maybe if I asked around—"

Just then Jack saw some movement on his tracking application, and his attention was drawn to it.

Chapter 16
Signs of life in the bog

Jack's eyes became glued to his cell phone.

"I'm sorry," he finally said to the man he had been conversing with. "I'm tracking my nephew's cell phone, and he seems to be moving. He and a friend are hiking in Strangmoor Bog—pretty treacherous area. If you will excuse me?"

"Wow. Strangmoor Bog," the man said. "Yes, of course. It was nice talking to you."

Jack smiled and disengaged.

He checked his watch. It was 4:47 p.m.

That's very interesting, Jack thought, his brow furrowing involuntarily. *They're taking a different route back. Wonder why they are not using their GPS to find their way out. Must be it's lost or broken. That cannot be good.*

Jack followed the boys' progress for a few minutes and then lost the connection.

He began packing up his personal materials, returned the Seney book to the librarian with his gratitude, and walked briskly to his car.

He made several efforts to call the boys' cell phones, but to no avail. Either they were just not answering their cells, or the connection was too marginal.

The drive to Creighton Truck Trail was uneventful. In fact, Jack shaved some time off the trip because of his eagerness to see the boys, and his becoming more familiar with the road.

Initially, he had dropped the boys off at the point where Highwater Truck Trail branched off Creighton. But this time he yanked his Tahoe to the left and headed east down Highwater. He had initially chosen that spot as a drop-off point because he saw on his Google Map that Highwater was a dead-end road, and he did not want to get himself in a position where he'd have to back up a great distance to extricate himself from the bog.

This time, however, he wanted to get as close as possible to where he anticipated the boys might emerge. He would worry about turning around later.

He checked his phone tracker on his cell phone. It indicated that communication with the boys' cells was still lost. The last location noted had not changed from what it was before he'd left the library.

Jack continued down Highwater until he neared a position that he surmised would place him closest to where he suspected the boys might be. Of course, now that they appeared to be operating without a Garmin, there would be no way to predict with any certainty what route they might take.

As near as he could tell, the boys had lost the use of their GPS over a mile in from Highwater Truck Trail, and perhaps as much as a mile east of Creighton Truck Trail.

Jack checked the bars on his cell.

"One bar," he said out loud. "That's probably about what they've got as well. Or maybe worse."

He proceeded down the bumpy trail, checking his cell phone as he slowly moved along.

"Whoa!" he blurted out. "Three bars!"

He slammed on the brakes.

It immediately dropped back to two bars, so he backed up a little, and the signal returned to three.

Jack again tried to call the cell he had been tracking, but could not get through. He decided to park right there—in the spot where he had three bars. He checked his phone several times and found that if he didn't move he was able to maintain a decent signal.

Waiting was torturous. Jack glanced again at his watch. It was now 5:40.

"Only three hours before it starts to get dark," he grumbled. "Maybe less."

Another check of his cell phone tracker indicated no movement.

If I head in to look for them, based on this last position, he reasoned, *I could be heading in the wrong direction. There's nothing to indicate that they are not still moving. But in what direction? There's no way to know. I need a confirmation as to where they are. And then I need assurance that they will wait right there—at least before I even think about heading in.*

He decided to hold his position.

Chapter 17

Struggles continue in the bog

Red had become virtually immobilized. The pain in his foot was so intense that he could not put any weight on it at all. In fact, the only way he felt any relief from the throbbing was to elevate it. So he stretched out on the fallen tree as best he could, placing his left leg on its upward slope. He kept himself from falling off by anchoring his right foot into the soft peat soil.

Robby continued scouting around for an improved signal. Actually, he would have been happy for *any* signal. Since the time he had found the two bars earlier, which was nearly an hour ago, he had not seen any similar indication.

Gradually he widened the distance from Red, walking a curved perimeter nearly one hundred feet from where he had left his friend.

Suddenly it happened. He had a signal. And it was a good one—three full bars. He tried to call Jack, but the call would not go through. He tried again.

His battery was down to ten percent.

He tried again. This time he had success.

"Robby! Are you okay?" Jack shouted.

"Yes, but Red hurt his foot."

"Can you stay put? I will come get you."

Robby's phone died. But before the call dropped, he got Jack's message: "Stay put."

"Red," Robby shouted. "I reached Jack! He's gonna come after us."

There was no response.

"Red!" Robby shouted. "Where are you?"

Still nothing.

"Red! Please answer me! I need to know where you are."

Even though Robby was certain he was no more than one hundred feet from his friend, he had wandered around looking for a cell tower. He was counting on Red responding when he called out to him.

Robby stopped in his tracks. *Okay,* he reasoned. *Jack knows where I was when I called him. And that's where he will head. I've got to find Red. But I cannot just move about looking for him. If I do, and fail to locate him, Jack will not find either one of us.*

"Red, can you hear me? ... Please answer me."

I should have taken the compass from Red, Robby thought in his frustration. *Then I would at least have an idea where he was.*

I think I stayed south of his position. But I don't know that. I sure wish he'd answer me.

"Red! Do you know where Buddy is? Where's Buddy? ... Buddy. Come here, Buddy. Good boy."

Robby had correctly surmised that Red had passed out. By calling for Buddy, he reasoned that he might get through to his friend and coax an audible response from him.

Robby turned his body a few degrees to what he thought was northwest and shouted again:

"Buddy, here Buddy. Good dog. Come here Buddy."

This time he thought he heard a noise.

I don't dare go far if Jack is on his way, Robby thought. *But I think that could have been Red.*

Robby made up his mind that he would walk fifty feet in the direction of the noise, and then repeat his calling for Buddy.

As best he could, he walked a straight line for thirty steps. He called, "Buddy. Buddy. Come here, boy. Good dog. Buddy, come here. Red wants to see you."

Again he heard a noise, and this time he was certain it was Red. It sounded as though it was coming from no farther than another fifty feet.

That's it! Robby determined. *I'm going. I can call to Jack from there and he will hear me.*

As he walked, Robby kept calling to Red. And Red responded, but barely.

Finally, he almost stumbled over his injured friend.

Red had momentarily blacked out and had toppled off the tree and onto the ground. He was nearly unconscious. Robby did not know it, but the wound on Red's foot was rapidly becoming infected from the massive amount of bacteria in the water.

Robby removed Red's backpack and turned his friend over on his back. He felt Red's face, and it was hot.

Robby slid Red's cell phone out and turned it on. He then began walking in the direction of the spot he had just vacated. Within minutes, he had a two-bar signal. Again he called Jack.

"The earlier call dropped," Jack said. "Is this Red?"

"This is Robby. I'm using Red's phone. He's hurt. Are you on your way?"

"Yes. How serious is it? And what's the injury?"

"He ran a sharp stick into his foot. He's got a bad fever. He needs a doctor. Pretty sure it's infected."

"I've got a fix on your location now," Jack advised. "So don't wander."

"We're not going anywhere. Red really can't walk at all."

"Sounds like he's hurting pretty good," Jack said.

"We're almost gonna have to carry him out. At least I think so. He's pretty much out of it. He's got a good-sized piece of wood broken off in his foot. Sort of between his toes. We must get him to a doctor. But, like I said, we're pretty much going to have to carry him out."

"We'll manage somehow," Jack replied. "This is very tough going. And I don't have waders. Do you think I can make it without them?"

"There's some water. Actually, a *lot* of water. You're gonna get really soaked. But you'll be okay as long as you watch your step. Be nice if you had our map. The one Red worked up before we left."

"Might not help a lot, because you did not take the same route back," Jack said. "Why was that?"

"When Red broke through the bottom of the creek, our Garmin went flying. I didn't know it at first, so we think it just floated downstream."

"Well, that explains why you took a different route back," Jack said. "So you just headed directly south from where you lost the Garmin?"

"Right. At least as close to south as we could manage."

"I'll keep that in mind," Jack said. "We might want to go looking for that Garmin on another day—like maybe tomorrow. They're not cheap."

"We might want to find it for another reason," Robby said.

"And what might that be?" Jack asked.

"Red found something really interesting in his soil sample."

"What does that mean?" Jack asked. "What sort of *something interesting?*"

"Like a ring. A gold wedding ring."

"Really? That is *very* interesting."

"Especially since it has a piece of finger bone in it," Robby added.

Chapter 18
Jack's shock

Jack was momentarily speechless. Finally, he blurted out, "A *finger* bone, and a gold ring? Are you quite sure about the bone?"

"Not positive about the bone," Robby said. "But that's sure what it looks like to us. It's definitely a gold ring though. Looks like a wedding ring. I suppose what we think is a bone could be a stick. But where it broke off, it was sharp like a bone. We didn't open the plastic container after we removed it from the driving tool. Mr. Idestam insisted that for us to win a merit badge, we must present the samples unopened."

Scout leader Idestam did things by the book—literally by the book. He carried the Boy Scout Handbook in his briefcase all of the time. And when he was without his case, another copy of the Handbook was tucked away in the glove box of his car. But even if he happened to be caught without access to one, he could recite most of it by heart.

He wasn't a huge man, but his two hundred pounds were distributed well over his six-foot frame. Even though it had been twenty years since his college days as a Division One linebacker, no one doubted that he could still lay some hurt on any running back who might venture up the middle.

Imposing as he was physically, and tough as he was as a disciplinarian, it was the goodness of his heart that endeared him to the boys and their parents. He was always the perfect example of what a leader should be—whether it was in class, on the athletic field, or as a scout leader. He led with discipline well tempered by love.

As the father of four daughters, everyone suspected that his immense dedication to scouting was partly the result of his desire to have a son. Whatever his motivation, everyone loved Mr. Idestam. Whenever he asked for fathers to help out on a scouting event, nearly every father volunteered—Jack included. Even though Jack was old enough to be the boys' grandfather, he frequently took up Idestam's offer and joined the boys' outings.

"We did just like Mr. Idestam told us," Robby said. "We didn't open either of the samples. Of course, you can't see through the soil. But there is some air in the tube. If you turn it so the bubble is at the ring, or what we think is a ring, you can see it a little better.

"And the way the soil sampler cut through, it slid right along the smooth outside of the ring. I know you can't see much of it, but it sure looks like a gold ring to me.

"And the finger bone. That's not quite so certain. I thought it looked more like an old bone than a stick."

Jack was again slow to respond because there was a lot going on in his mind.

"First things first," he finally said. "It's going to be dark soon. And I've got a lot of work ahead of me. Let's concentrate on getting you and Red out of the bog. And then we'll deal with the ring and finger."

Jack was not equipped for this type of rescue—at least not out of the middle of Strangmoor Bog. He had been wearing a summer jacket and jeans. While he did have boots with him, they were low hiking boots. He needed waders. Right at that moment he did not concern himself with what he didn't have. His adrenalin level was kicking in. He knew time was critical.

"I'm going to bring up a map to find the best route to get to you,"

Jack said. "One providing the fewest water hazards. I've got boots with me, but it sounds like they'll be worse than useless for this hike. I'll just wear my cross-trainers.

"Are you with Red right now?"

"No," Robby replied. "We don't have a signal where he is. I'm probably a hundred feet away."

"He's okay by himself?"

"Yeah," Robby said. "He's hurtin', but other than that, if he stays off his foot, he'll be better off. But, like I said, he should see a doctor as soon as possible. That piece of stick is still in his foot, and it's pretty nasty."

"If you stay right where you're at," Jack advised, "I can head straight for you. Keep the cell on and call me if you have to. But if it's not searching for a tower, it will prolong battery life. I'm not sure how long it will take me, but I'll navigate it as best I can."

"Thanks, Jack," Robby said as he disconnected the call.

Chapter 19
Jack gives Sheriff Green the finger

Five hours later, Red was out of surgery and resting comfortably in recovery with his bandaged left foot slightly elevated. Fortunately, War Memorial Hospital in Sault Ste. Marie had an emergency room doctor available to treat him immediately. They had given him a local anesthetic, along with antibiotics.

Jack had considered taking Red to Helen Newberry Joy Hospital and Healthcare Center in Newberry, but decided to drive on into Sault Ste. Marie because it was closer to the resort, and should the doctors wish to keep Red overnight, it would make it more convenient.

Another reason for Jack's having chosen War Memorial was that Sault Ste. Marie was located in Chippewa County, and Jack knew he would eventually have to report the boys' find to local authorities. While Jack did not consider himself to be Sheriff Bill Green's friend, Sheriff of Chippewa County, he at least was very familiar with him.

"How long before you can put some weight on that foot?" Robby asked.

"Now," Red texted.

"I don't think so," Kate countered. "The doctor said that if your fever does not come back, that he would consider fixing you up with a walking boot. Maybe even as early as tomorrow. That means you could go home then, or maybe the following day … but you will not be walking around on it for a while—probably in a week or so."

"I'd say you were real lucky," Jack said. "That was the biggest sliver I've ever seen. And it came out in one piece, right through the bottom of your foot."

"How'd that happen?" Robby asked.

"Apparently it had pierced the skin when you guys were walking back, and all the doc had to do was latch onto it and pull it out. The whole thing came out in one piece. Of course, he had to do some cleaning, but no bones or nerves were damaged. Your fever is already headed down. Prognosis is very good.

"But Kate's right about walking around on it," Jack continued, after catching a frown from Kate. "You should stay off it until it has begun to heal. No point aggravating the injury."

"The walking boot doesn't mean you can start walking on it right away," Kate said. "He will put the boot on it to *protect* it. We have to keep an eye on it to be sure it starts healing up. He was concerned that there might be more slivers from the stick still in your foot. He thinks he got it all, but he can't be positive. If there are, they will probably work their way out over the next few days.

"Otherwise, you might have to come back for some minor surgery."

"Go home tomrow?" Red texted.

"Maybe," Jack said after Red had shown him his text. "We'll have to see."

Jack then glanced down at his cell.

"Sheriff Green is on his way up to see you," he said. "I am not sure about the nature, or significance, of what you boys found. I just know that I am eager to hand it over to the sheriff."

"Jack. Why did you get me down here at this time of night?" Sheriff Green asked as he walked into the recovery room.

"I wanted to have you take a look at what the boys found. I think you will find it interesting."

Jack then handed the transparent tube containing the soil sample to the sheriff.

"Unless this contains a murder weapon, or a body part, I'm not going to be very happy about this inconvenience," Sheriff Green said.

"Take a look at it and tell me what you think," Jack said.

The sheriff examined the cylinder, turning it slowly in his hands.

"I'd say we had a ring here. A gold wedding ring. It might be a man's wedding ring. At least that's what it looks like."

"And what else?" Jack asked.

"Well, I'll be damned!" the sheriff said. "That sure looks like a piece of a finger bone—a *human* finger bone. Is that what you're thinking? That it's part of a human finger?"

"That's what it looks like to me," Jack said.

"Where did this come from?" the sheriff asked.

"Well, that could be a problem," Jack replied. "The two boys were taking soil samples in Strangmoor Bog. And this is what they came up with."

"Strangmoor Bog," the sheriff repeated. "Correct me if I'm wrong, but isn't that part of the Seney Wildlife Refuge?"

"Yes, it is," Jack replied.

"And isn't Seney located in *Schoolcraft County*?" Sheriff Green asked.

"Sheriff," Jack said, wanting to end the game playing. "You and I both know that this was not retrieved from within your jurisdiction. The problem is that I had to bring Red into the hospital. As you can see, he is not able to get around very well. He was injured in the process of obtaining that soil sample. I brought the boys directly to the hospital. And I would like you to take possession of what I think might be evidence of a crime.

The cylinder has not been tampered with."

"And what do you expect me to do with it?" Sheriff Green asked, obviously thoroughly frustrated with the whole matter.

"If you could, I would like you to enter it into evidence, somehow, and then see to it that it is made available to the sheriff of Schoolcraft County when the time comes," Jack replied.

"But there's no crime to connect it to," the sheriff said, handing it back to Jack. "How can this be evidence?"

"I'm sure you can do something with it," Jack replied. "It's evidence that someone died. Of causes yet unknown. And it is *currently* in your county. I'm sure you can take it off my hands."

"Every time ... *every* damn time I run into you, you somehow manage to make paperwork for me. And now you're dragging me down here in the middle of the night, for what might or might not be a crime, and even if it is, it did *not* take place in my county. You, my friend, are a pain in my ass. A *major* pain in my ass."

"I love you too, Sheriff," Jack said. "Do you need me to sign something?"

Sheriff Green raised his eyebrows in genuine disgust. "I'm not taking responsibility for it. You can drive it to Schoolcraft later today. It's not my problem."

"Do you have an evidence bag in your vehicle?" Jack asked.

"What difference does that make?"

"If you would be so kind as to go get one, we can bag it and date it—"

"Damn it, Jack! Just give it to me," the sheriff barked.

Jack handed the sample back to the sheriff.

"Here, this will do for now," Sheriff Green said, impatiently snatching the empty plastic liner from a small wastebasket and stuffing the sample cylinder into it. "We'll worry about getting this to Schoolcraft tomorrow.

"Thanks a lot, Jack. I really appreciate hearing from you again. It's always such a pleasure doing business with you. Now, if it's okay with you, I'll go back home and see if I can sleep. I'm sure that Sheriff Griffen will want to talk to you and the boys about this."

Sheriff Green turned and walked out of the room, not waiting for a response.

However, on his way back to his car Sheriff Green had second thoughts about the soil sample, and what might be in it. So, instead of going home, he retrieved an evidence bag and dropped the cylinder into it. He then returned to the recovery room and asked Jack to sign it.

"I'll get this locked up tonight," he said, obviously having calmed down, "and I'll notify Schoolcraft tomorrow."

Sheriff Green then turned his attention to the two boys. "What, pray tell, were you two boys doing in Strangmoor Bog? And you, Red, looks like you got yourself nicked up a bit. How'd that happen?"

Sheriff Green was fully aware that Red would not be answering his questions. His intention was to draw Kate out, and perhaps have her explain the circumstances.

She would have none of that.

"Red really should not be talking anymore tonight," she said. "How about we continue this conversation tomorrow?"

Chapter 20
The report

When Red awoke the next morning it was clear that the foot was healing well. But the doctor was not yet ready to sign his release.

By the following day, however, Red felt he was ready to go home. And the medical staff concurred. After he had completed his rounds, the doctor returned to Red's room and declared that he had conferred with the nurses, and that if Red could get around with a boot and crutches, he could go home.

"But don't put any weight on that foot," he said, looking directly into Red's eyes. "And elevate it as much as possible."

He then turned his attention to Kate. "I will want to see him again in two days. Call my office for an appointment. We'll see then when he can start to put some weight on it."

* * *

"It's just amazing what twelve stitches and a bottle of peroxide will do," Jack said the morning after Red had been released. "It's been less than four full days, and already the swelling is nearly gone. Oh, to be young and healthy. If that were my foot, the doctor would probably have kept me a week for observation … or amputated it. But that foot of yours is really looking great. You'll be running around the resort without crutches before you know it."

"You're joking. Right, Dad?" Kate said over her morning coffee. "Didn't you see what he and Robby were up to yesterday? We had barely got back from the hospital, and these two fellows decided to do some afternoon fishing on the St. Mary's.

"And you didn't know I was watching, did you?" Kate continued, now looking directly at Red. "But I *saw* you. You ditched the crutches on the bank and picked them back up when you returned."

"Can't use crutches on a boat," Robby chimed in, coming to his friend's defense.

"That's right," Kate said. "But you dressed out your catch, wrapped them, and stuck them in the fish fridge, all without using your crutches. I don't think you used them again until you came in for dinner.

"Look, I know you're not going to stay off your feet. And that's okay. I'm sure a little exercise isn't going to hinder the healing process. But just be careful to keep it clean and dry."

Jack and Kate exchanged smiles.

"Red, I just hope you don't expect me to keep waiting on you once your foot heals up," Robby quipped as he held the storm door open for Red. All four of them were headed outside to enjoy the breeze off the St. Mary's River.

Red sneered at him, poking a crutch against the door just in case Robby let go of it.

"Do you think I might be eligible for a nursemaid merit badge for taking such good care of Red out in the bog?" Robby asked, directing his question to Kate. "Or maybe lifesaving. I think I might have saved his life. I'm sure there's a merit badge for that."

"I don't think there's an award for what you did," she said. "Actually, if anyone should win a merit badge for the Strangmoor expedition it should be your Uncle Jack. But he's not a Boy Scout. Maybe I should have his sneakers bronzed and mounted on a plaque."

"They are *already* mounted … in the dumpster at the hospital," Jack said. "Didn't you see them? They were *really* messed up."

Just then, Jack's cell vibrated.

"Well, Jack, looks like you were right about that bone," Sheriff Green reported.

"Human?" Jack asked.

"Sure is," the sheriff said. "Schoolcraft got it yesterday and ran some preliminary tests. The bone fragment is from the ring finger of a male. The manner it was broken suggests that when your boys hammered the device into the soil, it caught the ring and finger just right, or just wrong. Anyway, it severely scored the ring, and broke the finger off on both sides of the ring. It's an absolute miracle that it—the ring—didn't just push out of the way and get missed altogether."

"DNA?" Jack asked. "Are they going to be able to pull some DNA from the bone?"

"Doubtful. According to the Schoolcraft sheriff, preliminary examination suggests that the bone could be thirty to fifty years old. Even if they *could* get a sample, what are the chances of making any kind of a match at this late date? Besides, there's probably not enough there to test.

"It might be a different matter, though, if we had the whole body. Is there any way we can get back to where the boys took their sample? Maybe we can find the rest of our victim?"

"Did you just call him your 'victim'?" Jack asked. "Are you suggesting that he *was* a victim of a homicide? And that you are investigating?"

"You're reading too much into my little slip of the tongue," Sheriff Green said, quickly covering his tracks. "Sheriff Griffen, the Schoolcraft County Sheriff … he and I go way back. We both graduated from LSSU at the same time. And we've stayed good friends through the years. We even go hunting together. Strangely, we hunt just off the Creighton Truck Trail. Isn't that something? It's not that hard going when it's all frozen over.

"But he and I have been talking about this dead guy, and how he might have ended up at the spot where your boys found him. Rather, how his *finger* might have ended up there. Wherever that was. Which brings me back to the main question—do you think they could lead us to where they found the ring?"

"There is a way," Jack said. "It's a bit convoluted, but it might be worth a try. Can I have a few of your friend's boys tomorrow? Schoolcraft deputies? If so, we just might work our way back to the body."

"I know I'd like to go," Sheriff Green said. "And I'm sure Sheriff Griffen could put together a few of his elite."

"I'm not so sure that's what we need," Jack countered. "I'm thinking more along the line of a few major mud trucks."

Jack sat back in the wooden Adirondack chair. The breeze off the St. Mary's was cool and refreshing. The sun was turning the scattered clouds into flaming gold and navy blue streaks and then reflecting them in the still deep waters of the river.

A perfect end-of-day repose with my three favorite people in the world, Jack thought. *Life is good.*

* * *

The next morning, when Jack, Kate, and the two boys turned off M-28 onto Creighton Truck Trail, both Red's and Robby's jaws dropped.

"Jack! Look at that!" Robby blurted out as he jumped up from his backseat and lunged halfway to the dash. He was pointing at the torn-up surface gravel covering Creighton Truck Trail.

Chapter 21

Mudders

"It sure looks like we're going to have company back here today," Jack said. "And from the size of those treads, I think it could be *quite* impressive."

For the most part, the clearing through which Creighton Truck Trail ran was only wide enough to allow for one large vehicle to squeeze past an oncoming one. But wherever there was any room at all, invariably the side of the roadway was shredded by one or more of the mudders exploding off the road to tear through puddles of water and brush.

"It's almost like the vehicles themselves were uncomfortable with smooth road surface and sought out the rougher terrain," Kate said.

"That looks like an excavator," Robby said. "It's leaving a track like an excavator ... or a bulldozer."

"You're right," Jack replied. "This ought to be very interesting."

"Okay," Kate said, getting serious. "We need to decide just how involved the boys are going to get in this business. From the evidence I've seen so far, there are going to be some very large and dangerous vehicles out here today. Where are we going to have the boys stay? In *this* vehicle?"

"Actually, I'm going to need the boys to come out into the bog, at least part of the way," Jack said. "They are the only ones who have been to where the soil sample was taken."

"Really?" Kate responded. "You know that we cannot take a chance on re-injuring Red's foot. We can't even allow it to get wet. How's that going to work?"

"We'll find the best vehicle, or vehicles, for this terrain. And leave the others parked in reserve. We'll just have to wait to see what the sheriff's boys are going to make available to us."

"And Red," Kate said. "How are we going to protect his foot?"

"He isn't going to have to get out of the vehicle," Jack assured her. "At least, that's my plan. I brought a drone. It has a two-mile range. But you never know. I will try to get Red and Robby as far back as possible. Ideally even beyond where I found them the other day. And then we'll see if we can find where they lost the Garmin.

"Shouldn't be too hard. Just locate the point in the creek where Red got stuck, and then use the drone to search out all the locations along the way where the Garmin might have got hung up. As much brush as there is out here, I think it's quite likely that it did not float very far downstream."

"And the drone has a GPS transmitter," Kate said. "That's how you determine where the Garmin is, once you find it with the drone?"

"Exactly," Jack replied. "Once we locate it with the camera, then we can determine what we will have to do to get back to it. But the boys will not be a part of that activity.

"Once they point out the spot where Red hurt his foot on the screen, we will take it from there."

Red did not want to be left out of what he anticipated would be a new adventure. Before they had left Sugar Island that morning he had tossed a set of waders in the back of Jack's Tahoe, along with his backpack (with two bottles of water and some granola snacks) and a new hiking stick. Of course, he strongly sensed Kate would not allow him to take off his walking boot.

His red curly hair, which had not seen barber shears for quite a few weeks, made him look like a cross between an angelic cherub and an unabashed Huck Finn character, full of spunk and ready to get rid of the boot he believed was tying him down.

"Any idea how long this might take?" Kate asked.

"I'd like to think that we will locate it quickly with the drone. Maybe within a couple hours. And then the hike back to where they took the sample. That part is unpredictable. So many difficulties and hazards. That last part is all going to have to be on foot."

"Those tracks look like they've got some pretty heavy-duty equipment back here," Kate said. "Couldn't they just drive over the brush and through the water?"

"If there were something substantial underneath," Jack said. "The problem is that parts of the bog are virtually floating on top of water. Heavy equipment will have a tendency to tear through the surface and just drop. It would be possible to get so stuck that the only way out would be with a helicopter. And some equipment is just too heavy for most transport helicopters.

"Besides, it could cost more to get a big enough chopper in here than any mud truck would be worth.

"That means if we get something out there, and get it stuck, we just might have to leave—"

"Oh my gosh!" Robby excitedly exclaimed, again nearly jumping over the back of the front seat.

Chapter 22

There are mudders, and then there are MUDDERS

Lined up and facing outward on the west side of Creighton Truck Trail were numerous very mean looking vehicles.

The first one in line was a Jeep Wrangler with wide tires, but a pretty standard undercarriage.

The second, a Chevy pickup, also had wide tires, but still with less than ten inches of clearance.

The third one was a different story altogether. It looked a lot like the monster trucks that perform in auditoriums and on television. It was equipped with four tractor-sized tires, each standing nearly five feet tall and measuring nearly two feet in width.

The chassis was totally customized, providing over two feet of road clearance.

But the ones chosen by the sheriff to venture out onto Highwater Truck Trail were a twin cab Chevy pickup equipped with aftermarket tank-like tracks that bolted on in place of ordinary wheels, and a Polaris ATV, also fitted with tracks.

The Chevy did not look much different from what you might see in a used car lot, except, in place of wheels, it was equipped with four sets of rubber-tracked devices manufactured by a company called Mattracks.

This equipment allowed a vehicle to ride on top of the bog, instead of trying to obtain traction by digging through it. That's what made it so effective.

Each wheel had been replaced with an assembly that provided about three feet of flat traction on the bottom. The vehicle turned just like one with standard wheels, because the Mattracks narrowed at the top in order to fit into the wheel wells.

Not only did they provide great traction, but they also raised the vehicle off the ground considerably, providing substantially greater clearance over standard treaded tires.

Also, being mounted on a standard four-wheel drive pickup, the relatively light weight of the vehicle aided in its ability to ride on top of the bog.

It was not, however, as maneuverable as the similarly equipped Polaris.

Once Jack saw what they had available, he quickly adapted his plan to accommodate the vehicles.

"Okay, boys, this is how we do it," Jack said. "Robby, you grab the drone out of the back. And Red, you carry the bag with my laptop.

"We'll use the Chevy as our base of operations.

"And, Kate, you can also monitor the drone's camera from here in the Tahoe. Keep your eyes peeled for the Garmin. It will have a tendency to blend in with its surroundings. But, I think we have an excellent chance of locating it, especially if it is still encased in that plastic bag you insisted on."

"Have to use the two-way radios," Kate suggested. "Cell coverage out here is spotty at best."

"We've got at least a couple miles on the two-ways," Jack said. "If we start to break up, go ahead and pull on down Highwater until we're good. The only problem there is that when the time comes to leave, you'll probably have to back out. Maybe. There is one place where you can turn around, but only one. At least as far as I saw. But I do want to maintain communication with you. You might spot the Garmin before we—"

"Jack Handler. You *do* remember me?" came a voice from the other side of Jack's Tahoe.

* * *

"Sweet are the uses of adversity
Which, like the toad, ugly and venomous,
Wears yet a precious jewel in his head."
— William Shakespeare, *As You Like It*

Chapter 23

Yes, I remember you

Jack had just stepped out of his vehicle but was still talking to Kate.

Looking up to see a familiar figure walking toward him, Jack smiled and replied, "Of course, Mr. Tanner—the skin-headed Zane Grey fan from Germfask."

"Zach. My first name is Zach. I actually live just outside of Curtis. And I'll bet that this is your beautiful daughter, Kate. The homicide detective from New York City. I think you should introduce us."

Jack no longer intimidated Zach Tanner. In the restaurant, Jack had caught him by surprise and then cornered him.

Today it will be different, Zach thought.

Zach had taken some time to do a quick but thorough investigation of Jack and his daughter. Actually, Zach did not do the research. Instead, he employed the services of New York's Binder and Bosch, one of the top private investigating firms in the nation. Jack, who had friends in the firm, had been given a heads-up that they had been hired to run him.

"Hope you don't mind, Jack, but I took a little time to check you out."

"I don't mind at all," Jack replied, "I hope you didn't spend much money. All you would have had to do is ask. I would answer your questions—and it would have been free."

"It didn't cost me that much," Zach replied. "But don't worry, I've got lots of money. I can afford it."

"That's what I've heard," Jack said, not appreciating the man's cocky demeanor. "Please tell me, what brings you out here today? Hope you're not driving your Porsche."

Sizing him up, Jack noted, *This guy's cowboy boots sparkle like Montaigne's toe—hopefully he brought something more appropriate for hiking in the bog.*

"No, that's my silver Wrangler over there," he said, pointing southward. "Good looking Jeep, isn't it?"

"Fine looking," Jack said. "But that doesn't explain what you're doing out here dressed like that."

"I came to help you locate the rest of that body. That's all they're talking about around here. The phantom fingerless body. I'm gonna help you find it."

"I don't think that Wrangler of yours is going to make it very far into the bog."

"Oh, I'm not going to drive it any farther than where it's parked right now. I really don't want to get it dirty."

Zach then looked again at Kate and said, "The girls like my Wrangler. I drive it mostly to please them. How about you, Kate, do you like Wranglers?"

Kate knew the man was merely fishing for some sort of reaction, so she didn't look at him or respond verbally.

Zach then pulled out a pack of Camels, slid one into his mouth, and with a snap of his wrist, clicked open a gold Zippo. He lit up and took a long drag.

"Do you have extra batteries for these two-ways?" she asked Jack, continuing to ignore Zach's advances.

"There should be a pack in the glove compartment," Jack said. "Open it, and split it with me."

And then, turning to Tanner, he said, "I don't think you're going to have much luck with my daughter today, Mr. Tanner. Is there anything else you can do to make yourself useful?"

"I thought I'd like to ask your daughter out on a date. ... Just kidding. You wouldn't mind that, would you? If I asked Kate out? But, to answer your question, I think I can be useful today. I've got a pair of waders in my Jeep. I'll slip them on. I'm sure I will find a way to make my contribution."

"How the hell did you hear about this project, anyway?" Jack asked.

"I find everything out," Zach said. "I'm good friends with Sheriff Griffen and most of his deputies. I even know Sheriff Green. He and I used to hang out. When we were younger. And, like I said, everyone's heard about the body. Can't keep something like that a secret.

"You don't have a problem with that, do you, Jack? You don't sound too excited about my being here. If you want me to, I'll just explain to Harvey, that's Sheriff Griffen, in case you didn't know, that you want me to leave. And I'll split. No problem. Of course, if I go, Kate will be *very* disappointed."

Jack smiled at Zach, but did not reply. Instead, he slid the batteries that Kate had given him into his pocket.

"I'll bet that's the redheaded kid who started this whole thing," Zach said as he approached the seat where Red was sitting. "Hey, kid, whaddaya got to say about all the hullabaloo you've caused?"

Red looked at Zach, but, of course, did not respond.

"What's up? Cat got your tongue?" Zach said sarcastically.

"And what's the deal with the walking cast?" he said, noticing Red's walking boot. "Can't talk and can't walk. Damn, Jack, what the hell did you do to this kid?"

Jack smiled broadly even though he was not amused. He walked around the front of the Tahoe and over to where Tanner was standing. It had become obvious to Jack and Kate that Zach's only interest today was in getting under Jack's skin. And at that, the younger man was successful.

"Uh-oh, boys," Kate said to Red and Robby. "Maybe you ought to plug your ears and cover your eyes."

Chapter 24
Just like a rag doll

Jack continued smiling until he reached Zach Tanner. Then his countenance changed dramatically.

Reaching his left hand down to the man's belt buckle, he gripped him by the top of his shirt just below the chin with his right, picked him straight up, carried him over to the front fender, and slammed him down hard onto the hood of the Tahoe. The man landed like a sack of grain on his back, with his head banging so hard on the hood that it bounced.

Jack then pressed his left thumb into Tanner's throat and countered the pressure by pushing on the top of the man's head with his right hand.

Jack then leaned over and whispered in Tanner's ear.

When he was finished, he again grabbed Tanner by his belt and slid him headfirst into the mud.

"Damn it, Handler," Zach said, lying on his back in the mud and propping himself up on his elbows. "Can't you take a joke, old man? All I can say is you need to get yourself laid!"

Jack placed his left boot just below Tanner's chin and pushed him back in the mud.

"Zach, my young friend," Jack said. "We need to have an understanding—you and me. Starting right now, you need to do your best to avoid me. Now you can go tell your buddies about how you almost became a hood ornament on my truck. Or tell them whatever the hell you want. Just don't be poking your nose into my business. And keep outta my way.

Especially when it comes to my daughter and the boys. Because, if you keep this shit up, Kate or I will have to shoot you. And that would just make more paperwork for your buddy Griffen."

When Tanner got to his feet he was not smiling. In fact, Jack thought he spotted a tear in Tanner's left eye.

Immediately after the humbled man had walked away, Kate smiled at her father and asked, "And just who is your mouthy friend?"

"*Friend*?" Jack chuckled.

"Who is he?" Kate asked again.

"His name is Zach Tanner. But exactly *who* he is, or *why* he came out here today, I don't have a clue.

"According to the owner of the restaurant in Germfask, he comes from a family with a lot of money. And a lot of power in the area. Apparently he wants to buy her restaurant, and she doesn't want to sell. He is threatening to open up a competing business just down the street if she won't comply with his wishes.

"I'd guess you could say he was a spoiled brat in his youth. And now he's just an obnoxious slug."

"But a slug with money," Kate said.

Jack did not respond.

"Well, I see you've met my friend," Sheriff Green said, walking up with a smile that was out of control.

"You've no idea how many times I've wanted to put him in his place. But his family is just too powerful around here for an elected sheriff to engage in that sort of thing."

"I don't know what you're talking about," Jack said through his smile.

"Well," Sheriff Green said, turning a little more serious. "I'm sure you've dealt with guys like him before. But just so you know, his family is not only filthy rich, *land* rich, but they have a reputation for being terribly ruthless on top of it. At some point down the road, Zach, his brother, or some of the dirtbags that work for him, *one* of them is going to come after you. Probably more than one. And they are pretty good at revenge. Had a lot of practice. So just watch your back."

"Duly noted, Sheriff. And I do appreciate the warning. But this sort of shit just seems to stem from being Jack Handler. I'm sure he'd like to hurt me—maybe he'll try," Jack said stoically. "But in the end, I can assure you that he and his family have more to be concerned about than I do."

"Jack, I wouldn't dispute that. But, please, whatever you do, don't bury the bodies in Chippewa County … or even in Strangmoor Bog, for that matter. This is *not* my favorite place in the world. I don't even know why I'm out here today—it's not in my jurisdiction."

"That's a deal. But I do have a question for you," Jack said, turning to face the sheriff squarely. "Why was this Tanner guy out here this morning? I gave him a pretty difficult time at the restaurant the other day. Why would he get in my face like that now? And why is he even here at all?"

Chapter 25
The Tanners

"There's the long version, and the short version," Sheriff Green said, looking at his watch. "Today we'll settle for the short one."

Jack did not object.

"Zach's family goes way back in this area—but only on his mother's side. Her name was Emily, and her family's surname was Daine. The Daine family was quite wealthy. They made their fortune during the 1880s and 1890s in the lumber industry. When the timber was exhausted, her family still owned the land—a lot of it. As the only child of Tim Daine, she inherited everything.

"She never worked. Never had to. She traveled all over the world. Apparently it was during one of her trips to New York that she met and fell in love with Isaac Tanner Sr. He was a wild fellow—drinking, gambling, and who knows what all. There are a lot of stories about him. Some of them I suppose might even be true.

"Anyway, he seized the opportunity and married Emily Daine and moved to Curtis. Even though Isaac made this area his home, he frequently spent long periods of time out East. Some said he had business interests out there, others thought that he might have had a mistress. But eventually he became a full-time resident of Curtis. This was during the early '70s.

"His family did not have money—at least not like the family he married into. What he brought into the marriage was guile. Some have even called him unscrupulous. The stories are endless. But, at any rate, over time through numerous business dealings, he parlayed their combined wealth into a sizable fortune—exactly how much, no one actually knows.

"And no one really understands how he did it. He attributed it to luck. But no one believes that. He just kept buying more and more land. And businesses. Today Zach and his older brother own thousands of acres, entire lakes, and a whole shitload of businesses from the Soo to Marquette."

"Soo" was short of Sault Ste. Marie.

"You said that there are numerous 'stories' surrounding the old man," Jack said. "What sort of stories? The short version, of course."

"There have been many rumors about Old Man Tanner, but the one that seems to hold the most water was his reputation for gambling, and a penchant for good whiskey.

"The story is that he could deal poker 'crookeder' than any other shark in the UP. He always carried a snub-nosed .32 in a holster he'd sewn to his boot, and a big hunting knife. He apparently knew how to use both of them, and reputedly did on a few occasions … when he was young.

"The thing that set him apart from all the other gamblers in the area, aside from his unscrupulous tactics, is that he always went after real estate. Not so much directly, but in the end he would come out with a man's property.

"The story goes that he would become friends with a man—drinking buddies, if you will. And then get him hooked on the camaraderie, the whiskey, and on gambling. After he'd taken all the man's money, and I mean *all*, he'd then offer to give it back to him on the condition that the fellow would write out a quitclaim deed for a small portion of the land the man owned.

"Strangely, he would come into a game with the paperwork already drawn up. Apparently he would have done his homework before inviting a man to play in his game.

"Sometimes it was just an acre. Sometimes a lot more. But by doing this Tanner was able to get his fingers into dozens of pieces of property throughout the area. And then, one way or another, he would find a way to weasel his way into obtaining the entire homestead.

"Well, that's about it. The family has continued grabbing land around this area, and now they are *the* major player in everything that gets done, or doesn't get done."

"And that's the *short* version?" Jack quipped.

"Yeah, it really is," the sheriff said. "There's the modern-day version too. It involves Zach and his brother Isaac. They still have their poker games. And they still pull some of the same shenanigans, or so it's said. And they've been known to flirt with questionable if not *illegal* activities. But nothing has ever been proven. Their net worth is about that of the rest of the county combined. The truth is, *nothing* gets done around here—and no one gets elected—without their approval. I think you get the picture."

"That still doesn't explain why this Zach character turned up here today," Jack said.

"It'd be a little hard to say exactly *why* he came out this morning," the sheriff replied. "But I'm sure his father had something to do with it. This finger bone is the biggest news in the area, and old man Tanner would want to find out about it as directly as possible. He may be old, but he still runs the family."

"Then the old man is still alive?" Jack asked.

"He is, but barely," the sheriff replied. "He's on oxygen with twenty-four-seven nursing care. Emphysema, and just about every other ailment common to a man who lived the wild life he has. He won't be around much longer. At least that's what I've heard.

"And, another reason Zach's here this morning is that he's a personal friend of Sheriff Griffen's. It's a simple fact that the sheriff would not be able to keep getting elected without the Tanners' support. So, it figures.

"But whatever Zach's motives, I think he could come in handy today. He is quite the woodsman. He and his brother know a lot about the area. And he even hunts in these woods. So he could be useful. Unless, of course, you bruised his ego too severely."

"Well, if I did," Jack said, "that's just too damn bad. He needs to keep out of my way, and out of my face. I just don't like guys like that.

"Anyway, we've got to get a move on," Jack said, satisfied with the sheriff's explanation. "This is how I see it. We'll put one vehicle in as close as possible to where the Garmin was lost. I'm assuming that you like the Chevy with tracks for that.

"I will have the boys with me in that vehicle. We will send up the drone, and find the location where Red hurt his foot. As long as we keep the drone within range, we'll be fine."

Jack then pulled out two pairs of waders, one for him and one for Robby. The two of them put the waders on while Jack continued to talk to the sheriff.

"Once we find the Garmin, we'll log the coordinates, and your guys will go in and retrieve it."

"Sounds simple enough," the sheriff said. "That is until someone actually has to go out and physically locate it on the ground—or in the water. What if in trudging through the creek the men dislodge it, and it floats further downstream? Can you keep the drone in the air to follow it?"

"Time is a consideration. Once we've located the Garmin, we'll have to bring the drone in. The batteries are good for half an hour. But I'd like to keep the cycles short—fifteen to twenty minutes. I've got plenty of charged batteries, so I can keep swapping them out.

"Whoever you have close to the Garmin, if you keep in contact with me, I can send the drone back in to pinpoint, or to relocate it if it gets away from him."

"I'll have three men on the ground," the sheriff said. "They will all fight their way into the spot. There are no trails out there. And nothing is charted. So they will each take a different route. They'll keep at it until one of them gets to the location."

"Kate," Jack said, turning to his daughter. "After we get set up in the bog, I'll call you to make sure you are able to monitor the camera in the drone."

"Sounds good," she said.

Kate, sipping a coffee from the thermos she had packed, stepped out of the Tahoe to see Jack and the two boys off.

She was wearing a navy blue NYPD hoodie. It had a gold emblem and a zipper up the front.

She looked at the boys and said, "You fellows take care. And Red, I want you to keep that foot dry—no matter what. Okay? … Robby, you help him remember that."

She then flashed them a thumbs up—her way of sending a hug, but without embarrassing them.

"God, I love those characters," she said out loud, but only after they were out of earshot.

When they reached the Chevy, Jack first situated the boys and his equipment in the rear seat. And then he walked to the back of the pickup to address the three men who would be doing the footwork. They were seated in the open box of the pickup. A now quiet Zach Tanner was one of them.

Chapter 26

The hunt is on

Gentlemen," Jack said. "I assume each one of you has a Garmin. I would like all of you to fire them up, and we'll run a little test."

Jack checked his own unit and said, "I've got 46.219904, -86.163062. Does anyone have something different?"

The men checked their units. All three reported that they showed the same reading.

"What was that reading?" a fourth man asked. He had just pulled up behind the Chevy. He was sitting on a tracked Polaris ATV.

Jack repeated the coordinates.

"Yup, that's what I got too."

"Great," Jack said. "Then let's get going."

Sheriff Green had positioned himself in the front passenger seat of the pickup. He couldn't help but grin as Jack addressed Zach Tanner as though he had never met the man before.

Jack then slid into the rear seat with the boys.

Immediately after the sheriff fastened his seatbelt, he introduced the driver to Jack and the boys.

"This is Deputy Manford," the sheriff said. "He will be our pilot today."

After they exchanged greetings, Jack took over.

"Deputy, let's get started. Just head straight down Highwater until I have you pull off. It will be to the left. And it will be in about eight-tenths of a mile, give or take."

"Yes sir, Mr. Handler."

"Let's just go with *Jack*. Is that okay with you?"

"Sure, Jack, you tell me where to go, and I'll do my best to get you there."

"How do these tracks handle in the bog?" Jack asked. He was directing his question to the sheriff, but he deferred to the deputy.

"This truck actually belongs to the deputy," the sheriff said. "What do you think about it, Deputy Manford?"

"I think it gives us the best chance to get in close to where you want to go. As soon as we hit a lot of brush, we'll have to stop. That's what the Polaris is for—to scout around for the best routes through the rougher terrain.

"*Neither* vehicle will get in all the way. But between the two of us, we can manipulate our way in pretty—"

"There!" Jack interrupted. "That's where I pulled off. Now, if you can see how far in you can get from that point. I walked almost directly north from that location. So try north.

"It was a little west, too," Jack continued. "I seem to remember that there was a bit of a clearing on the other side of this brush. If you can somehow get through it, we should have it easy for about a hundred yards, and then it gets a little more dicey."

The deputy stopped and motioned for the Polaris to come alongside.

"Junior," Deputy Manford said. "See if you can find me a clear path to get beyond this growth of brush. Jack says that just beyond it is a bit of a clearing. See what you can come up with."

The deputy put the Chevy in park while Junior explored.

"This is a very nice truck," Jack said to Deputy Manford. "Who did you get to fit it with these tracks?"

"I did it myself," the deputy said. "With a little help from my friends and a company called Mattracks. It's really not that big a deal with these tracks. All you do, basically, is jack it up, take a wheel off, slip the Mattracks on, and bolt it down.

"They are pretty heavy, so I prefer to have a little help installing them. But if you jack your truck up to the exact height, you can almost just slide them in.

"I think the company advertises that they take thirty minutes to install. That sounds about right—for each one. At least for me. If I pushed it I could probably put all four on in an hour—with some help."

Barely ten minutes had passed until Junior came shooting up from behind and pulled alongside the Chevy pickup.

"Piece of cake," he declared proudly. "Even your Sherman tank can make it through the clearing I found. Just follow me."

Deputy Manford shifted into drive and followed the Polaris closely as they drove off to the northwest. He was only twenty-four years old. His sandy blond hair was cut short and he wore a CAT cap to keep the sun out of his eyes.

They had traveled only about fifty yards when Junior threw out his right hand, forecasting a right turn.

"Yeah," Deputy Manford said loudly as he cranked to the right. "This is gonna work just fine."

The deputy kept his Chevy right on Junior's tail as the two vehicles sped through standing water sometimes knee-deep.

"You and he have done this before, haven't you?" Jack observed.

"Lots," the deputy replied. "Just not much in Strangmoor. How can you tell?"

"You can't be fifteen feet off that Polaris," Jack chuckled. "He hiccups, and you're all over him. You seem to know what to expect from him."

"I should," the deputy said. "After all, he is my little brother."

"That figures," Jack replied.

They pushed through to the far edge of the clearing, and the deputy signaled with his hand as he started to slow.

"How far in do you think I should go?" the deputy asked. "We have to be sure we leave ourselves room to turn around. If I remember right, the creek you're talking about is only a mile or so beyond the point where this clearing ends."

"That would be just about right," Jack said. "I think if we even park it right here, we will easily be within range for the drone. But still get in as far as you can.

"I'm thinking the point where I met up with the boys was right over there," Jack said, pointing to a location east and north of where the Polaris had turned around and stopped. "I think if we got in just a little closer, and get turned around, we'll be in great shape."

"No problem. I think I'll whip it around right here, and then back it in to where Junior is sitting. How does that sound?"

"That works," Jack replied.

"Looks like your brother's putting on a mosquito net," Jack said. "I suppose we should follow suit."

"Surely you wore one when you were out here the other night?" the deputy asked.

"I did, but I was hoping to avoid wearing one today," Jack said. "I didn't want to have my vision obstructed when I fly the drone. It'll be hard enough to find that Garmin even without additional hindrances.

"I'm sure I'll get a little better range if I operate it from outside the vehicle."

The deputy slowed and turned sharply to the right. He then backed the Chevy up to within ten feet of the Polaris.

Jack did not wait for him to stop. Slipping a mosquito net over his baseball cap, he jumped out and keyed his two-way radio.

"Kate. Do you copy?"

Chapter 27

Kate here

"Dad," Kate responded. "Are you all the way in?"

"About as far as we're going to be able to drive," Jack said. "I'm launching the little bird in a minute. I just powered up the camera. Can you see anything?"

"Yeah, I'm getting something. Hold it up and pan slowly," she instructed. "There, that's very good. As long as you move it slowly enough, I can see very well. You are also monitoring it—right?"

"Not yet. The monitor is still in the truck."

"And the boys. Where are they?"

"They're in the truck as well," Jack said. "As soon as I am ready to send it up, I'll have to bring them out with me. Will need their input. Maybe we can all work from the back of the truck. Red will for sure. Mosquitos are really bad. The nets and gloves should do the trick, though."

"You've got some Deet, right?" Kate asked.

"Yeah, but I'm keeping it in reserve—as a last resort."

Jack pounded on the rear window and signaled the boys to put on their nets and gloves. They knew that he meant they were getting out.

Jack told the men seated in the back of the Chevy to jump out and prepare to head into the bog on foot. As they stood, Jack stopped Tanner. "Zach, let me borrow your jacket for a minute. It'll make a nice launch pad for the drone."

Zach frowned, but did not verbally object.

Jack spread the new-looking camo out on the hood. His hand detected the distinct shape of a snub-nosed revolver in the zipped-up right pocket.

Jack had earlier noticed that the jacket hung a little crooked and suspected that Zach was carrying a handgun in one of its pockets.

Jack smoothed out a square-foot area of the back of the jacket and placed the drone in the middle of it.

"When I bring it in I'll have to land it on the ground," he explained. "But I need a good surface for takeoff, and the cab of the truck is a little too slippery.

"Okay, fellas," Jack said. "As soon as we get a fix on the Garmin's location, I want all three of you to head out, all taking slightly different approaches. We are not sure which will be the best route. It might turn out that the most circuitous is the one that works. But it is important that we move as quickly as possible. While I do have several batteries, flight times are limited.

"Once we locate the Garmin, and get coordinates, we're going to keep at it until we find and retrieve it."

Jack then started it up and prepared for takeoff.

"Once I get it up, I'm going to head it straight for where I met up with the boys," Jack said. "I know that location from my cell phone. But once we get there, I want you boys, Robby and Red, to tell me where to point it. We have to be as quick as possible. This drone can stay up for only thirty minutes. Maybe a little longer, but we're not going to take chances.

"So stay alert. Red, you can point on the screen if you want me to fly in a particular direction."

"Jack, I don't know how far we walked after Red hurt his foot," Robby said. "Most of all we were looking for a cell tower. I think we headed pretty much south, but I can't be sure about it."

"We've got more batteries. If it looks like time is getting away, and we still have not found the Garmin, I'll bring the drone back in and change them out.

"And we have liftoff," Jack said, taking the little bird nearly straight up to a height well above any of the nearby trees.

"Go ahead and grab your jacket, Zach," Jack said, keeping his eyes on the drone. "I'm done with it."

Within seconds the drone disappeared above the trees and into the airspace over the bog.

"Robby, key the radio. See if Kate is monitoring the flight with us."

"Kate. Are you watchin'?"

"Sure am," she said. "It's working well."

"Key it again, and hold the radio up so I can talk to her," Jack said.

"Kate, right about here is where I found the boys the other day," Jack said, as the drone approached a familiar area. "They are going to direct me in to where they lost the Garmin."

Red then reached toward the screen and indicated the direction he thought would take the drone in the vicinity of where he'd hurt his foot.

"Yeah!" Robby agreed. "I think over there too."

"You think that we should head in this direction?" Jack asked as he held the drone steady with camera pointed almost due north.

Red haltingly nodded.

"I'm pretty sure," Robby agreed. "But maybe a little to the east. Actually, if you head directly north, and a little to the east, once you reach the creek, we should be able to find where we crossed. It was down from a beaver dam. I just don't know how far down.

"Just downstream there was a pretty good sized tree across the creek—roots on the north side. Find that tree, and you'll be real close to where we dropped the Garmin."

"Bet you wish you'd of had this puppy the other night," Sheriff Green said. "Would have made reaching the boys a bit easier."

Jack acknowledged the sheriff with a nod but did not respond verbally.

"There's the creek. Obviously the dam is west of this point."

"The dam has to be west," Robby said. "The creek is too narrow here for it to be on the upstream side of the dam. But I'm not sure if the place we crossed is east or west of this spot."

"Okay," Jack said. "Let's head west and find that dam. And then work our way back. If you spot anything in the meantime, anything that looks familiar, just give me a shout."

Jack leveled the drone off to determine the height of the trees upstream. The camera was a GoPro Hero 3+ Black Edition equipped with a custom extended-range video transmitter that could send a signal over a mile.

"I've got to be very deliberate here," Jack said aloud, although he was speaking mostly for his own benefit. "Those trees can come up very quickly. So I want to stay above them. But, when I'm up that high, I don't get a great view of the creek. That Hero might be a bit too wide angle for this.

"So, I'll come in high—above the trees—and then tilt the camera downward to get a panoramic look at the creek. And then we'll take it in slow."

"How much time do you have left on those batteries?" Sheriff Green asked.

Jack looked at his screen and then over at the sheriff.

"We're sixteen minutes into the flight," Jack said. "I don't want to cut it close. I've got another ten, max, and then I start bringing it back in."

Chapter 28
The flight of the drone

Jack maneuvered the drone upstream a hundred feet, made sure that he was clear of nearby trees, and then held the position to observe the creek.

"Don't see the dam yet, or that tree where you crossed," he said. "Let's go up and take a longer view. I'd like to locate the dam—be certain we've got it—and then bring the little bird back for fuel."

"Couldn't we just look for the spot on Google satellite images?" Sheriff Green asked. "They're pretty good."

"That's how the boys found the dam on their way in. But they chose to take a different route out—one downstream from the dam. And there are so many trees across the creek, it'd be impossible to pick the right one using Google. Besides, we don't know how old the Google images are. They could be from a year ago, or even more. Beavers don't pay any attention to Google."

"Hey," Robby yelled. "There's a tree. Can we get a closer look?"

Jack moved the drone only a short distance when Red started shaking his head and pointing at the root system on the south side of the creek.

"Wrong tree," Robby said. "Sorry."

"That's okay," Jack assured him. "We'll just keep looking."

With time on his battery slipping away, Jack took the drone above the trees and made a beeline to the dam.

"There it is," Robby said. "That's exactly where we crossed on our way in. If we look just a little east of this point, we'll find where we crossed on the way out."

Jack turned the drone around and headed slowly eastward, looking carefully for the right tree crossing.

"Too small," Robby said, as Jack started to take the drone down to inspect another fallen tree.

Red nodded in agreement.

"Must be down a little further," Robby continued.

"We'll go another minute and a half," Jack said. "And then we'll bring it in."

About forty-five seconds later Red started tapping on the screen.

Robby bent forward to get a closer look.

"There, that could be it!" Robby exclaimed. "Can we get a closer look at *that* tree?"

"Only for a few seconds," Jack said, as he carefully maneuvered the drone down closer to the creek.

Both boys studied the screen.

Red then pointed at a limb sticking straight up. It was broken off about a foot from the trunk.

"I think that is the limb that Red was hanging onto when his foot was stuck," Robby said.

Red nodded his agreement.

"Okay," Jack said. "Then you're pretty sure this is the right tree?"

"Pretty sure," Robby said.

Red enthusiastically confirmed.

"I've got a few seconds left," Jack said. "Let's take a look downstream. Robby, hit Kate on the radio and ask her to pay close attention for the next few seconds."

Robby did as Jack told him, all the while keeping his eyes glued on the screen.

Slowly Jack dropped the drone down to within ten meters above the creek. Taking care not to hit any limbs or encroaching brush, he cautiously maneuvered the drone downstream along the surface of the water.

"There!" Robby shouted, pointing at a white object lodged in a bush hanging into the stream. "Can you get in closer to that?"

Using software installed on his Mac, Jack zoomed in on the object.

"Clearly it is a plastic bag," he said. "And clearly it contains an object about the size of a Garmin. I think we've located it."

Because the signals to Kate's screen reached her via a repeater in Jack's equipment, she was able to view exactly what Jack and the boys were viewing at virtually the same time. "Is that it?" she said. "I think it might be the Garmin."

"We think so," Robby answered.

"Now, let's log those coordinates and get this little bird back to base."

"46.244781,-86.144007," Jack said. "Sheriff, could you write those numbers down and give them to your men? I'm going to fly the drone back while I still can."

The sheriff had earlier dispatched the three men who had ridden out in the back of the Chevy, as well as Junior, and asked them to move fifty to a hundred yards into the bog, and wait there for further instructions.

He radioed the coordinates to them and told them to proceed the best way they could in order to retrieve the Garmin.

Jack brought the drone up high enough to safely clear the trees and headed back.

All of a sudden he grumbled, "What the hell is going on?"

Chapter 29

What happened?

He had barely reached altitude when suddenly his screen went totally blank.

"What happened?" the sheriff asked. "Did you run out of battery?"

"No," Jack replied. "I still had fifteen percent."

"I didn't see or hear it crash," the sheriff said. "Do you think it went down?"

"We wouldn't have been able to see or hear it yet," Jack said. "It was still too deep in the bog.

"And we might never know. It could be very difficult to locate."

"Dad, my screen went blank," Kate reported. "How about yours?"

Jack took the radio from Robby and said, "Yeah, mine did the same thing. I think we lost the drone."

"It crashed?" she asked.

"Don't know for sure," Jack said. "We didn't see anything. And the battery would be just about gone by now. So I think we have to assume it went down. The last contact I had with it was just a few seconds after we located the Garmin—or what we think might be the Garmin.

"When the guys get there I'll have them check around for the drone. They might be able to retrieve it as well."

* * *

Nearly two hours passed before the sheriff heard back from the four men.

Finally, Zach radioed in, "Damn, this is hard goin'. Much easier during the winter."

"Did you retrieve the Garmin?" the sheriff asked him.

"No," Zach said. "I just reached the location. Haven't spotted it yet, but will continue to look. I'm down in the middle of the creek as we speak. I *should* be seeing it. I'm right on the coordinates you gave us. But don't see anything. You're sure it's still in that zipper plastic bag?"

"We saw it with the drone," the sheriff said. "Jack got in pretty close, and for sure it was a dark object in a clear plastic zipper bag—like a freezer bag. We actually saw it. It was tangled up in some brush on the north side of the creek. You don't see *anything*?"

"Well," Zach said. "Actually, I didn't see anything like what you're talking about, but I did find something."

Chapter 30

No Garmin?

What are you saying?" the sheriff asked. "You found *something*? But not the Garmin?"

"Exactly," Zach said. "I imagine it's Jack's little toy plane—the drone. It's pretty messed up. Looks like it came straight down. Smashed up pretty good. I left it where I found it but recorded the coordinates. I thought Jack would like to see it right where it crashed.

"In fact, I didn't even touch it. Handler's a genuine *asshole*, you know."

Zach knew that Jack could hear what he was saying.

"I'm not touching his shit. I'll look for the Garmin. But I don't want *anything* to do with his ... junk."

Zach had paused a moment before selecting what he thought to be the stronger pejorative—shit or junk.

"Are you sure the Garmin is *not* there?" the sheriff asked again.

"I suppose I could be missing something," Zach said. "Like I explained, this place is virtually impossible to get around in.

"Here, let me get this out of my pocket again—the coordinates you gave me. I'll read them back: 46.244781,-86.144007."

"Those are correct," the sheriff said. "And that's where you are right now?"

"Precisely, and I have a pretty good view up and down the stream."

"Take some pictures with your cell phone," the sheriff said. "And bring them back to me. Unless you can send them."

"No service here," Zach said. "But I'll shoot some images and show you when I get back."

"Why don't you poke around there a little more," the sheriff said. "And wait until the other three arrive. Maybe a fresh pair of eyes."

"Will do. But I haven't seen any of the other guys yet."

"Just hang in until they arrive," the sheriff said. "And when you get out of the creek, take some pictures of the downed drone. Just like you found it. And I will ask Jack if he wants you to bring it back with you."

"But I ain't touching it," Zach said. "I already told you, I want *nothing* to do with Handler. I don't like him."

"Some people do find Jack a little hard to get along with at times," the sheriff said loudly, smiling at Jack and making sure he was able to hear him. "At least take some pictures of it, and I'll ask Jack if he wants it disturbed. If so, I'll have one of the other guys gather it up.

"Keep in touch," the sheriff continued. "Let me know when the other fellows show up. Especially if one of them finds the Garmin."

"Will do, Sheriff," Zach said. "But right now I think I hear someone coming my way. I'll check it out and get back to you."

Chapter 31

What the hell!

Did I hear him say that the drone was heavily damaged?" Jack asked the sheriff.

"He said it was in pieces."

"Then that could *not* have been a battery issue," Jack said. "If it was a battery failing, the software would have brought it down slowly. That's how it's designed.

"It was above tree level, so it didn't hit a limb. Had to have been a catastrophic failure—of some sort.

"Can't see the motor stopping and the camera failing at the same time either. They run on separate power supplies. It's like something hit it. Or it hit something. But I was way above any possible obstacle.

"I'd just say have him leave it there after he logs its location. I'll investigate after we locate the Garmin. Better notify the others as well, so no one disturbs it."

The sheriff agreed to Jack's plan and set about contacting the searchers. The first one he talked to was Zach.

"Still no luck with the Garmin?" the sheriff asked.

"None. I'm still in the creek looking," Zach said. "Maybe it got dislodged and floated on downstream. Too bad about the drone. It'd be nice to shoot it back up and take another look."

"That's not going to happen," the sheriff said. "About the drone. You indicated that it was bunged up pretty good. Is that right?"

"It's in pieces," Zach said. "I'd say *that* was bunged up."

"Yeah," the sheriff agreed. "Sounds like. This is how I'd like you to proceed. Don't touch the drone. Jack wants to do an inspection of it right where it crashed. Okay?"

"No problem there, Sheriff. I promise I'll not touch Jack's toy. I might take a piss on it. But that's all. I promise."

"Hit me as soon as you learn anything new about the Garmin."

"Will do, Sheriff," Zach said. "I'll just keep poking around the area until I'm otherwise instructed."

"That's cool," the sheriff said. "I'll keep you informed. And as the others come up, tell them what I said, and have them radio me."

"Sheriff," Zach said. "Does Jack have another drone out here? A red one?"

"Another drone?" the sheriff asked. "You've got another drone out there?"

"Sure do. It's about twice the size of Jack's. It's bright red, and noisy as hell. Are you saying that this one is not Jack's? Then whose is it?"

"Jack!" the sheriff shouted in Jack's direction. "Zach is saying that he saw another drone out there. He *just* saw it. He said it's about twice the size of yours, and it is red."

Jack was shocked.

"Can I have that radio?"

The sheriff handed the radio to him.

"Zach. Are you saying that you've spotted a *second* drone out there? After you visibly verified that mine was on the ground?"

"Pretty much," Zach replied. "Your drone, the dark-colored one, is about one hundred feet south of the creek, and it is in pieces. It must have come down very hard. The drone that I just saw was on the north side of the creek, it was over twice the size of yours, and it was red. It sounded like it took off maybe two hundred feet … maybe a hundred yards northeast of here. I'm in the creek right now. It took off straight up, and then flew directly north. It was quite loud."

"Was it powered by an engine?" Jack asked.

"No. It was electric. It was loud because of the size of the rotors. It was pretty big."

Jack thought for a moment.

"Are any of the other guys there yet?" he asked. "I take it you got to the scene first."

"Haven't seen anyone else yet," Zach said. "So far I'm the only one on-site."

"And you can't find the Garmin?" Jack asked.

"No. I explained all that to the sheriff. I have searched thoroughly at the coordinates you gave us. I even went downstream a bit. But found nothing."

"Let us know if and when any of the other guys show up, or if any of you find the Garmin."

"Sure thing, Jack," Zach replied.

"How's it coming?" Jack asked the sheriff. "Any luck reaching the other three?"

"I talked to Junior," the sheriff said. "He's attempted to get the Polaris in from three different angles. But has had no luck. He decided to park it and go in on foot. He thinks he might be less than fifty yards away, but the going is really tough."

"How about the other two?" Jack asked.

"I talked to Ralph. He has about the same story as Junior. He thinks he might be near the location as well. But he's having a hard time.

"I was not able to get a response from Milton. He doesn't answer."

"Really? Don't you think that's curious?" Jack asked.

"I'll keep trying him," the sheriff said.

"Ask the other two if they know anything about that drone."

Suddenly Junior's voice broke loudly over the radio.

"Sheriff! We've got a *big* problem!"

Chapter 32
Where's Milton?

"Junior. What's up?" the sheriff asked.

"Milton! I just found Milton," Junior said. "And I'm pretty sure he's dead!"

"Shit!" the sheriff said. "You can't be serious! Are you sure?"

"Sheriff," Junior said. "He's right here on the ground. And he ain't breathin', and there's blood. I'm guessing—just guessing—a gunshot wound. Quite a lot of blood."

Jack told the two boys to get in the truck and to stay there. And then he called Kate.

"We've got a problem out here," Jack told her. "I don't know what's going on, but our drone crashed. I think suspiciously. And one of the men said there was a second drone flying around out there.

"But, worst of all, one of our guys has apparently died, maybe killed."

"Died?" Kate asked. "How?"

"Don't know yet," Jack said.

"Murdered? An accident? What do we know so far?"

"Only that Junior, one of the searchers, said that he found Milton lying on the ground, and that he *appeared* to be dead."

"But we don't know that for sure?" Kate asked. "Not yet, at least? Just that one of the men *thinks* he's dead. Where are the boys?"

"In the truck," Jack said. "They're fine. But we've got to get them out of here. This is not an appropriate place for them to be—not anymore.

You stay put for now. I'll find a way to get them out to you, and you can see they get home. Maybe call Mary and have her meet you halfway. I could sure use you here."

"Mary is in Munising all day. I'll see if she can get away and meet me at the highway."

* * *

Kate was able to reach Mary Fletcher. And Deputy Manford drove the boys out to Creighton Truck Trail, where Kate was waiting in Jack's Tahoe.

Kate delivered the boys to a waiting Mary Fletcher, and then she returned with Deputy Manford to the place in the bog where Jack and the sheriff were waiting.

"Hear anything new?" Kate asked her father as she jumped out of the Chevy.

* * *

"Regardless of the situation, don't let the bastards win … and have no regrets … for it will be a good day!" — Richard Wakinyan (Martian Fleet Commander) in R.G. Risch's *Beyond Mars: Crimson Fleet.*

Chapter 33

A complicated matter

Jack was glad to see Kate. While he totally trusted Sheriff Green, he liked having Kate close by when he was bouncing ideas around. After all, as a homicide detective in a large city, she had investigated dozens of murder cases involving numerous different motives. And while the death of Milton Stenos had not yet been officially declared a homicide, all those present viewed it as such.

"We've got a chopper on the way with a forensic pathologist on board," Jack said.

"Then we're pretty certain your guy is really dead?" Kate asked.

"All three of the other searchers have converged at the point where the body was discovered," Jack said. "And one of them, Junior Manford, has had medical training. He stated categorically that Mr. Stenos is dead."

"Did he have any theories as to how he died?"

"Shot," Jack said. "At least in Manford's opinion Mr. Stenos appears to have died from a single gunshot wound to the chest."

"Did anyone hear it?" Kate asked.

"Not really. Zach said he thought he might have heard something. But it didn't sound like a gunshot to him. More like a branch cracking underfoot—but louder."

"Suppressor," Kate said. "Sounds like the shooter was using a suppressor."

"That's what I'm thinking," Jack agreed. "But Zach wouldn't have known that—or at least he *shouldn't* have. No reason to think he's ever heard a suppressed gunshot. To him it might have sounded like someone walking through the woods."

"No one else heard it?" Kate asked.

"Right," Jack said. "But there is an interesting wrinkle. Before the guys headed out, I thought I noticed Zach's jacket hanging a little crooked."

"Like he was carrying?" Kate asked.

"Exactly. So I asked to borrow his jacket to launch the drone. When I spread it out, I felt a pistol in the pocket."

"Do you suspect him for the shooting?" Kate asked.

"No reason to. Not yet. Wouldn't be unusual to want to carry a handgun if you're going into a bog like this. And besides, the gun I felt was not equipped with a suppressor."

"Could have attached it in the bog," Kate suggested.

"That's possible," Jack agreed.

"Especially if he does not want to have to explain why he was carrying concealed with a suppressor. Could have had the suppressor in another pocket, or in his pants pocket."

"That's possible," Jack agreed. "Guess we'll just have to take a look at Zach's gun when he comes back. To see if it's been modified to accommodate a suppressor."

"And to see if it's been fired lately," Kate added.

"I asked Sheriff Green to request Zach's firearm as soon as possible," Jack said. "He's on his way back to the scene now—the hard way."

"How are we going to get back there?" Kate asked. "The *hard* way too?"

"The chopper's going to drop a line for us, and then take us, along with the doctor and Sheriff Griffen, up to the crime scene."

Kate laughed. "I guess there are some perks that come with age."

"Age! What are you talking about?" Jack responded with a big smile. "I told the sheriff that we needed you back there, and that you didn't have the proper gear. I'm just hitchhiking."

"Suppose we won't be needing crime scene tape for this one," Kate said.

They both smiled.

"God," Kate continued. "I hate dealing with asymmetrical cases like this. If you don't do everything by the book, when it goes to trial you're screwed. And if you try to do it the right way, you're still screwed by the logistics of the whole mess."

"That's assuming we are able to catch the killer in the first place," Jack countered. "But say we do—catch him that is. At that point maybe we'll figure out that there is an easier solution to the whole conundrum."

"Yeah, right," Kate said. "Sometimes I just wish it could be that easy. How long before the chopper gets here?"

Jack looked at his watch and then off to the northwestern sky.

"Coming from Marquette?" Kate asked.

"Right. And it should be getting here any time now."

* * *

"Sheriff Green," Zach Tanner said as the sheriff struggled through the final few yards of thick brush and sometimes knee-deep water.

"Gentlemen," the sheriff responded. "Couldn't you have found a better place to hold this meeting?"

The sun had dropped deep into the southwestern sky. It was after seven p.m., and it was overcast. That meant that soon they would need additional light.

"Hopefully the doc can get here and do his stuff. Before it gets too dark."

The sheriff looked off to the east and saw what looked to be Mr.

Stenos's form lying in the mud.

"Anyone touch the body?" he asked.

"Well, *I* did," Zach quickly said. "When I found him I pulled him from the water and turned him over to see what was wrong. But as soon as I saw the blood, and his eyes, I knew he was dead. So I just pulled back and did not further disturb the body. When I originally found him he was face down in about three inches of water."

"And I checked him as well," Junior Manford said. "But you knew I was going to take a look, and you said I should. I felt for a pulse. And I could also see that he was dead. I didn't move him. I could see the bullet wound in his chest, and all the blood. I briefly examined the rest of his body but found only that single gunshot. I don't know if there is an exit wound."

"Were you wearing gloves?" Sheriff Green asked.

"Yes."

"The doc will be here soon and formally declare him dead," Sheriff Green said. "And hopefully, he will be bringing Sheriff Griffen with him."

"Zach," Sheriff Green said, turning his full attention to his unruly friend. "Could we take a couple steps over here? I have a favor I have to ask you."

"Sure," Zach replied. "There's a small clearing over here to the north. That's where Jack's little helicopter crashed. I'll show it to you. I wouldn't let the guys get too close to it, because Jack said he did not want it disturbed."

"Let me get this straight," the sheriff said, first looking at the downed drone, and then turning his eyes toward the dead body. "You found the helicopter, but you *didn't* see the body? They can't be more than forty feet apart."

"That's right," Zach said. "I didn't walk through right here, so I might have missed it the first time. But when I returned to the drone to take pictures for Jack, that's when I spotted Milton."

"Yeah," the sheriff said after thinking about it for a moment. "But that's not the main reason I wanted to talk to you."

"What's up?" Zach asked.

"I understand that you are carrying a pistol—a snub-nosed revolver. I would like to check it out."

"Damn," Zach said. "How'd you know about that? *Handler* told you, didn't he? He went through my pockets when he borrowed my jacket. Funny, I didn't see him do it. That bastard is really slick."

"Doesn't matter how I found out," the sheriff said. "I would still like to see it. Would you please turn it over?"

"I can't, Sheriff," Zach said.

Chapter 34
And there's more

"You're *refusing*?" Sheriff Green said, taking a step backward to provide separation.

"No, I'm not refusing," Zach said. "I somehow lost it out here, or on the way out here."

"You *lost* it?" the sheriff said with a tone of skepticism. "How could you lose it?"

"Hell if I know," Zach said. "The only thing I can think of is while we were waiting to receive the coordinates, I decided to take a dump. I took my jacket off and tossed it on a bush.

"It sort of slid down the side of the bush toward the creek. I grabbed it before it hit the water. The gun could have tumbled out when I jerked the jacket back up on the bush. I don't know. I thought I had my pocket zipped. But that's the only time I can imagine.

"It was a nice little Smith and Wesson. I would really hate to lose it. My dad gave it to me on my twenty-first birthday. When this stuff is all finished, I intend to retrace my steps. If that's where it fell out, I should be able to locate it."

"Sheriff Griffen should be tagging along with the pathologist," Sheriff Green said. "I am going to have to tell him that you lost a gun out here in the bog. So get prepared for some questions. He can be tough."

"The sheriff is actually a friend of mine," Zach said, again exhibiting a cocky attitude. "But you're right, he can be a hard-nosed SOB when he wants to. And I know he's gonna have a problem with that—my losing a gun—especially with Milton getting shot and all. Griffen's not gonna like that coincidence."

"You said it was a Smith and Wesson?"

"Right," Zach said. "A .38. It's not new, but it's in great shape."

"Sheriff Griffen is going to wonder if Stenos was shot with your gun," the sheriff said. "The entry wound looks like a .38, or a 9 mil. Can't tell for sure which it was because they are the same size. But my guess is, the bullet was not fired from a 9 mil., because it's too hard to hang on to the casings with a semi-auto. Most likely Milton was shot with a revolver. Maybe like yours."

"I'm going to have you slip on a pair of latex gloves," the sheriff said, pulling a pair out of his pocket.

"Gunshot residue!" Zach was getting nervous and loud. "You think I might have GSR on my hand? You consider me a suspect, don't you?"

"Hell no," Sheriff Green said firmly. "This is how I clear you. If I can say that I had you put on latex gloves, and if there is no GSR found on your hands or in the gloves, that will help you. Just do as I tell you. It's procedure."

"Sure, Sheriff, whatever you say," Zach said, angrily slipping on the gloves with a snap. "But I was in the creek. I got my hands wet. If I shot Milton, there'd be nothing on my hands anyway. It would have washed off."

"That's all fine," the sheriff said. "Just leave the gloves on until Griffen says you can take them off."

* * *

"Dad," Kate said. "Do you hear that?"

Chapter 35

Their ride arrives

First, they dropped the bucket down and Jack strapped Kate into it. The pilot was able to get down to within thirty feet of the ground to pick them up.

Once Kate was safely inside the chopper, they dropped the bucket down for him.

"Jack Handler, I presume?" the neatly uniformed Sheriff Harvey Griffen said. "Pleased to meet you. I'm Harvey Griffen, sheriff here in Schoolcraft County. My good friend Sheriff Green tells me that you and your boys have turned my county upside down. But that's okay. I like to keep busy."

"Sheriff," Jack said. "I guess that this is turning out to be some kind of a major big deal."

"It sure is," Sheriff Griffen agreed.

"Sheriff, have you met my daughter?" Jack asked as an introduction.

"I sure have. She and I had a nice conversation while you were getting hoisted up here. Homicide detective in New York City. You must be very proud of her."

"Very much so," Jack said.

"I don't know just how extensively you've been briefed regarding—"

"Maybe I can save you some time," Sheriff Griffen interrupted. "Why don't I tell you what I do know, and then you can fill me in.

"First of all, this thing got started when two young men, both of whom are associated with you, found a wedding ring and a human finger bone here in Strangmoor—a *partial* human finger bone.

"The problem was that they lost their Garmin, and so they couldn't lead my men back to the spot where they had originally found the bone.

"And that's why the excursion today—to locate the Garmin, and then hopefully the site of the body, if there even is a body.

"But that didn't happen. Instead, one of my good friends, Milton Stenos, gets himself shot and killed. And no one finds the Garmin. Even though at one point you had a visual on it using that drone of yours.

"Would you say that is about the whole gist of the story?"

"I think that's about it," Jack said, sensing that Sheriff Griffen was not pleased with the outcome of the search.

"I should have been out here from the start," Sheriff Griffen said. "I should have put off my testimony, put on my waders, and joined your party in the bog.

"Not that it would have made a difference. I'm not suggesting that Green or you did anything wrong. It's just that this is Schoolcraft County—my county. I was the one elected to protect its residents. And it should have been *my* job to get my ass out here with you guys today.

"Had I any notion that someone might get hurt. Hell, it even looks like Milton was murdered. Is that how you see it, Jack? Milton Stenos, he was shot; but was it murder? Is that what you think?"

"Mr. Stenos apparently died from a single gunshot wound. At least, that's the preliminary report," Jack said. "And Sheriff Green did not say anything about finding a gun near the body. So that would make it highly likely that some sort of homicide was involved. After all, who would commit suicide out in the middle of the bog? And then by shooting himself in the heart? Can't rule anything out at this point, I suppose. Could have been an accident. But it will take some serious evidence to convince me that forensics is not about to rule it a homicide. But to call it a murder, at this point, that would be a stretch."

"Kate," the sheriff said, turning toward her. "Any thoughts yet?"

Kate was deep in thought about the recent events. So much so it produced a series of scowl lines on her normally youthful appearing face. She had just tied her long auburn hair back in a ponytail to keep it out of her way and pushed up her shirtsleeves—a habit she had developed back in her early days in New York when she was pulling files and going through evidence.

Now that she knew the boys were safe with Mary, she was about to pour herself fully into the details at hand.

"Kate?"

"Not murder at this point. I would agree with my father. We need to allow forensics to do its thing, and then see where the evidence leads."

"I suppose," Sheriff Griffen said.

"Now, I want to send the doctor down first," the sheriff continued. "Then I'll go down. And then you and your daughter.

"Deputy Grant," the sheriff said, turning to a uniformed deputy sitting behind the chopper pilot. "I want you to keep the crime scene fully lit up. Hit it with everything you've got. Be looking for any movement outside the perimeter as well. Something strange has already taken place here. We have to guard against … I suppose we don't actually know what we have to guard against. As I understand it, there was another drone up here, just about the time of the murder. A big red one. I suppose you need to be on the lookout for something like that as well.

"And, I'm talking to you now, pilot. How long can you hover? Have we got a full tank?"

Neither the pilot nor the co-pilot responded because at that moment they were not monitoring the headsets the passengers were using. So the deputy tapped him on the shoulder, and then pointed to the fuel gauge. The pilot then held up two fingers.

"I had talked to him earlier about fuel," the deputy said. "He says now we are good for two hours. And then he will want to head back in. But we have another chopper on the ready if we need it. As far as lighting is concerned, I have a whole crime scene lighting assembly I'll lower down after all of you are on the ground."

"Okay," the sheriff said, satisfied that a suitable plan was taking shape. "We'll get this wound up in an hour. I don't want to spend any more money on choppers.

"I hope you heard that, Doc. I want you to get your end tidied up quickly.

"And deputy. When it comes time to go, I'm taking the doc, Handler and his daughter, you, myself, Sheriff Green, and, of course, the body. The rest of them are going to have to hike back out.

"We'll drop Green and the Handlers off where we picked them up. And the rest of us will head directly to the morgue. I want that bullet tonight. You heard that—right, Doc? I want that bullet *tonight*."

The doctor, who also went by the name "Dr. John," was used to the drill and the barking. Having spent nearly two decades doing this same thing in Detroit with the Metropolitan Police, he had seen more than his share of gunshot wounds, stabbings, and other types of violent deaths. And he had been yelled at by the best of them. He just sighed and nodded his head, indicating that he was in agreement.

Dr. John, a diminutive man with horn-rimmed glasses, was as meticulous about his appearance as he was with his work. He always wore his white lab coat and a black tie. Even though he knew just how miserable performing his duties would be out in the bog on this day, still he looked the part of the professional.

Dr. John always wore his uniform when on the job. Even in the most miserable of winter storms, if you looked carefully you would see the lab coat and black tie, along with his neatly trimmed silver goatee, peeking out from the doc's hooded down coat.

"Then we all understand each other," Sheriff Griffen said. "If for some strange reason we are able to make an arrest, then I will leave it to one of my deputies to bring the perp in. But the doc and I are going to stay with the body until I have the bullet."

"Sheriff!" Deputy Grant said, careful not to interrupt. "Take a look over there. That shiny object."

Chapter 36
The shiny object

After lowering the pack of auxiliary lighting to within grasping distance of the men on the ground, Deputy Grant began flooding the area with the onboard spotlights, looking for the best possible location to receive his passengers. Suddenly, some distance from the group of men, a brilliant beam bounced off the ground and caught his eye.

"What do you suppose that is?" the deputy said out loud. While none of the others heard his words, he retrained the light on the object and pointed it out to them. He, Jack, Kate, and the sheriff were all engrossed with the prospects of what the object could be and what it might be doing out in Strangmoor Bog.

"I have no idea what the hell that is, but I'm sure gonna find out," the sheriff said. "But how best to do it—that's another question.

"That is treacherous going down there—how do we get to it?" he asked, checking with his eyes to be sure that the others understood.

"What do you think, Jack?" the sheriff continued. "You've poked around down there a bit. Would it be best to drop someone down directly from the chopper? Or navigate someone on the ground over there to check it out?"

"We've got the tools to work with right here," Jack replied. "That looks to be nearly a hundred feet from the guys below. To get them over there, and then to direct them specifically to where it is. It'd take too long, and use up too much fuel.

"I'll take the ride down and snatch it. It'll save a lot of time and aggravation."

The deputy explained to the pilot that they needed to take a look at an object he'd spotted. He then guided the pilot to a point directly above it.

Jack was ready. His intention was to drop down using a winch rescue strop, inspect the reflective object, mark the area with yellow crime scene tape, and photograph it.

If he deemed it appropriate, he would collect any portable evidence and then have the deputy hoist him back up with it.

But before Jack even hit the ground, he recognized the source of the reflection and chuckled out loud.

"You guys are going to get a laugh out of this," he said. "Looks like someone was down here passing some time."

Before he retrieved the top and bottom of an empty can of Copenhagen snuff, he carefully opened a Ziploc plastic bag and, wearing latex gloves, placed both pieces of the can in the bag, zipped it, and slid the bag into a nylon pouch attached to his strop.

He was about to signal to the chopper to pull him up when another object caught his eye. Underneath a small pile of brush just a few feet away, he spotted a patch of camo cloth.

"What the hell!" Jack said, reaching down to pull off some of the twigs strewn loosely over the top of the object to further conceal it.

Chapter 37

Now this is weird!

Pulling still more branches aside, Jack could see that what initially looked like a small swatch of camouflage fabric was actually a sizable zippered camo bag.

As he felt around for a handle, he could tell that there was an object inside of it and that it was substantial.

"Hey, guys," Jack spoke into the mic. "I've got something pretty big down here. Appears to have been freshly placed in a camo bag. Can't tell just how heavy it is, but I'd guess it could go as much as a hundred pounds. Any suggestions?"

"You want to bring it up, right?" Deputy Grant asked.

"Not sure," Jack replied. "What does the sheriff think?"

"We're not seeing it," the sheriff said. "Can you move it out so we can get a look at it? Is there a handle that we could get a hook on?"

"I'll see what I can do," Jack replied. "But first I'm going to take a couple snapshots of it right where it lies."

After securing his cell, Jack lifted the bag by the handle and found that he could quite easily lift it. He pulled it out from the brush and set it down in a manner that would allow the sheriff to view it in its entirety.

"How much do you think it weighs?" the sheriff asked.

"I think seventy-five pounds."

"Let's bring it up and take a look."

Jack disconnected the rope from his harness, looped it around the bag and through the handle, and then snapped the hook onto the rope. He then cinched it tightly around the object of interest, and made sure that there was nothing above that could cause it to hang up.

"There you go," he said. "I'm off and it's on. Take it up, but don't forget to drop the rope back down."

Immediately the slack in the rope disappeared and the camo bag with its mysterious contents lifted off the ground. Jack guided it up so that it did not swing back and smack him in the head.

Once the deputy had disconnected and secured the bag, he sent the rope back down for Jack.

After Jack had hooked the strop back to the rope, he looked up and signaled with his hands that they should reel him in.

As soon as he and the sheriff had pulled Jack into the chopper, the deputy asked, "We gonna open it up in the chopper?"

"I don't know," the sheriff quipped. "What if it's a bag of snakes?"

"Too heavy," the deputy fired back. "I'd like to see what's in it. Wouldn't you?"

"Kate. Whaddya think?" the sheriff asked. "Should we open it?"

"Whatever you decide," Jack snapped. "But maybe we should get the doc down so he can do his job."

"Right," the deputy agreed. "What do you think, Sheriff?"

"Yeah," the sheriff said. "It's critical that he get started. I'll follow. After we check out the contents of that bag, of course. And then Jack. You're going to want to go down as well, right?"

"Kate and I would at least like to inspect the drone," Jack replied. "And then gather up the parts. I want to know what brought it down."

"This is what we do," the sheriff said. "We'll drop the doc. And then we'll take a look inside that bag. See what that's all about. And then the three of us—Jack, Kate, and I—will go down.

"Deputy Grant. You stay with the chopper ... and this mysterious package. And after they get the lights set up on the ground, you go back with the chopper and refuel. We've already lost too much time. I do not want to rush the doc. And even more, I don't want to run this bird low on fuel.

"When we wind this up, I will radio you and you can have them come back and pick us up.

"I really have no idea how long it's going to take the doc—"

"I don't think it will take me very long to declare the man's dead," the doc said. "Seems like we've already got a consensus about that."

"I'm sure you're right," the sheriff said. "But I'll be damned if I'll rush this investigation just because of a fuel issue. And I sure as hell don't intend to be on CNN tonight trying to explain how I allowed my chopper to run out of gas. Or worse.

"We'll do it just like I said. Deputy Grant, get the doc on the ground. And give them a heads up below that they're about to have company. They probably can't see what we're doing up here with those lights blasting them in the face."

"Yes sir, Sheriff," the deputy said, signaling the pilot to center the chopper over the scene.

"Okay, Jack," the sheriff said. "You do the honors. Open up that bag and let's see what you found."

Before Jack unzipped it, he lifted it up by the handle.

"Easily it weighs seventy pounds," he said. "Too heavy for snakes, or any other living thing that might fit into a bag this size."

Setting it back down gently, he pulled the C-shaped zipper that extended three-quarters of the way around the bag. He then laid it wide open.

"Well, Sheriff," he said. "Ever seen anything like this before?"

Chapter 38
What is it?

Yeah," the sheriff said. "In *Back to the Future.* I think it's some kind of flux capacitor. What do you think?"

"Got a flashlight around here?" Jack asked. "I'd like to get a look at some of the components."

"Here ya go, Dad," Kate said, handing him her keys with an attached LED flashlight.

"Perfect."

Jack removed his reading glasses from his jacket pocket, put them on, and knelt down closer to the mysterious contraption.

After sliding the device around several times in order to get a better look, Jack finally rose up from his knees and stared at the sheriff.

"Well, what do you make of it?" the sheriff asked. "Any idea what it is?"

"Better than that," Jack said, "I know exactly what it is. And you're not going to like what you hear."

"What is it?"

"I'd bet we've got some sort of EMP weapon."

"Electromagnetic pulse?" the sheriff said after a moment. "*That* is a weapon?"

"Powerful enough to bring this chopper down," Jack said. "If it is properly prepared and aimed, it will send a magnetic pulse for quite a distance, and fry any electronics in its path."

"I thought those puppies had to be huge?" the sheriff said. "And nuclear. Are we talking about the same thing?"

"Some EMPs do use nukes," Jack said. "Those would be considered strategic weapons.

"But what we've got here is a portable tactical device. It looks to me like this one was made in China. That's no surprise. And instead of the older Marx pulse generator, it apparently uses a flux compression device. That allows it to be portable.

"My guess is that to fire it, a small explosive charge—almost like a blank round in a firearm on a movie set—is triggered, forcing an armature through a magnetic coil. When this happens, a strong magnetic field is compressed and discharged from the business end of the device.

"And, depending on the protection that is provided for electronic devices in its path, the magnetic pulse this weapon produces can be very destructive, even incapacitating.

"This is what was used to bring my little bird down. I'm quite sure about that. When I analyze the electronic components in my drone, I'm certain I will find them fried."

"And my friend," the sheriff said, "Mr. Stenos, he just happened to have seen something that he wasn't supposed to see. Is that what you figure happened?"

"That's entirely possible," Jack agreed. "It will be interesting to see if the victim has any stippling on his clothing. I'm starting to think that he was shot from the same place where I found this bag. Probably with a rifle using a suppressor. I'm not sure why there was no exit wound. Generally you'd expect one if the shot was fired from a rifle. But this could be some sort of specialized weapon. Perhaps even using a smaller load.

"I suppose it's possible that the killer left his hiding place and walked over to where Stenos was standing, and then shot him.

"But it seems more likely to me that Mr. Stenos heard the discharge of the EMP weapon, turned to face the man who was wielding the weapon, and was then shot. Probably had a scope as well. A bullet directly through the heart. That shot was very well placed. Especially if it was fired from a distance."

"What the hell kinda guy is going to have a weapon like this?" the sheriff said, gesturing toward the bag containing the EMP device. "What would be the point?"

"As I understand it," Jack said. "These EMPs are about to become the weapon of choice for terrorists—specifically, those who act on their own."

"So, is our killer a terrorist?"

"That assumption would be a stretch," Jack said after thinking for a moment.

"If we were in New York," Kate contributed. "We'd be engaging profilers. People have different reasons for possessing weapons such as this. One of them being, simply because they can. Some people just like to accumulate exotic weaponry. I'm not suggesting that is the case with this killer. But I've seen it. A guy—almost certainly it's a male—who has more money than he needs. He doesn't like to invest. Or more likely he's obtained his money through illegal, or at least questionable means and doesn't want to run the risk of it being traced back to him. So he pours his extra cash into various material objects—and sometimes that includes exotic weapons.

"I'm no profiler. But I would agree with my father, simple possession of an EMP device does not necessarily suggest terror connections.

"But, that's not to say that this guy is not a serious threat—perhaps even a terrorist. This type of weapon could be used to bring down a large commercial passenger plane.

"Unless those who own or lease the plane have taken specific precautions to protect the electronics in that plane, if a perpetrator can get close to it, like during takeoff or landing, he can fry enough of the circuits to bring it down."

"Well," the sheriff said, "it sure as hell brought your dad's drone down."

"Sheriff," Jack warned, "I would advise you not to handle that piece of equipment. First, we're not sure how it works. And if accidently discharged it could cripple this bird.

"Also, we know that this type of EMP requires an explosive charge to generate the magnetic pulse. Who knows what damage that alone is capable of creating?

"Besides, the FBI now has to be contacted. And they are going to want to get their hands on it just the way it is. When they interview you, for instance, it would work to your advantage to be able to state that you personally did not touch it. It will save you a lot of time and trouble just to leave it alone, and to put it back right where we found it.

"I think we should zip it back up, drop me down with it, and I'll tuck it back under the brush exactly where the perpetrator left it. And then let the FBI have at it as they see fit. Of course, you must tell them that I brought it up into the chopper. But as soon as you saw what we had, you made me return it.

"That device is evidence, and it would simplify matters if we did not have to establish and defend an extended chain of custody. Just leave it on the ground, and post a deputy to guard it until the FBI gets here. The deputy can answer all their questions, and we can then all go about our business."

The sheriff heard Jack out but did not appreciate his telling him what to do. Carefully the sheriff zipped the bag up and slid it as far out of the way as possible.

"That weapon, or whatever the hell it is, it is going to stay with me. I'm not putting it back in the bog.

"Okay, Kate, it's your turn," the sheriff continued. "Ready to get lowered?"

* * *

After Kate, Jack, and Sheriff Griffen had all been lowered to the ground, the sheriff ordered Deputy Grant to have the pilot take the helicopter back into Marquette for refueling.

"And after you're finished there," he said. "have them set the chopper down in Manistique on your way back, and run this *thing* over to my office and secure it. You'll have plenty of time. I won't want you heading back here until the doc is finished and we've got the site marked off."

Jack and Kate both heard the sheriff's orders. They looked at each other and grimaced.

"That's a *big* mistake," Kate mouthed silently.

Just as quickly as the sheriff gave the order to head out, the pilot took the helicopter straight up, pointed its nose to the northwest and lowered it. As the nose dropped, the pilot revved up the RPMs and sped off toward Marquette.

Deputy Grant had just settled back in his seat for the ride back to Marquette when he heard a beeping noise.

At first he assumed that it was emanating from some of the instruments in the cockpit, but soon he realized that it was actually coming from the camo bag containing the mysterious EMP device.

Carefully he unzipped it.

"What the hell could this mean?" he grumbled as he took a close look at a small digital display that had before been dormant.

It was counting down by seconds: "52, 51, 50, 49 …"

He looked for anything that resembled a cutoff switch, but found none.

"37, 36, 35 …"

He slid the bag out and considered dumping it over the side. But that would cost him his job. So instead, he reached over and grabbed the pilot's arm and signaled for him to set the chopper down.

The pilot disgustedly waved him off and signaled for him to retreat.

"12, 11, 10, 9 ..."

Deputy Grant did as told.

Dropping to his knees beside the device he again looked for some sort of disable mechanism.

"4, 3, 2, 1 ..."

When the display reached "0," the countdown ceased, and a flashing character appeared on the screen. He had no sense as to its meaning or significance, except that he believed it could not be good.

Chapter 39
Not very far at all

The Sikorsky S-76D hit an altitude of three hundred feet, and had flown barely a mile downrange, when it blew up.

"Holy shit!" Ralph shouted. "Did you see that? The chopper just exploded. Holy shit! I can't believe it!"

Jack took a look around at all the men who were gathered there. He was looking for some sort of weapon that might have been used to bring the helicopter down. He saw nothing.

"Booby-trapped," Jack said to Kate after some deliberation. "That chopper did not just explode. Sikorsky helicopters are as safe as they get. It did not explode without help. The EMP was booby-trapped. Probably had a sensor that triggered when it got too far from a transmitter. I'd bet that somewhere close by we will find it—the transmitter. Most likely over by where the perp left the weapon. Wouldn't have to be very large. Maybe the size of a pack of cigarettes, or a little larger.

"We're lucky it didn't go off when I moved the weapon the first time. Must not have reached the necessary distance."

"You saying it had an explosive built into it?" Sheriff Griffen asked.

"Must have," Jack replied. "The shooter intended to come back and pick the EMP up—probably after a day or two. Perhaps longer. But, just in case someone beat him to it, he activated a mechanism that would explode if it were removed from this specific location sufficiently. That is, far enough so that it was no longer able to receive the signal being sent to it.

"That was not a huge explosion—just enough to totally destroy the device. Possibly five or six ounces, or even less, of C-4. That would easily do it.

"But the destruction of the chopper—that was unintended collateral damage.

"Of course, this is all conjecture," Jack continued. "But if we find a transmitter near where we found the snuff can, then that would definitely support my theory.

"What do you say, Sheriff?" Jack asked. "Okay if Kate and I poke around over there to see what we find? And you'd better get word to the FBI, ASAP."

"And who the hell do I call about a chopper crash? The NTSB?" the sheriff asked Jack.

"The FBI ... start with the FBI," Jack replied. "They will determine when other agencies should get involved. But right now, the first call goes to the fire department, and the second to the FBI. And I would try to get some of your guys over there. One of them was driving a Polaris on tracks. Which one of you was that?"

Junior spoke up. "That was me. I got in as far as I could with it. It's sitting about a hundred yards west and south of here."

"Do you have extinguishers in it?" Jack asked.

"One for sure. Maybe two. I know I have a twenty-pounder. There might be a second smaller one."

"Sheriff," Jack said. "I suggest you send two of these men over to the Polaris. And see if they can get to the crash scene.

"The problem is, if the water content of that peat is less than fifty-five percent, the fuel from that chopper could set the peat on fire, and it could take months or even years to fully extinguish the bog.

"Your guys are not going to have much luck putting out an underground fire like that, but the sooner they can direct the firefighters to the location, the better."

"Junior, you and Ralph head over there as quickly as possible," the sheriff commanded. "As soon as you are able, call the fire department. When you arrive on the scene, lend whatever assistance you can. Let me know what you find. And provide my office with the coordinates. And then have them—the fire department—contact the FBI."

"Kate, you come with me," Jack said. "I could use a younger pair of eyes."

"What exactly are we looking for?" Kate asked.

"There is probably going to be a transmitter close to where we found the EMP."

"Couldn't the killer have triggered the explosion from the ground?" Kate questioned. "With a portable transmitter?"

"Could have," Jack replied as he led Kate away from the group for privacy. "But I'm thinking that whoever hid the device did so planning that he would return later to retrieve it. That means that he has probably left this area altogether. And if, during the time that he was gone, someone found and tried to remove the EMP, our perp would not want him to be successful.

"But, if our guy does still happen to be on the ground here with us, he would not want the portable transmitter to be found on his person during a search. So he would have concealed it close by. I suspect something is hidden over there where I found the EMP, and I think we just might be able to find it. Turn on your flashlight and follow me."

The bog was filled with the noise of the night insects, amphibians, mammals, and birds. A coyote howled in the distance, and the screech of an owl made the scene feel like the set of a Hitchcock movie.

Illuminating their way with only one small flashlight, Jack and Kate immediately headed over to the area where he had found the EMP.

No moon or stars aided their effort. When the chopper pulled out it left only the stark blackness of the bog surrounding them. Aside from a few flashlights, and four Streamlight Portable Scene Lights deployed surrounding the Stenos body, the night was as dark and damp as an empty cave.

"Who do you like for this?" Kate asked as they fought their way through the bog. "Got any favorites?"

"It would be easy to think that one of the guys down here on the ground must have been involved," Jack replied. "But no evidence suggests it … yet. That device was too large for any of these fellows to have concealed. It almost had to have been brought in earlier, or by a third party. But I'm not sure how. Or why, for that matter. That's some major weaponry just to bring down my little drone."

Jack, the former homicide detective, had been sorting through and analyzing the facts in his mind, much like he did back in his days in Chicago, when he stopped suddenly and turned toward Kate. They were by then well out of earshot from the others.

"This is what I think to this point," he said. "A person, or persons—it's likely that there are two or more involved—for some reason did not want the rest of the body the boys discovered to be found.

"And, strange as it might seem, I think they have some connection with the group out here today."

"It makes sense, but do you have a specific reason to think that?"

"The EMP. Whoever brought my drone down had to have been aware that I was going to use a drone to find the Garmin, and they surmised the best way to bring it down would be to use the EMP.

"You can't put a suppressor on a shotgun," Jack continued. "And it would be impossible to shoot it down with a pistol or a rifle.

"I think the profile you came up with earlier makes sense. Whoever is behind this had the EMP in his arsenal already. They're not very difficult to build—all the necessary components are available from online sources.

"And the manner in which it was rigged to explode if tampered with or removed—that's not terribly sophisticated either.

"Federal security agencies use similar devices on laptops containing sensitive material," Jack continued. "If one gets stolen, a small explosive device will destroy the hard drive when the laptop is separated too far from the party assigned to it."

"And how do you think they managed to get the device into the bog to begin with?" Kate asked.

"Dropped it from an airplane earlier. A chopper would have been noticed. Probably dropped it from a small plane."

"By parachute?" Kate asked. "But if they did that, wouldn't we have seen someone running around down here? Someone who didn't come out with us? *Unless!* Unless they marked the target with a laser, used a skydiving canopy, with a homing device to fly the equipment to the spot marked by the laser. I'll bet that's what you're thinking."

"Pretty much," Jack agreed. "But I'm thinking a high-altitude drop, perhaps as high as ten thousand feet, using GPS instead of laser targeting. For precision drops like this the military uses a JPADS technology—Joint Precision Airdrop System. If our military has it, most likely the Chinese have knocked off the technology and are selling it to anyone with deep enough pockets. And anyone who would know where to buy an EMP would also be able to procure this GPS technology."

"So," Kate said, "that means that somewhere around here there is a parachute, and some superfluous electronic and mechanical equipment."

"By now the chute is probably buried somewhere in the bog," Jack said. "Unlikely it'll ever be found."

"Does that mean one of our guys out here is responsible?"

"It'd be my guess, and it's only a guess, that someone out here today at least knows some of the details."

"You had a serious confrontation with that Zach character earlier," Kate said. "Do you suspect him?"

"I wouldn't characterize that as a serious confrontation," Jack said. "He's got a big mouth—that's all. But to your point, I can't rule anyone out. Except you and the two sheriffs. However, all the rest of these guys—they're all still suspects in my mind."

"Except for the dead guy—Milton Stenos," Kate said. "He didn't shoot himself."

"There is another angle," Jack said, as he and Kate began to poke around where they suspected the killer might have hidden a transmitter. "When you look at the larger picture, there is nothing to say that the killer has not already left the area—that perhaps he was waiting down here before all this went down. Maybe he intercepted the signal as to the location of the Garmin. And then, wishing to terminate the video, he destroyed my drone, killed Stenos, secured the Garmin, and afterward took off. He might not even be anywhere around here at this time."

Kate mulled over in her head what Jack had just said but did not respond to his statement. Instead, she continued to search the area, until ...

Chapter 40
Finding the crash

Within ten minutes from the time they left the group, Junior and Ralph found they had cell service, and so they followed the sheriff's orders and called Schoolcraft County Dispatch to report the downed helicopter.

"What do you think?" Junior said to Ralph. "I'm thinking that the best way to do this would be to go back the Highwater Truck Trail, hit Creighton, and take it north. From where the chopper looked to go down, I don't think it would be that far from Creighton."

"I like that idea," Ralph replied. "Sheriff Griffen didn't specify as to how we make it to the crash. Only that we get there as quickly as possible."

"No matter how we go about it," Junior said, "it's not going to be easy. Who knows what's between here and the crash? At least if we go back to Creighton, we might run into the fire responders on the way, and we can just follow them in.

"But if we just take off through the bog on a beeline, we probably won't make it through. I think using Creighton is a reasonable approach."

"I agree," Ralph said. "If we go back to Highwater, and take it to Creighton, we might even come out real close to the crash site.

"Besides, I don't know what the sheriff thinks we can accomplish with a couple of fire extinguishers; about all that will burn on that bird is the fuel. But there's definitely plenty of that, and our extinguishers couldn't possibly even touch it. And if the bog starts to burn, then all bets are off."

"He had to send us," Junior said. "Even if we fail to find the crash site, he will have covered his ass. If he doesn't at least make an effort it could cost him his job."

"I suppose you're right," Ralph said. "But we're not equipped to make a rescue effort. It seems like such a waste of time to me."

"You really think the boss sent us on a rescue mission?" Junior asked. "We're not about rescuing anyone. They're all dead. Everyone knows it. And certainly Sheriff Griffen can see that."

"You're probably right," Ralph said. "But I remember reading about that Detroit plane crash in '87—Flight 255. It killed over one hundred and fifty people. One little girl, four years old, she somehow managed to survive."

"That was before I was born," Junior chuckled. "But I did read about it recently. She just got married. And the fireman who pulled her out of the burning wreckage walked her down the aisle. That was quite a story."

"So those things do happen," Ralph said. "Sometimes people do survive against terrible odds. It does happen."

The Polaris had reached Highwater Truck Trail and was moving quickly along it toward Creighton Truck Trail.

"No one survives a helicopter crash," Junior countered. "They're different. When a chopper comes down, it comes straight down—no forward momentum to carry it past the explosion field. Whoever happens to be in the chopper ends up right in the middle of the burning rubble, strapped in and dead.

"With an airliner crash, like Flight 255, the speed of the plane can distribute debris over a long stretch of the terrain, especially when the crash occurs on takeoff. So if for some reason a passenger is strapped in, and the fuel burns some distance away from him, or in this case her, a passenger can survive.

"That's what happened in the case of this girl. All the stars were aligned just right for her survival on that day."

The two men reached Creighton Truck Trail and turned north onto it.

"See that orange glow off to the right?" Junior said. "The chopper's still burning."

"That doesn't look to be very far in," Ralph said. "Not far at all. Looks like you made the right call—using Creighton and all."

"And we beat the fire department," Junior said. "If you see a good place to enter the bog, shout it out. I'd like to get the Polaris in as close as possible."

"This is something," Ralph said. "I deer hunt in there. Right up here, there will be a sign. And one hundred feet past it is a bit of an opening. Not sure if you'll be able to drive the Polaris in, but it's passable on foot in the winter. I think I can find it if you slow down."

"There!" Ralph shouted. "There's the sign. Slow down. It's not far. Take it very slow."

"That looks like a bit of a clearing," Junior said, pointing off to the right. "Is that it?"

"Could be," Ralph said, splashing the area with a five-cell flashlight. "Yeah! That's it. Think you want to try it with the Polaris?"

"How deep is that water?" Junior asked.

"Not bad. You can get through it. But on the other side—there's a lot of thick brush."

"But you can walk it okay?"

"Right. But I don't know how this is going to work. Worst that can happen is that you end up parking it and we go in on foot."

"I can't believe it," Ralph said after only a few seconds. "I can't believe that we were able to get in this close. The crash can't be more than forty, fifty yards in."

"We're done," Junior said. "This is all the farther we can take the Polaris."

Both men jumped off, each grabbing a fire extinguisher.

"This look familiar to you?" Junior asked.

"Yeah," Ralph said. "The trail, if you can call it that, will take us a little north of the crash—at least that's how it looks to me from here. But we should be able to get in closer if we take it."

"You lead the way," Junior said. "I'll follow."

Junior and Ralph fought their way in on the trail until they were close enough to see sparks drifting upward. They were within fifty feet of the helicopter.

"Looks like it crashed into a pool," Ralph said. "Not much still burning, except for the remaining fuel. That's good."

"We should still press in as close as we can," Junior said.

"Roger that," Ralph agreed.

As they fought their way in even closer, the heat of the fire nearly singed their faces. Right before them lay the stinking blackened carcass of the huge Sikorsky helicopter. Orange flames still licked at everything that would burn, casting an eerie glow to the flora surrounding it.

"Hold it!" Junior shouted, grabbing Ralph by the shoulder. "Did you hear what I heard?"

"Hear what?" Ralph asked.

"Help!"

"Where the hell did that come from?" Ralph said.

Chapter 41
Help!

"Hello! Hello! I hear you," Ralph shouted. "Where are you?"

"Help! Please help me. I'm hurt real bad."

"Where are you?" Junior shouted. "We can hear you, but we don't know where you are."

"Oh my God! I'm hurt real bad! Please help me!"

Just then there was a flare-up of the fire, as though the flames found something that would burn and devoured it. The heat from the flame ignited a nearby scrub pine, and for a few moments it illuminated the sky.

"Up here," the voice said. "I'm up here."

Both men on the ground looked up. There were a number of trees nearby capable of supporting the weight of a human being.

They began walking around one tree at a time until they were certain the voice was not emanating from it.

"Oh my God! Oh my God! I think I'm dying! Please help me."

"Over here!" Ralph exclaimed. "I'm pretty sure it's coming from this tree. Right here. This pine. Listen."

"Here. I'm here. Help me. I'm hurting."

"I'll climb it," Ralph said, pointing up into the branches of a tall pine. "I think this is the right tree. I think it's coming from up here."

Ralph did not wait for Junior to comment. He walked around the tree looking for the best way to attack it. And then he dropped his waders.

"Are you up here?" he called out after he had scaled the larger limbs to a height of fifteen feet.

"I'm here. I'm stuck. And I have two broken arms. I can hardly breathe. I can't stand the pain."

Ralph could tell that the cry for help was directly above him.

"He's up here," Ralph called down. "And he says he's got some broken bones, and that he can't breathe."

"Okay!" Junior shouted back. "I'm going back to the road and wait for the fire department. We shouldn't move him until they get here. You go on up and see what you can do, and you can direct us back when they get here."

"Right," Ralph said. "I'll see what I can do."

Ralph carefully made his way through the maze of the smaller limbs toward the upper part of the pine. Finally, he reached the victim.

"Deputy Grant!" Ralph said excitedly. "I didn't know you were even working today."

"Volunteered," the deputy said. "They told me no one would get hurt. They told me. Now look what's happened. Milton's dead. And I'm hurt bad. Real bad. And the others on the chopper. Are they okay?"

Ralph did not want to answer that question, so he asked a question of his own.

"What happened? Do you know what happened?"

"I guess it blew up."

"The chopper blew up?"

"No," Deputy Grant said. "The thing Handler found in the bog. He called it an EMP weapon. Suddenly it started beeping. And there was a screen. It started counting down the seconds. I don't remember the blast itself. But that thing must have exploded. I jumped just before the chopper impacted."

* * *

Nearly twenty minutes later Junior led a group of fire rescue workers out into the bog.

"Ralph!" Junior shouted. "Where are you?"

"Over here. I'm over here."

Junior had pretty accurately retraced his steps, arriving almost exactly at the precise location. Ralph had climbed back down the tree and had put his waders back on.

"How is he?" Junior asked.

"He didn't make it," Ralph said. "It was Deputy Grant. I didn't even know he was on the copter. He didn't make it."

Standing off in the distance, a hundred feet from the crash, was the old man, the faint glimmer of dwindling orange flames dancing across his wrinkled face. He watched sadly, silently, and undetected.

Chapter 42

The ring

Jack and Kate spent the next day piecing together all the facts and suppositions regarding the events of the past few days. They had just finished clearing the dinner dishes, and all four were seated around the table at their resort on Sugar Island.

"So, Dad, what have we got?" Kate asked. "What do we actually know?"

Kate had opened her iPad and was prepared to take notes.

"For one thing," Jack said. "We know we're awfully damn lucky. That booby-trapped EMP could easily have detonated while you and I were still on the chopper.

"You boys ought to be particularly happy about that. Otherwise, you'd be cooking your own chicken soup."

"I don't know about that," Robby said with a snicker. "Red's a pretty good cook, and he—"

Kate interrupted his comment by pouring a teaspoon of ice water down the back of his collar.

"Careful there, bub," she said. "You'll be on dish detail for the next month. And I can sure dirty a lot of them when I want to."

"Just kidding, Kate," Robby said. "You know I *love* your cooking. You are the best!"

"That's more like it," she said, messing up his hair.

"But, seriously," she said. "What do we really know about this whole mess? What do we *really* know?"

"To start with," Robby said. "We know that there is a body out there somewhere in Strangmoor. I suppose we don't know for certain that there is an *entire* body, but we do know that there was at least a finger of a man. And that he was married. That was a *wedding* ring."

"Let's start with the ring," Kate said. "We have a ring, and part of a human finger. Forensics tells us that it is likely fifty years old, and that it belonged to a man—probably a younger man.

"The inscription on the inside of the ring was 'G&A Forever.' That would have been their first initials. The man's would have been first. That means his first name started with a 'G.'

"Now, it's possible that the 'G' stood for a nickname rather than his real first name.

"And the 'A,' the same thing would be true for her. Her name could be something like 'Ann,' or it could be the first letter of her nickname."

"That means we've got Greg and Ann Doe," Robby said. "I think we should call them that until we find out different."

"We know that we were unable to come up with any DNA," Jack said. "Just too much decomposition, even with peat-bog preservation.

"If we could find the rest of the body, chances are that we would be able to come up with something. We might be able to match it with the DNA of current families residing in the area. Or at least to eliminate some families."

"It would be real good to find the rest of the body," Kate said. "Just a couple initials are not going to get us very far."

"Unless," Jack countered. "Unless we can somehow narrow the date, and find some corresponding data, such as marriage licenses, at that time, that include couples with those first initials."

"Goes back to narrowing the time frame," Kate said.

Just then Red began to text.

Kate leaned over his shoulder and read aloud, "Check missing persons."

"That's something we can do," Jack agreed. "But again, narrowing the time frame is virtually essential. Pretty much have to have more evidence to do that. Or dental records."

No one talked for a moment. And then Red again began to text.

Kate glanced over at Jack and smiled, and leaned over Red's shoulder.

"Who made the ring?" she read.

"Yeah," Robby said. "Some jeweler had to have engraved it. Maybe there's some records."

"That's really not a bad idea," Jack said. "I looked at the ring—closely. It was made for a larger man. At least he was not a small man. And it is barely worn on the inside. That would indicate that the victim had not worn it long before he died. Odds are, that would make him a younger man."

"Or a man who had recently remarried," Kate tossed in.

"That could be," Jack agreed. "But I would bet that it was a first marriage, and that the man was younger—probably under thirty."

"Reason?" Kate asked.

"I just think that the nature of the inscription would better fit a younger couple. Young people entering into a first marriage would be more likely to stipulate that their relationship was *forever*. A couple going into a second marriage, or one later in life, would be less likely to think in terms of eternity.

"First marriage, younger couple," Jack said. "Can't know that for sure, but I think it would be a logical deduction."

"It would sure be useful to find the rest of the body," Kate said.

"We marked it, you know," Robby said. "We poked a walking stick into one of the sample holes, the one where we found the ring, and we stuck a water bottle on the end of it to mark it."

"That's right," Kate said. "You guys mentioned that earlier. It had slipped my mind because I was so caught up in finding the Garmin. But that's not going to help us much unless we get in very close first."

"Wait a minute," Jack jumped in. "Was that in a dune, or the wet section?"

"Wetter," Robby said. "We did the dune first. And then just moved over into the wetland."

"On that basis, I think we just might have some luck locating it," Jack declared. "However, we'll need a little help from Roger. If it's in the wet section, he just might be able to spot something with a satellite."

The "Roger" Jack was referring to was Roger Lawrence Minsk, a close friend of Jack's.

He was also known to his friends and associates as Roger Burnside, because of his admiration for the great blues singer, RL Burnside.

But more importantly, Roger was considerably high on the food chain of the Secret Service. Not only did he head up the Secret Service detail charged with guarding former first lady Allison Fulbright, he was also tight with the former president—Bob Fulbright.

Jack dialed his friend.

* * *

"In the realm of the unknown, difficulties must be viewed as a hidden treasure! Usually, the more difficult the better. It's not as valuable if your difficulties stem from your own inner struggle. But when difficulties arise out of increasing objective resistance, that's marvelous!"
—Aleksandr Solzhenitsyn, The First Circle

Chapter 43

The stick

Rog. Jack here. I need your help."

"Haven't heard from you for a while. Thought you were dead."

"No such luck."

"So, what can I do for you? I should say what can I do for you that won't get me fired? Or killed?"

"Just a little favor—this is no big deal."

"If it was a piece of cake, you wouldn't be calling me. … My friend—what is it you need?"

"This is something you can handle right from the seat of your pants."

"You called me at the perfect time."

"Why's that?"

"I'm playing poker with a mutual friend," Roger said. "And he's up. And I do mean *way* up."

"Who you got? Or who's got you?"

"Here, I'll let him tell you," Roger said, reaching across the table and handing his cell to the man sitting across from him.

"Handler! How the hell are you?"

Jack recognized the voice. It was former President Bob Fulbright.

"Mr. President!" Jack said. "This is awkward."

"Well, spill it," the former president said, laughing out loud. "Just what sort of favor are you after? If you're trying to bring down a foreign power, you're out of luck tonight. I'm not in that business anymore."

Jack was not intimidated. He had worked for the Fulbrights on numerous occasions, handling the dirty work that goes along with being president. But he was not comfortable with describing the nature of his request because of the heavily technical aspects it involved. Nevertheless, he knew it would not be appropriate to refuse to explain it to the former president.

"I need to borrow a satellite," Jack said.

"Oh, hell, is that all you're asking for?" Fulbright said, laughing again. "Maybe I don't really want to know anything about that. Well, Jack, I can't really say that it was a pleasure talking to you. I've got your friend here in a whole bunch of trouble, and I'm thinking you might be getting him off the hook with this interruption."

Fulbright, handing the cell back to Roger, said, "He needs a date, Rog. Can you fix him up?"

"Jack, I'm back. What is it you need?"

"I need to borrow one of your KH reconnaissance satellites," Jack said.

KH satellites, or Keyhole-class reconnaissance satellites, are a type of satellite used by the military and intelligence agencies to surveil using overhead photos.

While Keyhole satellites have been in orbit for thirty years, the newer ones, such as those of the KH-12 class, are capable of discerning clearly an object five or six inches in size. Jack believed that if he could provide Roger, with reasonable accuracy, the general location of the bottle on the stick, perhaps it could be found using the Hubble-like camera in the satellite.

Roger did not respond immediately.

"Hold that thought for a minute," Roger said. "I'm going to excuse myself, and escape from the president's ear."

With that Roger stood, and, facing President Fulbright, he said to Jack, "Plausible deniability. We must protect the president."

Once Roger had moved to the far side of the room, he said, "First of all, these satellites do not belong to me. So, when you say you want to borrow one of my satellites, as though I keep them in my pocket like a pack of Marlboros, you're way off base.

"Second, even if I wanted to help you with this, I can't. While these satellites can be moved and redirected, they are not subject to discretional deployment at my whim. What you are requesting would have to be approved by the Joint Chiefs, or at least a director. And the only way I could get their attention is if it was a matter of national security."

"How about a terror threat?" Jack asked.

Roger paused for a long moment, and then said, "Really?"

"I just had a drone shot out of the sky by a fairly powerful EMP weapon."

"How powerful?"

"It could easily have brought down a commercial airliner," Jack replied. "Or any plane with unprotected electronics."

"Can you produce that weapon?"

"Not now," Jack replied. "It was equipped with an explosive device to prevent capture. It detonated, and when it did, it brought down a Sikorsky S-76D."

"I heard about that," Roger said. "I should have known. When I heard that it was in your neck of the woods, I should have just assumed you'd have had something to do with it."

"It was a close call," Jack said. "Kate and I had just dropped out of the chopper, at a crime scene, and when the Sikorsky pulled out, the charge in the EMP weapon exploded—some type of proximity device, I'd guess. Anyway, it was big enough to bring down the big bird."

"So, what's the terror connection?" Roger asked.

"I would imagine that the feds like to keep their eyes open for devices like that," Jack replied. "The mere existence of a portable EMP weapon, inside our borders, must be of concern to Homeland Security. Regardless of what it was used for this time. Not to mention the bringing down of a helicopter."

"It could take a day or more to get it cleared—"

"That won't do," Jack said. "I need it now."

"Hold on a minute," Roger said. "I'm going to get a third opinion on this."

Jack knew exactly what that meant.

"So much for *plausible deniability*," he muttered.

Chapter 44
Just do it!

Bob," Roger said, walking back to where the former president was seated. "Jack has a problem."

"And exactly how is *that* news?" the former president quipped, still sporting a playful grin.

"He wants to use one of our satellites, a KH-12 class, to locate a rogue EMP weapon. He suspects that it might be used for a terror attack. But we don't have time to go through regular channels."

"Damn it!" Fulbright said. "Is he serious?"

"Jack's always serious," Roger said. "One has already been used in his presence to bring down a drone and to drop a Sikorsky, with loss of life."

"The FBI must be involved already," Fulbright said.

"He didn't say, but I'd assume so. What he is seeking is immediate deployment—outside of regular channels.

"I think I could twist some arms and get it done, but it could cost me."

"Give me your phone," Fulbright said.

"Jack. Fulbright here. I take it that everything Roger is telling me is based on solid intel. Is that correct?"

"That is correct."

"Then I'm going to make a call. Roger shouldn't put his career on the line for this. But I don't have a job to lose. You fill him in on all the details, and I'll deal with the director of the CIA. I did appoint him, after all. He owes me."

The former president handed the phone back to Roger.

"Okay, Jack, fill me in on some of the details," Roger said. "What are the coordinates? We might not even have a satellite capable of handling this."

"It will be in the general vicinity of Seney Wildlife Refuge, in Michigan's Upper Peninsula."

"Of course," Roger said. "That would be where that chopper went down. Right? But can you be more specific?"

"That's the area," Jack said. "I can't give you much more than that. What I need for you to do is to locate a marker in Strangmoor Bog. The best I am going to be able to provide are topographical descriptions."

"What exactly are we looking for?" Roger asked.

"A plastic bottle on the end of a stick," Jack said. "One end of the stick is poked in the ground, and the bottle is on the other end of it."

"A plastic bottle?" Roger snickered. "And the whole point of this scavenger hunt—just how does it relate to the EMP weapon?"

"That's a long story," Jack said. "Maybe I can get into all the intricate details later. Right now, I need to locate that marker before the killers, perhaps terrorists, are able to find it and remove it. If that happens, we might never be able to locate it again. It is virtually impossible to navigate the bog. And I cannot emphasize enough—time is of the essence."

* * *

Jack explained to NASA that he needed the camera to search the southwestern part of Strangmoor Bog, specifically in the northwest edge of a wet section, searching for the plastic bottle on the stick. He provided them with these approximate coordinates: 46.251544,-86.142125.

D. L. Grover, the NASA technician assigned to the project, was in the middle of explaining just how impossible it would be to locate such a small object, especially at night. He told Jack that it would be a difficult task to accomplish in daylight, but he held out no hope that he would be successful until sunrise.

And then the unexpected happened.

"What the bloody hell!" he exclaimed! "How could this be?"

Chapter 45
What the bloody hell!

Kate and the boys were keenly following Jack's efforts. He had turned on the speaker so they could hear both ends of the conversation.

When the technician voiced his excitement, Kate tilted her head slightly, furrowed her brow, and looked firmly into Jack's eyes. It was as though she were seeking an explanation. But Jack offered none.

Finally, in a whisper she asked, "What's the deal? What's going on?"

"Excuse me," Jack finally said. "Mr. Grover. Are you seeing something?"

"You could say that," he replied. "I have two subjects, at a location similar to what you described. I picked them up on infrared. Would not be able to identify them; it's too dark. But I am pretty sure they are digging around. It does not appear to be going particularly well—digging in that muck. But that's obviously what they are doing."

"That's going to be the spot," Jack said. "Log those coordinates. And, Mr. Grover, what does it appear that they are using? What sort of tools? Can you tell?"

"No exotic equipment. Just shovels."

"It'd be real nice if we could track these fellows," Jack said. "Any chance of that?"

Roger was listening to the conversation, along with the former president, who was shaking his head.

"I'll answer that question," Roger said. "Zero. Absolutely a zero chance that we will be locking on and tracking. You've got everything you're going to get. We got lucky with it. Just happened to have a KH-class satellite in the vicinity. You've got what you were after. We're not gonna be repositioning any assets—not with the info you gave us. I'm really glad we could help, Jack, but we're going to be losing that satellite shortly. It's not Geo-synchronized, and the world does turn, you know."

"You've been a huge help," Jack said. "And be sure to thank Bob for me, too."

"You just did," the former president said. "Now, Jack, if you turn up anything on that EMP weapon, you be sure to hand it over to the FBI."

"Of course," Jack said with a broad smile. He knew that he'd not be voluntarily passing on any information to the FBI. He had no doubt that they would be following up on his use of the spy satellite—it might be as soon as the next day. But, sooner or later, they would want to find out everything he knew. And then they would order him to keep out of their way.

"Thanks again, guys," he said.

"We need to get together and play some poker," the former president said. "You, Roger, and me. Like in the old days."

"Sounds like a plan," Jack said as he disconnected.

"You used to play poker with a president?" Robby asked.

Jack smiled at Robby but did not answer his question.

"Your Uncle Jack did a lot of things he isn't going to talk about," Kate said. "So don't even bother to ask him."

"Do we have to stop those people from digging up the body?" Robby asked.

"No," Jack said. "They're not going to have any success with shovels. Especially at night. And, besides, it is unlikely that the body was ever buried out there. If he, the victim, was murdered, chances are that his body was simply dumped.

"And then, after the coyotes, raccoons, and wolves got done with him, the rain and the snow would have moved the remaining pieces, mostly bones, around. Probably there are body parts strewn over a fairly large area … and who knows how deep.

"We're not going to be in as big a hurry as our friends are—the fellows who are there right now. And we're going to have better equipment. They might turn up something, but I think their goal was actually to remove the marker, and see if there was any obvious evidence lying around. Something large, like a pelvic bone, or a skull. Anything visible to the naked eye.

"But it comes down to their obscuring the site—to make it difficult for us to find it without the aid of that Garmin. There's little doubt that they are the ones who knocked my drone down, stole the Garmin, and killed Stenos. And by their efforts tonight, I'm sure they are confident that they have made it impossible for us to locate it using any markers left by the boys. They've got to be feeling pretty good about themselves right now."

Before Jack had completed his sentence, he had already dialed Sheriff Harvey Griffen.

"Sheriff. Jack Handler here. I've got some good information for you. And, I need you to do me a favor."

Chapter 46

What sort of favor?

"Handler. It's late," the sheriff said, not happy with Jack's call. "Don't you ever rest?"

"We've got a couple guys trying to dig up the rest of your body—the one in Strangmoor."

"Where are you?" the sheriff asked.

"Home," Jack said. "I'm with Kate and the boys on Sugar Island."

"Then how do you figure someone's digging around in the bog? And just what sort of favor are you expecting? Every time I talk to you, someone else dies. I'd really rather not have anything to do with you. You're nothing but trouble."

"Funny, but that's exactly what your buddy says—Sheriff Green."

"No shit," Sheriff Griffen said, "Now, what exactly is this favor you're looking for?"

"I think you should send as many cars as you can spare to the vicinity of Strangmoor," Jack said. "No doubt they will be driving vehicles with tracks. So they won't necessarily be using roads. In fact, they will probably avoid roads. But, at some point, they will have to be moving around out in the open. Maybe some of your guys will spot something that gets their attention. Any info like that could be useful.

"I'd head out there myself," Jack said, "but it will probably take me too long to get there."

"Do you think I should call the FBI on this?"

"Do what you think you have to," Jack said. "But they're going to want to know where you got your information, and by the time they're finished debriefing you, our guys will be long gone."

"Now I can see why Sheriff Green is scared to associate with you," Sheriff Griffen said. "You step on too many toes."

"I only step on the toes that need stepping on," Jack said. "Now, how about the cars? Will you send them?"

"Of course," the sheriff said disgustedly. "Anything else I can do for you?"

"Actually, yes," Jack said. "What's forensics learned on the shooting in the bog—Mr. Stenos? Do you have anything definitive on that yet?"

"Let me get some cars on the move," the sheriff said, "And then I'll talk to you about what we've got so far."

Chapter 47

Now that's curious

Ten minutes later Sheriff Griffen called Jack.

"Where are you right now?" the sheriff asked.

"Kate's just sending the boys to bed, and then we're headed out to Seney."

"Good time to talk?"

"Sure," Jack replied. "It's going to take a few minutes before she's ready."

"Well, we didn't learn much from the bullet we retrieved from the victim," the sheriff said. "Not as much as we'd like. We received the ballistics report. It indicated that the bullet was fired by a *smoothbore* firearm. A .38 caliber."

"Really?" Jack replied. "Nothing at all? As far as rifling?"

"Perfectly smooth. Obviously machined. Someone went to a lot of trouble to take the bore out."

"That Zach fellow—he claims to have lost a handgun in the bog," Jack said. "A .38."

"Yeah," the sheriff said. "That is really curious. But somehow I don't think that was the weapon used. I suppose it could have been, but I have my doubts."

"Your reasoning?" Jack asked.

"First of all," the sheriff said, "there was no stippling on the victim's clothing. That suggests that the shooter fired from some distance. For a round to be placed that accurately, from a distance, suggests a firearm with a longer barrel. Especially if the firearm had no rifling."

"Did forensics pull any foreign fibers out of the wound?" Jack asked.

"Such as would be the case if the shooter fired through a jacket, or something like that, to dampen the sound," the sheriff said. "We considered that too. That would certainly explain the absence of stippling. But the lab didn't find any unexplained fibers in the wound. At least none that did not come from the victim's own clothes."

"So, you're suggesting that the shot was fired from some distance, using a longer barreled weapon," Jack said. "And since the shooter had obviously gone to some trouble to machine the bore out of the barrel, he just might have made a custom shoulder stock to improve aim. Affixing a suppressor on it—that would not be a problem. And a twelve-to-sixteen-inch barrel would explain the accuracy from a distance.

"Another possibility is that the shooter used something like a Kel-Tec SUB-2000. I'm sure you're familiar with that firearm. It comes with a sixteen-inch barrel and uses some standard pistol rounds—not the .38, at least as far as I know. He might have adapted parts of a SUB-2000 for his purposes, possibly affixing the shoulder stock and longer barrel to a .38 caliber revolver."

"Something like that makes sense to me," the sheriff said. "Might seem a little farfetched, but machining the bore out of a .38 isn't exactly garden-variety behavior. And we know that happened. So most anything must be considered as a possibility.

"Anything else?"

"Well, there is one thing," Jack said.

"Fire away," the sheriff said. "Might as well get all your questions answered at one time."

"The FBI. They've not interviewed me yet. I find that a little curious.

Seems as though they would have picked up on the portable EMP weapon. That's got to be on every terrorist list out there."

"Yeah," the sheriff said. "I'm sure they are. But I didn't describe it exactly in that way."

"No? In what way, exactly, did you describe it?"

"I simply said we found an electronic device of some sort, and when the chopper headed back to refuel, there was an explosion."

"I don't understand," Jack said.

"Damn it, Jack. When *you* talk to them you're welcome to tell them anything the hell you wish," the sheriff said, obviously a little agitated. "What you showed me gave me no *definitive* proof that it was one of those electromagnetic weapons. In my view, it could have been anything. The idea that it was some sort of exotic weapon is pure speculation on your part. At least in my opinion.

"Before I make any statement to the FBI," the sheriff continued, "I have to know beyond a shadow of a doubt that what I am saying is factual. If they can put it together and convince themselves that it was the weapon you think it was, then that's cool.

"But I'm no expert on that sort of shit. All I saw were a bunch of coils and electronic components. I don't know what the hell it was. It could have been some sort of bad-ass hairdryer, for all I know."

"Really, Sheriff," Jack retorted. "A 'bad-ass' hairdryer, hidden in a camo bag, out in the middle of Strangmoor Bog."

"Look, Jack, say what you want. If you think it was a weapon, then you should tell them that. But I'm not in a position to make that type of declaration. It's as simple as that."

"I can assure you that my story is going to be a little different from yours," Jack said. "I know beyond doubt precisely what I found out there. And it was an EMP weapon. Not a terribly large one, but one capable of bringing down some airliners. Its existence absolutely posed a terrorist threat. And we have no reason to think that there could not be more of them. Units like that are custom made. If you have a problem with one, you really do not have a factory to repair it. So, if the shooter bought one, there's a decent chance he bought a second.

"The FBI needs to be aware—"

"Then, Jack old buddy, you had better get on the phone and call SAC Dollar—he's the special agent in charge—and fill him in on your little theory. I think his full name is SAC William Dollar. My God, Handler, you are such a royal pain in the ass. Sheriff Green has really got your number."

"That's cool, Sheriff," Jack said, trying to calm the situation. "I'll wait until I hear from him. I don't want to stir the pot unnecessarily. I'm sure he'll get to me, eventually."

"Well, if he's smart he'll avoid you. I sure as hell wish I had."

Neither man wanted to say the next word.

But finally the sheriff spoke, "Hey. I'm going to head out to Strangmoor to see what my guys turn up. Thanks for the lead. And sorry about the crap I just dished out. It's just that this is turning into one messed-up case. I am an elected servant of the people. I serve at the pleasure of Schoolcraft County. I can easily be fired if I am perceived not to be doing my job. I, like all elected officials, seek simplicity. Not expediency, but simplicity. And so do the voters. It's just the way it is in my little world. This case, my friend, is beginning to worry me."

Jack did not immediately respond, so the sheriff continued, "Hell, it's way beyond the beginning stage. I'm scared about where all this shit could lead."

"I understand," Jack said. "Let me know if your guys turn anything up."

As Jack was disconnecting the call, Kate said, "Dad, there's a reflection. Or a small light. Something's shining out from beneath your Tahoe. And it looks like it's moving. Come here and take a look."

Only two months ago Jack and Kate had decided to replace the crushed limestone driveway with sandstone pavers. So on this night, with a steady light rain falling, even the slightest spot of light reflected off the smooth, wet surface.

At first Jack was skeptical. While he did see the small sliver of light bouncing off the rain-slicked driveway, instead of immediately suspecting wrongful activity, he searched for a more benign explanation.

And then the light disappeared.

"Grab your gun," Jack said, pulling his Glock from its holster. "I'll come in from the south—from the river—you head straight for the road. Take cover behind that big oak. If there is something going on, whoever it is would have come in by boat, or from the road. We'll pinch him between us. Be very careful. And don't shoot me!

"Boys," Jack said stepping into their room. "You wait here and do not come out until one of us comes and gets you. I don't want either one of you leaving this room for any reason. If everything's cool, one of us will step in and give the *all clear.* … Got that?"

Chapter 48

Pinball—Jack's recovery

Three days later, Jack began to stir. He had been totally unconscious from the time he dropped over in Kate's car until he asked for a drink of water.

"Dad," Kate said. "Nice to have you back."

She placed a damp sponge on his lips.

The nurse had told her that when he woke up he would probably ask for a drink of water, and that she should dab a little moisture on his lips.

The nurse had said that Jack was receiving all the liquids he needed intravenously, but that his lips would feel parched from all the tubes they had pushed down his throat.

Jack slowly opened his eyes as she squeezed a little more moisture from the sponge.

He moaned.

"You gave us a bit of a scare," she said.

Jack groaned again, but not loudly.

"What happened?" he asked.

"You got shot. Do you remember that?"

"Sort of," he said. "I remember seeing that man in black. And that's all I remember."

"Well, the man in black had a friend," she told him. "A friend with a suppressor. And he shot you from the tall grass along the river, just as you suspected."

"Shot me?" Jack asked.

"Sure did," she said. "And you almost didn't make it. It was a good thing I drove you to the hospital. Another five minutes and you would have bled out."

"I was shot in the right arm," Jack said. "Or, rather *under* my right arm. That thing still hurts like hell. You said I almost bled out?"

"Came pretty close," Kate said. "The bullet entered under your right arm, and struck a rib. But you've got a pretty good set of bones, because the bullet broke apart. Unfortunately, a small part of it bounced upward and severed your right subclavian vein. That's what caused the extensive bleeding—internally.

"The larger part of the bullet pinballed off of another rib and exited out of your back, just like you thought. You might not remember, but the night you were shot, before you passed out, you said that it felt like the bullet might have exited below your shoulder blade. Well, most of it did."

"Did the doctors find it?" Jack asked. "Was it trapped in my clothes?"

"It was," Kate answered. "But about the only thing that could be made out was that it was from a .38 that had no rifling."

"Same gun then," Jack said. "Probably the same gun they used in Strangmoor."

"That's what the sheriff is saying.

"Is it starting to come back?" Kate asked. "Are you starting to remember more about the night you got shot?"

Jack paused, silently thinking for a moment, and then became very agitated and tried to lean forward. "The bomb! Was there actually a bomb in my Tahoe?"

Chapter 49
The bomb

"Take it easy, Dad," Kate said in her most comforting voice. "Everything is okay. Really. The sheriff came right out and evacuated the area. He immediately brought in the FBI, and they *defused* the bomb … if you can actually call it that."

"Then there was a bomb?" Jack asked rhetorically. "Someone really wanted me, us, dead that badly?"

"Looks like," Kate said.

"Tell me more about the bomb," Jack requested.

"Once the FBI determined that it was a real bomb, and calculated its strength, they figured it would be better to detonate it still attached to the Tahoe. They thought it would be safer.

"So they covered your vehicle with a couple huge heavy blankets, wired a small explosive to the bomb, and blew it up."

"You're joking. Right?" Jack asked. "They didn't really destroy my Tahoe. They didn't actually blow *it* up. Did they?"

"Oh yeah—they sure did," she said. "They had everyone wait behind a barrier out at the road. There was a muffled explosion. But that's it. Those bomb-blankets sure do dampen an explosion.

"Our guys on the bomb squad in New York have them, but this is the first time I've ever seen one used in the field, with a real bomb. Actually I didn't see it, but the boys did—and they shot a video for me. … I was with you in the hospital that whole night and the next day."

"Probably for the best they blew it up," Jack said. "At least from their standpoint. No point trying to defuse a small bomb like that from under a vehicle. Too much could go wrong. But, did they recover a transmitter?"

"They did. Once the bomb situation was defused—sorry about the pun—they brought in a different group, and they looked *specifically* for a transmitter.

"And they found one down by the river. They said if we had tried driving the Tahoe, we probably would not have made it much past the end of the driveway. The range on the transmitter was five hundred yards at most.

"So, it's impossible to know exactly where the blast would have occurred. Most likely we would have barely reached the road before it detonated. At least, that would have limited injuries at the resort. But it would have killed us. It's just a darn good thing we caught it."

"That's right," Jack agreed. "If you hadn't looked out of the window at exactly the right time we wouldn't be talking right now. And, again, the boys would have no one to take care of them. Damn, that makes me mad. Someone's going to pay a severe price for this."

Kate then leaned in toward her father and whispered, "The FBI wants to talk to you in the worst way. They've posted a guard at your door, making sure no one stopped by to finish the job. At least until Special Agent in Charge William Dollar debriefs you."

"There's a guard out there right now?" Jack asked.

"Was when I came in," Kate said. "In fact, every time I stopped by I had to show ID before they'd let me in. They have another agent posted in the lobby. Maybe more than one. There was only one down there that I made for sure.

"Sheriff Griffen is a little nervous about the whole thing," Kate added.

"As he should be," Jack said. "He totally mishandled this case so far. He should never have left that EMP weapon in the chopper. It needed to go back to the spot where we found it, and then the FBI would have been responsible for it.

"Truth be told," Jack continued. "I should have performed a preliminary examination of it right where I found it. I could have ID'ed it for what it was, and we could have avoided all this garbage. So I share some of the culpability, I suppose. But I think we'd better keep our mouths shut regarding that."

"Dad, you tried to convince the sheriff to leave it in the bog for the FBI, but he insisted," Kate said.

"I guess I didn't do a very good job of convincing," Jack retorted. "From here on out, I'm going to have to walk a fine line. I have to give the FBI as much information as I can, but not put the sheriff in jeopardy. I think I'm going to claim some level of amnesia. I did suffer physical trauma, you know. I just need to see the sheriff so we can compare notes and come up with a story we both can live with."

"Don't count on doing that right away," Kate said. "I'm sure that the FBI won't let you talk to the sheriff before they get their chance at you. I heard that directly from the sheriff. I told him that I would let him know as soon as—"

Just then the door opened, and a tall, well-groomed thirty-something man poked his head into the room. "I see you're awake, Mr. Handler. I have someone here who wants to talk to you."

Chapter 50

Nattily dressed and bespectacled

Special Agent William Dollar did not wait for Jack's response. Bursting past the man holding the door, he strode through the room like one of Hitler's SS Stormtroopers. He pushed himself in front of Kate and flung his leather satchel down on Jack's knee.

Feigning a brief and insincere smile in Jack's direction, he then quickly turned to face Kate.

"Young lady," he said. "My name is SAC Dollar—FBI. If you don't mind, I would like to speak to Mr. Handler in private. So, say your good-byes. You can come back later if you wish. You can check with Agent Snyder. He's the gentleman who announced me a moment ago. You can check with him later to see if Mr. Handler can talk to you. Now, if you would excuse us."

Jack was doing a slow burn. If he did not need to play sick at that moment, he might have slapped the special agent across the room. Of course, that might have been difficult to do without the use of his right arm. But he was still tempted to give it a go.

He's one rude SOB, Jack thought. *There's no excuse for that. Maybe I should have a little fun with him.*

SAC Dollar continued to face Kate until she had exited the room. And then he turned to Jack.

"Mr. Handler," he said. "It's so nice to see you're doing better. It was a little curious that you remained unconscious for so long. Am I correct that you did not suffer any head trauma?"

"I'm told I took one under my right arm," Jack said. "I'm still a little groggy. I guess I don't really know what happened. Do I have bandages on my head?"

"No. You look perfectly fine to me. I did hear that you'd lost some blood. I guess the bullet grazed a vein. Not very serious, I understand. You should make a full and speedy recovery."

"That's nice to know," Jack said. "I haven't seen my doctor since I woke up. I have a lot of questions for him. Could you call him for me?"

Jack was making every effort to terminate the meeting with the rude special agent.

"Certainly," SAC Dollar said. "As soon as you've answered some of my questions, I will get the doctor for you. The staff gave me permission to ask you a few questions. But when we're done, I'll get him for you."

I'll just bet he did not ask my doctor if it was okay for him to interrogate me, Jack thought. *This guy has never asked anyone for anything.*

"I've got one hell of a headache," Jack said. "And I feel like I might drop off. But you go ahead and ask your questions. I'll see what I can remember. I'm very foggy about what happened. All those drugs you know."

"What can you remember about the man who shot you?" SAC Dollar asked. "That is, assuming it was a man. *I'm* thinking that it was the same guy, or guys, who brought down your little drone with the EMP. What do you think about that? Can you describe the shooter?"

"No. The first thing I can remember about the whole incident is waking up here and seeing my daughter. You know, I think she spent the whole time here."

"And how long was that? Since you were shot? Hours? Days? Weeks? How long ago was it that you got shot?"

"My daughter said it was three days," Jack replied. "I don't remember.

Is she right? Was it that long ago?"

"You don't remember?"

"No. Nothing," Jack said. "I don't feel so good. I think I might throw up. Could you get my doctor? I think I've got a button here someplace. Do you see it? The one that calls the nurse. I can't find it. Could you help me find it? I don't feel good."

"I just need you to think, Mr. Handler. I really need your help. Maybe I can jar your memory. What do you remember about the night you found the electronic device in Strangmoor Bog? What can you tell me about that?"

"Where? What electronic device? Could you please call my doctor?"

"Strangmoor Bog. Do you recall anything about the drone you lost to that electronic device?"

"Drone?" Jack mumbled. "Yeah! I have a drone. Haven't used it in a long time. Battery's probably discharged. Did you want to borrow it?"

"You don't remember anything about the helicopter that exploded?"

Jack faked a thoughtful expression, while actually struggling to keep himself from laughing out loud.

"No. You've got that wrong," Jack said. "I don't have a *real* helicopter. I have a little battery-powered drone. Is that what you're talking about? My drone?"

"Then you don't have any memory concerning the electronic device? The one you thought was an EMP weapon?"

"What? What are you talking about? Those things are dangerous. And *very* illegal. What would I be doing with an EMP? I wouldn't mess with anything like that. I have a drone with a camera. That's it. Period. I don't mess with any of that illegal shit.

"Look. Special Agent. Your name is Dollar?"

The special agent nodded his head.

"SAC Dollar. I'm very sorry. But I don't feel well. I need to talk to my doctor. I don't remember anything about what you're talking about. I think there are rules about when you can and cannot question a patient. I don't think what you are doing right now is legal. I'm sick. And anything I might say … it's going to be conjecture … or delirium. I can't talk to you until I get my doctor to say I'm okay. I'm sure I'm *not* okay right now.

"Would you please go get my doctor?"

Jack looked around and found the nurse's call button, and pushed it.

"There," he said. "My nurse should be here in a second. She'll tell you that I am in no condition to be talking to you.

"So, would you please go now? And get that damn briefcase off my knee."

Jack's temper was rising. He did not wait for the special agent to remove his satchel. Instead, Jack picked it up with his left hand and hurled it across the room. It hit the window with a loud thud and spewed papers all over the floor.

"Oh," Jack said. "I'm so sorry about that. I'm just not myself. I need to see my doctor. Please forgive me. I don't know what came over me. Must be the medication. I think I need to get some sleep now. So, if you will excuse me."

Jack closed his eyes and faked drifting off.

"Handler!" SAC Dollar shouted as he stormed around the room picking up his papers. "This is inexcusable! You have just assaulted an officer of the federal government! And that's a *very* serious crime!"

Jack continued to feign sleep, fighting the urge to smile.

"Mr. Handler, is everything okay?" Nurse Conner asked as she slid past the agent guarding the open door.

She walked up to Jack and placed her hand on his forehead. "You pushed the button? Do you need something? And what is this gentleman doing in your room? You're not supposed to have visitors."

* * *

Down in the hospital coffee shop, Kate was sitting with Sheriff Griffen sipping a cup of detestable vending-machine coffee. She had spotted him when she walked in and had just joined him.

He looked concerned.

"What does he remember?" the sheriff asked.

Kate smiled, but didn't answer.

"What does that grin mean?" he asked.

"He's meeting with SAC Dollar as we speak. Before he makes any sort of statement to the FBI he wants to talk with you. To get your stories lined up.

"I'm not really sure just how much he remembers right now, but I'd imagine it will all come back to him. There was no head trauma. And his emotional condition is solid. I don't think there will be any permanent loss of memory. Not after a cup of good coffee."

"Dollar doesn't waste any time," the sheriff said. "Wish he'd get off my ass."

"Don't expect that to happen," Kate said. "He's on a mission. And part of that mission is to make people like you, me, and Jack squirm."

"That's sure the way it feels from my perspective," the sheriff said.

Kate and the sheriff locked eyes for a moment. *I think this is the time to ask him some questions,* she reasoned.

"Tell me again," she said. "What, if anything, did you find out the night Dad was shot? When he called you and asked you to dispatch some cars to Strangmoor. I understand one of your deputies intercepted Zach Tanner in the area. What was *he* up to?"

Chapter 51
Who and what

Zach was by himself," the sheriff said. "He was very surprised to be pulled over. Embarrassed is probably a better word."

"And he readily admitted that he had been in the bog earlier that night?" she asked.

"That's what he told my deputy. Zach said that he wanted to find the gun he had lost the night the helicopter crashed. He had been waiting until after I had pulled my men out.

"I guess he had seen that there were no longer any vehicles near the murder scene and thought that this would be a good time to go look for it."

"Do you believe him?" Kate asked.

"Definitely," the sheriff said. "He showed the deputy the metal detector he had used. He even had night-vision equipment, just in case his search carried on into the night. He was prepared."

"And he actually did find his gun. Is that right?"

"He retraced his steps. Spent all day out in the bog. And then, just after sunset, he said he found it."

"And you believe his story?"

"No reason not to," the sheriff replied. "He gave the gun to the deputy, and we had it examined. Forensics came back with their report today. The gun he said he found was the one registered to him. And it looked like it had been underwater for several days—it was starting to rust."

"Had it been fired?" Kate asked. "Could they tell?"

"The gun had not been fired recently," the sheriff said. "Not since it had been cleaned last. Still had oil residue in the barrel. And, believe me, it had not been cleaned in a while. It was full of mud when he turned it over."

"How about the rifling?" Kate asked. "Had it been ground down?"

"No. Definitely not," the sheriff said. "The gun had a crisp bore. And the barrel was not threaded to accommodate a suppressor. Plus, I think we're looking for something with a little longer barrel. The pistol Tanner gave me was a snub-nose."

"So, I guess that means that Mr. Tanner's handgun, at least *this* one, was not the one used to shoot Mr. Stenos?" Kate asked.

"Can't see how it could have been."

Just then SAC Dollar came charging at them.

"That sonofabitch attacked me up there!" he said, mostly to Kate. "He had damn well better watch himself, or I'll be pressing charges! He assaulted a federal officer. The day he's discharged, his ass is mine."

She was not surprised.

"What exactly did my father do to you?" she asked.

"He grabbed my satchel away from me and threw it across the room. I spent five minutes picking up my papers."

Kate looked over at the sheriff, and then back at the special agent. "Is that really what happened?" Kate asked. "Before you kicked me out of the room I distinctly recall you slamming your briefcase into my father's groin. If any assault occurred, I'd say you were the one committing it. My poor defenseless dad. In a coma for three days, on all sorts of medication, and you *attacked* him like that.

"Are you sure you didn't just drop it? My father is in no condition to be attacking anyone."

Dollar was furious at her comments.

"I did no such thing!" he said. "Just all of a sudden Handler lunges at me, misses, but grabs my satchel and throws it across the—"

"I'm glad I found you," said a very agitated man who was obviously a doctor. "I'm Jack Handler's physician. Which one of you is from the FBI?"

* * *

"There is always a storm. "There is always rain. Some experience it. Some live through it. And others are made from it."

—Shannon L.

Chapter 52

That sounds serious

SAC Dollar sized up the doctor and decided to ignore him.

"I asked a question," the doctor said. "Which one of you is from the FBI? I'm looking for a Mr. Dollar. Is one of you Mr. Dollar?"

"I'm Special Agent in Charge William Dollar. What can I do for you?"

"My name is Dr. Jeremy Johnson. I'm the physician in charge of Mr. Jack Handler's care here in the hospital. I understand you interrogated him without my permission. Is that true?"

"I don't have to ask your permission for any—"

"The hell you don't," Dr. Johnson said, taking a half step into the special agent's space. "You have no right to interfere with my treatment. Mr. Handler had one visitor cleared to visit him, and it wasn't you."

"Okay, Doctor, you've made your point. I don't want any trouble with you or your patients. I should have checked with you first. I just thought that if a New York City homicide detective can talk with one of my witnesses, I should be able to do the same."

"Kate might be a detective, but she is also my patient's daughter. There's a big difference."

"Granted," Dollar conceded. "I understand that I might have jumped the gun on this. But national security is involved here. And I have reason to believe that Mr. Handler has information that could be helpful in bringing down a group that might have terrorist ties."

"That doesn't excuse your behavior," the doctor said. "Mr. Handler is still my patient, not your prisoner. At least not yet, as far as I'm aware. Have you arrested him?"

"Mr. Handler is a potential witness—"

"Then you haven't arrested him?" Dr. Johnson barked.

"I have not arrested Mr. Handler."

"In that case, when I am convinced that it is safe for you to talk to him, I will let you know. But if you try to pull this trick again, I will have a talk with your boss."

"You've made your point, Doctor," Dollar said, desiring to end this conversation. "I would like to talk to your patient, Mr. Handler, as soon as you deem it safe. Do you have any idea when that might be?"

"For one thing, I haven't had a chance today to check him—not since he woke up. Once I have, I'll let the nurses know what I think he can and cannot deal with. I assure you that I will make him available to you as soon as he is able to do so without jeopardizing his care."

"That would be just great," Dollar said. "I would appreciate that."

"Now, if you would excuse me," the doctor said, "I will continue my rounds."

Kate made no effort to conceal her smile as she excused the doctor.

And then she glanced over to the sheriff and said, "Seems to have a handle on the situation, wouldn't you say, Sheriff?"

Sheriff Griffen did not respond. He did not want to do anything that could set Dollar off against him.

"I will come back tomorrow," Dollar said to Kate. "You had better talk to your father. Let him know that I will not tolerate the sort of behavior he exhibited today. I will bring a witness, and if he pulls anything like that again, I will place him under arrest right here. I'll cuff him to his bed, and as soon as he is able, I'll stick his ass in jail. Have I made myself clear?"

Initially, Kate had thought that she would do what she could to placate the hotheaded special agent. But when he decided to go off on her, she was less inclined to be the peacemaker.

"Completely clear, SAC Dollar. I'll let my father know what you said. But I doubt that he'll remember it. And next time—when his doctor says it's okay for you to meet with him, I intend to be present as well. Besides, I don't think he *has* to talk to you at all, unless you actually do intend to place him under arrest. Is that what you intend to do?"

Dollar did not respond. He turned and stormed off toward the elevator.

"A genuine *fart gate*—that agent Dollar," the sheriff said with a broad smile. "A real flamin' fart gate, if you get my drift."

Chapter 53

The little ice cream shop

Buddy," Robby said. "Stay."

Buddy, Red's golden retriever, circled once and then lay down on the sidewalk outside the local ice cream shop in Curtis.

Quite possibly the most ornately bedecked spot in the center of town, the shop sat on Main Street, overlooking South Manistique Lake. Large windows facing north, on either side of the front door, provided a panoramic view of the street as well as the shops opposite it.

Three white ceiling fans turned slowly, almost as though their purpose was as much to soothe tension as to move air.

Everything inside was painted crisp white. Even the tablecloths on each of the eight round metal tables were white. Accenting the middle of each of those tables like a cherry on a sundae was a small vase containing three freshly cut red flowers.

The sepia and black and white photographs hanging on the walls were mostly from times gone by. They depicted landscapes, notable members of the community, and area sports teams.

The floor was spotlessly clean, with its black and white tiles giving it a retro timeless appeal.

"How long is Uncle Jack gonna be in the hospital?" Robby asked as they walked in and looked through the glass covering the ice cream dipping cabinet. "I'm asking for Red. But I wanna know too."

"That's up in the air," Kate said. "If *he* had a choice, he'd be on his way home today. But his doctor is still not ready to release him."

Kate stood in front of the chalkboard menu, looking at the choices of the treats. Millie kept herself busy during the decisions, slipping on a new pair of disposable latex gloves and swapping out the ice cream scoops with freshly washed ones.

"Red, you're my butter pecan man," Kate said. "But, Robby, what kind of ice cream would you like?"

"Chocolate."

"Of course," Kate said. "I should have known."

"Millie," Kate said. "Would you make us two double-dip cones—one butter pecan and one chocolate? I'll have a single chocolate. And I'd like that single chocolate in a dish. The other two should be in sugar cones."

Millie smiled as she snatched a small plastic bowl from a shelf behind her. She placed one generous scoop of chocolate into the bowl as she set it on the counter. And then, holding two sugar cones in her left hand, she piled them high—one with dark brown chocolate, and the other with creamy butter pecan. She then carefully handed each boy his ice cream and left Kate's on the counter, pulled her gloves off, and took a twenty-dollar bill from Kate.

Kate marveled that Millie's smile never left her face, even as she wiped down the counter.

After Kate and the boys received their ice creams, they looked around for a place to sit down. Red was interested in keeping an eye on Buddy, so he headed for a table in the middle of the shop and took a seat facing the front door. He couldn't actually see Buddy from there, but he figured it offered the best view available.

"Hello, I am Sean Bronson," said a tall, good-looking, forty-something man at the next table. He was primarily addressing Kate.

"And this is my wife Stacy. I don't think I've met you folks before. Are you from Curtis?"

The man was being more friendly than flirtatious. He was enjoying a cup of coffee and a small strawberry sundae with his wife. The strawberry seeds in his dessert cup had long since been abandoned by the ice cream and syrup, suggesting that Sean and his wife had been sitting in the shop for a long time.

"Kate Handler," Kate replied.

"And these two characters are with me. That's Red, and that's Robby," she said, pointing to each boy as she introduced him. "We are not from Curtis. We're visiting from Sugar Island. Are you familiar with Sugar Island?"

"Of course," he replied. "The home of the famous Hilltop Bar."

"Exactly."

"Oh my God!" Sean said as though someone had just flashed a strobe in his face. "I'll bet these are the two boys that discovered the body in Strangmoor. Am I right? And that would make you Kate *Handler*, the big-city detective."

Kate did not audibly reply. She simply smiled.

"I've heard all about that," he said. "And so has everyone else around here. What a terrible tragedy that was. Milton, and Deputy Grant, they were both good friends of mine. And now they're dead. Could have been me. I was out of town when that all went down. Or I would have had my Jeep right out there with those guys. Harvey, Sheriff Griffen, is a good friend of mine. What a shame."

Stacy, realizing that her husband might have been one of those who ended up in the morgue this past weekend, just sat there shaking her head.

Suddenly Kate realized that her ice cream was melting faster than she could eat it, and she wanted to end this conversation quickly.

"It was a tragedy," Kate said. "But I really can't talk about it because there is an ongoing investigation—"

"FBI," Sean interrupted. "The FBI's taken it over. Right? I play cards on the weekend with Griffen, and he won't talk about it either. Doesn't seem too happy about the whole thing. I don't think he appreciates the way the FBI has been treating him. But I should probably be keeping my mouth shut. What do you think about it? Are they getting closer to solving it?"

Jeez, Kate thought, *this guy's really pushing my buttons.*

"Sorry. Can't discuss it," she said. "But, it is safe to say that when the feds get involved in cases, good things generally happen, and usually sooner than later."

"Endless resources," Sean added. "I've heard that the reason they are so good is because they are willing to devote an enormous amount of resources. Not just money, but human resources as well. And they have access to the big databases—that's how they get to the bottom of just about anything. Wouldn't you agree, Kate?"

"No question about it," Kate said. "They've got a terrific track record."

She then stood and walked over to snatch a few more napkins for the boys, and to hopefully transition out of the conversation.

Outside the door to the shop, an old man and a very beautiful young redheaded girl were approaching. She was walking about twenty feet in front of him, and at a brisker pace. When she reached the door, she entered. But the old man stopped and just looked in. For a few long moments, he studied the people inside, cupping his hands over his eyes to block the glare. And then he stepped backward.

He noticed that Buddy was looking up at him, and he knelt down and lovingly petted the ever-eager golden retriever.

"I'll bet you're with those boys inside," he said audibly, but mostly to himself. "They look like good boys. I'll bet you're a great friend to them. I used to have a dog that looked a lot like you. But that's been years ago. He got old and died on me. That happens, you know. We all die sooner or later."

From his knee he turned back and looked into the shop. His eyes met Red's, and they both smiled.

"Those are the boys I saw in the bog that morning," the old man muttered, again to himself. "The ones who found that wedding ring."

The old man stared blankly for several moments, and then he took a piece of paper and a pencil and wrote a short note. When he was finished, he rolled it up and slid it into one of his Xikar aluminum cigar tubes. He thought for another long moment, and then unlaced his boot three hooks and cut off a few inches from both ends of one of his leather shoestrings.

After he had knotted the two pieces together, he wrapped the leather string securely around the Xikar tube and tied it tightly to the bottom of Buddy's collar.

He then turned again to look inside the ice cream shop. Red still had his eyes fixed in the direction of the old man.

Standing, the old man took one last look inside, flashed Red a thumbs-up, and then knelt down and petted Buddy on the head, and walked away.

Without explanation, Red stood and walked over to the front of the shop. He opened the door to check on Buddy. He did not notice the note tied to Buddy's collar. Red then returned to Kate's table.

"What was that all about?" Kate asked.

Red just scrunched up his mouth and shook his head. Kate knew that this meant Red simply wanted to check on Buddy's status—nothing more. Had it been important to Red, he would have texted an explanation.

Red then glanced over at Robby, and then at the cute girl. The boys looked again at each other. They were both in love with this attractive young redhead.

Chapter 54
The call

I don't think I've met you guys," the girl said. "My name is Angel, what's yours?"

"My name is Robby, and this is my friend Red. He doesn't talk. *Can't* talk. But he can text like a wild man. We're from Sugar Island."

"I know where *that* is," she said with a gorgeous smile, happy to find some common ground with the two boys. "I always go there with my friends, to the music festival. What fun that is. Do you guys go to the festival? It's in August."

"We didn't this year," Robby said. "But we are next. Maybe we could hang out together."

Robby surprised himself with his comment. He was not used to flirting.

Kate was equally taken aback.

"Yeah," Angel said. "We could probably do that. My friends—the ones I go with every year—they have a camper. They live on the island, but they park their camper at the festival for two nights. I would be spending most of my time with them. But I'll watch for you. We can talk, and maybe hang out some. We usually build a big bonfire and have marshmallows and hot dogs after dark. My friends are musicians, and I like to sing a little too. Maybe you could join us. It'd be fun.

"But whatcha doin' in Curtis?" she said, abruptly changing the subject. "This is a long way from Sugar Island."

"We have a room at Christopher's," Robby said. "You know, that restaurant. It also has a bed and—"

"Yeah," Angel said. "I know all about the bed and breakfast. My mom runs the place. And we live there."

Millie was listening to the conversation, and she decided that she needed to interject herself.

"Hold on, Angel. I don't *run* anything, except for this ice cream shop. All I do is make sure everything gets cleaned on time, the beds get made, and no one ruins the furniture."

"So," Kate said. "Angel is your daughter?"

"She sure is," Millie replied, slipping her arm around the girl. "Can't you see the resemblance?"

"Mom, please!" Angel said, prying her mother's hand from her shoulder.

Millie was an attractive young woman. But her daughter was as beautiful as a fourteen-year-old girl can be beautiful.

Even without her precocious self-confidence, Angel stood out.

Her hair was a mixture of blonde and red. Her mom called it *strawberry blonde*—but Angel preferred to be called a redhead. She wore it tied back into a short ponytail that hung beneath a black beret. She was wearing white shorts, a baby blue T-shirt with an Old Navy logo, and dock shoes. She was thin and wiry—but not skinny. Not quite five feet tall, and weighing just under ninety pounds, she had the muscle tone of a long-distance runner.

It was, however, her blue eyes and an adorable row of freckles across her turned up nose that made her stand out.

"Angel is one of the most popular people in town," Sean said. "Everyone knows her, and everyone likes her."

"She is pretty special," Millie said. "She actually takes after her father more than me. He was very outgoing, just like her."

"Never met him," Sean said. "He was gone long before I moved here."

"Sometimes I wished I'd never met him either," Millie said. "Except for this girl. She is an angel. She is the only good thing that came out of that marriage."

"Mom, you shouldn't put my dad down. None of us really knows why he left. Maybe he would like to come back, if he could. We just don't know."

"You've got a point, I guess," Millie said, although she didn't really mean it. "I have no idea why he left, and I don't know why he never came back. I guess there are some things in life that you just can't find the answers to.

"But," Millie added in an attempt to put a gentle end to that conversation. "He gave me you. And for that, I will always be grateful. You are a blessing beyond measure."

"Mom, you're making me blush," Angel said, even though she was not at all embarrassed. She was so practiced at graciously accepting praise that feigned humility just came naturally to her.

"If you're staying at the Christopher," Angel said, "why haven't I seen you? I thought I'd met all the guests."

"We just checked in," Kate replied. "The boys carried the luggage up, and we came down here for some ice cream. We'd heard that this was the place to go."

"Hope you weren't disappointed," Millie said.

"Not at all," Kate replied.

"This place does have the best ice cream for miles," Sean said. "It's just a shame that Millie wants to sell the business."

"Sean isn't big on desserts," Stacy said. "I come for the sundaes, he mostly drinks coffee, and talks to people."

"I had a dessert today. But you're right. Usually, I just drink coffee.

Millie roasts her own, you know. You can't get coffee this good anywhere else in the UP. Unless, of course, you drive to Brimley, or the Soo."

"Why would you want to sell?" Kate asked. She knew her question was inappropriate, but the detective in her wanted to know.

"It's just too much work. I spend so much time down here. And not enough quality time watching my girl grow up. While I certainly don't run the Christopher's Bed and Breakfast, I am responsible for the housekeeping crew. That takes time as well. I thought if I could sell the ice cream shop, when the next housekeeper quits, I could then just replace her. With what I would gain from the sale of the shop, plus the extra I could earn working full time at Christopher's, I'd do just fine.

"And I would get to spend more time with my daughter."

Just then Kate's phone vibrated.

Chapter 55
Ain't got time to take a fast train

Kate checked the caller ID before answering. It was Janet Beckett, the prosecutor handling an important case Kate was involved with in New York.

"A new charge?" Kate inquired. "You're filing a new indictment against Joe Tuco?"

"That's right, Kate," Janet Beckett replied. "You recall we discussed this earlier? We just didn't think we had enough evidence. The D.A. believes that this new charge just might bring Tuco around and convince him to testify against his boss."

The "boss" to whom she was referring was Randall Croft, a notorious New York criminal who specialized in contract killings.

"It's worth a try," Beckett said. "I think our case against Croft is pretty good without Tuco, but it would be even better if we could make a deal for him to take the stand against Croft. Anyway, if you're able to, we would all feel a lot better if you could appear at his arraignment. It's scheduled for Thursday afternoon. I think his lawyer trusts you. Or maybe *fears* you. Whatever the case, I think it would be great if you could be here. I know how badly you want to see Croft get what's coming to him, and this would get us one step closer.

"We all understand that you've needed to be there with your father.

So, if you can't get away, we will understand. … And just how *is* he doing?"

Kate and her father had personal knowledge regarding Croft's ruthlessness. Jack was pretty certain that the Croft family was responsible for the murder of two lawyers who were visiting him on Sugar Island. Both were killed in broad daylight while riding back to Sault Ste. Marie on the Sugar Island Ferry.

And Kate narrowly escaped death when her plane crashed in Upstate New York. It was believed that Croft had placed a bomb on the turboprop shuttle in his effort to kill the prosecutor whom he believed was hounding him. The bomb did bring the plane down, killing all on board except for Kate and two other passengers. The prosecutor, who was a close friend of Kate's, and the target of the bomb, was one of the passengers who died in the crash.

"Dad is doing much better—thanks for asking. I'll try to get a flight out of here Wednesday morning, spend the night in the city, show up at the courthouse on Thursday morning, and then I'll catch a flight right back. Any chance that the hearing will be delayed?"

"That's good news about your father," Beckett said. "Happy to hear he's making progress.

"Of course, delays are always a possibility in cases like this. But it's one of those chances we think we have to take. We've got an okay case against Croft, but his lawyers are some of the best money can buy. The DA would really like it if you could get here. If we can convince Tuco's lawyers that it will be in their client's best interest to turn, it will make it easier to get something out of Croft's attorneys. The DA thinks it best to get him to plead down, rather than to go to trial. I know that's not what you want, but we need to get him on something, and then hope the judge throws the book at him. Right now they are not even willing to talk. Tuco might give us what we need to get Croft on financial improprieties, taxes, money laundering—*something*."

"Aren't you worried about his safety? Tuco, that is?"

"We don't think it will go that far," Beckett said. "We've got Tuco in isolation at Rikers right now. And we're prepared to keep him there until Croft's trial. But it won't come to that. Croft knows Tuco can bury him. As soon as news gets out that we're bringing new charges against Tuco, Croft will know what this is all about, and make a deal. At least that's what we're counting on. I'm so pleased that you will give it a shot to be here."

"Oh, you can count on it," Kate said. "I'll be there. Connections aren't the best out of Chippewa County, but at least they're reliable. If I get delayed, it will most likely be in Detroit or Philly. This time of year, it should all work out. I'll call you if something comes up and it looks like I might not make it."

Kate disconnected the call, leaned back in her seat, and stared at the ceiling.

Robby looked over at Red, and then at Kate.

"What are you gonna do with us?" Robby asked. "Isn't Mrs. Fletcher gonna be gone for a while more?"

"Good question," Kate said, turning her attention to the boys. "Right now I don't know. Mrs. Fletcher will be in Spokane all this week, *and* next. And I'm not sure when your Uncle Jack will be coming home. And when he does, it might not be such a good idea to have you on the island with him—at least not until we get some of this other business sorted out. So, I'm not sure where you'll be staying. Maybe I should pack you guys up in a suitcase and take you with me."

"Do you mind if I make a suggestion?" Sean Bronson asked after making extended eye contact with Stacy.

Sean was the sort of person everyone liked and trusted. Part of his popularity was because he always seemed to find a solution to every problem.

"I know this might seem like a bit of a stretch, because both of these boys are already nearly grown young men, and are obviously quite able to take care of themselves. But Millie here is a licensed care provider, and her daughter has taken the Red Cross course. Isn't that right, Millie?"

"You're thinking about two or three days?" Millie asked.

"Right," Kate said. "I'd leave Wednesday morning early, and get home late Thursday night. Or possibly as late as Friday, depending on the connections. I'll have to check and see what's available."

"I'd be happy to watch them," Millie said. "I might have them hang out over here some of the time. But, since we are both staying at Christopher's, it shouldn't be any problem at all."

"Millie's the greatest," Sean said. "And so's Angel. Everyone in Curtis swears by them. Your boys would be in great hands. If *we* were going to be in town, I'd keep my eye on them too. But I'm going to be in Minnesota on business the rest of the week."

"You'd be willing to do that?" Kate asked Millie.

"Not a problem, as long as you don't mind if they hang out here part of the time. Fifty dollars a day sound fair?"

"Not really," Kate replied. "I'll pay you a hundred a day. You've no idea how much these two boys can eat. And, hanging out in an ice cream shop—they just might break the bank."

"I don't know if you are aware of it," Sean said, "But one of the FBI agents working on the case here in Seney is also staying at the Christopher. Along with his daughter and mother."

"*Really*," Kate said. "Do you know his name?"

"No, but he's one of the agents assigned to guard your father's hospital room."

"No kidding," Kate said.

"He's the one with the daughter in the wheelchair. I heard she suffers from severe autism. I guess when he is assigned to a case like this—for an extended time—he flies his mother and daughter out to be with him."

"Autism?" Kate asked. "I thought that mostly boys had that condition."

"Usually is," Sean said. "Four out of five cases are boys. At least that's what I've read. But, from what I've heard, that's the situation with this agent. His daughter is *severely* autistic. Gus Christopher, the owner, is a friend of mine, and he filled me in on the story. Great people. That's how he describes the family. But a very sad story, nonetheless. I understand that the mother did not want to deal with having a daughter so disabled, and so she just took off—simply ran away to avoid facing the problem. Of course, there're always two sides to every story. But that's the version I've heard. According to Gus, the agent's mother likes to talk and sip martinis in the evening.

"Whatever the case, apparently the agent and his mother are raising the child."

"Well," Kate said. "If they are staying at the Christopher, then I'm sure I'll get a chance to meet them. Probably already have met him, if he's assigned to the hospital.

"So, Millie," Kate continued, turning back to her newfound caregiver friend. "The boys are all set with clothing and bathroom necessities. How do you suggest we handle sleeping arrangements?"

"I have an inflatable mattress," Millie said. "Do they have sleeping bags?"

"They sure do."

"Then that will work just fine. It's not like they're moving in for good."

"Oh," Kate said. "I totally forgot. Buddy. The boys have a dog. A golden retriever. Buddy. Does that make a difference?"

"I'm guessing that's him sitting by the door."

"Right."

"He seems like a well-behaved dog. And Mr. Christopher is not objecting to his staying with you now? Right?"

"Buddy's probably got better manners than my two boys," Kate said.

Kate looked over at Red and Robby and apologized. "Just kidding, guys. But Buddy is the best dog I've ever seen. Red has trained him very well."

Kate then turned her attention back to Millie. "The owner, Mr. Christopher, said Buddy's staying would be okay with him as long as the other residents don't complain."

"Then that won't be a problem."

Robby and Red looked at each other and sneaked a smile.

Red texted, "Ths gonna b real cool!!"

Robby stole a peek at his phone.

Chapter 56
Life at the Christopher

"Agent Snyder," Kate said as she was unlocking her room on the third floor of the Christopher. "I just learned that there was an FBI agent staying here too, but I didn't know it was you."

Jack had introduced Kate to Agent Snyder earlier, so Kate had already become somewhat familiar with him. Actually she had asked her father to introduce her to Snyder, as she was impressed with his good looks and pleasant personality.

"Hi, Kate," he said with a smile. "I'm the guy. And my mother and daughter are here with me as well."

Snyder was a big, well-built man—six feet three inches, and two hundred pounds. While many FBI agents were satisfied with wearing cheap blue suits, Snyder dressed more like a stockbroker or network news anchor than a cop. As far as his obtaining and maintaining the expensive wardrobe was concerned, it helped that his older brother owned a high-end men's store in SoHo. Every Christmas Agent Snyder was gifted by his brother to his choice of suits and sports coats—as many as he could pack and carry on a plane.

The tailor at the clothing store always threw a fit when measuring Snyder for a new jacket. "Can't you do *something* with that ... that *gun*? How am I supposed to make you look good with that *thing* bulging out? Maybe you could get a smaller gun?"

Despite the tailor's tinkering, Snyder kept his Glock, and the tailor adapted to the objectionable bulge.

"A gentleman at the ice cream shop told me earlier that there was an FBI agent registered here—I wondered if it was you. So, I guess we are now sort of neighbors. At least for right now."

"Right. You could say that," Agent Snyder said. "I didn't know you were staying here either. I thought that you had a place on Sugar Island—where your father was shot."

"We do," she replied. "But I wanted to be closer to the scene of the original crime, and our friend that usually watches over the boys is on vacation. So this bed and breakfast just seemed to work out. Terrific place, don't you think?"

"Absolutely," he said. "And that's why I booked here as well. Didn't know that I'd be spending most of my time in the Soo. But, that's okay. Mom and my daughter Sarah, they love it here."

"And I'm sure Dad's not going to be in the hospital forever. I think the nurses are ready to send him home."

"He told me that he might be heading back to the island as early as tomorrow," Agent Snyder said. "I'll miss him. He's a bit crusty, but I really like him."

"Yeah, he likes you too," Kate said. "A lot better than he likes your boss. In fact, he told me that he is going to request you be given the job of guarding him when he goes back to Sugar Island."

"No comment regarding my boss," Agent Snyder replied. "But I did hear something about my being assigned to your father when he gets released."

"Say," Agent Snyder said before Kate had entered her door. "Maybe the six of us can have dinner downstairs. I'm buying, of course. I'd like to have you meet my daughter."

"We'd love to," Kate said. "I'm going to be in New York for a couple days starting Wednesday. But I'm hoping to be back Thursday night. I'd love to have dinner with you on Friday—if that works."

"Friday it is," he said, smiling broadly. "Goodnight."

Kate smiled back and ushered the two boys into the room.

"Kate's got a boyfriend," Robby whispered to Red, just loud enough for both Kate and Agent Snyder to hear.

As soon as Agent Snyder had closed his door, a tough looking man who appeared to be in his early-to-mid-sixties walked up the steps and into the small corridor. The back of his neck and the exposed parts of his upper hands and arms bore evidence of his extensive gang and prison history. He was carrying two Walmart bags. He unlocked the room next to Kate's and entered.

He closed and locked the door behind him, tossed the bags on the bed, and made a call.

"I'm here," he said. "I got a room right next to the Handler woman. She's got the two boys and the dog here with her."

A female voice on the other end said, "Perfect."

Chapter 57
Kate visits Jack

By eight o'clock the next morning Kate was loading Buddy and the boys into her car to visit Jack in the hospital. If all went as hoped, Jack would be released after his doctor made the morning rounds.

As she left the Christopher's parking lot and turned north on H-33, also known as Manistique Lakes Road, she observed that a black Escalade had pulled out behind her. She monitored its position as it quickly seemed to drop back a considerable distance.

She slowed to see if it might catch and overtake her, but the Escalade slowed down further, maintaining a distance of about six hundred yards between them.

Realizing that the driver might be an older area resident, one who was not particularly in any hurry, she sped up to see if she could widen the gap between them.

But that didn't happen. When Kate hit sixty-two MPH, which was significantly above the posted speed limit, the Escalade appeared to be keeping up with her.

Finally, when she reached and passed the road leading to Germfask, the driver of the Escalade turned on his signal and headed west.

Coincidence? Kate asked herself. *Most likely.*

However, she did keep her eyes open for other suspicious vehicles.

Robby had been busy checking sports scores from the night before, but Red had noticed that Kate's attention had been drawn to her rearview mirror, so he did a head check and had been monitoring the black Escalade as well. While no audible communication occurred between Kate and Red, both acknowledged the fact that the Escalade was no longer following them, if, indeed, it had actually been following them at all.

When they reached the hospital, Kate asked Red and Robby to take Buddy for a walk. She did not want to leave Buddy in the car, and she wanted to discuss her plans for the boys with her father.

"Who exactly is this Millie?" Jack asked.

Kate explained in detail to her father her dilemma regarding what to do with the boys while she was in New York. She assured him that Millie seemed to her to be the best bet for them, at least until he was able to leave the hospital.

"Even after I get to go back to Sugar Island, until this whole mess shakes out a little, I wouldn't think it wise to have the boys come home."

"I agree," Kate said.

"As far as my going home," Jack said. "I'm hearing that I might get discharged as early as today."

"That's what I heard too," Kate replied.

"Who told you?"

"Agent Snyder. He said that the word going around was that you were headed home," Kate said. "I imagine SAC Dollar is preparing to post a guard at the resort when you go back."

"When did you talk to him? To Agent Snyder?"

"That's another thing," Kate said with a large smile. "Agent Snyder is staying at the Christopher too. He's there with his mother and daughter. So he'll be keeping an eye on the boys as well."

"What's he doing way over *there*?" Jack asked. "Can't he get a room around here?"

"I'm sure he could have. But up until you got shot, he didn't know he'd be spending so much time in the Soo."

"Babysitting me," Jack scowled. "That's what this amounts to. I'm ready to get the hell out of here and go home. And I think the staff would second that motion."

"He'll probably go with you to Sugar Island," Kate said. "I doubt that he's done with you yet."

"Oh, I don't mind Snyder a bit. He's a pretty straight-up guy. But if he's going to be coming to the island to babysit me, he's going to be eating a lot of my cooking. I hope he likes whitefish."

Chapter 58

He never gave up

Russell Cox stood just outside of the section of Strangmoor Bog that had been cordoned off by the FBI. Three days earlier they had taped off nearly half an acre, designating it as an "FBI Crime Scene." Russell Cox had stationed himself there before sunrise and had not budged.

Actually he had spent most of the previous days there as well. He had spotted the detectives from the sheriff's department when they originally ran the tape for the murder of Milton Stenos. He had returned to that area daily.

When the FBI took over the case they moved the whole investigation to the location where the boys had discovered the ring and human finger. So then Mr. Cox began visiting that site every day.

After their technicians initially examined the crime scene area, the FBI determined that they needed additional equipment to properly search for and process evidence, so they did not return to the site for the following three days. Instead, they positioned cameras on the perimeter, installed a generator, and established a satellite uplink.

While the ribbon was designed to keep people out, Russell Cox regarded it as a target marker. So, after waiting outside the ribbon for the first day, and not seeing anyone guarding the area, Russell Cox arrived early the second morning and spent nearly six hours poking around inside of it.

Even though the old man had combed that very real estate dozens of times before, now he did so with intensified interest.

Because of the nature of the terrain, the FBI requested that the Schoolcraft Sheriff's Department monitor the cameras. In the event of an alarm, the sheriff was supposed to send an appropriately equipped emergency vehicle to investigate.

In order to respond quickly, the sheriff requisitioned a two-man tracked ATV and left it on the Highwater Trail, just outside the bog.

Unfortunately, on the first night, the camera system was activated numerous times by raccoons, deer, and bears. After a while, the dispatchers stopped paying attention to the alarms. *After all*, they reasoned, *who in their right mind would ever venture out into such an inhospitable area*?

SAC Dollar had another idea.

The second day after the cameras had been installed, he sent Agent Randy Frank into the dispatch office to view all the video.

After having a nice laugh with the dispatchers and Sheriff Griffen about all the wildlife caught on camera, suddenly he let out a shout. "What the *hell* is that?"

"Hey!" he called out to the head of dispatch. "Take a look at *this.* Tell me—just how the hell could you have missed something this obvious?"

Sheriff Griffen, who had earlier been joking around with Agent Frank, closely scrutinized the monitor as the agent zoomed in on his object of interest.

"Who the hell is that?" Agent Frank asked.

"That's old man Cox," Sheriff Griffen said. "What the shit does he think he's doing?"

"One thing is obvious," Agent Frank said. "The old fart is *inside* the tape, and he is compromising, maybe even contaminating, my crime scene. How did your people miss *that*?"

Sheriff Griffen knew the answer to that rhetorical question, but he did not wish to register a comment.

"What time did that happen?" the sheriff asked.

"This morning, just after sunrise," Agent Frank replied.

"Check the previous day," Sheriff Griffen suggested. "Let's take a closer look at that video. Chances are he was in there then as well."

The sheriff was correct. On closer examination of the video recordings, they could see the distinct outline of an adult male walking around inside the taped-off area.

"He was there yesterday as well," the sheriff said. "And now he's back. We're going to have to post a guard out there until after you're finished. Just no other way. We could bring Cox in. But who's to say that someone else might not violate it. Besides, bringing the old man in for questioning would probably kill him."

"You got anyone you can spare?" Agent Frank asked.

"It's *your* crime scene—not ours. We're not even being compensated for monitoring the cameras. But if we have to provide manpower to guard your crime scene, then that becomes something else altogether. We will have to expect something. The county will require it."

"I'll clear it with my boss," Agent Frank assured him. "I'm sure it'll not be a problem. Just get one of your men out there. Now. And keep someone on the scene until further notice."

Sheriff Griffen did not trust that Agent Frank could make such a commitment, but he was quite eager to get back into the case. So, after voicing his reservations, he ordered the deployment.

From that point on, at least one deputy stood guard over the crime scene, day and night.

And during that time, from sunrise to sunset, Russell Cox maintained a vigil at his post just outside the tape.

Only one time during the first several days of the investigation did SAC Dollar observe that the old man's chair was empty.

"Where's the old man?" Dollar asked the guard. "Did he die?"

"No, he was here earlier this morning. I think he stuck around for about an hour. And the next thing I noticed he was gone. He didn't say anything to anyone. But, he never does. He just sort of appears, and then disappears."

Chapter 59
Only one finger

Just as Sheriff Griffen suspected, SAC Dollar merely sneered at Agent Frank's declaration that the FBI would be reimbursing Schoolcraft County for additional manpower, but he wasn't present when the agent broke the news to his boss.

Cringing with displeasure at the thought of more paperwork, Dollar initially barked something like it'd be a "cold day in hell" before he'd consider reimbursing the county "for doing their job." But he didn't know Sheriff Griffen very well and so was not certain just how insistent the sheriff might be in protesting for payment, so Dollar expedited the exploratory and forensic investigation of the Strangmoor Bog crime scene.

"Couldn't we have saved money by flying out of Munising?" Dollar asked. Commanding the operation from his mobile communication center located in a semi tractor-trailer parked at Sawyer International Airport in Marquette, he was remonstrating against Frank's choice to use Sawyer, as opposed to Munising's Hanley Field.

"Forty-five miles—give or take," Frank confidently responded. "In the grand scheme, I think my choice of Sawyer was the right one. The chopper pilots were pretty insistent about using Sawyer as well. They said they had no problem with Hanley as an emergency refueling station, should it be necessary. But they were more familiar with Sawyer. Besides, the company that we leased the choppers from, they pretty much insisted on Sawyer.

"And, you know, they'd already lost one chopper in the bog. I did not feel like arguing this point with them."

Dollar did not persist in his protest.

"How many trips are we talking?" Dollar asked, continuing to calculate the cost.

"Two or three to set up," Frank said. "At least that's what they estimated. But you know how that goes. Once we get boots on the ground we will probably discover that we're missing something. Logistics can be a real bear in situations like this.

"And a lot of it will have to do with how quickly the crime scene can be processed. So far, all we have is that one finger. No telling just how far from the rest of the body it might have migrated."

"Well, one thing for certain, we're not going to be turning the whole bog upside down."

"It's a huge crime scene, by any standard," Frank said. "And given the nature of the terrain—"

"We will give it three days maximum," Dollar interrupted. "We've got a finger. Actually, we have only *part* of a finger. And that might be all we get."

"I'll not share that with the agents on the ground," Frank chuckled. "I think they might work a lot more efficiently not knowing just how long they might be stuck out there. This crime scene is just about as bad as it gets. Maybe we should think about getting Mike Rowe in there."

"I can justify three days, counting today," Dollar said, appreciating Frank's humor but not responding to it. "After that, if we don't turn up something significant, we're pulling out of this shithole."

Neither man spoke for a long moment, and then Dollar asked, "Two trips to set up?"

"Given the three-day scenario," Frank replied, "I'd guess three trips the first day, two the second, and three to pack up and get out. That'd be a total of eight flights, if everything went reasonably well. Personally, I see us here for a minimum of five days, particularly if we start finding evidence."

Frank looked over at his boss, but Dollar did not respond. Instead, he began operating the joystick and switches that controlled the on-scene camera system.

A few minutes later Frank blurted out, "Hold it! Go back with that camera, and zoom in. I think that's him. The old man. Can you zoom in a little better? And focus?"

"Here, *you* run it," Dollar commanded. He was frustrated at the prospect of all the paperwork awaiting the conclusion of this case, in particular, the costs associated with the chopper rentals, and the possible hassle with Sheriff Griffen seeking reimbursement for additional man-hours. Plus, he was a little irritated with his subordinate telling him what to do.

"You've played around with this stuff more than I have. You take my seat," he continued as he got up and walked over to the restroom. "See what you can do."

It was true. Frank was much more proficient with the electronics than was his boss, and both men knew it.

Eagerly, Frank took the vacated seat and switched to a camera located closer to where the old man was standing. He then panned the camera over toward the man and zoomed in.

When Dollar returned, he sat down in the seat beside Frank.

"So that's him?" Dollar said.

"It is."

"Leave that camera on him—at least for now. How many cameras do we have?"

"This system supports sixteen," Frank said. "But we have eight hooked up."

"Do we need more?"

"No. I don't think so. The purpose for the cameras is to monitor the scene until we're finished with it. We'll actually have two forensic photographers on the ground for the duration—"

"Is that enough for such a large crime scene?"

Dollar's question was rhetorical. He was not about to add personnel to the investigation, regardless of what Frank said. Frank knew that and did not respond.

After a moment, Frank said, "Technically, it remains to be established whether or not a crime actually took place here. We have a finger. That's it. And at this point we don't know anything more than that. If it weren't for the chopper exploding, I doubt we'd even be in the bog right now."

"Take a look at him," Dollar said. "His somber demeanor. Has he ever said anything to the agents? Have they taken a statement from him? Do we really know who he is?"

"His name is Russell Cox," Frank said. "He lives in the bog. That's all the old man told us. I know it seems weird that anyone would choose to live in the bog. But that's his story."

"Does he indicate why he is so intent on watching the investigation?"

"Not really. But, what else is there to do? This has got to be the best show in town for him."

"There's more to it than that," Dollar said. "Look at the expression on his face. He's no casual observer. I want to talk to that man. Get me a chopper. *Now*! Notify Agent Rolly to keep an eye on the old man. If he looks like he's leaving, detain him. I'll get there as quickly as possible."

Agent Rolly was the agent in charge on the ground.

"Better put your boots on, sir," Frank advised.

His boss did not find his comment as humorous as Frank had intended it.

Chapter 60
Where do you live?

Agent Frank arranged for the chopper to pick up his boss at the command center. Twenty minutes later, SAC Dollar was on the ground.

"Mr. Cox. My name is Special Agent William Dollar. I'm with the FBI. I understand that you live in the area. Is that true?"

Cox did not respond. Instead, he stared at the investigators searching for the body.

"Your name is Russell Cox. Is that correct?"

This time Cox responded with a deliberately slow nod.

"Do you have some identification with you? Driver's license maybe?"

Cox shook his head.

"You have no identification at all?"

Cox, still not looking at the special agent, reached into his front pants pocket and pulled out a small chain—again moving in spiritless motion. His hands were dark and wrinkled with gnarly fingers, his nails worn jagged by his lifestyle. His gray eyes matched his gunmetal gray thinning ponytail, most of which was tucked under his cap. His deeply wrinkled face bore evidence of decades in the harsh environment of Strangmoor. He'd stopped shaving longer ago than he could remember, opting instead for an occasional once-over with scissors.

With shaking hands, he continued to tug on the chain until the dog tag that was attached popped out of his pocket. He handed it to Dollar but did not talk to him.

Dollar took the dog tag from him and read it. "'Cox, Russell L.' What does the L stand for?"

"Lawrence," the old man responded slowly in a gravelly voice.

"So, your full name is Russell Lawrence Cox. And you live somewhere nearby? Is all that correct?"

Cox nodded his head slowly.

"Well, Mr. Cox, you have been spending a lot of time out here watching my men. You even ventured across the tape here. You weren't supposed to do that. I could have you detained for crossing that ribbon. Do you know that?"

For the first time, Cox turned his head and glared into Dollar's face. But he didn't speak.

"Don't worry, Mr. Cox. I have no intention of arresting you. At least not at this point. But I would like you to answer some of my questions."

And then, handing the dog tag back to the old man, he asked, "Where exactly is your house from here? You can just point if you wish."

Slowly Cox raised a shaking index finger and indicated a direction to the northeast.

"So, how far would that be? One mile? Two?"

The man did not respond.

"How far, Mr. Cox?"

Still the old man ignored the question.

"Mr. Cox. You can answer my questions here, or I will take you into custody," Dollar said, placing his hand on the old man's shoulder.

The second his hand touched his shoulder, Cox took a half step backward and knocked the special agent's hand away.

"Young man," he said. "You keep your damn hands to yourself. If you're gonna be arresting me, then do it. But you don't need to be pushing me around. I ain't done nothin."

"Mr. Cox, I apologize for that. I didn't mean anything by it. I just need to have you cooperate with me a little and answer some of my questions. Will you do that for me?"

"I don't know you," Cox said. "You say you are from the FBI. But you did not show me any identification. And you want to know where I live. What're you gonna do? Rob my house?"

"You are correct, Mr. Cox," Dollar said, showing the old man his ID. "I apologize for that oversight."

Cox lowered his head to get a good look at the special agent's credentials.

"What is it about this site that you find so interesting?"

"My brother."

"What about your brother? What is his name?"

"George."

"Where is he? Your brother George? Does he live with you?"

Slowly Mr. Cox pulled an old tattered wallet out of his left pocket. The tan leather was cracked. It had a zipper on three sides, but it was falling apart. Stamped into the leather was the image of a Native American.

"Here," Cox said, handing the wallet to Dollar. "I found this out here in 1978, one year, two months, and six days after my brother went missing. I was out here deer hunting, and I found George's wallet. Nothing else, just his wallet."

"You're sure this is your brother's wallet?" Dollar asked.

"Hell yes. It's got his pictures inside, and his driver's license. It was his wallet all right."

"Your brother went missing, you said?"

"That's right. I don't know what happened to him. He gets married to this girl from Curtis. His childhood sweetheart. Buys her a huge house.

And the next thing I know, he disappears. Never heard from him again."

"What do you think happened to him?"

"Hell if I know," Cox said. "It wasn't like him to just go away. He was happy, and hardworking. His wife was pregnant. And he was excited about becoming a father. I never believed that he would just run away. But that's what the police said—that he must have had a fight with his wife, and left town. That's crazy. That's just not the way he was. George would not have run off like that. And besides, if George had run off like they said, how'd his wallet end up out here in the bog? Don't make sense."

Dollar recalled the inscription on the ring the boys had found, *G&A Forever*, and asked, "your brother's wife—what was her name?"

"Andrea," Cox said. "George and Andrea."

Dollar did not react to the old man's words, but both he and Agent Rolly, who had just joined his boss and Cox, immediately recognized that the wedding ring that started it all quite possibly had belonged to George Cox, Russell's brother.

"Where exactly did you find the wallet? Was it near here?"

"No. It was nearly a quarter mile to the north. I spent the next ten years searching that area, but never found nothin' else. For the past thirty years I have searched the entire bog. But never found another damn thing. I'm getting so old and tired. It's too much for me anymore. I get so tired."

With that comment, the old man started to cry. He didn't say any more. He just looked down and shook his head.

"I think we've got something over here," one of the investigators said, bending down and pulling a piece of metal from the damp soil.

"Mr. Cox," Dollar said, "I do not want you to move. Agent Rolly and I will come back and talk to you as soon as we check this out. You wait right here."

Dollar then ducked under the tape and walked through the bog over to where the investigator was standing.

"What have you got?" he asked.

"I was using a metal detector. Right in the area where the boys found the ring. And I discovered this about an inch or two beneath the surface."

"What is it?" Dollar asked.

"Looks like a dog tag to me."

"What's the name? Can you make it out?"

"It's Cox, George W. … Do you think that would be the name of our vic? That would fit perfectly with the inscription on that ring the boys found—*G&A Forever*. That *G* could be for George—George Cox."

"Is that your mark? Where you found it?" Dollar asked.

"Yes. It's about fifteen feet from where the boys found the ring."

"Keep looking, agent. It'd be good if we could find the rest of the body. Might be able to positively identify it through dental."

"What was your brother's middle name?" Dollar said as he turned and walked back to where Mr. Cox was waiting.

"William. His name was George William Cox. … Why? What did your guy find?"

"A dog tag. I would say that there is a very good chance that it belonged to your brother. The name on it is Cox, George W. Blood type B Positive. Was he B Positive?"

"Yes, he was. We both were."

"Then this dog tag most likely would have been your brother's. Could he have somehow dropped it out here?"

"What kind of a fool are you? He's dead. George is dead. This proves it. I've always suspected it, finding his wallet. But this proves it. He never took his dog tag off. It would have been around his neck when he died. Probably the rest of his body is nearby. I would like to give him a proper burial. Your men will keep looking, right? They're not gonna give up?

Right? They're gonna keep digging?"

"Now that we've found the dog tag, we'll keep looking. Chances are that the rest of the body, if there still is one, will be located pretty close to where we found the dog tag. And the chain on it was not broken. So, while we don't know much for certain, it still seems likely that other body parts should be in the vicinity. Of course, it could have slipped off, or been pulled off, and then washed over here during a rainstorm or a flood. Can't tell about that. But there seems a decent chance we will find more. … At any rate, we *will* keep looking.

"Mr. Cox. It could take a very long time to finish up here. It could be several days. I suggest that we have one of my agents walk you back to your house, and stay with you if you wish. But there is no point in having you wait out here in the elements. This is going to be a long and drawn out process before we wind it up.

"I cannot express to you how sorry I am for your loss. But it is pretty certain right now that the ring and finger that we found did belong to your brother. And I will promise you that I will personally see to it that we share with you any additional findings. But I think you should go home now, and rest. I will want to question you later, once we determine the cause of death. Okay? Will you go to your home now?"

Chapter 61

The long walk home

Initially, Mr. Cox totally rejected SAC Dollar's offer to send an agent to accompany him back to his cabin. But, eventually he realized that he had no choice in the matter, and he complied. Agent Rolly volunteered, but Dollar instead sent Agent Manuel Alvarez to walk with the old man.

"Hope Alvarez doesn't get lost coming back," Rolly quipped. "Good thing he's got a Garmin."

The team of investigators was employing the primary method for a search of this type—that is, the inch-by-inch visual inspection of the suspected location.

Initially, they had brought in a corpse-sniffing cadaver dog, but it did not prove fruitful.

They also performed a chemical analysis of the air and soil of the entire crime scene, also to no avail.

As the day wore on, technicians uncrated another piece of equipment—a lawnmower-sized Ground Penetrating Radar device, known by its acronym, GPR.

The GPR can be a very effective tool in locating various types of subsurface evidence, such as tunnels and chambers, building foundations, disturbed soil, explosives, caches of drugs or money, guns and knives—and, of course, buried bodies.

Of all the equipment available to law enforcement and crime scene investigators, when it comes to detecting the presence of buried evidence, only manual excavation comes close to GPR's effectiveness.

It was GPR that proved effective for Dollar's crew in Strangmoor Bog on that late summer evening in 2014.

Less than an hour after Alvarez returned from walking Cox back to his cabin, one of the technicians called over to Dollar.

"Sir, I think we might have something here."

Dollar was talking to Rolly regarding whether they should keep working into the night or break off until morning. There was no furniture at the crime scene, so it was virtually impossible for them to find a comfortable place or position from which to observe.

"What do you think you see?" he asked the GPR operator.

"There's definitely something down there. And it's not very deep. The top of it looks to be about three hundred millimeters, or about a foot, below the surface."

"How large is it?" Dollar asked. "Can you tell what it might be? What does it look like?"

"It has a rounded portion, and it is about the size of a skull. Worth digging up, I'd say."

Dollar thought for a moment and then said, "Before we do that, see if you can find anything else in the surrounding area. Keep in mind that the body was probably not buried—just dropped on top of the bog. And that wolves and coyotes could have ripped it up pretty good, and then spread it around.

"It follows that the head might have been severed from the torso, possibly by wolves. The fact that the chain on the dog tag was intact suggests that possibility.

"There's no point in trying to dig around in this mud. Let's just assume for a while that you have actually located a skull. And that's sure as hell what it looks like to me. Mark its location, and then let's think about where the rest of the body might be. Maybe it got washed down a bit. Work your way out into a twenty-foot radius, and let's see what else you turn up. Would probably be about the same depth. Mark anything that looks like a bone.

"I'll work at getting some pumps in here and at least take the surface water off. The bog is too large to drain, but if we can determine that we have a body, and then demonstrate that we have a crime, then we will have to expand our search—*considerably* expand our search."

"If the wolves got him, they could have dragged the carcass off a long way," the GPR operator said. "And no telling in what direction."

"I understand," Dollar said. "If, indeed, we do have a skull. There is a very good chance we can make a positive ID from the dental records. The dog tag is great, but it could have been dropped here when George Cox was hunting. I want to get as much as we can."

An hour passed, and then a second. Finally, after four straight hours, the GPR operator shut down his machine and looked over at Dollar and said, "Sir, I'm not finding anything else."

"Well then," Dollar said, "let's see what we've got."

During the time that the GPR operator was scanning the scene, the rest of the team ceased what they were doing and set about placing three gas-powered pumps around the perimeter and two additional pumps with screened points that were pushed into the soft soil close to the marked target area. These two pumps drew the water out from the soil directly in contact with the possible skull.

Once the pumps were all operating, everyone gathered around to watch the excavation of what they hoped would be an intact human skull.

What they found shocked them all.

* * *

"The larger crimes are apt to be the simpler, for the bigger the crime, the more obvious, as a rule, is the motive." —Sir Arthur Conan Doyle

Chapter 62

Let's not get *ahead* of ourselves

With painstaking care, Agent Michael Mallory, the forensic specialist charged with this part of the investigation, carefully removed the peat soil from a three-square-foot area above the object.

Every spoonful of soil was placed on a large piece of plastic to be saved and water-sieved later.

As he reached a depth of about nine inches, he began using a stiff brush to separate the soil from the bottom of the hole.

Leaning backward to stretch out his back muscles, he looked up at Dollar and moaned, "This is like lopping through a lava cake looking for a lost marble. My back is killing me."

Finally, after nearly two more painstaking hours, his brush caught into something. Immediately he stopped sweeping.

"Hit me with some light here," he said. "I want to get a good look at this."

Agent Rolly was closest, so he removed one of the lights nearby and held it to within a foot of the brush.

Carefully, he shot a stream of air onto the soil beneath his brush. As he did, it became clear that his brush had become entangled in human hair, and that the hair was still attached to a human scalp.

"Holy shit!" he said. "We've not only got a human skull, but it is virtually mummified. At least this part of it is."

Dollar snatched the light from Rolly and dropped to his knees beside Mallory.

"Let me see that," he said.

"That's for sure a human skull, right?"

"Yes sir, it is," the forensic investigator replied. "And it is a very unusual human skull. It has been mummified by the surrounding peat of the bog. I might be wrong, but it is quite possible that once we retrieve it, we will be able to get the old man to identify it. It could be that well preserved. And judging from what I can see so far, it's very likely that it is."

"Well, carry on," Dollar said as he stood. He handed the light back to Rolly.

"Do you still need this down here, or shall I reattach it to the stand?" Rolly asked.

"Go ahead and hook it back up. I'm going to take a little break."

"Is he serious about that skull being mummified?" Rolly asked.

"There's definitely precedent for it," Dollar replied. "I've read about it happening, but mostly in Europe. There's one instance in particular. It occurred in Denmark in the 1950s. Women digging up peat found a full skeletal mummy. It was so well preserved that they thought it was from a recent murder. But carbon dating placed it in the fourth century BC. It was over two thousand years old. Perfectly preserved. He, the mummy, was known as the 'Tollund Man.'

"So there's nothing new about it. We just don't see it happening here very much. I think it is just one of those special characteristics about a peat bog. These mummies are called *bog bodies.*

"But I doubt that we'll be asking the old man to ID his brother by showing him the mummy. The shock would probably kill him. Maybe if it comes to that. But we should get something out of the dental records."

* * *

The process resumed after a short break. It remained slow and tedious. Once a substantial amount of soil had been removed near the perimeter of the area being excavated, Mallory began brushing the debris away from the skull and into the empty space he had just created. And once the perimeter had filled, he would again empty it.

Finally, he cleared the forehead of the skull down to the bridge of the nose.

"Looks like something tore him up a bit," he said. "Possible evidence of a K-9 having dinner. Much of the skin on his forehead has been torn away, and part of his nose. And, there is something very interesting here—*very* interesting. Hey, boss, I think you need to see this."

Chapter 63
Possible cause of death

SAC Dollar, even though he was growing a bit antsy, had still been keeping a keen eye on the progress.

Affecting an exhausted effort to pry himself from his seat on the wooden GPR storage case, he finally dropped both feet into the bog and sloshed his way over to where Michael Mallory was working.

"Whatcha got for me?" he asked.

"Right here," Mallory said, shining a flashlight square on the exposed forehead of the victim's skull. "I'm not sure how well you can see this, but there appears to be a bullet hole above the vic's right eye. Appears it entered at a slight angle, right to left—from the vic's perspective."

"How certain are you that it is a gunshot wound?"

"Pretty sure," Mallory answered. "We can't be one-hundred percent until we get the skull back to the lab, but my experience tells me the vic was shot in the head by a small-caliber handgun—possibly with a .32.

"Given the angle, it would be a good chance that the shooter was left-handed and shot the vic at close range. The shot was too well placed to have been done from a distance. Unless the shot was fired from a rifle. But the shooter appears to have used a small-caliber round. And that would most likely be from a handgun. Could have been self-inflicted. Provided the vic was right-handed. What do we know about this Cox fellow? Righty or lefty? That's all very preliminary, of course. I know I'm getting ahead of myself. I think that the lab might find evidence of some stippling—given the level of preservation."

"Is there an exit wound?" Dollar asked.

"Won't know that for a while," Mallory replied. "But the images from the GPR would suggest that there are no bullets remaining inside the skull. I saw some fillings in the teeth, but nothing that looks like a bullet. So I think we might find that it exited. But it is going to take some time before I can be more definitive. The bullet might be in there, fragmented perhaps, and I just can't see it. I'll know more in a bit."

"Self-inflicted you think?" Dollar asked.

"Not likely," Mallory replied. "But possible. At least as far as I can speculate at this time. That peat bog preserved the skin on the forehead even better than you'd find on an Egyptian mummy. I have eyebrows, eyelashes, and a lot of hair. I might even be able to pick up stippling around the entry wound, if there were to be some. And right now I don't see any. Of course, my work on mummies is quite limited. Actually, I don't have a clue as to what I should be looking for.

"However, one thing is for sure," Mallory said, as though begining and then waiting for a response from his boss.

"Okay. You've got my attention," Dollar said. "What would that *one thing* be?

Chapter 64
The school of hard knocks

Our victim, George Cox, or whoever he turns out to be, he has a very interesting depression on the top of his head, above and slightly to the left of the entry wound."

"Really?" SAC Dollar said. "Why would anyone hit him on the head, and then shoot him? Or, the other way around? You can only kill a *normal* man once. Doesn't make a lot of sense."

"Either injury would have proved fatal," Michael Mallory said. "At least that's my take on it. We need to get as much of this fellow as we can find under the microscope."

"How much do we have?" Dollar asked. "Can you determine that yet?"

"It looks like we have separation at the third cervical vertebrae—between C3 and C4. ... And. ... And. ... This is also interesting."

"What's that?" Dollar asked.

"I would have suspected, given the post-mortem K-9 wounds on the head and nose, that the neck would have been severed with signs of tearing. I'm not seeing that. It looks more like a severe compression resulting in the fracture. Like maybe he was first hit on the head with enormous force. And then, after he had fallen dead, he was shot in the head. Whatever the nature of the blunt object used to kill him, it must have been removed by the killer when he left. Otherwise, we should have found it nearby."

"You're suggesting he was struck on the head *first*?" Dollar asked.

"And then shot in the head *after* he'd fallen to the ground?"

"That sure is what it sounds like if I listen to myself," Mallory said with a chuckle. "Regard it all as idle chatter. Forget everything I've said. I should just be keeping my mouth shut until we get this guy back to the lab."

"Maybe he *was* a zombie," Agent Rolly chimed in. "Maybe he *had* to be killed twice. How the hell do you kill a zombie, anyway? I think the only sure way is to destroy the brain. Even an intact severed head can bite you. So, Mallory, you'd better watch your digits. Don't let the guy bite 'em off. He even looks like a zombie—all mummified like that. Shot in the head. *Knocked* in the head. Then decapitated and buried. I'd bet you got yourself a genuine zombie mummy there.

"I'm callin' the *National Enquirer* right—"

"Shut the hell up," Dollar barked. "You never know who might be listening … and *recording*. We'd all have our asses handed to us if this conversation ever got out."

Chapter 65

Wednesday morning arrives

She's on her way to the airport right now," said the tattooed man who was staying next door to her at the Christopher. "Should I follow her?"

"No," Allison said. "It seems reasonable that she would be headed to the airport right about now. It's ten to four, and Flight 4605 departs Chippewa International at six thirty. Where else could she be headed this early in the morning?

"Now with Kate gone, I want you keep your eye on the boys. Monitor their activity. If they leave the Christopher and head to the swamp, or anyplace else, they will do it together. And when you get the chance I want you to check out their room. I want to know if you find anything that will tell us what they're looking for in that swamp. I have a lot at stake here, and I don't believe all this activity could possibly have to do with some Boy Scout merit badge.

"Not with Jack getting shot and everything. And now with the FBI getting involved.

"Jack might be leaving the hospital today. Knowing him, I wouldn't think it impossible for him to pick up the boys and head right out to the swamp. I know it would be highly unlikely. But keep your eye out for him, and stay out of his way. He would not take kindly to your poking around—especially where those boys are concerned."

"By swamp, you're talking about Strangmoor Bog?" the tattooed man asked.

"Yeah. Where the boys are supposed to have found the gold."

"And what exactly am I looking for in their room?"

"I'm not totally sure. But I have it on good authority that Jack commandeered one of our spy satellites to track down some specific location in that bog. Where something is buried. Apparently he lost the coordinates and had to enlist the help of my husband to use a military satellite to re-locate it.

"And I understand that there are other interested parties, including the FBI. Now, with Jack getting himself shot, he might be unable to retrieve whatever it is that is buried out there. I have reason to be concerned. And your job is to make me feel better."

The tattooed man was not the typical ex-con. If he were, Allison would not be dealing directly with him.

The tattooed man was actually a man named Warren Cardfield. He was well known to Allison from her days in the White House, and even before. Warren Cardfield, whom she and almost everyone who currently had dealings with him usually referred to as *Tatts*, worked as an advisor to the Fulbrights, both when they resided in the governor's mansion in Louisiana and later at the White House.

Warren Cardfield came into their lives through Allison. Before she married Bob, she had dated Cardfield while they were both students at Yale Law School.

At that time, no one who knew Cardfield could ever have guessed how he would end up, or that someday he'd be known as Tatts. It just wouldn't have seemed possible.

As a first-year law student with Allison, he was near the top of the class. Allison was attracted to him for that reason. She was shopping for a husband, and she viewed him as a man with potential—at least early on.

Allison was also near the top of the class, and she was rapidly developing a presence of her own on the Yale campus. While she did not openly boast about her 175 score on the Law School Admission Test, commonly referred to as the LSAT, she was not ashamed of it either. After all, the average LSAT score across the country was 150, and at Yale the average was 173. But when she learned that Warren Cardfield had scored a perfect 180, it took her breath away. She immediately homed in on him, and he didn't have a chance.

By the end of the first week, they were dating. And before Christmas they were an item.

That, of course, was before she met her soon-to-be true love.

During the first week of her second year of law school, she met a new man—Bob Fulbright. When she learned that he had scored an impressive 178 on his LSAT, she immediately took note. Soon she was focusing almost all of her attention on Mr. Fulbright.

Allison's attraction to Bob Fulbright was not based solely on the young man's scholastic aptitude. He was, as Allison herself described him, "absolutely beautiful in every conceivable way."

They did not even share a class together during his first year. But she did see him in the common areas, and when she did, she could not take her eyes off of him.

By the time Thanksgiving rolled around, she had virtually glued herself to him. Like Cardfield before him, Bob did not have a chance. Allison was on a mission. She warded off all competition like a pistol shrimp in heat.

But Allison did not totally discard her former lover. Instead, she convinced Bob to hire him as part of his legal staff when he became governor of Louisiana.

Cardfield then followed the Fulbrights to the White House. That's where Cardfield first met Jack Handler and Handler's good friend, Reginald Black.

Given the nature of the work in which Handler and Black engaged, and the many demands placed on all three of them by their bosses, it did not take very long before the DC Bar called Cardfield in and revoked his license to practice law.

Shortly thereafter he took the fall for one of Bob Fulbright's close confidants and was sentenced to ten years in the Federal Penitentiary at Leavenworth for racketeering. Everyone knew that had he named names, he could have gotten off. But Cardfield believed that it would be much safer for him inside than out—at least under those circumstances.

So, he did his time, getting out after eight and a half years. He had a nice paycheck waiting for him when he hooked back up with the Fulbrights. Plus, he was hired as an omnibus problem-solver by the former president at nearly a quarter-million-dollar salary. Of course, his association with the Fulbrights was totally off the record.

When asked if he bore any regrets for having hitched up with the Fulbrights he'd answer, "Hell no! Who do you know that makes two hundred and fifty thousand dollars a year for doing shit? I get all the women I want. I can get drunk whenever I want. I could snort drugs, if I wanted to, but that's not my thing. Never was. And check out these radical prison gang tatts. There's not an honest lawyer alive who would not trade places with me in a heartbeat. Or maybe there's just not an honest lawyer."

After he had done his time, no one ever questioned his loyalty to the former first family. And, because he looked more like a street thug than a former Ivy Leaguer, few had the guts to challenge his credentials in the physical arena either.

Once, in a bar, a young man fresh out of county lockup approached Tatts and asked him about his tattoos. "What gang did you join?" he asked. "AB, DWB, or maybe DMI?"

Tatts smiled, and then slapped the young man so hard on the side of his head the kid briefly lost consciousness. Catching him with his free hand before he hit the floor, Tatts steadied him on his feet and asked, "Just how bad do you want to know?"

"Al," Tatts said. "Jack Handler is my friend. I'm not comfortable working behind his back, if you know what I mean. So, please, just afford me the latitude to stay out of his way."

Allison knew exactly what Tatts was thinking. No one, herself included, wanted to rile Jack up. As it stood, she was fairly certain that Jack was not aware of her concern about what was going on in the bog. And he certainly did not know that she had dispatched Tatts to keep an eye on him and what he was up to.

She fully understood what it could mean should Jack somehow be faced with the fact that someone as dangerous as Tatts was poking around in his business.

While it was true that she had hired Jack to search for and return to her the one hundred million in gold that his friend Reginald had accepted from her as payment for the failed assassination of the sitting president, and while Allison totally trusted Jack's integrity to deal fairly with her, the fact that Jack had been shot—by someone whom she didn't know—made him appear weaker and more vulnerable in her eyes. Allison felt constrained to watch out for her own interests. That's why she dispatched Tatts to check out the find of gold in Strangmoor Bog.

Add to that the fact that for some reason Reginald had flown into Sault Ste. Marie just before his death. *Perhaps Reg had hidden my gold somewhere in Michigan's Upper Peninsula, and later traveled up there to retrieve it,* she wondered.

And then there was the matter of the FBI digging around in Strangmoor Bog. Ostensibly they were looking for a body, but she never bought anything the FBI said. For all she knew, the gold that the boys found might have nothing at all to do with a murder victim, and might have everything to do with her gold. Perhaps Reginald buried the treasure in the bog, the boys found out about it, and they were able to recover part of it.

Aside from Jack, Tatts was her most ruthless yet trusted associate. And having worked closely with Jack for a number of years, he had the ability to predict the way Jack thought.

While there was no better man than Tatts to send on this mission, were Jack to learn that he was acting on her behalf, his first reaction would be to take Tatts out.

Tatts recognized the awkwardness of the situation. While the only person around that could possibly ID him was Jack himself, if that were to happen, one of them would likely die. He did not want to be the one who killed Jack Handler, but in his eyes, he preferred that outcome to the alternative.

"Jack's still in the hospital," Allison said. "So as long as he's there he will not be a problem to you.

"But, while that's good for you, his being laid up does not help my case. I need someone to assure me that all this activity in the bog has nothing to do with my gold. Once that happens, you can get out of town.

"But until then, or until Jack gets on his feet, avoid him," Allison advised. "Shouldn't be too difficult to do that. At least for the time being, he will probably be either in the hospital or at his resort on Sugar Island. Stay out of those two places, and you shouldn't run into him."

"One thing for sure," Tatts said, "I do not want to show my face out in the bog with the FBI crawling all over it. My best bet would be to do like you said: search the boys' room, particularly now that Kate is headed out of the state for a couple days."

"Where are you right now?" Allison asked.

"I just went back to my room at the Christopher."

"And the boys? Where are they?"

"Right next door."

"Can you monitor their conversation? How soundproof are the walls?"

"Wouldn't matter," he said. "The redhead can't talk. So all they do is text."

"That's right. Can you think of a reason to pay them a visit?"

"Al," Tatts said. "I gotta go. Someone's at my door."

Chapter 66

Tatts meets the boys

Oh," Robby said apologetically. "We're sorry. We thought Millie, the ice cream lady, lived here."

"No, kid," Tatts said. "She lives on the other side of you and Kate."

Immediately Tatts cringed. *I shouldn't know where anyone here lives,* he thought. *This is a bed and breakfast for God's sake. I just hope the boys didn't spot my mistake.*

"Hey, aren't you those two *famous* boys? The ones who found the gold in Strangmoor Bog. Are you the ones?"

"We are the ones," Robby answered. "But we're not famous."

Tatts then reached out to shake Robby's hand and, afterward, Red's.

The boys had picked up on Tatts' overly familiar posturing and his having more information than he really had a right to. But they had grown used to strangers seeking their approval.

"Tell me, boys. Did you fellows find just that one piece of gold, or is there more?"

"Our Uncle Jack told us not to discuss this with anyone unless he or Kate were with us. We can only say that the police report is correct—we found one gold wedding ring. That's it. Beyond that, we're not supposed to talk about it—not even to the FBI, unless Uncle Jack or Kate is with us. So that's all we can say. Sorry."

"That makes perfect sense to me," Tatts said. "You just can't be too careful these days. Especially when it concerns all that gold. No telling who might want to get in on it."

At first Robby was inclined to say something to diminish the notion that there was or could be more gold, but he thought better and kept his mouth shut.

Tatts correctly read Robby's initial reaction as a sincere inclination to quash that notion. *I'm beginning to think that all they found is that one ring—no more,* Tatts reasoned.

"Hey, mister," Robby said, trying to excuse himself. "We've gotta get going. Two doors down you said? The ice cream lady lives two doors down?"

This time Tatts was a little more careful.

"You know, I really don't know who that would be—the ice cream lady. I did catch you coming in last night, so I knew you guys were staying next door. I would assume that the person you're looking for might be on the *other* side, because my room is the last one on this side of the corridor. So you might try two doors down. That could be it."

"Thanks, mister," Robby said as turned to follow his friend. Red had already headed down the hall.

Tatts stepped outside to see the boys off but quickly returned to his room and shut his door before the boys knocked on Millie's door.

"That sounded a little fishy to me," Robby whispered. "What do you think?"

Red looked at Robby and nodded. Both boys stopped and thought about it for a moment, and then shrugged it off.

"Hi, boys," Millie said, welcoming the boys into her apartment. "Angel, the boys are here. Want to come out and greet them?"

"Hey, guys," Angel said, bursting from her bedroom, her bright blue eyes flashing as brightly as her smile. "I've got today all planned. Hope you're up for some *Angel Adventure.*"

Chapter 67
The ground rules

Robby glanced over at Red. Both boys smiled in anticipation.

"Sounds good to us," he said. "We're up for it. For sure."

"Before you three adventurers get too far ahead of yourselves," Millie said in an authoritative but pleasant tone, "we need to establish a few guidelines. First, I need to know where you are *all* the time. I want you to have some fun, but I do not expect to be wondering where you are or what you're doing.

"Angel knows what I'm looking for. But I'm not making her your boss. Each one of you must be accountable for your own behavior. If I should get a call from Kate, I want to be able to say you guys are at such and such a place, and to explain to her what you are up to. I do not expect any surprises.

"Do we all agree on that?"

"Guys, she means it," Angel said. "Believe me, I've had to learn the hard way."

Robby then said, "Sounds fine to us."

"Good. The second thing is this—bedtime is flexible. But all three of you will be in this apartment before ten p.m. every night. Do not call me at nine-thirty and tell me you might be a *little late*. There is no such thing as a *little* late. You're back on time, or you're late. Period.

"You might be surprised just how understanding and permitting I can be. If it's legal and moral, I will most likely grant permission. But don't assume anything. Ask in advance.

"Now, I will repeat—Angel is not your boss. I am. But she does understand my rules, and what I expect. So do not hesitate to run stuff past her. But just because she thinks something is okay to do, does not make it so. You each remain responsible for your own actions. All Angel will be able to do is tell you that something *might* be permissible. And if she thinks it is, then you should give me a call. If I don't happen to pick up, consider it as 'permission denied.'

"So far, are we on the same page?"

"Yup," Robby said. "Sounds fine to me."

"Then that's about it. There are only two things that I expect you to do today. I want Angel to introduce you two boys to my mother. She is lonely, and she loves the attention. You can do that first thing—before I head down to the shop."

"And the second job?" Angel asked.

"Sometime before I close it up, I would like the three of you to come down so I can make you the best sundae you've ever had—in your *whole* life. Do you think you can handle that?"

"*Mom.*" Angel groaned, "You're being facetious."

"Yeah, well. I mean it. If the boys like what I make for them, they will come back, and invite their friends. I can use all the business I can get. Now don't these two boys look like they appreciate the finer things in life? And my ice cream treats—there's nothing like them in the world."

"We'll definitely take you up on that offer," Robby said with a chuckle in his voice. "And I'm not sure about facetious, but if it means you're being really nice to a couple of fun-loving boys, then we also think you're being facetious."

Millie smiled at Robby and said, "Aren't you the charmer. Well, that's about it, I'll take you over to see Mom myself, and introduce you to her. She absolutely adores young people. She says they keep her young. Unfortunately, she still seems to be getting older. So I'm not so sure how that's working out for her."

"You will not mind talking to Grams," Angel assured the boys. "I really enjoy spending time with her. She might be old, but she is a lot of fun. And she *does* like to talk to teens. Not every old person is like that. She's such a sweetheart. I just know you will like her. We told her about you guys and she is very eager to meet you."

Millie was just about ready to head down to her shop. She was wearing jeans, a green T-shirt with a Lake Superior logo and an orange hoodie, complementing her red hair and bright green eyes. She had her cross-trainers on and was ready to go.

Millie would not likely be the first woman in Curtis to come to mind when the word "beautiful" was used. But for those who knew her, she would certainly make the top twenty list if the descriptive was "attractive."

She was thin and kept herself in good shape. It was obvious that she did not overly indulge in the products she sold. Millie maintained her weight at one hundred and fourteen pounds. So, at five feet four and a half inches, she looked almost too thin.

She had the appearance of a young woman who spent hours at the gym. But such was not the case. Millie maintained her trim physique mostly by just keeping busy—very busy.

Six days a week she worked at her ice cream shop. And then in the evenings she would check the list of guests. It was her job to make sure every empty room was ready for the next day. Occasionally she would discover that the day crew had entirely missed a room. When that happened, she was responsible for cleaning it.

She would, of course, investigate the next day to find out exactly who had dropped the ball. Usually, it was not the fault of her employees.

Sometimes a guest simply was unable or unwilling to vacate the room by the eleven a.m. checkout time. Generally, when this happened, the cleaning staff would leave Millie a note with an apology. If there were two or more such situations on any given day, one of the day staff would stick around to clean at least one of the rooms so that Millie would not get stuck with an overwhelming task.

While Millie did not work out in a gym, she did run several times a week. The Christopher was just over a mile from the ice cream shop, and unless the weather was dreadful, she would slip her reflective running backpack over her shoulders and sprint the distance to her shop.

Even if she was carrying nothing in her backpack, she still wore it to work whenever she ran. It served as a reminder to her on days that she had driven that she should not run home—if the backpack was not hanging beside the back door of her shop, that told her that she had driven that morning and should drive home.

She developed her system after the third time that she ran home, leaving her car at the ice cream shop.

But the greatest contributor to her keeping in shape was not her running; it was the time spent working at the shop. Not only did these eight to twelve hours on her feet build up her leg muscles, but her upper body benefited from the workout as well.

"Most people probably don't realize just how difficult it is to scoop ice cream," Millie once explained to an admirer, "especially if it is deeply frozen. That's how I developed my upper body strength."

The benefits of ice cream scooping came as a surprise to her. One morning, about a year after she had bought the shop, while she was standing in front of the mirror getting ready to head to work, she noticed that the muscle development in her right forearm and biceps appeared more massive than did that of her left. The same was true for her right pec.

She took a closer look, flexing both arms and turning her fists as she did it. She was amazed at the difference.

I like what this has done for my bowling score, she chuckled to herself. *But I'm turning into a bit of a freak.*

From that day on she began switching back and forth, first using her right hand to scoop the ice cream, and the next time switching to her left.

Soon the size of her two arms balanced out.

So, while Millie Star was not considered beautiful by most, she was definitely in shape and very attractive.

Her daughter Angel, however, was genuinely beautiful.

As Angel turned to follow her mother out the door that morning, the two boys joined in the procession. Robby, walking directly behind her, pointed his face upward, placed both hands over his heart, and sighed so that only Red could see and hear. And then he looked back at Red to see if his friend got the message.

Red slugged him on the arm.

Chapter 68

The boys meet Grams

"Grams," Angel said, pushing past her mother and planting a big kiss on her grandmother's forehead. "You look *beautiful* this morning."

The old lady smiled broadly from her wheelchair, but she didn't respond verbally to her granddaughter's compliment.

"Mom," Millie said. "These are the boys I told you about. The adventurers. They're the ones who found the ring in Strangmoor Bog. The one everyone is talking about."

And then, placing her hand on Robby's shoulder, she said, "This is Robby. And Robby, this is my mother. Her name is Louise Breeze, but you can call her Grams. That's what Angel calls her."

Louise was a small, frail woman with thinning winter white hair pulled back in a ribbon. Her soft brown eyes looked fatigued, as though she carried a heavy weight on her shoulders. Her time-chiseled face bore the lines of decades of worry and stress.

Millie always made sure her mother wore bright colors, probably to neutralize her drab countenance. And today was no exception. Louise was decked out in a beautiful new-looking red sweater and a pair of black slacks.

As is the case with most elderly people, Louise was wearing warm slippers, not shoes. She wore shoes only when going out to see the doctor.

"And, Mom," Millie said, lovingly laying her hand on Red's far shoulder and pulling him to her side, "this is Red. He is Robby's best friend. He doesn't talk. He only does text messaging. That means he will have to talk to you through Angel, or Robby. It was actually Red here that dug up the ring. But they're both amateur geologists. The boys were working on a Boy Scout merit badge in the bog when they made their discovery. It's had the whole town in an uproar."

The old lady reached out to the boys. They each took one of her hands and held it for a moment.

"Doesn't she have the coldest hands you've ever touched?" Angel said.

Finally, she pulled her right hand free and motioned toward a small table setting at the end of the couch.

"Ahhh," Angel said. "She wants to show you her pictures. She *loves* those pictures. I'll get them for her."

"Here, Mom, hold on for a second," Millie said, heading toward the kitchen sink.

A moment later she returned with a damp cloth to clean the large tray that attached with Velcro to her mother's wheelchair. The unit was designed for snacking, but recently Louise had taken all of her meals in her wheelchair using that tray.

In fact, for the past two years Louise's list of home activities consisted of those she did in bed and those she conducted from a wheelchair. During the day she rested, ate, and watched TV in her Nova Lightweight Wheelchair. When she wanted to take a shower, Millie helped her switch to her new Invacare Shower/Commode wheelchair.

She never left her apartment anymore, unless it was to see her doctor in his office.

Every morning before she went to work, Millie would help her mother out of bed, get her showered and dressed her for the day, secure the tray to the armrests, and then prepare her breakfast.

Louise loved to watch TV. So Millie would attach the TV remote to her tray using Velcro.

In the event of an emergency, Louise wore a dual-button waterproof medical alert pendant around her neck. When the pendant buttons were pushed, it activated three communication stations throughout the suite. One was in the kitchen, one in the bathroom, and one in the bedroom. Those units then served as microphones/speakers for a two-way connection to Millie's cell phone.

Millie had purchased the system when it became clear that her mother would be spending the rest of her daytime life in a wheelchair. So far Grams had not found it necessary to use the emergency pendant.

The next logical step in the progression was assisted living or a live-in caregiver—neither of which fit into Millie's budget. When asked about her plans for her mother, she would reply, "We're taking it one day at a time. Can't tell the future, so I won't worry about it."

Millie tested to be sure the tray was secured firmly to the armrests. Angel then laid the larger of two photo albums in front of her grandmother.

The first photograph she turned to was that of Millie. Angel had observed that her grandmother always looked for that picture first, so she folded down the top corner of the page to make it easier to open the album to it.

The old lady's eyes immediately sought and found her daughter's image. She reached her right hand to the picture and gently stroked it with her shaking fingers.

Up to that point of their visit, Angel's grandmother had not said a word. While she displayed a pleasant smile, it seemed to Angel that it was more affected than sincere.

Finally, looking into Robby's eyes to be sure he was paying attention,

Louise said, “Young man, this is my daughter. She was a very beautiful young lady, wouldn’t you agree?”

Her comment caught Robby by surprise—not because of its content as much as the very fact that she spoke with such clarity and volume.

“Very beautiful,” Robby replied with a blush. “What do you think, Red? Wasn’t Millie good-looking back then? Still is, actually.”

Robby was clearly embarrassed.

Red smiled at the old lady and signaled an affirmation of his friend’s observation with an emphatic nod. His cheeks demonstrated the degree of his embarrassment as well.

Both boys were infatuated with Angel, and it made them both uncomfortable to express an opinion regarding the relative attractiveness of their new friend’s mother.

“Mother!” Millie complained. “What kind of a question is that? You’re making the boys nervous.”

“Grams was just stating a fact,” Angel said, “You were, and still *are*, absolutely gorgeous.”

The boys were visibly pleased that the focus of attention moved from them to the women in the room.

“That’s a huge house,” Robby said, pointing to a picture in the album. He was seeking to change the subject altogether.

“Is that where you lived when you were younger?” he said, turning to address his question to Millie.

“That’s where Mom and I lived until I got married. And she continued to live there until Angel and I moved back to the UP.”

“So,” Robby said. “Where did you move to when you got married?”

“My husband sailed the Great Lakes. When we got married he was a crewmember of a freighter that carried iron ore from Duluth to the Soo—to Algoma Steel Company, Sault Ste. Marie, Ontario.

"In '98 he signed on to a freighter that sailed out of Cleveland. So we moved there, and that's where Angel was born."

"And then Daddy decided he didn't want to be married anymore," Angel jumped in, realizing that this part of the story always made her mother uncomfortable. "That's when we moved back to Curtis, and Mom bought the ice cream shop.

"Grams sold the big house, along with some other property, and used the money to buy the business.

"At first we moved into the apartment above the shop, and Mom and Grams ran the business. But ten years ago Grams had a stroke, and she couldn't get up and down the steps at the apartment, so we all moved into the Christopher—they have an elevator.

"So, for the past ten years Mom has run the shop by herself."

"Not entirely by myself, sweetie," Millie said, tossing her arm around her daughter and hugging her. "You're a *huge* help."

Angel smiled at her mother and said, "Mostly I help with the eating part of the business."

"Millie tells me that Angel is the reason all the young people hang out at the shop," Louise said, boasting about her granddaughter. "She is like a beam of sunshine on a cloudy day. Everybody loves Angel. Especially me."

"Grams, now you're embarrassing me."

"I gotta get going," Millie said. "You kids have some fun today. When you figure out what you want to do, give me a call. Remember, save some time to stop and see me over at the shop. I'll make you a surprise. And don't tire your grandmother out too much."

"Don't worry, we'll find plenty to do," Angel said as she hugged her mother. "And I will call you later. I think I'd like to take them to the library for a while, probably on our way to the shop, or maybe after. But I'll check with you."

As soon as Millie had closed the door behind her, the old lady's countenance morphed more somber.

"I understand you boys found a ring in Strangmoor Bog," she said. "Is that true?"

"Red found the ring," Robby said. "We were acquiring a core sample of the soil in the bog. It was all just to get a Boy Scout merit badge. We drilled down and pulled the sample out. And there it was—a man's gold wedding ring. It sure has attracted a lot of attention."

"That's exciting," the old woman said. "Can you describe it to me? Has anyone figured out who it belongs to?"

Chapter 69

Picking brains

"It was just an ordinary man's wedding band," Robby said. "But it did look like it belonged to a pretty big man."

"Was there an inscription in it?" she asked.

"Yes. But it did not give a name."

"Do you remember what it said?" she asked.

"No," Robby answered.

"Do you remember what was written in the ring?" he asked Red.

Red shook his head.

"We never saw it after we turned it over to the police. Uncle Jack told us that it said something about *love* and *forever*," Robby said. "Pretty general stuff, I guess. Isn't that about what all wedding rings say?"

Just then Red began to text Robby.

"Initials. I thnk 2 initials & forever," Red texted. "Dnt thnk love mentioned."

Robby read the text out loud so the old lady could hear.

The old woman did not respond. Instead, she leaned back against the backrest of her wheelchair and closed her eyes.

"I think that's our signal to go," Angel told the boys. "When Grams gets tired she lays her head back and closes her eyes. We should really let her rest now."

"Goodbye for now," Robby said as he gently laid his hand on her shoulder. "Hope we get to talk to you some more later."

The old lady did not respond to his comment. Red thought he detected a tear pinched in the corner of her left eye. But he wasn't certain. He brushed it off with this thought: *All old people leak.*

Angel circled around to follow the boys out. She bent over and again kissed her grandmother on the forehead and said, "See you later, Grams."

Again, the old lady did not react.

As they entered the corridor on the way back to Millie's room, Red sent a text, "Unk Jack. Wht was carved on ring? I 4got."

Jack was talking to his doctor when the text hit his phone. He read it and decided to respond later. Too much was happening right then. He had more pressing matters to attend to.

Chapter 70
Jack released

I guess you could say that I am signing your release papers because I have no other choice," the doctor told Jack.

"And what is that supposed to mean?"

"I think you know exactly what I mean. You stopped cooperating with me days ago. The nurses have been filling me in on your activities. You are treating this hospital as your own personal office—your hotel. You are running around all day long, and show up in your room at night to sleep. You might as well go home. We're not doing you any good like this."

"Doc," Jack said. "I didn't intend to get you so agitated. You did a great job getting me fixed up, but I'm ready to get back to the grind. I've had good days on the outside where I felt worse than I'm feeling right now. Honestly, I'm good to go. Right now I'm wasting your time and resources."

"Jack, your blood pressure is way too high. I am not happy about the way your heart sounds. If I had a few more days I could help you get things—"

"Doc, I didn't come here in the first place because of my heart. I had a hole in me where I shouldn't. And you fixed it. Now it's time for me to get back to work. So, when can I leave?"

"I'll drop your release form off at the desk, and they will send a chair up to taxi you down. Do you have someone to pick you up?"

"I'll check with my FBI buddy. He's going to accompany me anyway. If you're releasing me right now, I can take it from here."

"That's not how it's done. The paperwork will take a few minutes. Someone will be up to escort you out when it's completed. Well, Jack, can't say that you've been my best patient, but I have enjoyed being your doctor. You added some excitement to my day. Don't get to treat that many gunshot wounds, at least not many that aren't somehow involved with hunting accidents."

"You did a great job, Doc. Especially when you put Dollar in his place. I heard all about that from my daughter. I would have paid to have seen it."

"Don't know anything about that," the doctor replied. "I'm just pleased that we were able to help. You take care, Jack. And next time duck a little quicker."

After the doctor left, Jack walked out and requested that Agent Snyder join him in his room.

"You're going to be going back with me to Sugar Island—right?" Jack asked.

"That's what the boss said. I did overhear the doctor say he was releasing you. I think we all saw that coming. I'll check to see if my orders still stand."

"Do that. I'd like to get out of here before the doc changes his mind. Kate left my replacement Tahoe in long-term parking. You've got a car here? Right?"

"I do."

"How far from where I check out?"

"It's right there in the lot."

"Great. You can walk me down. I imagine they're going to want to run me down in the chair. We'll take your car over to where Kate left the new Tahoe. And I'll drive it back to Sugar Island.

"Here's where she parked it," Jack said, handing Snyder the note Kate had given to him. "Does that make sense to you? I didn't pay much attention to local geography on my way to the hospital."

Snyder looked at the parking location and confirmed that he knew exactly where it was.

"I suppose I could go drive it up for you," he said. "But that could get me in trouble with SAC Dollar. I suggest that you let me drive you out to the island, and we can send for your car when Kate gets back."

"I'm not leaving my vehicle here," Jack countered. "We'll do it my way. The sooner I can get back to normal, the better off we'll all be. I don't give a shit if you tail me, but I'm driving my own car back to the island."

Just then Jack remembered that he had not responded to Red's text. "G&A Forever," he texted. "Why?"

Snyder chuckled at Jack's c *What if this guy knew that I was having dinner with his daughter on Friday night?* he thought. *I don't suppose I will be breaking that news to him right now.*

"Just heard from SAC Dollar," Snyder said, checking a text. "He says that I should accompany you out to your house, and that I should stay with you until further notice."

Jack then received another a text from Red: "No reson. Jst wondered. U home yet?"

Jack responded, "Headed home now. Just got out. Kate's in NY. U guys ok?"

"Met real nice people. Millie and Angel. Angel is our age. Thnk Rob likes her."

"Enjoy ur self. B good. U can come home when Kates back."

"My car's dead ahead—the dark Silverado Crew Cab. Actually it's not really a car, is it?"

"All you FBI guys drive those Silverado Crew Cabs?" Jack asked.

"Not all of us," Snyder said. "But a lot of us do. The bureau pays for everything, so what the hell."

Jack got in the Silverado, Snyder again checked Kate's directions to Jack's Tahoe, and he pulled away from the curb.

Parked four spaces in front of where Snyder had just pulled out was a dark, late-model, four-door sedan. When Snyder's Silverado passed it, the driver pulled out behind them and followed at a discreet distance.

Chapter 71

Getting to know Angel

"This is what I have in mind for today," Angel told the boys. "Hope you like adventures. First we take a tour of Christopher's. I know you and Kate looked around already, but I have some secret places I like to go. And no one knows where they are but me.

"This place was built in the 1800s," she continued. "At first it was a hotel. It still is, sort of. But now it's more of a bed and breakfast.

"Back then they did things different. For instance, there are rooms on the third floor that no one ever goes in anymore. And some more little rooms in the basement. Except for me, and a few of my very good friends, no one even knows they exist."

"Why do they let you go in them?" Robby asked.

"The owner doesn't exactly let me," she said. "But I work here helping my mom. And we have master keys that fit every door in the whole place."

"How can you do that?" Robby said. "Won't they see you?"

"The secret places in the basement," she explained. "Those will have to wait until night. After Mom goes to sleep. But we can sneak up to the attic. There are some rooms up there, rooms that they rent out. So people go up there a lot. We just wait until no one is looking, and then we can sneak into the secret rooms."

Red texted, "Get ur mom in trouble????"

"No, sometimes we have to go in there to get stuff for guests, like foldup beds, if they need them. I've helped Mom get them out and set them up many times. As long as we're quiet, we'll be okay."

"Hang on," Angel said. Her cell was vibrating.

"Mom."

"I did. Sorry. I brought it home to make cookies with Brittany. I'll run it right down there. See you in a few minutes."

Angel then turned to the boys. "I goofed. I borrowed the vanilla flavoring from the shop a couple days ago, and forgot to take it back. I'm gonna quick run it down to the shop. She's making a dessert that calls for vanilla. It'll only take me a few minutes. She could walk over to the store and buy some, but I think she wants to make a point. I don't mind. It *was* my fault."

"Want us to go with you?" Robby asked.

"No. I have only one bike. I'll just be a few. We have satellite TV. Lots of books. The fridge is pretty full—feel free to help yourself."

Red texted so Angel could see, "OK if we talk to your gram?"

"Sure. If she's awake," Angel said as she walked out the door. She had stuffed a commercial-sized bottle of GFS vanilla in her backpack and was carrying it in her hand. "It's unlocked. You can take a peek in."

But the girl did not head down the steps immediately.

"Come on with me, I'll pop in before I go and see if she's awake," she said, taking a detour to her grandmother's room.

The old lady was wide awake and watching TV.

"Grams. I have to take something to the shop for Mom. Is it okay if the boys wait with you? I'll only be a few minutes."

"Sure," she said. "I'd love the company."

Chapter 72

The picture album

As they were walking into the room, Red was texting Robby, "Tell her G&A Forever. That was carvd in ring we found."

Robby looked down at the message and said, "Red wanted me to tell you that the inscription in the ring was this: 'G&A Forever.' Do you think you recognize either initial?"

"No," she said. "I had heard about a hunter a few years ago who went missing in Seney, but his name didn't start with a G or an A. So I guess I don't know anything about it."

"Are you originally from this area?" Robby asked. "From the Upper Peninsula, like when you were growing up—when you were our age?"

"No," she said. "Originally I was from New York. I got married to a man I met in New York, and moved here. *He* was from this area. Seems like only yesterday."

"Do you have some pictures of you when you were young?"

"Some, not many. Mostly I have pictures of Millie, and then Angel when she was a baby."

"Can I look at the pictures with you?" Robby asked.

"Sure."

Slowly, Robby and Red paged through the album. Whenever they ran across a picture that looked like Millie or Angel, they would ask about it. Clearly that's who the old lady wanted to discuss.

"Do you have any pictures of Millie's father?" Robby asked.

"No, probably not. We were not married very long. He stayed with me long enough to give me my beautiful daughter, and then he left. I guess the responsibilities of being a husband and father proved too much for him."

"How old was Millie when he left?" Robby asked. "Did she get to know him?"

"He left before Millie was born," the old woman said. "She never saw her father."

"That's really sad for your daughter," Robby said.

"It is, but you can't make people do things they don't want to do. Or be what they don't want to be."

"Is that you?" Robby asked, pointing at a beautiful young bride dressed in a vintage satin and lace wedding dress. "That is you, isn't it?"

"Yes, I suppose it is. My husband took this picture on our wedding day."

"Hey! That looks like this building in the background?" Robby asked.

"Yes," she said slowly. "We were married right here at Christopher's. The service was held outside. It was so beautiful. Not a cloud in the sky."

"But no pictures of your husband?" Robby asked. "Why's that?"

"My husband was taking the pictures. We didn't have a real photographer."

"There was one picture," Robby said, "back toward the front. I noticed it earlier. It's a picture of you with a man by your side. I thought he might be your husband.

"I'll see if I can find it again. Is it okay if I look for it?"

The old lady did not answer. Instead, she lifted both hands from the album and held them up as though granting reluctant permission. Red sensed that she was not pleased by Robby's boldness, and he looked over at his friend. But he did not intervene.

Robby remembered almost exactly where he had seen the photo and turned immediately to it.

"I'm sorry, but I assumed that this was your husband," he said, pointing to a picture of a man with his arm around the old lady.

"No, that's my cousin Joe," she said. "He came up for the wedding. He's from New York too."

"Oh," Robby said. "That makes sense. Do you have any other family living in this area?"

"Not really. My husband's family was not close to me. I never see them, not since Michael … left me. It's like I, like Millie and I, don't exist.

"But that's okay. I have Millie, and Angel. They are both angels to me."

Chapter 73

Kate lands in NY

Kate had spent her time on the plane wisely. She reviewed all the evidence in the two cases awaiting her in New York.

First the case of Randall Croft. While the arraignment she would be testifying at was that of Joe Tuco, the real target was Randall Croft. Tuco was just a means to an end—the end of Randall Croft, if everything worked out right.

Even though Kate had been the detective who initially arrested Tuco some months ago, she could barely remember what he looked like. All she recalled was that he had beaten up his girlfriend. Normally, because it was not a homicide, she would not have been called in for a case such as this. However, because Tuco was reputedly close to Randall Croft, when she learned that there was a warrant out for Tuco's arrest, she picked it up and aggressively pursued it. Randall Croft was the big fish she wanted to cook.

Within three days she had tracked Tuco down and taken him into custody.

What she did not know at the time was that the instrument Tuco had used to beat the girl up was a stolen 10mm Glock.

There was, in fact, blood still on the Glock when she brought him in. And tests proved that the blood on the pistol belonged to Becky Menendez, Tuco's live-in girlfriend.

Furthermore, when the pistol was run through the system, it was discovered that not only was it stolen, but that it was one of a half-dozen firearms taken in the burglary of a gun store in Ohio six months earlier.

And, one of the other guns proved to be the weapon used in the murder of Steve Williams, one of the co-conspirators involved in Allison Fulbright's plot to assassinate Barry Butler, the sitting president of the United States.

Randall Croft was suspected in that killing, so if it could be established that Joe Tuco sold or gave the murder weapon to Croft, and if Tuco could be enticed to testify against Croft, then Croft's lawyers might convince him to produce the name of the party who had hired him.

While Kate acknowledged that the labyrinthine nature of the plan to nail Croft left a great deal to chance, she was still eager to do her part to sell it.

No one seriously thought that Croft would name names; he was, after all, the consummate professional hit man.

However, if Tuco could be persuaded that it would be in his best interest to turn on Croft, it would strengthen the stranglehold the prosecutor felt she had on Croft already.

The FBI was backing the move as well. They wanted to find out where the other four guns ended up. And, depending on indictments that might follow those firearms, they were willing to grant Tuco immunity on the initial theft, and for transporting them across state lines, if he helped them track down the stolen firearms, and if he could be convinced to testify against Croft.

Fortunately, the FBI was also willing to provide Tuco access to their Witness Protection Program. That came as a surprise to Kate and the prosecutor, because the FBI tended to be a bit stingy when it came to their witness program.

So, it was a great deal for the soon-to-be three-time loser. Instead of facing life in prison, he would be able to start over as a free man. If he could avoid getting into further trouble, he would be able to leave his past behind.

That is, of course, if he could stay alive.

Not only did Croft now want to kill him, but other very dangerous elements were lining up to take a whack at Tuco as well. The old metaphor about the vulnerability of the weakest link in a chain fit.

Former first lady Allison Fulbright had earlier contracted Croft to murder the two lawyers hired by Pam Black to represent her interests against the former first lady. Pam Black was the widow of Reginald Black, Jack's good friend and confidant. In that instance, Croft traveled all the way to Sugar Island and consummated the contract on the Sugar Island Ferry, which was right under Jack's nose.

Later Ms. Fulbright hired Croft again, this time to kill Steve Williams, who was a long-time Fulbright associate and a co-conspirator in the failed plot to kill President Butler.

And then Kate crossed paths with Croft again. When she and an assistant prosecutor were getting too close to him, Croft arranged to have their turboprop blown up. The prosecutor and most of the other passengers were killed. Kate, who was also riding on that plane, narrowly escaped death herself.

For several years Tuco had stolen firearms, and then sold them to low-level criminals. But in recent years he had moved up in the world. He found that by providing weapons to professionals such as Croft, he could get a premium price. Plus, thinking that powerful characters such as Croft would be less likely to get caught, he felt safer about doing business with them—safer and significantly richer.

However, what Tuco had not considered was the fact that when professional killers get caught, they hire other professional killers to go after potential witnesses.

Kate's job on this trip was to convince Tuco that it would be in his best interest to cut his losses and provide evidence against his former customers.

Kate understood all the tenuous contingencies involved, but she and the prosecutor remained hopeful that the house of cards they were building would help to put Croft away for a very long time.

The plan was for Kate and the current assistant prosecutor, Janet Beckett, to meet with Tuco and his lawyer before his arraignment on the new charges and convince him to work with them and the feds.

In return for his cooperation, he would not go to jail, and he would be protected—both until they were finished with him and afterward.

Kate had helped Tuco cut a deal earlier, and both he and his lawyer trusted her. That's why Prosecutor Beckett was so adamant about having Kate come to New York for the hearing.

Plus, it was her job. Kate had made the original bust, and even though she was on vacation, she felt it was her responsibility to come through on this one.

Kate smiled as she walked down the jetway at LaGuardia, reading a text from her father: "I'm a free man at last! Call me."

That was the last time she smiled on this trip.

Her next text was from the assistant prosecutor, Janet Beckett.

"Major event in case. Fill you in when you get here."

Oh shit! What could that mean? she thought.

As she entered the terminal, Kate was met by a very somber-looking Janet Beckett—one NYPD officer on her right, and another on her left.

"Kate," Janet said. "We've got a *big* problem."

"What's up?" Kate asked.

"Do you have any check-ins?"

"No, this is it," Kate replied, holding up a small carry-on.

"Good. I've got a patrol car waiting. We can talk in the car."

Chapter 74

The trip to Sugar Island

"Is this it?" Agent Snyder asked as he pulled up beside Jack's Tahoe to drop him off.

"Must be. Looks just about like the one they blew up—except cleaner," Jack said, handing Snyder a piece of paper.

"I penciled out a map on how to find the cottage on Sugar Island," Jack said. "I assume you've never been there before."

"Actually I have," Agent Snyder replied. "When the boss told me I would be assigned to you upon your release from the hospital, I took a drive out there. That is some beautiful view you have of the Saint Mary's River. And that resort—pretty cool. I told the boss that, depending on your cooking, I might not want to leave."

"Funny," Jack said. "Then I assume you discovered that there were not many gas stations on the island."

"Yeah. I didn't see any so I figured that there weren't any. I will have to gas up on the way."

"Actually there are three, but you never know about their hours. You're better off fueling up in the Soo. As long as you know where you're going, I'll not worry about you. You just head out, and I'll meet you there."

"Sounds good," Snyder replied as he slid the shifter into drive and eased forward. "What could possibly happen between the hospital and your house, anyway?"

Jack jumped behind the wheel and breathed deeply. "Love that new car smell," he said, sliding the key into the ignition. As he did, the doors locked, and the driver's side airbag inflated, smashing his head back against the headrest.

A thick vapor filled the Tahoe as the airbag slowly deflated. Jack slumped forward. He was unconscious.

* * *

Thirty minutes later Snyder pulled into the resort. He drove all the way past Jack's cottage looking for the Tahoe. Not finding it on the property, he tried to call Jack on his cell. A man's voice answered, "Hello."

"Jack, is that you?"

"I'm sorry," the voice said. "I just found this phone on the ground. I am on my way into the hospital to leave it there. Do you know who it belongs to?"

"It was just lying on the sidewalk?"

"Right. Sort of. It was lying on the pavement between parking places."

"Was there a white Tahoe nearby?"

"No. But I did see a white Tahoe pull out, and I waited around to see if the owner would come back for his phone. But no one showed up. I've got an appointment and have to take off. I'll have to leave it at the front desk, unless you think you know where the owner is. I really don't have time to—"

"You wait right where you are," Snyder said. "My name is FBI Special Agent Thomas Snyder. I am *ordering* you to stay right where you are. I want you to carefully place the phone in your pocket, out of the way so it doesn't get damaged, and wait with it. And don't move it or touch it again. There might be fingerprints on it."

Chapter 75
Burnt Island adventure

"Hey," Robby said as Angel walked back into her grandmother's apartment. "Got your errand done?"

"Mom's all happy," Angel replied. "Mom wants to make Texas Sheet Cake for tonight. This will be the first time, I think in three years, that she's made it. If you ask me, I believe Mom is trying to impress you guys."

"She shouldn't go to the trouble—" Robby started to say.

"Oh yes she should," Angel interrupted. "It won't be finished until after dinner tonight. And she doesn't want us to come down to the shop until after it's ready. Soooo. That means we have all afternoon—*all* afternoon for a Burnt Island adventure."

Red and Robby exchanged glances—long ones.

"I don't think we've ever heard of it," Robby said. "How do we get there from here? And what's there?"

Robby and Red had both been thinking about fishing since they first learned they would be staying in Curtis. They had their poles ready inside of their room, and were already wearing their typical fishing gear—Detroit Tigers caps and camo pants. Robby was wearing his favorite drab green T-shirt, and Red the Bass Pro shirt that Kate had given him on his last birthday.

But Angel had other plans for them—and hers did not involve worms or any other forms of live bait.

"If the lake were a little lower we could walk over," she said. "But all the lakes are up this year. So we borrow a canoe. It's about half a mile from Christopher's—directly north. Kayaks would be more fun, but we would need three. And I don't want to ask for three. But they will let us take one canoe. The hotel rents them. If they have one, they will let me use it. We just have to be back in time for dinner."

"If it's only half a mile," Robby said. "We can easily be back in time."

While Robby was talking, Red was texting.

He leaned over and showed it to Angel, "Bring Buddy?"

"They're large canoes," she replied. "Big enough for a whole family. I'm sure there's plenty of room for all 'fur' of us—get it? *Get it*?" she giggled.

Robby and Red smiled, and Robby asked, "Do people live on the island?"

"There are two rental cabins, but I doubt they're rented right now. I almost never see anyone else go to the island."

"What's to do there?" Robby asked.

"Probably no adults. We'll be entirely on our own. We can keep an eye on the dock and tell if we are getting company. But not many people go there during the week. So we should have the entire island to ourselves. There's a huge fire pit. We can build a fire if we want to. And, we can explore.

"Have you guys heard about the ancient Native American grave on Burnt Island?" she asked, lowering her voice to add an aura of mystery. "I've seen it with my own eyes. There are a bunch of names and dates carved on it. The chief's name was Chief Menowamee. I Googled him, but couldn't find out anything else.

"Six other men were buried there as well—their names are carved on the marker along with the chief's.

"Very few people have ever seen the gravestone—only one other person that I know of for sure.

"A friend of mine told me about it. He was hiking on the island and virtually tripped over the marker."

"That would be great!" Robby said. "Do you remember where it is?"

"My friend gave me directions. It's in a secluded part of the island. If we take the directions with us, I think I can find it again.

"My friend said that when he went back to it recently, it looked like looters had been digging around, so he covered the headstone with leaves and stuff. I didn't brush the whole thing off when I was there. But he said it's quite large, three feet by one-and-a-half feet. And it's made out of solid rock—granite, I think. I can't tell. It just looked like a rock to me. But it is very interesting. Are you guys game?"

Robby looked over at Red and then said, "Sure, I guess. Are you sure it will be okay with your mother?"

Both boys were taken in by Angel's adventurous spirit and were eager to spend more time with her.

"We won't even have to get special permission. She lets me go out in a canoe whenever I want."

Angel whipped herself around, her ponytail flying sideways with the move.

"Grab what you need from your room. Good idea to take a jacket. I'll throw some PB&Js together, and some water. Meet you in the hall in fifteen minutes."

Tatts had been eavesdropping. This was his chance. He knew that Kate was flying to New York and Jack was at the hospital, and most likely would be headed directly to Sugar Island to recuperate. And now he learned that the boys would be spending the day on Burnt Island. He had no idea where the island was, but if they were taking jackets and lunches, they'd be gone for quite a while. And as long as they were not headed to

Strangmoor Bog, he didn't have to follow them.

Once he had heard the three young people head down the stairs, he left his room and followed them down. Standing on the porch that wrapped halfway around the hotel, he lit a cigarette. He had been trying to quit smoking for almost a year. In fact, the pack of cigarettes he carried in his pocket was nearly a month old. He could not believe how foul the smoke tasted to him.

Part of the repulsive flavor had to do with its being so terribly stale. But perhaps even more significant than that, his body was beginning to free itself from its need for nicotine.

However, even though this smoke registered a zero on his pleasure meter, it accomplished what he had wanted it to—it had afforded him a good excuse to wait on the porch to make sure that the three teenagers managed to procure a canoe, and that all of them, including the dog, were on their way to Burnt Island.

By the time he had finished smoking the filtered Marlboro, he had almost begun to enjoy smoking again. Almost.

He flicked the still-lit cigarette into the grass, turned, and headed back into the Christopher.

On his way up the stairs his cell vibrated. He checked the caller. It was Allison.

Chapter 76
Tuco has been shot

Once Kate and Janet Beckett were seated in the patrol car, Kate asked, "What's up? What's happening?"

"Joe Tuco's been shot," Beckett said. "He was shot and killed in lockup about one hour ago."

"You can't be serious. How'd that happen?" Kate asked. "Who could have got to him?"

"One of us."

"What!"

"He was being transferred from the general population to a private cell for his own protection, and one of the two officers assigned to protect him, a Corporal Lester Anderson, virtually unloaded his Glock into him. Preliminary report states that as many as seven 10mm rounds struck Tuco. He was wearing a vest, so the ones that hit it just knocked him on his ass.

"But while Tuco was lying face down, Officer Anderson then shot him three times in the head—point blank. While Anderson was still shooting, the other officer assigned to the detail with Anderson shot his partner, hitting him once in the vest, and then disarmed him. Actually Anderson simply handed his pistol over to the other officer. That's all we've got to this point."

"Did the shooter give any reason?"

"None," Beckett replied. "We have no comments from him at all. He's not seriously injured. His vest did its job. Detectives tried to talk to him, but he lawyered up as quickly as he gave up.

"And get this. He's hired that same big buck law firm that represents Croft. Which makes me suspect that this was a hit. What else *could* it have been? We might find out that Anderson's wife is dying from cancer, or something like that. Or maybe he is. And maybe he needed a boatload of cash for treatments. Or maybe he has loan shark debts. Who knows right now?"

"We know that sort of thing happens," Kate commented. "Croft has a lot of well-heeled clients who would not like to see him go to jail. Sometimes people talk, once the big doors slam shut behind them.

"I guess the real question right now is how does this affect the Croft case? If at all?"

"Of course it's a setback," Beckett said. "But I think we still have a strong case against him. And New Jersey is vigorously pursuing the case against his daughters. I'm not involved in those proceedings, but I talk a lot to the ADA there. You do recall that Croft works with his daughters?

"No doubt about it, it would have been nice to have Tuco point his finger at Croft during the trial, but that's not going to happen now."

"Do you think this might frighten off other witnesses?" Kate probed.

"That's a possibility," Beckett said. "Fortunately, much of what we have is forensic evidence.

"I'm almost afraid to talk to my boss after this. Sometimes he can be so gutless. He might want to pull the plug on the whole thing.

"That's what I liked about the new Tuco indictment. It let in a little fresh light on the Croft case. The problem is that the DA does not like pushing cases forward that he thinks we might not win. And given the high-profile defense counsel, I think he's worried."

The officer in the driver's seat turned to the women in the back and asked, "What do you want me to do? Shall I escort you ladies back to the courthouse, or do you have someplace else in mind?"

"Give us a second," Beckett said.

"What do *you* want to do?" she asked Kate. "Obviously, we're not going to be arraigning Tuco tomorrow. Have you got some pressing business back in Michigan, or do you want to spend the night? I realize you are on vacation."

"I have reservations in the city," Kate said. "I should make an appearance at my office tomorrow. I let my boss know I was coming to the city, and he wanted to meet with me.

"Besides, if I headed back to Michigan without at least checking in, I doubt that my trip would be reimbursed—at least not without *serious* discussion. I really need to at least pop my head in. My hotel's within walking distance of the courthouse. So I'm all set."

"Why don't you spend the night with me on the island?"

"Thanks for the invite. But if I were going to go to the island, I'd just sleep in my own bed. It'll be quicker and more convenient to catch a taxi to LaGuardia in the city. … But we could still do drinks tonight, if you want."

Beckett then turned to the driver and said, "You can drop my friend off at her hotel, and then me at my—"

"Hold it!" Kate interrupted. "Can you pull back to the curb? I've just received a disturbing message from the FBI. It's about my father. I might have to change my plans."

Chapter 77
Jack's in trouble

Jack remained unconscious for a long time—exactly how long he did not know.

The first thing he sensed upon awakening was how badly his head ached. The next was that his wrists were duct-taped together behind him, as were his ankles. He was lying on his stomach. When he tried to turn over, he discovered that his entire body was secured to a collapsible ambulance-style gurney. But the vehicle he was riding in did not feel like an ambulance.

He could not move. He was blindfolded. And his head throbbed with pain.

Okay, what can I remember? he asked himself. *I got in the Tahoe, and the airbag hit me in the face. That's it. And then I woke up in here—in this vehicle. And it's moving.*

His shoulder hurt as well as his head. Having his hands tied behind his back put added strain on his healing wound. Plus, whoever was responsible for transferring him from his Tahoe to this vehicle probably treated him a bit rough. *Made it this far okay,* he concluded. *My original wound wasn't life threatening, so that shouldn't be a problem. I would sure like to know how long I've been out, and where they are taking me.*

"Handler. You waking up?"

Jack did not recognize the voice. He didn't respond. *If they want me to talk to them,* he reasoned, *then they can remove this blindfold.*

"Talk to me, Handler," the man barked as he gripped Jack's injured shoulder and squeezed.

Jack refused to give his antagonist the satisfaction of knowing just how much pain he was exacting. Jack still kept his mouth shut.

Finally, the man ripped the cloth bag off of Jack's head. "You bein' a tough guy? I know that shoulder hurts like hell. It's okay. You can moan and groan. I would if I were you."

"Who are you and where are you taking me?" Jack demanded, twisting his head around to try to get a good look at the man who was tormenting him.

"That's better," the man said. "Talk to us a little. Tell us what we want to know, and we let you go. And then we won't hurt that pretty daughter of yours."

While Jack was able to get a good look at the man standing beside him, the fact that the man was wearing a ski mask prevented identification. But that is not to say that he didn't gather information.

First of all, Jack reasoned, *my abductors know me, or at least have done their homework.*

They're after specific information, and they will be ruthless in obtaining it. And once I've given them what they're after, or they become convinced I either don't have what they're after, or am not willing to give it up, they will kill me. No matter what I do, they intend to kill me.

And, most worrisome of all, Kate is in play. They don't think that she has the info they're after, but they will use her to break me. It's good that she's in New York right now. I hope she stays there.

This is going to be a long, miserable experience, and one that will most likely end badly.

If I tough it out and refuse to cooperate, they will snatch Kate when she gets back to Michigan.

I'll just wait to see what they want, and if I have it, I just might give it to them before Kate gets involved.

Or ... maybe I escape.

"Where are you taking me?" Jack asked.

"You'll find out soon enough. When we get there, I suggest you tell us everything you know right off the top. Resist, and you will suffer a great deal. Resist too long, and you'll get to see your daughter mutilated."

Jack carefully considered what the man had told him. T*his has nothing to do with Allison*, he concluded. *She would never threaten to hurt me or Kate. It must be—*

"Good night, Jack Handler," the kidnapper said as he slipped a chloroform-moistened cloth over Jack's face.

Chapter 78

Tatts takes advantage

"Al," Tatts said, "I'm going in their room in just a bit."

"Where are the boys?" Allison asked.

"They're on a canoe trip with a cute redhead."

"In Curtis?"

"Right. I watched them head out—the girl, the two boys, and the dog. It looked like they packed a lunch, so I should have plenty of time."

"Don't do anything that could hurt the boys," Allison ordered. "Jack will kill both of us if they are harmed. See what you can find. If need be, make it look like a bungled burglary."

"They spent a lot of time this morning with the old lady—the girl's grandmother. I think I'll pay her a visit first."

"What's she got to do with it?"

"Don't know. But the two boys made two separate trips to visit her. You said the kids are pretty sharp. I'll just find out what they talked about, and then I'll take a look in their room. And the girl's room. They spent time there this morning as well. I'll give you a full report.

"Well, I'm here. I should go. We'll talk later."

"Hi," Tatts said to the old lady as he opened her unlocked door and stuck his head in. "Sorry to bother you, but Robby asked me to look for his hiking boots. He thinks he carried them in here and maybe set them down."

Tatts still had not entered the room.

"Do you mind if I take a quick look around?"

"Who are you?"

"My name is Jimmy. I work for Christopher's—in maintenance. I just got a call on my cell from Robby asking me to check around for his hiking boots. May I look in here? He thinks he might have brought them in with him, and accidently left them. Can I take a quick look around?"

"Sure. Sure. That's fine. You said your name was Jimmy, and that you do maintenance for the Christopher?"

"Yeah. I just started a week ago. Millie, your daughter, got me the job."

A little preliminary checking by Tatts taught him that the old lady did not have a landline telephone or a cell. She had the pushbutton around her neck for emergencies, but as long as she didn't push the button or scream, she could not communicate outside the room.

"I didn't see them leave anything. Which one was Robby?"

"He was the one who talks. Red, the other boy, has a speech impediment."

"They are sweet boys. I think they like my granddaughter, Angel. But who wouldn't. She is as cute as a button. Do you know Angel?"

"Yes. I know her well. And she is very pretty. Did the boys use the bathroom while they were here? Or go in your bedroom?"

"No. They were right here by me. I really don't think they brought anything in my apartment. But suit yourself and look around."

"They are pretty smart young men, don't you think?" Tatts asked, trying to draw her out.

"Very smart. And polite. They were so kind to me. And I'm just an old lady. Young people don't always treat old people very well. But they're nice. I even think they liked talking to me."

"What did you talk about?"

"They wanted to see my picture albums. From when I got married.

I don't know why, except that they might have wanted to impress Angel. I think that was probably it.

"They were in the news lately, you know. Those are the two boys that found that gold ring in Strangmoor Bog."

"I heard about that. So, they are the ones. That's amazing. Makes me want to go prospecting out there. Did they say they found other gold, or was that just it—one ring?"

"Oh, I think that was it. Just that gold ring. Young man, I'd like you to leave now. You're asking personal questions, and I'm not comfortable. You didn't find the boots, so I think you should leave. Besides, I'm getting tired."

Tatts had not expected the old lady to go feisty on him.

"Absolutely," Tatts said apologetically, holding both hands palms out in front of him. "I'm so sorry to have intruded. I'll be on my way."

"I think I want to go out in the hall," she said, "I feel a little uncomfortable with you in here. I've never seen you before. Please let me past."

"Of course," Tatts said, "Let me help you."

He then put his left hand over her mouth, pinching her nose with his thumb and index finger. He wrapped his right arm across her chest preventing her from lifting her arms to fight him off. It took nearly two minutes before she ceased squirming. Not taking a chance on her reviving, he continued to block her breathing for another two minutes.

He then felt for a pulse. There was none. She was dead.

Looking around the room, he spotted a wooden cane near the door. Taking a pair of latex gloves out and holding the cane in both hands like a baseball bat, he struck her above her left eye with a vicious but glancing blow.

Even though the strike did severely break the skin, her heart had already stopped, so she didn't bleed.

He then laid the wheelchair on its side next to a coffee table to make it look like she had tipped it over and bumped her head.

She's old, so chances are there will be no autopsy, he reasoned. *This will go down as an accidental death.*

He wiped the cane off on the old lady's clothes, set it back where it was in the corner near the door, and then took a moment to briefly look through the two photo albums the old lady had mentioned. He tore one picture out and slipped it in his pocket.

On his way out, he wiped down the door to remove fingerprints, and quickly picked the lock on the boys' room.

No one noticed him.

Chapter 79

Kate interrupted

"Oh my God!" Kate said. "He's been kidnaped!"

"You're shittin' me!" Beckett said. "Not *Jack*. Couldn't happen!"

"Well, it did. I've got to find a way to get back."

"Hang on," Beckett said. "Maybe I can help."

Beckett then turned to the officer who was driving and said, "I'm going to see if I can help my friend. She has an emergency. This could take a little time. Maybe you can park it somewhere out of the way. I'll call you when I'm ready."

"Look, Miss, I'm not your personal driver. I'll stay right here until my boss pulls me off. Sorry, but that's the way it is."

"Fine!" Beckett barked. "But just keep in mind that Kate here is a *lieutenant* of detectives. I think she outranks you and your sergeant. When we're done, I'll come back to this spot, and I expect you to be here waiting. Lights on—lights off. I really don't give a shit. But you had just better be here waiting for me."

Kate heard the prosecutor berating the officer. While she did not approve of her tone, she did not comment. She had more pressing issues on her mind.

"NYPD," Kate said, flashing her badge and cutting into the front of the line. She was dressed in her black suit and red heels with a matching leather bag. "I need a ticket to Sault Ste. Marie, MI. Chippewa International Airport. As *soon* as possible. This is a police emergency."

"We have a two thirty-five. I can get you on that," the ticket agent said. "You would get into CIU at eight fifty-six p.m. Will that work for you?"

"That's the next flight?"

"Yes."

"Would you check the other airlines to see if they've got something that will get me there a little faster? This is an emergency."

The agent checked all the other airlines and said, "I'm sorry, but Chippewa International Airport does not have a lot of flights in or out. The two thirty-five is the best bet for you. I have plenty of seats left on that flight. It's one stop in Detroit. I've got seats all the way through. Will that work for you?"

"Yes," Kate said. "Please book it. And thank you."

"Kate, I have a friend who is part owner of a Lear Jet. I could see what he could do for you. But I doubt that it would be much better than what she's offering."

"I know. That's not too bad. Hang on for a second. I've got to make a call."

Kate then dialed Roger, Jack's friend in the Secret Service, and told him about Jack's situation.

"You're headed back to Michigan, I'd assume?" Roger asked.

"That's right," Kate replied. "I'll get in this evening."

"I'll see what I can find out in the meantime," Roger replied. "Give me a call as soon as you hear anything."

"Right. I'll call you from Michigan," Kate said. "Maybe it will all be sorted out by then. Could be this is all one big mistake. I can't see anyone kidnapping my dad."

"I'm going to hang around with you until you board," Beckett said. "If that's okay."

"You need to get back to work," Kate said. "I'll be just fine."

"What's this kidnapping all about? What is the FBI saying?"

"Very sketchy. Agent Snyder just texted that Dad was kidnaped right after he was discharged from the hospital. He's not sure exactly how it happened. They found his Tahoe abandoned at a nearby gas station. The airbag had been activated. That's weird. There was no blood. That's good. And no demands … at least not yet.

"But I wouldn't expect anyone taking credit. The only reason I can think of that someone would kidnap Dad would be for some information that they think he has. Anyone familiar with us knows that we would not pay a ransom. If I ever did, Dad would disown me. All told, the longer he holds out, the better our chances. I don't think they, whoever they are, have any notion as to what they are in for. They just may have bitten off more than they can chew with my father."

"The airbag was activated?" Beckett asked. "Is that what you said?"

"Right. That's what Agent Snyder says."

"That's pretty sophisticated shit," Beckett said. "It's not easy to tie the airbag to the ignition switch, or so I've heard."

"You're familiar with that?"

"One of the girls I went to law school with," Beckett said, "she's now with the FBI, down in Florida. She investigated a kidnapping just like that. It was a professional job, of course. It involved a major drug deal that went south. When they retrieved the vehicle, they found that the driver's side airbag was wired to activate when the car was started. And there was also a canister of gas that was released at the same time.

"The airbag stunned the driver, and pinned him to his seat. And the gas knocked him out. Don't know what kind of gas was used, but it dispersed quickly, allowing the vehicle to be driven off by the perp."

"Ever catch the guy?" Kate asked.

"No."

"And the victim. How did he fare?"

"Not good," Beckett said after a lengthy pause.

"Does the FBI have any suspects?"

"I wouldn't be privy to that info. I can check with my friend. But I'm sure that the special agent in charge in your father's case will be aware of the Florida kidnapping.

"Tiffany—my friend in the FBI—told me that this was the topic of chatter for some time. So, the special agent in Michigan should be up to speed on it. But it wouldn't hurt to bring it up with the agent you've been texting."

"That was good information," Kate said. "Now, I want you to get out there so that patrolman can get back to work. Thanks for your help."

"I apologize for the way I talked to him. I know I was out of line. Now, Kate, I want you to call me as soon as you hear something," Beckett said. "And if there is any delay with your flight out of here, let me know, and we'll find you an alternative."

The women hugged, and Beckett left.

Chapter 80
Jack wakes up

Damn," Jack mumbled. "What I wouldn't give for a couple aspirin."

"Handler," said a man whose voice Jack did not recognize. "Glad to see you're coming back to me. Never know when you put a man to sleep if he's gonna wake back up. Some don't."

"Is that what happened to my friend, Reg?"

For the past several minutes Jack had begun to regain consciousness. But finding himself bouncing around in the back of a strange van, with a thick bag over his head, and with both hands and feet securely restrained, he thought it prudent to feign unconsciousness, at least until he was more fully awake.

As he lay there thinking, Jack correctly deduced that his abductors were the same men who had earlier kidnaped and killed his best friend, Reginald "Reg" Black.

"You are just as smart as they said you were," the man quipped. "Unfortunately, your friend's body did not handle as much heroin as we anticipated. That could happen to you, too. But if you give the boss what he needs, you'll avoid the hard drugs. I really recommend you choose that route. That is, answer all his questions. Save yourself some pain."

Just as I suspected, Jack thought.

"Breath deeply," the man accompanying him said, sensing that Jack was more fully awake than he wanted. He was pressing something moist over the hood that covered Jack's face. "This will help you get a little more rest."

Those words became Jack's last thought until he found himself strapped securely to a heavy wooden chair, his clothes and hood missing, and his only covering consisting of a large white towel wrapped around his lower body.

Jack suspected that he would meet a similar fate as did his friend, whether he cooperated or not.

Adding to Jack's concern was the fact that the hood was gone. Apparently the man assigned to administer the next stage of the interrogation wanted Jack to look him in the eyes because he also was not wearing anything over his face to disguise his identity.

This can mean only one thing, Jack reasoned. *They do not intend to let me leave here alive. Otherwise, one of us would be masked.*

"Do you know what we want from you?" the man asked.

"I could guess."

"And if you were to guess, what would that guess be?"

Initially, Jack just dropped his eyes pretending to think. What he was actually doing, however, was checking to see if the legs of the chair were secured to the floor. If they were somehow fastened it could be a problem. But while the chair appeared to have been constructed from very heavy wood, there was nothing connecting its legs to the floor.

That's a very good sign, Jack thought.

He looked up and into the eyes of his interrogator and said, "I would imagine that you want to know where Reg hid the gold. And because he came up here to see me, you're wondering if he might have hidden it somewhere in this area. You are also thinking that I might have been in on the theft from the start, and that I might know exactly where he stored it. Am I close?"

The man chuckled. "Jack, my friend, you're more than just close. You've hit the nail right on the head. Now, all you have to do is tell us where the gold is, and you walk out of here with only a headache. How does that sound?"

"It sounds like a big lie," Jack said. "You're planning to kill me regardless."

"Jack, you hurt my feelings. How could you possibly think that of me? I'm not a heartless animal. All I want is to know where you and Reg stashed the gold. That's all I want from you. You tell me what I want to know. And if it checks out, we'll retrieve the gold, and you'll walk out of here a free man. It's that simple. In fact, if most of it is still intact, we'll match Allison's deal. I think she offered you ten million."

"You seem to have all the answers," Jack said. "You obviously know that I don't cheat clients. The real owner of the gold has hired me to find it. And so far I have not. Doesn't it make sense that if I knew where it is, I would have returned it to my client and collected the money?"

All the while Jack was talking he was considering just how it was that these fellows found out about his deal with Allison—right down to the dollar figure. As far as he knew, only he and Allison were aware of the details. *Must be some sort of a leak on Allison's end*, he reasoned. *I wonder if she's got someone checking up on me.*

"It seems to me that you would prefer one hundred million over ten—that's how it seems to me."

Jack then bowed his head slightly and sneaked a glance over to his left. There, on an eight-foot white plastic folding table, was a torture device Jack had seen before. However, he recognized it not because he had ever been subjected to its painful application; he knew what it was because he had used one like it before, when he was trying to get a man to answer his questions.

Shit, he thought, *I'm not looking forward to this. Not one bit.*

"I see you find my toys fascinating, Mr. Handler. May I assume that you know what they are, and how I intend to use them?"

"I'm not sure what you are talking about," Jack said. "Are you talking about these wires and light bulbs? Who are you, anyway? Mr. Wizard?"

"Mr. Wizard? Jack, you date yourself. That's not my name, but you can call me that if you like. About my toys—I think you know exactly what they are, and how they can be used when in the right hands."

"Not really," Jack said, trying to buy time. "Why don't you enlighten me?"

"Your friend, Reginald, he found out what these tools could do. I'm sure they would have worked on him if it weren't for the smack. Sometimes smack, as some of my friends refer to heroin, can help loosen the tongue. But not in the case of your friend. His body was so intolerant to foreign substances that it reacted in a very negative way.

"We had made him virtually the same offer as we just made you. All he had to do is tell us where the gold was hidden, and we would have let him go. We would even have rewarded him handsomely. We told him that. But he thought he could handle this table. Too bad he resisted.

"Jack Handler, I hope you are smarter than your friend."

Jack was seething. *If I can survive the torture, this asshole is going to die tonight*, Jack determined. *And I'm going to make it as unpleasant for him as I possibly can.*

"I thought you were going to explain to me how all this shit works," Jack said calmly.

Chapter 81

Four-point restriction

Jack was encouraged by the fact that only his wrists and ankles were tied. That meant his neck and head were not secured, which was critical, given the fact the chair was so terribly well made. *No way I'm going to be able to break it up*, he determined. *Can't break the nylon ropes securing my wrists either. Must cut them with something.*

The cord used was three-eighths of an inch thick. He knew how strong it was. It would have to be cut.

However, he was very pleased that the kidnapper had opted for the rope over plastic handcuffs. *If they'd used flex cuffs, I would not be able to break or cut them.*

But, most of all, Jack was delighted by what happened next. Mr. Wizard's assistant, who was standing by the door, succumbed to his appetite.

"Boss," he said. "I'm starvin'. Looks like everything's under control here. If you're good with it, I'd like to go back into town. Remember that Chinese restaurant we passed? They have really good food. We've used them before."

That brief interchange told Jack two things. First, he most likely had about an hour to work with—maybe more, maybe less. And second, the man staying back with him was the boss.

"This is how we're going to do this, Jack," Mr. Wizard said. "We are going to start out by pouring a little salt water on your right wrist, and then on your ass. I'm afraid it's a little on the cool side, hope you don't mind."

The man then lifted a pitcher of saline solution from the table and poured part of it on Jack's right wrist, and a sizable portion of the remainder on his lap.

The water was very cold, but Jack did not flinch.

"Now, this is where it will get interesting for you," Mr. Wizard said with an air of glibness. "You are sitting on a copper plate. And that copper plate has a fourteen-gauge copper wire attached to it. You have another similar wire connected to a copper strap that is wrapped around your right wrist. The saline solution I just poured on you will help facilitate an electrical current to pass through your body."

"You've created an electric chair," Jack said. "That's what this is."

"In a manner of speaking," Mr. Wizard agreed. "But it is not designed to kill you. On the contrary, it is intended only to make you very uncomfortable. Of course, if you don't tell me what I want to know, it certainly will kill you—just very slowly. But I think you will decide to help me out before it gets to that. At least I hope you will. I sort of like you. But, whatever. It's all up to you.

"On your left, I have a switch. When I flip it, one hundred and twenty volts of alternating current will pass into your right wrist, through your arm, your torso, and then down to your ass. To say that it won't be pleasant would be an understatement.

"Now, I am going to give you a little test, just to show you how it is going to feel."

With that, the man reached over and turned on the switch.

Jack's body jerked with the shock. He could not control his body's reaction. The man left the switch on for nearly five seconds. And then he turned it off.

"That was just a little taste—a tease, if you will," Mr. Wizard said. "As you can see, I have this circuit wired in series with this ten-watt light bulb. Did you notice that the bulb lit up when I hit the switch? You might not have seen it. It wasn't very bright. And I'm sure you were slightly distracted.

"But this next bulb, it's a little brighter. It's twenty-five watts. That's still not very bright. It's a little bigger than you might find in a refrigerator, but it is about the same physical size. What will make this bulb interesting is that it will allow a little more current to pass through it. And, because it is wired in series, a little more current will pass through you. But I'm sure you get all that."

The man then unscrewed the smaller bulb and installed the twenty-five-watt bulb in its place.

"Jack, I want to warn you," Mr. Wizard said. "This one is going to hurt you—a lot. I want you to understand that I get no pleasure in making you suffer. And, I'm sorry, but from now on, you will begin to suffer. If you tell me what I want to know, we can stop this right now. What do you say?"

"I don't have the information you want," Jack said. "If I did know where the gold was, I would have retrieved it, and I wouldn't be sitting here now looking at your ugly face."

"Sticks and stones, Jack. Now, we both know that all that digging going on in Strangmoor Bog—that does have something to do with the hidden gold. Is that where it's at?"

"That's crazy," Jack said. "If you think that has anything to do with Reginald's hidden treasure, you're nuttier than I thought you were."

The man did not like Jack's response. He reached over and activated the switch again. This time he had a smile on his face. Jack fixed his gaze on that evil grin and the single gold tooth it revealed. The tormentor allowed the current to pulse through Jack's body for nearly eight full seconds this time.

When he turned the switch off, Jack's body went limp in the chair.

The added electrical current clearly made Jack uncomfortable, but he did not utter a sound.

"I'll have to admit it—you are a tough guy," Mr. Wizard said. "You're my first patient who did not cry out at this point. Even Reginald spouted off a few expletives—and he was high as a kite. But you soon will. Everyone does. Are you ready to talk to me yet? Or do we have to move on to the forty-watt bulb? I will guarantee you that this one will make you squirm. It could even stop your heart. Talk to me, and we can put an end to this … experiment. I really do not want to hurt you anymore.

"And, God forbid, if you don't make it—say your heart does give out. We are gathering up your boys right now. I'll bet you don't even know what they've been up to. Do you? You probably think that Millie, the ice cream lady—you probably think that she's watching them while Kate's in New York.

"I've got news for you. I know where they are, and they are not with Millie.

"Red, Robby, and that cute red-headed girl, Angel. I don't think you've even met her yet. Well, you're soon gonna get your chance. That is, if you're still alive when she gets here. She's quite a sweet kid, or so I've heard. The boys really seem to like her.

"We'll be bringing them here to watch you. And maybe to participate. Kate will be getting back from New York. We'll have one big party. *Somebody* will talk. Even if those boys don't know where the gold is hidden, they might know more than you think they do.

"So, I'll ask you again. Did your friend hide the gold in Strangmoor Bog? And if not, where did he hide it?"

Jack's head was bowed down to the point that his chin nearly touched his chest. Lifting his head only enough to look his tormenter in the eyes, he said, "Go to hell, you bastard."

"Have it your way, Mr. Handler.

"Let's see. This one is almost fifty percent larger than the previous one. So that means it will make you considerably more uncomfortable than before. And to make it even more fun—fun for *me*, of course, not so much fun for you I'm afraid—I just might leave the switch on for a little longer. Keep in mind that it could stop your heart. But that's the chance you're forcing me to take.

"Are you sure you really want to continue? Never mind. You've already made it clear that this 'bastard' should light you up a little more. So, here goes."

The pain was exponentially greater than before, and it seemed to Jack that it would never end. He could not help but groan in agony. His tormentor, face fixed in a Himmleresque smile, ground the switch vigorously with his thumb as though the added pressure might force more electrical current through Jack's body. And then, just as it seemed Jack would succumb, evil lifted its thumb and abated the torture.

When the power finally ceased flowing, Jack's body at first reeled backward over the top of the chair, and then fell forward until his face was within inches from his knees.

Jack went silent.

* * *

"In the realm of the unknown, the path I walk lights up in flames"
—Roberta Karim

Chapter 82
A sense of urgency

While Tatts had initially not intended to kill the old lady, the fact that he had did not overly trouble him. She was not his first. Sure, he would prefer never again to be in a position where he had to end another's life. But, if so doing suited his purpose, he would kill without hesitation and without remorse. Such was the nature of the person he'd become.

Once inside the boys' room, he began to rifle through their belongings—wearing latex gloves, of course.

He was tidy. Everything that he examined, he placed back exactly where he'd found it. If he were careful enough, the boys would never suspect anyone had been in their room—especially once the old lady's body was discovered. He believed the revelation of her death would suck all the oxygen out of everyone around.

It did not take him long to discover what he'd been looking for. Tucked into an interior pocket of Red's suitcase was a lightweight mailing envelope. The title of its contents was neatly written on it with black permanent marker: "Notes relating to our effort to earn a Geology Merit Badge by gathering and analyzing soil samples from Strangmoor Bog."

The first page of the enclosed notes outlined the boys' effort to gain the esteemed Geology Merit Badge by conducting the difficult task of taking soil samples in Strangmoor Bog and then writing a report on their findings.

It explained how that, while drilling for the second core sample, they hammered through what they thought might be a small branch or twig, but in reality it was the bone of a human's ring finger. When they examined the core more closely, they spotted a gold ring and what looked like the bone from a human's hand.

There was no mention of their having unearthed any large quantity of gold, or even a small stash. The only gold they turned up, by their own admission, was a single gold ring. *Allison's concern that the boys might have stumbled upon the gold she was looking for was obviously unfounded,* Tatts concluded. *I'm going to put this matter to rest and get out of here.*

Carefully, Tatts slid the notes back into the envelope and then returned the envelope to where he'd found it.

He took one long look around the room. *Is there anything that I moved around?* He asked himself. He'd heard that the boys were themselves becoming very astute amateur detectives, and he did not want to give them any reason to suspect an intrusion.

"Looks good to me," he finally said aloud. "Time to blow this popsicle stand."

He was pleased to be winding this case down. He knew just how clever Jack and Kate were. And he feared that the longer he poked around in their business, the more likely he'd be found out. He did not want to suffer the wrath of Jack Handler.

He removed the latex gloves before opening the door to leave, but he still used them to grip the doorknob.

He cracked the door slightly—just enough to check the hall to be sure no one would see him leaving the room.

"Elvis is about to leave the building," he muttered as he opened the door fully. But as he switched the gloves to the outside knob to pull it closed, one slipped out of his hand and fell to the floor. At first he didn't notice it. Not until the door had closed and latched, with the dropped glove stuck between the door and the jamb, where they met at the floor.

Realizing he retained only one glove, he looked downward. "Shit! Shit! SHIT!" he muttered. "What the *hell* have I done?"

He bent over to see if he could pull it free. It started to come, but then it stuck. Placing his toe against the door and digging his heel into the carpet, he pushed as hard as he could against the bottom of the wooden door. It gave just enough so that he was able to reach down and slide the glove out.

As the glove snapped free, Sylvia Snyder, Agent Snyder's mother, along with Sarah, his autistic daughter, got off the elevator and passed directly behind where Tatts was working. He stood erect and faced them as they entered their room. Sylvia Snyder smiled at him, and he smiled back.

Damn! he thought as he headed for the stairs. *This is not good.*

Chapter 83

Time to get out of town

Tatts was concerned. He knew that he had to downplay any concern he might have regarding what had just transpired in the Christopher.

Were he to tell Allison that he had been forced to terminate the old lady, or that he might have been spotted exiting the boys' room, she just might have him killed.

He knew that he'd been careless, but he dared not share that knowledge with Allison—whom he considered to be one of the most dangerous women in the world.

I'll keep my mouth shut, and maybe this will all just go away, he reasoned. *There's no purpose to be served in my sticking around here any longer, anyway. My work is done. So, if I disappear right now, the worst that could happen is that I will be leaving a few lingering question marks.*

Fortunately, Tatts was leaving nothing in his room that could readily be used to identify him. While he had slept there since arriving, every night before retiring he would carefully spread out a bed sheet, one that he had brought with him, on top of the hotel's bedding, and he would sleep on it. In the morning, he'd carefully wipe down everything he'd touched, and then he'd fold the sheet he'd slept on and store it in his car for the day. He did this in order to minimize the likelihood of his leaving fingerprints or DNA.

Not knowing exactly when or how expeditiously he would be leaving, he followed this routine every day.

He had checked in under an alias, and he was quite certain that the Christopher did not employ any significant CCTV. *I'll be fine if I leave right now,* he thought.

"Allison," Tatts said when his call went to voicemail. "False alarm. Thoroughly checked out the work being done in Strangmoor, and it does not have anything to do with what we suspected might be the case. Only one object has been found, and it was discovered quite by accident. I'm heading back."

The Buick he was driving had stolen plates on it. Because many hotels maintain a record of plate numbers, he pulled into a large supermarket in St. Ignace. Quickly, he removed the license plate from his vehicle and swapped it with that of another car in the parking lot. He then put the newly stolen plate on the Buick he was driving.

He then put on a pair of large sunglasses and a Detroit Tiger baseball cap, headed south, and crossed the Mackinac Bridge. He knew that cameras would record his face and his license plate as he passed through the tollbooth.

Three hours later, he parked the car in long-term parking at Gerald R. Ford International Airport in Grand Rapids, placed the ticket stub on the center console, tucked the key beside the gas cap, and purchased a one-way ticket to Washington, DC.

While he was waiting to board, he called an associate in DC and left this message: "The 2013 black Buick is parked in long-term parking at GRR. Second level. License plate number is LSS 2666. Key is where you'd expect."

Tatts knew that before his plane would touch down at Dulles International Airport, employees from a Grand Rapids chop shop would have removed the Buick and begun dismantling it for parts.

However, something else was taking place in Curtis, MI. After mulling it over for a few hours, Sylvia Snyder finally succumbed to her suspicious nature and called her son.

"Yeah, Mom," Agent Snyder said. "What's on your mind?"

"You know those two boys, and that woman detective?"

"What about them?" he said. "I've got big problems here. Tell me quick."

"I saw a strange man in the hall when Sarah and I were coming up after breakfast. It looked to me like he was coming out of their room?"

"I'll check with Kate when she gets back in town," Agent Snyder said. "She's in New York today. She should be back tomorrow. I can't talk to you right now. Is Sarah okay?"

"Sarah's fine," Sylvia said. "We had a wonderful breakfast downstairs. I'm sorry to have bothered you. It just struck me as really strange—that guy. I'm pretty convinced he was coming out of their room."

"No problem, Mom. He might have been maintenance. And you're never a bother. You can call whenever you feel like it. But right now I am in this situation up to my neck—it's an emergency. I know I'm going to be late tonight. I'll call you when I know more. But I think you and Sarah should plan to have dinner without me. Talk to you a little later. And I will make it a point to catch Kate tomorrow and see what that man by her room was all about."

Chapter 84
Trouble on Burnt Island

"This place looks absolutely amazing!" Robby said excitedly when their canoe was about half way across. "How did you find out about it?"

"You live in a place long enough, you eventually discover all the cool spots to hang out," Angel said.

"I don't like to fish, but some of my friends do," she continued. "I sunburn too easily. But I do like to explore. And that's what I find intriguing about Burnt Island. It's never crowded, and there are so many little things to see."

"Who owns it?" Robby asked. "Does anyone care that we're here?"

"Burnt Island is owned by a nearby resort," Angel said. "So, I suppose they could ask us to leave. My friend said that they sort of have a 'don't leave anything but your footprint' policy. But I don't know about that. No one has ever kicked *me* off. But I don't come here that often."

"Here," Angel said, reaching for Robby's paddle. "Let me do this for a while."

"Are you sure?"

"Positive. I'm pretty good at it."

Robby traded positions with the cute redhead, and began stroking the ruff on the front of Buddy's neck. He was a little concerned that the dog might decide to jump off and swim ahead.

"What's this?" he said, sliding to the side the aluminum tube the old man had attached to Buddy's collar. "I don't recall having seen this before."

Red glanced back at it and shrugged.

"Angel, had you noticed it before?"

"No," she said. "Open it."

Robby removed the cover and looked inside.

"Looks like there's a piece of paper rolled up and stuffed into it," Robby said. "But I can't get it out."

Angel stopped paddling and took a look for herself.

"We're not going to get that out without tweezers. You should put the cover back on and wait until we get back to the hotel. I have a pair in my room."

Robby thought that was a good idea. But when he tried to re-attach the cover, Buddy twisted his body around to get a look at some strange looking birds on the shore, and the cap went flying into the lake.

"So much for that," Robby said. "Whatever is in there is stuck pretty good. I'm sure that it won't fall out."

Buddy then started to bark at the birds as the canoe approached the island.

"Are those wild chickens?" Robby asked.

"They're called range chickens. But they are wild. They've pretty much claimed Burnt Island as their home."

The three teenagers paddled their canoe up to the shore. Buddy was the first to get out. He loved it. He was not too sure about the ride itself, but the opportunity to stretch out and run around a bit—those things excited him.

"Do we have to tie the canoe up?" Robby asked.

"We're by ourselves here," Angel said. "And there are no storms on the horizon. It's fine like it is—just pull it up on the shore. Come on, follow me. I want to show you that Native American grave. It's so cool."

Angel took off running, and the two boys followed close behind. It was only a few minutes until she abruptly stopped. "Well," she said, "what do you think of it?"

"Think of what?" Robby asked. "I don't see anything."

"Right there," she said, dropping to her knees.

She began brushing the leaves and twigs aside. And there it was, just as she had said—a large rock with six names carved in it. And beside each name was a date, with the earliest dating from the mid-1800s. On the top of the marker was a carving of a bear.

"Can you see this?" Angel said, rubbing her fingers across the name of Chief Menowamee. It was the first name that appeared.

"I'd like to take a picture of that," Robby said. "Do you think that'd be okay?"

"I did when I was here earlier. I don't think it's a problem."

Just then Red stood and looked back toward where they had left the canoe. He grabbed Robby by the shoulder and pointed.

Buddy had also spotted movement and was already standing at attention.

"What's up?" Robby said.

Red pointed again in the direction of the canoe.

Robby then stood as well.

"Looks like we have company," Robby announced. "Do you think we've got a problem?"

Two men were walking in their direction.

All three of the teenagers watched attentively as the men approached.

"We're from the Mackinac County Sheriff's Department," the man leading the way said. "You do know you are trespassing on private property?"

The three kids looked at one another.

Red held his phone over for Robby to see. It said, "Ask thm for badges."

"Could we see some identification, sir?" Robby said.

"Sure," the first man said, pulling his tan windbreaker aside to expose an official looking badge attached to his belt. Right next to the badge hung a not-so-official-looking tattered brown leather holster. In the holster was a very shiny stainless steel Service Six revolver.

"Now, answer my question, please," the man said as he rested the palm of his hand on the pistol. "Do you kids know that you are trespassing on government property?"

"We know that the island is owned by a resort," Angel said. "But we thought it was okay to be here, as long as we were careful."

"Well, you're wrong about that. The county bought the island earlier this year, and we use it for exercises and training. It's no longer open to the public. I'm afraid we are going to have to detain you until your parents can pick you up. Is that dog going to be a problem?"

"Buddy is cool," Robby said. "He won't bite you."

"He'd better not," the second man said, sliding his jacket open to reveal a black revolver.

"As long as he behaves himself, I won't have to hurt him. So, you see to it that he minds his manners."

Just then, the second man spotted Red checking his cell phone.

"What the hell do you think you're doin', Red? You give me that cell phone. And you other two, hand 'em over. All your cell phones. Now!"

The two boys looked at each other. They both thought it strange that the man would have known Red's name. Red was first in handing over his cell phone, and then Robby followed.

"How about you, young lady. Where's your cell phone?"

Reluctantly Angel also complied with the demand. Her mother had recently purchased a smartphone for each of them, and she did not want to give it up.

Red began shaking his head slowly to signal his dissatisfaction with the whole situation. The men, fearing the kids would run away, drew their pistols.

Red tried to run, but he made it only a step or two before the first man tripped him with his foot, and then grabbed him by his curly red hair.

Buddy lunged, sinking his K-9s into the man's calf.

The second man extended his revolver and shot at Buddy. The bullet struck the dog in the neck, causing him to immediately release his grip on the man's leg and fall to the ground. Buddy did not move.

Chapter 85
Jack being Jack

Jack reeled in pain with the last round of electrical current. But he was not unconscious, as he would have his antagonist believe.

"Jack," the torture-minded Mr. Wizard said when Jack feigned falling forward. "I hope you haven't up and died on me.

"Let's take a look," he said, standing and leaning over Jack to check for a pulse.

This was the moment Jack was waiting for. He and Mr. Wizard were the only ones in the room. *All I have to do is take this asshole out, and I'm home free—maybe*, Jack thought.

Jack could tell by the location and posture of Mr. Wizard's torso that the man's face would be directly above the back of Jack's head.

Furthermore, because Jack had leaned forward earlier, while at the same time pulling his feet as far back under the chair as possible, his center of gravity shifted to a point just slightly in front of his feet.

Now is the time all those squatting exercises will pay off, Jack thought, as he shot to his feet.

At the same time, he snapped his head backward.

And just as Jack had planned, the back of his head caught the man flush in the face, breaking his nose and rendering him instantly unconscious.

Jack, afraid the man would fall too far away, swung the back legs of the chair around, catching the man on the buttocks.

Then using the chair to apply pressure to the falling man, Jack propelled Mr. Wizard onto the floor next to the table of torture.

Somehow Jack maintained his balance, although just barely. He was able to stumble to where the man was lying and direct the right front leg of the chair to a position above the man's neck. And then, with all the force he could muster, he drove the leg of the chair into the man's neck, crushing his spine and instantly paralyzing him. Jack remained seated until he was certain his attacker could not move.

Jack was limited in his ability to control his movements. He knew he needed to somehow bring the table of torture to the floor, but he was not able to use his feet to kick it over.

Struggling mightily, he again pulled his feet far enough beneath him so that he was able to balance himself in a somewhat upright position. Looking a little like an alligator snapper standing on its hind feet, he managed to engineer a major face plant on top of the table. His weight and momentum easily brought it crashing down.

Several of the bulbs burst when the table collapsed. By an elaborate series of minimal maneuvers, he was eventually able to bring his right wrist into contact with the jagged base of one of the broken light bulbs.

After what seemed to him an interminably long length of time, he successfully cut the rope that secured his right hand.

Once he had fully freed himself from the constraints of the makeshift electric chair, he took a close look at the man on the floor.

Seeing the man's eyes move, Jack said, "Good for you. Looks like you're still alive. Let me assure you, that's a temporary situation. I do want to thank you for using these old-fashioned incandescent lights! If you'd been a little more green conscious, I'd never been able to free myself."

Jack then adjusted the towel he still was wearing, set the chair back to where it originally was, and lifted Mr. Wizard into it.

He then removed the man's belt, ran it through the back of the chair, and attached it tightly to the paralyzed man's limp neck. Using the ropes that had earlier bound him to the chair, Jack now secured Mr. Wizard's arms and legs. He did that not so much to restrain the paralyzed man as to stabilize his position.

"Wouldn't want you to fall out and hurt yourself. Would we?" he joked.

He then attached the wires to the man—one on his right wrist, and the other one on his left ankle. He then poured the remaining saline solution over the man.

"Well, my friend," Jack said. "Let's see how you like it. Just wish you were a little more alive so you could enjoy it better."

Jack looked around until he found the two hundred watt bulb, and screwed it into the socket. But then he thought better of it. He replaced the big bulb with a twenty-watt.

"If we do this too quickly you might not live to fully appreciate what is happening to you."

When he threw the switch, the man's body quivered, and smoke began flowing from where the cables were connected—slow at first, but more profusely as his body heated up.

"I know you can't feel your extremities, asshole, but just believe me when I tell you that they're smoking."

Still totally naked aside from the towel, Jack looked around and found his clothes. They were unceremoniously dumped in a pile close to the door leading out of the cabin.

"Oops," Jack said. "Almost forgot. I'm going to have to borrow your keys … *and* your Glock. Hope you don't mind."

Jack flipped the torture switch off long enough for him to locate the man's car keys and gun.

"I'm going to take your cell phone as well. You won't be needing it I'm sure. And, I suppose I should also take your wallet. I might want to track down some of your friends and family. I just thought you might want to know that—just something to think about as you drift off."

He then turned the switch back on and headed toward the door. But before he left, he took one more glance back at the man.

"This is just too clean," he said. "You don't deserve to have an open casket funeral. Not for what you did to Reg."

Jack walked over to the gas range and turned on a burner. It lit. He turned the burner on low, and then poured a cup of water on it to snuff the flame.

"What a beautiful smell," he said, as a sulfur-scented invisible cloud began to fill the room.

"Let's see if we can speed this up a bit," he said, turning the gas valve to its fullest open position. He then cranked the furnace thermostat up to seventy-five degrees Fahrenheit.

In Jack's mind, he suspected that the electric current had already stopped the man's heart. But that's not how he wanted to remember it. He turned back to the man one last time.

"Normally I might say something like 'May you burn in hell for what you did to Reg.' But that wouldn't be necessary. Would it? I think you're just about to get a bit of a jump on that burning part in the here and now. Cheers."

But before he reached the car, Jack heard the second man driving up with the Chinese. *What good timing,* he thought.

Jack crouched behind the car until the man had headed toward the door with the food, and then as quick and quiet as a cat, he slid in behind him.

"I'll take that," he said, removing the bag of food from his hand and pressing the cold barrel of the Glock against the man's neck. "You're just in time for my party. Now open the door and we'll see how things are going in here."

As the man stepped in, Jack clubbed him over the head with the Glock, knocking him to the floor. He yanked a fifteen-foot extension cord from the wall and tied the man up.

Jack then leaned over the man to be sure he was not unconscious.

"Good. You're awake," he said. "I was concerned I might have hit you too hard. I just wanted you to know that I am throwing this little party for you and your boss in honor of my friend, Reginald Black. You probably knew him just as Reg. He's the fellow you killed last year. You remember him, right?"

The man nodded his head.

"I'm going to take your wallet. But don't worry, I'm not interested in your cash. I just want to see if you have any pictures of your family. I might want to pay them a visit."

"Mister," the man said. "Please don't hurt my family. Do what you want with me, but don't take it out on my family. Please."

"It's getting a little hard to breathe in here," Jack said, fingering through the man's wallet. "I think it's time for me to go."

Chapter 86
Kate's back

Jack was eager to vacate the area. He did not know how long it would take for the cabin to explode, and he did not want even to be in the vicinity when it blew.

He was telling the truth when he observed that Mr. Wizard had started to smoke. But Jack didn't think that the current from the electric chair would provide an open flame or even a spark, and that's what it would take to ignite the gas.

Most likely the pilot from the gas water heater will do the job, he reasoned. *Or maybe it'll be the furnace. Whichever, I don't intend to be nearby.*

It was not until Jack had driven nearly one hundred yards along the winding driveway before he realized where his kidnappers had taken him.

"Oh my God!" Jack said when he spotted the St. Mary's River. "I'm on Sugar Island! I can't be more than a mile and a half from the resort! ... I'll bet I may have even passed Agent Snyder on my way out here. That's just too damn wild."

The more he thought about it, the more sense it made. *Why not bring me to the island?* he asked himself. *There's no resident law enforcement presence on the island. Hundreds of secluded cabins. And only six hundred or so neighbors, and they all like to mind their own business. Perfect place for this creep to practice his trade. I'll bet that was where they murdered Reg—right under my damn nose!*

As he drove along South Brasser Road, Jack began to scroll through the numbers stored in the boss's telephone.

"I should call Kate," he mumbled. "She's probably worried about what's going on up here."

However, before he could dial her number, a text came in: "Got the kids. Comin' in w/thm. Shot Dog. Left it on island. Waitin' for instructions."

Instead of calling Kate, Jack called Roger—his friend in the Secret Service.

"Rog. Need your help."

"Kate already called me. We've got a satellite watching the Soo Locks. That turned out to be significantly fortuitous for you. ... I take it you managed to escape. What can I do for you this time?"

"I'm gonna make a call using this phone. The phone I'm going to call is to a man, or a group, who are holding Red and Robby. I want you to find their location."

"I'm ready right now," Roger said.

"Okay, here goes."

Jack dialed the number. "Boss?" said the voice at the other end.

"Yeah," Jack said. "Where are you?"

"Boss?" the man said again.

"Where the hell are you?" Jack repeated.

"*Who* is this? And where's the boss?"

"He's right here with Handler. He asked me to give you a call to see where you were."

"Who are you?"

"This is Sammy," Jack said. "I'm just up from Florida. Didn't the boss tell you about me?"

"Put the boss on. I want to talk directly to him. We're gonna wait right here until we talk to him."

"Okay. Okay. Keep your pants on. I'll tell you right now, he's not going to be happy that you're screwing around with me. You know, he looks like he's pretty tied up right now. I'll have him call you as soon as he finishes this round with Handler."

Jack disconnected the call before they could ask him any more questions, and he called Roger back.

"Did you get what we needed?" he asked Roger.

"Sure did. We not only located the phone, but we found them with the satellite camera as well.

"There are two men in the cab of a red Chevy pickup. Right now it is parked on Ashmun, just north of Portage.

"I see three heat signatures in the back of the truck, perhaps under a tarp. Could be the boys, and Buddy. Do they have the dog with them?"

"I think they shot Buddy," Jack said. "At least that's what they said in their text."

"That would make sense," Roger then said. "It looks more like a third person. I was just guessing about the dog. Who would that third person be? Do you have any idea?"

"Not at this time," Jack said. "Unless it's that girl. Mr. Wizard mentioned something about a redheaded girl. But I don't know. I'm heading toward the kids right now. I'm going to disconnect and call Kate. Hang on, I think we can make this a conference call. Kate? Is that you? Where are you?"

"Dad? I thought you'd been kidnaped," Kate said.

"Long story. They've got the boys."

"*Who's* got the boys?"

"Friends of the guys who had me."

"Where are they? Do you know?"

"Yes. They are in a red Chevy pickup, with a tarp on the back. Right now they are parked on Ashmun Street, just north of Portage."

"I'm ten minutes away—maybe less," Kate said. "I have Agent Snyder with me."

"Take up a position and wait for me, unless you have to move in. I've got Roger keeping an eye on them for us."

"How long before you can be there?" Kate asked, as she put her car in cruise, slipped out of her heels and put on a pair of Nike cross-trainers. She then switched off the cruise and, steering with her thighs, twisted and clipped her long auburn hair back off her face. She was getting set to kick some serious ass.

"I'm just exiting the Sugar Island Ferry," Jack said, "on the Soo side of St. Mary's."

"They brought you to Sugar Island?" Kate asked. "That's weird."

"I thought the same thing, at first," Jack said. "Anyway, I will be coming in from the east. If you have them from the west, they'll have no place to go."

"Who are these guys, anyway?" Kate asked.

"They are the ones behind Reg's murder. They were after Allison's gold. They somehow thought that because Reg came to the UP, that he must have hidden the gold up here. And when the FBI started digging around in the bog, they assumed that the gold must be buried there. They're stupid. What else can I say?"

"How'd you escape?"

"Like I said—that's a long story."

"I'm just pulling up," Kate reported. "I see them. They are parked on the east side of Ashmun—"

"That's right, Kate," Roger said. "I think I might have spotted you. You're in that dark sedan? You just parked on Portage?"

"Right," Kate replied.

"I'm now on Portage heading west," Jack said.

"Dad!" Kate yelled. "I don't like this. The driver is getting out. I see a pistol, with a possible suppressor—I've gotta move on them right now!

Jack hit the gas and blasted past the slower traffic.

Kate had taken only a dozen steps toward the truck when it became obvious to her that the boys were in imminent danger. Snyder was following close on her heels. The driver of the red pickup had reached the rear of the truck and was beginning to remove the vinyl snap tonneau cover that Jack and Roger assumed covered the boys, and perhaps some mysterious third party.

Kate was not quite within range of her Glock. But she couldn't wait. The gunman had, as Kate suspected, already attached a suppressor to the barrel of his revolver and was pointing it into the bed of the truck.

"Police! Stop right there!" she shouted loudly.

Snyder had taken a position slightly behind her and to her left.

The man snapped around and pointed his gun. He fired twice, missing her both times.

But Kate did not miss. She got three shots off before he began to fall. One was squarely between the eyes, and the other two were no less deadly.

As soon as the volley of shots had ceased, the passenger in the truck opened his door and bolted on foot north up Ashmun. Kate aimed her Glock at the man but did not attempt to get a shot off because he was fleeing.

When he reached East Water Street, he commandeered a Jeep, forcefully yanked the female driver out, and threw her to the pavement.

"One of them is now in a Jeep," Roger announced. "No place to go. He's got to swing back to Portage—probably on Bingham."

Roger was right. The driver sped off on East Water and turned right at Bingham toward Portage.

see where the bullets intended for her had gone.

While Kate had not expected Angel to be among the kidnap victims, she was not surprised.

As soon as Kate reached the truck, she verified that the man she had shot was dead, and then she kicked his pistol under the truck.

She then jumped into the back of the truck and began freeing the three teenagers.

When she removed the gag from Robby's mouth, the first words he uttered were, "They killed Buddy. They shot and killed Buddy."

Red's eyes were huge and red. He'd been crying.

"I'm pretty sure you're gonna want to see this," Kate said with a big smile. She held her cell down so both boys could read a text she had received earlier.

Chapter 87

Good news

Jack had also received that same text. And, like Kate, he had glanced at it briefly as he sped to rescue the boys.

It read, "Am tld a very wet Gldn Rtrvr showed up at the hotel. Bad bruise on neck. Looks like a bullet struck cigar tube and collar and bounced off. BAD bruise but othrwis dog ok—SAC DOLLAR"

The fact that Buddy suffered only a superficial wound to his neck from the gunshot indicated to Jack that the shooter had used full metal-jacketed target rounds. He suspected such because target rounds contain significantly less gunpowder, and therefore they do not have the velocity of a normal round.

That's why, when he observed the rounded ends of the bullets in the revolver of the Jeep's driver, Jack was able to conclude that the man he was about to shoot was probably the one who earlier had shot Buddy.

Without a doubt, that likelihood provided Jack with some added incentive—it was probably worth an additional round or two.

* * *

When Red realized that Buddy was still alive, he let out a groan as only he was capable of. Fortunately, he was still gagged.

Once Kate removed his gag, he blasted out with another, but this second one was more subdued.

"And, Angel," Kate said. "I suppose I shouldn't be too surprised to find you here. What do you think about hanging out with my boys now?"

"Wow!" Angel said, "Your guys sure know how to have fun!"

Kate laughed out loud.

And then, scooping the still-bound girl up in her arms, Kate hugged the little redhead and said, "Angel. You are definitely my kind of girl."

"I'm not kidding," Angel said as Kate was freeing her. "It was a *little* creepy when the man shot Buddy. It was so loud. But now that we know that Buddy's gonna be okay. It's all good. And the boys were great—from start to finish. They didn't seem worried at all. Like they just knew that you'd show up to save the day. I have not had so much fun in my entire life."

Kate then used her Gerber Mark II to cut off the tie wraps from around their wrists and ankles.

As soon as she had freed them, she instructed them to remain exactly where they were lying.

"Don't get up yet," she said. "There's something I've got to take care of first."

The three teenagers complied, even though they did not yet understand why she had said that.

Kate slipped off her jacket and spread it out over the dead man's bloody head.

"Okay," she then said. "Come over to the side of the truck, and I will give you a hand getting out."

Lew, the nearby shop owner, had now joined them behind the pickup truck.

"Here, kids," he said. "I'll help you out."

"How about I take them over to the store?" he asked Kate. "If that's okay."

"That would be great," Kate said. "They need a little change of scenery."

"Go with this man, and wait with him."

And then Lew said, "Kate. Your name is Kate. Right?"

"Yes. I'm Kate Handler."

"Kate. I'm not sure you are aware that the man with you is down. I don't know what happened, but I think he might have been shot."

"What!" she screamed. And then, turning around, she spotted her father administering first aid to a man on the pavement. She immediately recognized that it was Agent Snyder. She ran to him.

"Tom! Are you okay?"

Agent Snyder looked at her and forced a faint smile.

"How is he, Dad? Is he going to make it?"

"I hope so. I saw him lying behind you, and made it over here as fast as I could. He took one in the neck. He's lost a hell of a lot of blood. But he's pretty fit. He seems to be holding his own right now."

Jack was applying pressure to the man's jugular vein.

"His vein's pretty well nicked, I'd guess. But probably not severed. I got to him as quickly as I could. Should be fine."

Kate was familiar with the way her father dealt with situations such as this. She knew that Agent Snyder was in serious trouble, and that her father was doing his best to calm the wounded man. Whether or not he really believed the agent would be fine, that was another matter.

"Great!" Kate said. "Is an ambulance on the way?"

"I just heard them," Jack said. "Should be only a minute longer."

Then Jack spoke directly to Agent Snyder. "Looks like I'm going to be visiting you in the hospital. Bit of a switch on things, don't you think? I'll make sure to get Dollar in there to hold your hand. I'll bet he has some really good bedside manners. I know he's just the fellow I would want visiting me."

Agent Snyder looked up at Jack and again forced a smile. And then he blacked out.

"Dad! Is he gonna make it?"

Chapter 88
Putting things back together

For the next week, Kate spent most of her time sitting with Agent Snyder as he mended at the War Memorial Hospital in Sault Ste. Marie.

It was later determined that the bullet that did the damage was indeed intended for Kate. And it might have struck her, except she was able to fire her fatal shots before the kidnapper could zero in. So, instead of striking her, the errant rounds zipped past her left arm, and just as Jack had suspected, one of them clipped Agent Snyder in the neck, ripping through, but not entirely severing, his jugular vein.

Everything that day worked perfectly on behalf of Agent Snyder's survival. Had Jack not quickly pounced on the wound and properly applied targeted pressure, Agent Snyder would have bled out in minutes.

And if the paramedics had not arrived when they did, Agent Snyder might have gone into shock and never recovered.

Finally, had the hospital's emergency room surgeons not been prepared to properly treat Agent Snyder's wound, he again might not have survived.

Of course, the getting shot part was not exactly fortunate. But everything that followed certainly worked to his advantage.

Before Agent Snyder had even arrived, the paramedics had already notified hospital personnel that they had a gunshot victim with a wound in the neck and who was bleeding profusely. They believed it to be a partial tearing of the jugular vein or possibly a totally severed jugular.

Once in the emergency room, the trained surgeons carefully opened the neck to expose the damaged vein and then clamped it off above and below the wound. After that, they obtained a piece of suitable vein from Agent Snyder's leg and sutured it into the damaged area.

The surgery, while sounding like a straightforward procedure, was anything but simple. It took over five hours to complete. Fortunately, there was enough of the vein left intact so that no tension was required to make the repair.

The prognosis: excellent chance for full recovery. While there was some extraneous nerve damage, it was believed that, given time, his healthy body would totally restore itself.

Kate was with Agent Snyder when he woke up.

The first thing that he wanted to know was if his daughter and mother were okay. He had tubes in both arms, in his nose, and down his throat, so he posed his right hand as though holding a pencil.

Kate slid a pen into his hand.

"Mom and Sarah OK?" he slowly scribbled.

She assured him that Sarah and his mother were fine, and that they both were eager to see him.

He closed his eyes for a moment and then wrote, "See them later. U tell them?"

Kate nodded her head and went out into the waiting room to talk to his family. She explained that while Agent Snyder was going to make a full recovery, he did not want them to see him with all the tubes stuck in his body.

"He's going to be okay?" his mother asked.

"Definitely," Kate replied. "He took a bullet in a bad place, but the doctors fixed him up. And it went perfectly. Now he just needs to rest. I will stay with him, and I will talk to you often. And as soon as he gets some of the hardware out of him, he wants to see both of you. Just not now."

"You heard about Millie's mother?" Sylvia asked.

"I only know about Angel, her daughter," Kate replied. "Is there something I should know about Millie's mother?"

"She died this morning," Sylvia said.

"What happened?"

"An accident. She fell out of her wheelchair and hit her head."

The rest of the events of the day drained Sylvia Snyder. She had totally forgotten about having seen the man come out of the boys' room.

Had Tatts been around to hear this conversation he probably would have said, "Sometimes I'm good at my job, and sometimes just lucky. And if given the choice, I'd choose luck any day."

Chapter 89

Bodies galore

After forensics had finished with George Cox's skull, it was determined that death was caused by a single gunshot to the head by a handgun—a .38 caliber to be precise.

The bullet had entered the right side of the victim's forehead, passed through the right side of the brain, struck the back of the skull, bounced forward, and lodged in the upper jaw.

Initial presumptions made on-site were proved to be wrong. Michael Mallory thought the entry wound too small for a .38, and so he assumed it was likely a .32 caliber. His mistake was due to his inexperience at making determinations dealing with mummified corpses. Because the flesh was still on the skull, even after all those years, the entry wound appeared smaller than it actually was. And because a more powerful handgun was used, the bullet, a hollow-point, broke into fragments in the brain. The largest piece of the bullet had enough velocity to bounce off the back of the skull and travel all the way forward to the upper jaw area. It left fragments that looked to Mallory's equipment more like tooth fillings than bullet fragments.

When asked about his faulty preliminary conclusions, he said, "Well, I suppose that's why we have a lab to do forensics."

But one of the conclusions reached that evening in the bog was totally spot on. The body found was that of George Cox. DNA obtained from his brother proved a familial relationship, and the dog tag found near the body further substantiated that it was indeed the body of George W. Cox.

However, neither the identification of the body, nor the cause of death, turned out to be the most significant discoveries made in the bog during the course of that and the next two months.

Once the FBI determined that they did have a crime, they were forced to enlarge the perimeter of their investigation. They brought in dozens of pumps and virtually drained that whole section of Strangmoor Bog.

As it turned out, by the time they terminated the crime scene portion of the investigation, they had unearthed human remains from six different bodies.

In some cases, the bodies were largely intact. And in other cases only body parts were found. But the number remained constant after the first three weeks of digging—six separate bodies, all male, and all relatively young.

The causes of death in four of six instances could be determined—gunshot wounds to the head.

In the other two cases, where the cause of death was unclear, it was because the skulls were not found or were too terribly degraded to make a positive determination.

But, on the other hand, there was no definitive reason to think that in all instances the causes of death could not have been from a gunshot wound to the head.

And even more interesting is the fact that, of the three bullets that were retrieved intact, ballistics indicated that in each case the same gun had been used—a .38 caliber handgun.

One of the other interesting finds had to do with extraneous wounds found on two of the victims. For instance, George Cox's skull evidenced a very large blunt-force impact on his head, and a compression of his vertebrae. The same was found to be the case with one of the other bodies.

Officially, this conundrum was never fully dealt with in the final report.

When asked about it later, SAC Dollar simply shrugged his shoulders and replied, "Maybe someday we will understand better just how these men met their end. But for now, I think we've done all we can."

Jack was not pleased with that conclusion.

The FBI finally decided to end their search after an additional three weeks passed without turning up any further body parts. While they acknowledged that there could be more, the extreme cost of conducting a search in an environment as unfriendly as Strangmoor Bog mitigated against its continuation. Besides, cold weather was setting in.

Forensics determined that the bodies dated from the mid-1970s, as was the case with George Cox, to as late as the 1990s.

Most of the bodies could not be positively identified—at least not immediately. That part of the investigation continued unencumbered.

But the name of one of the other murdered men was determined. His name—Michael Patrick O'Malley.

He was positively identified by his dental records. Upon further investigation, it was discovered that he was a man of substantial means at the time of his disappearance, which was determined to have been in the autumn of 1971.

When the FBI ran his name, they found that he had left a will and a managed stock portfolio in the trusted hands of a law firm in Sault Ste. Marie.

The beneficiary of the will was a person named Millison O'Malley. This Millison O'Malley was the son/daughter of Michael O'Malley. It was concluded that the will had been drawn up before the birth of the child.

When contacted about the trust, the law firm indicated that they did indeed manage the portfolio, and had taken a healthy administration fee out of it each and every year, but that they had never made an effort to locate the beneficiary because there was never a death certificate issued for Mr. O'Malley.

When asked by the FBI to send all the records of the trust to an independent accounting firm selected by that agency, it was discovered that the value of the stock portfolio approached thirty million dollars. At first no one believed it possible, but the accounting firm read that in 1983 the account manager sold all the IBM stock and invested almost all the funds in an initial public offering on March 13, 1986. That fledgling company was Microsoft Corp.

But no one could ever locate Millison O'Malley, so the law firm continued to manage the account—not until one day when Robby, Red, and Angel were rummaging through an old tan suitcase they had found stashed away in one of the "secret" rooms on the third floor of the Christopher.

"This looks like your grandmother," Robby said after Red had handed him a picture. And I don't think I have ever seen her *with* this guy. Do you suppose that's her husband? He wasn't in any of the pictures in her albums."

"I don't know," Angel said. "What else is in this suitcase?"

As they rummaged through it, they found a stack of letters written by Louise Breeze to Michael O'Malley.

"Angel," Robby said, "that was your grandmother. She must have known that Michael O'Malley pretty well. These are quite the hot love letters."

Then they found it. Buried at the bottom of the suitcase was a different sort of envelope. It did not have an address or a stamp on it. They opened it. Its only content was a marriage license taken out in the name of Michael Patrick O'Malley and Amy Louise Breeze.

"Your grandmother was really Louise O'Malley," Robby said. "She must have taken her maiden name back when her husband disappeared."

Red then texted, "And tht Millison O'Malley tht FBI is looking 4—thts ur MOM!"

It took months, but eventually DNA proved that Millie Star was the daughter of Michael O'Malley, and, therefore, the rightful heir to his fortune.

After all legal fees had been paid, and the applicable fees and taxes, Millie still turned out to be one of the wealthiest women in Michigan's Upper Peninsula.

Both Jack and Kate were very pleased with that outcome.

Millie finally did sell her ice cream shop, and the two of them—Millie and Angel—became regulars every summer at Kate's resort on Sugar Island.

When asked what she thought about Angel hanging out with her two boys, Kate would say something like this: "We love her like family. Besides, you can never have too many redheads running around Sugar Island."

However, even though they liked the outcome, Jack especially sensed a gnawing at his gut that there remained too many loose ends regarding the murders.

Initially, Jack would call SAC Dollar every week to find out about progress on the case. After six months, Jack began calling every few weeks. Finally, he gave up calling altogether, as he sensed the FBI had pretty much decided to relegate the murders to cold-case status.

Something has to be done, Jack reasoned. *The souls of those murdered men and their devastated families are crying out for justice.*

Chapter 90

The interrogation of Russell Cox

Under normal circumstances, SAC Dollar would have ordered Russell Cox to come into Sault Ste. Marie to be interviewed. But the man was old and fragile. And beyond that, Russell was a genuine recluse. So the FBI veteran decided that the best way to help the old man open up would be to bring his office out to Strangmoor Bog and conduct the interview in the familiar confines of the old man's little cabin.

The interview was recorded on both video and audio and was witnessed by two FBI agents in addition to SAC Dollar. They were Agent Randy Frank, who was second in command under SAC Dollar in the Strangmoor Bog investigation, and Agent Manuel Alvarez, who had also been intimately involved in the investigation, and who had become personally familiar to and with Russell Cox.

All three were lowered to the cottage via helicopter. Dollar did not want anything to do with using land-based vehicles in the bog, which he continued to refer to as the "big damn swamp."

Dollar was very eager to wind this case up, and he was not hesitant about expressing that desire.

As for the interview with Russell Cox—it was his intention to frame it as the closing summary of the case.

"For the record," Dollar said, "this interview is with Mr. Russell

Lawrence Cox, the brother of the deceased George William Cox, whose partial skeletal remains were recently unearthed in Strangmoor Bog. Strangmoor Bog is located in the Seney National Wildlife Refuge in Schoolcraft County in Michigan's Upper Peninsula.

"My name is FBI Special Agent in Charge William Dollar. Seated with me on this interview are FBI Agent Randall Frank, also known as Randy Frank, and FBI Agent Manuel Alvarez.

"The date is October twelfth, 2014. We are meeting today in Mr. Cox's cabin, which is located in the general vicinity of where the body of George Cox was found, in Strangmoor Bog.

"Mr. Cox, would you please state your full name for the record?"

For a long moment, the old man just looked disgustedly at Dollar and then finally said, "Russell Cox. My name is Russell Cox."

"For the record, is your full name Russell Lawrence Cox? Is that correct?"

"Yes."

"And how were you related to the deceased, George William Cox?"

"He was my brother."

"When was the last time you saw your brother alive?"

"Four days before he went missing."

"And when was that? Do you recall an approximate date?"

"I know exactly when it was. I had breakfast with George on September ninth, 1977."

"That would have been the morning of September ninth, 1977?"

"I said I had *breakfast* with my brother on that day. Of course, it was in the morning. It was a *Friday* morning."

"Do you remember what you discussed?"

"Oh God," the old man said, "this is hard for me." He sat there for nearly a minute before continuing. He raised a wildly shaking right hand to wipe away the tears that were flowing down both cheeks. Alvarez spotted a roll of paper towels beside the kitchen sink. He pulled one off and handed it to the old man.

At first Mr. Cox did not notice the paper towel. His eyes were closed. Finally, he opened them and accepted the towel. He looked at Alvarez and nodded his appreciation.

"We talked about his future, and his finances, mostly. George had married just before he went off to Nam. He was drafted. I joined up. I wasn't married. But the draft got him. Don't get me wrong. He wasn't one of those draft dodgers. He never considered running off to Canada, or anything like that. He was willing to do his part. But he wasn't happy about leaving his wife and business."

"Okay, but he was already back from Vietnam when you had this conversation with him on September ninth—is that not correct?"

"Yes. When he got back, he wasn't the same. He drank too much. I think he might have used drugs a little too. You know, smoked some pot. And the gambling. He must have started gambling in the army. He never did it before he got drafted. But when he got back, he started playing cards—more than once or twice a week, sometimes. He had big plans. He was going to go to college on the GI Bill. But the gambling got the best of him. He dropped out the first year.

"Before he went in the army, he and I had planned to develop some property on the lake—the big one. Lake Manistique. Our parents owned a large piece of property on the lake and left it to us when they passed. That's what we were doing when he got drafted.

"But when he got out, all he wanted to do is drink whiskey and play cards. He was hanging around with bad people—I knew it, and he knew it.

"And that morning, the last time I talked to him, he told me that he had lost part of the land in a poker game. And it was not just an insignificant parcel. The portion that he quitclaimed over contained the only slice of the property where we could construct a drive to the lakefront. Without that particular piece of property, we were both up the creek. Access was blocked—as far as developing that property was concerned. And then he goes and disappears."

"What happened to the rest of the land?"

"Oh, I held on to mine for several years. Couldn't do much with it. And his widow did the same thing. I tried every way I could to find another access, so we could develop it. But came up dry. Finally, we both let our parts go—almost just for back taxes. Nothing else we could do. We just about gave it away."

"Did you think at first your brother ran off?"

"He wouldn't do that. He hadn't been himself for some time. And there was the drinking, he drank an awful lot of whiskey. And the gambling. But I never thought for a minute that he could have run off. He just wasn't that kind of a man. His wife, Andrea, she was pregnant at the time. He wouldn't just run off like some people said he did. I knew that much from the start.

"But I didn't know what happened. At least not at first."

"Your brother was left-handed, is that correct?"

"Yes."

"Our forensics lab indicates that your brother died from a gunshot wound to the head. The fatal shot entered your brother above his right eye, and passed through his head from right to left."

Dollar observed the old man grimacing as he listened to the description.

"Now," Dollar said, "I am very sorry to have to be so graphic in my portrayal of the event, but it is important for you to know the details. I'm going to continue, are you up to this?"

"Yes. I suppose I am."

"Given the trajectory of the bullet, our forensic technicians do *not* believe that the wound was self-inflicted. For one thing, a left-handed man would not likely shoot himself in the right side of his head. And for another, the stippling around the entry did not appear to be what would be expected from a self-inflicted wound. As you may or may not know, usually we are not able to see stippling on a body from that long ago. But the bog preserved it, and if there had been powder burns around the wound, such as would be consistent with a self-inflicted gunshot wound, we would have seen concentrated stippling."

"I don't understand all those big words. I just know that my brother did not shoot himself, if that's where you're going with this. He didn't run off, and he didn't kill himself either."

"Our conclusion is that your brother was murdered, and that his body was dumped in the bog. Is there anything you could add that would suggest otherwise?"

"My brother was going through some hard times—emotionally. But he wouldn't have done that to his wife, or to me. He was shot by someone else. And whoever that was, they put him in the bog. I've thought that for a long time."

"Would you tell me how you came to that conclusion?"

"His cap was found by hunters … in the bog. Not real close to where you found his body. But it was found in the bog. And, like I said, I found his wallet out here in the bog. It was in a different spot—that is, not around where you found the body. That's why I moved into this cabin, so I could search for … for his body. I knew it was there somewhere. That's what I've done every day for … I don't know for how long. But a very long time. I was fairly young back then. And now I'm old and ready to die myself. I'm ready. I can die now … now that I got my brother properly buried. I buried him in that old cemetery just outside Seney. In Boot Hill. That's what it is still called. It goes back to the 1800s. No one gets buried there anymore. But I took his ashes out there at night, dug a hole, and buried them right beside our parents. They're buried there too."

"Was there ever someone you suspected? Someone you thought might have wanted your brother dead?"

"No. George had no enemies. He wasn't that kind of guy. And his wife was very kind, … *is* very kind. Andrea. That's her name. She never remarried. After we lost the property, she moved into Curtis and got a job. Her daughter, Lesley, she got married and moved out of the state. I don't know where. Andrea still lives near Curtis. But now she's in a rest home. I really don't know how she's farin'. I always liked her—she's a good woman. But she doesn't want to talk to me, though. I think she believes I'm a little crazy. I probably am."

The old man smiled after this admission, but then quickly grew sober and began to sob uncontrollably.

"Would you like to take a break, Mr. Cox?" Dollar asked.

"No, I'm okay. It's just such a relief to have this over with. Now I can die. … I've got nothing else to live for. Finding George is all that kept me goin' for all those years."

"You didn't completely answer my question, regarding anyone who might have wanted your brother dead. Do you know of anyone like that? Who might have wanted to harm your brother? Or who might have gained from his death?"

"No. Like I said, he was a great guy. He had no enemies."

"No one you would suspect?"

"No. No one. Can we stop talking about this now? I'm really tired. And I've told you all I know. Can we just stop? Whoever killed George is probably dead by now. Or so old it wouldn't matter. I just want to be done with this."

The old man had already stood and removed the microphone that was hanging around his neck. He carefully laid it on the table and walked to the kitchen.

Alvarez whispered to his boss, "I think we end it. The old man looks like he's had enough. We can come back later if we have to."

Dollar nodded in agreement. "We've got what we need," he said.

After extending his appreciation to the old man for granting the interview, Dollar had Frank summon the chopper for their ride back. As they stood outside the cabin waiting for it, Alvarez asked his boss, "Why didn't you mention the shattered neck, and the massive injury on the top of his brother's skull?"

"Too graphic, and not necessary. I gave him all he could handle. And I was not pleased to have to do that. But we had to officially interview the man."

"How long do you think it will be before *his* body is found?" Alvarez asked.

"He'll die here," Dollar said. "Soon, probably."

Later that winter, hunters discovered the body of an old man. It appeared that he had passed away while sitting in a chair just a few yards from where the body of George William Cox had been found earlier. The dead man's head was bowed slightly, and his body frozen.

Investigators identified the body by the dog tag he carried in his pocket. It said "Cox, Russell L."

Gripped tightly in his left hand was another dog tag—that of his brother's, "Cox, George W."

Chapter 91
Spring break

Kate had returned to her job in New York shortly after the rescue of the three teenagers from the back of the pickup truck.

Initially, SAC Dollar protested her leaving town until the completion of the investigation of her shooting of the man on Ashmun Street, but it soon became obvious to him and his superiors that there could be no grounds to charge her in the shooting, particularly given the fact that the man she shot had already fired two shots at her, with one of those errant rounds striking and nearly killing one of his men, Agent Snyder.

But even though she was not actively investigating the Strangmoor Bog murders, neither she nor her father spent a single day without those killings haunting them.

The problem was that there seemed to be no loose ends to investigate. Sure, they had bodies and bullets, but they could not find motive or opportunity. And Dollar was quite satisfied to drop the investigation in the cold case file.

But there was one aspect that continued to get on her nerves. At the funeral for Millie's mother, Amy Louise Breeze, Kate learned that originally Louise Breeze hailed from out East. In fact, in her youth she lived on Long Island and worked in Manhattan as a hotel maid.

It was not until she met, and subsequently married, Michael O'Malley, a wealthy lifelong resident of Curtis, that she moved to the Upper Peninsula. Prior to that, she was known as Louise Breeze and lived with her family on Long Island.

Kate talked to Jack about it and decided that it might be interesting for her to pay a visit to the childhood home of Louise Breeze and see what she could turn up.

It wasn't as difficult to find as Kate had anticipated. In fact, the house and a substantial piece of property were still owned by members of her family. While no one lived at the location any longer, the acreage that was attached to the old homestead was leased out annually to a prominent livestock farmer. Crops such as corn and oats were rotated on the property, and occasionally it was allowed to go to hay. The past year it had been oats, she learned.

Kate had checked with Jack regarding her taking a one-day trip to check it out. He not only thought that it was a great idea, but Jack suggested that she do it over spring break—that way he could drive the boys out and they could investigate the homestead together. He indicated that he had friends out East that he needed to see, and so the trip would also give him the opportunity he needed. And then, once finished, they would all get back together and do some sightseeing in New York.

By "friends," Kate knew that Jack was checking something out, probably having to do with an investigation for which he would receive compensation. She never asked questions about his work unless it directly involved her. And even then she used discretion.

Initially, Kate suggested Jack get Millie's permission and bring Angel along.

Kate and Angel had become close. Angel referred to Kate as the big sister she never had. And, of course, Red and Robby were big fans of the idea of bringing Angel along for their spring break adventure.

However, that part of the plan, the part about bringing Angel along, did not materialize. Millie had already made arrangements to take her daughter to Florida for spring break.

* * *

"That's the thing about a human life— there's no control group, no way to ever know how any of us would have turned out if any variables had been changed."—Elizabeth Gilbert

Chapter 92
The barn

The farmhouse had long ago fallen victim to a bulldozer. There was nothing left except for the scattering of a few foundation stones.

"The house is totally gone," Robby said. "But back there—way back there—you can see the barn. It's still standing."

The three-hundred-foot path from where the house once stood back to the barn was a knee-deep jungle of broadleaf plantain, common blue violets, dandelions, and various wild and unkempt grasses.

"It looks like no one's walked back to the barn in the past twenty-five years," Kate said. "Do you think there could be snakes?"

Robby glanced over at Red, who was walking to his left and about one step ahead. Red looked back at him and smiled.

Both boys sensed an opportunity to have some fun with Kate, who was following in their steps a dozen feet behind.

Red immediately reached for his cell and texted Kate, "Diamondbacks u think?"

"Really?" Kate said upon reading his message. "I thought they'd disappeared from here generations ago."

"Should've known you would do your research," Robby said through a smile. "But there are snakes around here. It just has that feel. Maybe a black snake. They like rats, and this place looks like it would have rats. They're not poisonous, though. Black snakes, that is."

"I hate all snakes," Kate commented. "Even a *picture* of a snake freaks me out."

Just before they reached the barn door, Red saw his chance. Holding his right hand up as a signal for Robby and Kate to stop, he carefully poked the broken rake handle he had picked up earlier under a section of discarded black water hose and rapidly lifted it above the grass, making sure Kate got a good look at it.

"Nice try," she said, genuinely appreciative of his effort.

With a shrug, Red slid the stick out from under the hose and continued toward the barn door.

There was a large steel hasp with a rusted-closed padlock securing it. All the other openings on the front of the barn had been boarded up.

"Let's take a look around back," she said. "Maybe we'll find a door that's more inviting."

Just as Red rounded the right corner of the old building, he stumbled upon a group of wild turkeys that had been resting or feeding there. The cacophony of rustling wings and warning calls caught Kate and the boys off guard.

There were several birds that apparently preferred running to flying. Only two of them took flight, while the rest of them scurried off on foot into the cultivated field behind the barn.

"Whoa!" Kate blurted out. "I wasn't expecting that. Those were turkeys—wild turkeys."

"Holy cow! That scared me!" Robby exclaimed. "I was ready for a snake or a rabbit. But not a bunch of stupid turkeys."

"Rafter," Red texted. "Group of stupid trkys called a rafter."

"I can think of a couple of names I might like better," Robby added.

"Check that out," Kate said, pointing in the direction the birds' escape. "That certainly looks like it has been farmed recently. Like even last fall."

And then, after scrutinizing it more closely, she said, "That on the left looks like an old landing strip. See how long and narrow it is. And when they stopped using it for planes, they probably leased it out to be farmed along with the rest of the field. Let's see if we can get inside this building … maybe from back here. We might discover something interesting inside."

The three of them made their way along the side of the barn. Kate had picked up her pace and was now walking slightly ahead of the boys.

"Would you take a look at that," she said, pointing at a large set of double doors.

They were open just far enough for a person to walk through.

The doors were each nearly twenty feet wide. They were suspended at the top by a set of four pulleys that rolled on a piece of channel iron affixed to a 2x8 board above the openings.

Each of the two sections, when fully pushed to the sides, provided an opening of nearly forty feet. A huge steel beam ran over the opening to support the roof, with an angled steel brace at each end of the opening.

"That should be plenty large to roll a small airplane through," Kate said. "Let's check this out."

Chapter 93

Surprised, but not really

They stepped through the opening but stopped when only a few feet inside. Red saw it first and held up his hand to warn Kate.

"Whoa, Kate," Robby said as his eyes adjusted to the dark. "You're not gonna like this very much."

Lying there on the dusty floor of the old barn was a large black snake. At first Kate thought that Red was playing with her again.

"Enough theatrics," she said, also stopping to allow her eyes to become accustomed to the dark surroundings.

"We're not kidding this time," Robby said. "It's a snake. And it's a big one."

Kate finally saw it as well.

Red gently poked it with his stick to coax it out of the way. At first it coiled as though going into attack mode. But black snakes are not known to be aggressive against humans. So as soon as it realized that there was not actually a threat, it slowly slithered off and out of the way.

Robby sensed Kate's uneasiness and tried to be upbeat.

"On the positive side," he said. "If that snake felt comfortable enough to rest himself in the middle of the floor, then we don't have company in here. That's nice to know, because that door was open enough to let people in.

"Plus, he looked pretty fat to me. So it's likely that he's been feasting on rats and mice. Probably don't have to worry about stepping on a big rat either. Those are all good things."

Kate appreciated his humor because it gave her a chance to regain her composure.

"Let's see if we can slide those doors open a little further," she said. "We could use a little more light in here."

The two boys immediately headed for the doors. Using both hands, Red pushed as hard as he could on one of the doors, but he didn't budge it.

So he turned to the other door. It didn't move either.

Robby said, "Let's both push on it. It looks rusty—maybe we can break it loose if we gang up on it."

So that's what they did. Red went low, using his shoulder to push, while Robby pushed with his hands above him.

But the pulleys on the top of the door didn't turn.

Instead, the boys' pushing dislodged the pulleys closest to the opening, causing them to slip off the track. And then, pivoting on the third pulley, the part of the door closest to the boys dropped to the ground.

"Watch out!" Kate yelled. "That whole thing could come crashing down."

Robby and Red stepped back for a moment to size it up.

"That door isn't going to open," Robby concluded, "but if we don't mess with it anymore I think that it will balance on that one pulley and will stay where it is. Shall we see if we can get the other side open?"

"It would help to have more light in here," Kate replied. "Give it a try, but be careful."

"If we push down a little at the same time," Robby said, "maybe it won't jump off its track. I think *I* caused the problem on the other side. I had my hands too high up on it. Let's give the other side a try."

This time Robby slid in more closely beside Red and exerted his effort more horizontally.

Kate also gripped the door with one hand and aided the boys' effort.

Finally, two of the rusty pulleys broke free and turned. The two that did not turn slid on the track. And the door began to open.

"Keep it going," Kate said. "Let's keep it moving and open it as far as possible. At least another four feet."

Kate checked the track and said, "Let's stop here, before we get to the end. No point running it off. We'd never get it back on."

All three stopped pushing and stepped back.

As their eyes adjusted to the darkness inside of the barn, Kate exclaimed, "Would you take a look at that?"

Chapter 94
The Cessna

All three of them stepped deeper into the barn to get a better look.

There, in a place where it had apparently stood untouched for what looked to be decades, sat what was most certainly a single-engine aircraft. It was draped from propeller to cockpit with a drab green aircraft cover. A smaller piece of canvas neatly covered the windshield. This left the wings and the entire rear portion of the aircraft uncovered.

"That's definitely a Cessna 172 Skyhawk," Kate said. "One of the earlier models. Probably as old as 1960. And it's a beauty. What a great airplane."

As they walked closer to the plane, Robby observed, "Look at the dust. I'll bet it hasn't been out of this barn in thirty years."

"Just as we suspected, those extra-wide doors do tell us that this barn was adapted as a hangar for the airplane," Kate said. "It then probably reverted to a barn most likely when the plane ceased to be used. Let's check it out."

The floor was concrete. And it was covered with decades of dust and animal feces. Dung the size of a small dog's was piled on and around the front wheel fairing and on the horizontal stabilizers.

"I wonder who left us these presents," Robby quipped, pointing at the decaying defecations. "Red, have you been hanging out around here?"

But Red didn't respond. He had discovered that the left cabin door had been left unlocked, and he had opened it fully to look in.

When Robby realized what Red was doing, he yelled as he ducked under the plane, "Hey, Red. Whatcha up to?"

Red had already jumped into the cockpit. Robby stepped onto the wheel strut and leaned into the plane to get a better look.

Kate had not yet made it over to the vintage aircraft. She had spotted a bed-sheet-sized piece of drab green canvas loosely folded and lying underneath a half sheet of plywood next to an inside wall. It looked to her as though it had been casually tossed there years ago, covered over with plywood, and then forgotten.

She put on a pair of latex gloves, slid the board off from on top, and dragged it away from the wall and into a cleared-out section of the floor. There, she carefully unfolded it.

The inside was totally dust free. It had obviously not been disturbed since initially deposited on the floor.

Another clue suggesting that it had not been disturbed was the fact that it cracked in several places where it had been folded.

Once she had the canvas stretched out, she noticed that there were at least two large dark stains on it and that they seemed to overlap.

Kate stepped back. *I've never seen a fifty-year-old blood stain*, she thought. *But I'll bet that's what one would look like.*

She then glanced over at the boys. Red was still seated in the cockpit, and Robby was leaning over him.

"Out!" she shouted as she bolted under the engine. "Get out of the plane right now. And try not to touch anything else. Now!"

Red knew what that meant. And so did Robby. Both boys had witnessed Kate in action at a crime scene, and they could tell by the tone of her voice that this was no longer a casual fact-finding mission. They looked at each other, their faces only inches apart. In one motion, Robby pushed off from the door of the plane and hopped off the wheel fairing.

Red pulled his hands toward his body and swung his left leg out of the door. Within a few seconds, both boys had separated themselves from the plane and were standing free of it.

"I could be wrong," she told them, "but I think I've got blood on a piece of canvas. Maybe even multiple stains."

"This is a crime scene?" Robby asked, looking over at Red.

"Could be," she replied, slipping a pair of booties from her bag and putting them on.

"Here," she said, tossing booties and gloves to the boys. "Sit down and put these on. Better late than never. After you get them on, I want you to take a look around the barn. See if there's anything that might give us a clue. But don't walk even close to that piece of canvas in the middle of the floor. Not even close."

Chapter 95

Looking around the barn

This was a first for the two boys. Never before had Kate instructed them to don forensic gear—that is, latex gloves and booties. They were ecstatic.

Robby glanced over at Red. For a long moment, the boys just stared into each other's faces seeking silent communication.

Finally, Robby asked Kate, "Is it okay to sit down on the floor to put the booties on? Or should we go outside?"

"It's fine to sit down. We've already contaminated this as a crime scene. At this point, I have no idea what we might find. The gear is simply to minimize what we might introduce to it going forward.

"So, slip the gloves on first, and then just sit down and put the booties on. As you search the barn, don't move anything. Just look around and see if you find something that you think might be of interest. Keep your eyes open for anything that appears out of place. Like maybe someone set it down temporarily, intending to come back later and retrieve it. Or perhaps accidently dropped it.

"If you find trash, take a close look at it. Try not to disturb it, of course. Just scrutinize it. You've both got your cell phones. Take a lot of pictures. And if you see something that you think I might find interesting, give me a shout."

At first the boys proceeded as though glued to one another—Red generally leading the way.

But soon they separated. Robby spotted a small pile of what looked to him to be trash, and off he went.

Red poked around closer to the plane.

"Kate," Robby said loudly. "You might want to take a look at this. I've never seen anything like it."

Chapter 96
Trash pickin'

Kate was not eager to break away from the plane, but she had sent the boys on this mission, and so quickly made her way over to where Robby stood.

"Whatcha got for me?" she asked.

"I'm not sure what these are," he replied. "But they don't look like they belong in a barn, and they're just kinda sitting on top of this trash pile. And there's more of them on that bench … and over there on the floor. What do you think they are?"

Kate didn't need to think about it.

"Very interesting. Those are the throwaway tabs from an old Polaroid black-and-white camera. They are like the negatives."

"Never heard of them," Robby said. "Do you think they could be important? There are two right here, and several more over there," he said, pointing to another pile of litter a few feet away.

"Don't disturb them," she said. "We need to get them inside an evidence bag. There will most likely be fingerprints on them. I need you to head back to my car. In the back of it you will find my black leather bag. Inside of it are a dozen or so plastic evidence bags. Take your booties off first, but leave your gloves on. And bring me the bags. Here are the keys."

By that time, Red had walked over to where Robby had found the Polaroid tabs.

Kate read his puzzled expression and explained.

"Back in the '60s, this company called Polaroid developed a camera that basically contained its own darkroom. All the chemicals needed to develop a picture were contained in a special film pack. You merely pointed the camera at what you wanted to shoot and triggered the shutter.

"I remember all this because my dad had one of the earlier models.

"These things laying on the floor. A tab connected to them popped out of the camera after you had taken a picture. You gripped the tab and pulled the whole thing out. After a minute or so you could pull the picture off. And these are what you threw away—the negatives. People were always so eager to see the picture they had just taken that they would often simply toss useless tabs aside right where they were standing. That appears to be the case here."

Red texted, "No film?"

"Right," Kate said. "You pulled this tab, and after a minute you had a finished picture. You might want to Google that later. It was a fascinating process. It worked great. Might still be going strong except it got replaced by digital photography."

"Fingerprints?" Red texted.

"Possibly," Kate answered. "Actually it is likely that we will find prints on the tab. It could be degraded by now, but forensics will probably find something useful. Might even be DNA. Never know until you look for it.

"At any rate, this could be real evidence. We can easily find out who the plane belonged to. But these tabs might tell us who his friends were."

Red thought the whole concept of Polaroid photography to be fascinating. He continued to look around at the tabs strewn about. And that's when he found it. Leaning against an interior barn wall, with the blank side showing, was a slightly curved piece of paper. Carefully, he reached down and picked it up. It was a photograph of a woman.

Red immediately recognized the woman. It was Louise Breeze. She looked a lot like she did in the pictures he had seen in the old woman's photo albums. Except for one thing. In this shot she was standing in what appeared to be this same barn. The airplane was in the background, and she was posed with arms crossed in front of her, and with a pistol in each hand.

Red studied the picture—myriad thoughts racing through his mind. After a long minute, he walked over and silently handed the picture to Kate.

"What have we here?" she said as she received it.

"Oh my God!" she said in disbelief. "This just can't be!"

She stood there for an additional minute. One of the pistols was a Smith and Wesson .38 caliber snub-nosed revolver. The other looked like a .32 semi-automatic.

"Oh my God!"

Finally, she looked over at Red. He looked at her with an expression of utter disillusionment.

Robby, who had just returned with the evidence bags and was standing beside her, had observed the image and knew what it meant. He opened an evidence bag, and Kate dropped it in.

"Who do you suppose shot that picture?" he asked.

"Let's keep looking," Kate advised. "Carefully place these Polaroid negatives in evidence bags. Those that you find on the floor, label them as such. Those you find elsewhere, label them as well. Be as specific as possible."

"Can the pictures on these negatives be read?" Robby asked. "After all these years?"

"I really don't know," Kate said. "The crime lab can do some pretty fascinating stuff. I think that the newer Fuji instant film can be reprocessed, using certain chemicals. But I don't know about the old Polaroid.

There's probably something on it, but I don't know if it can be retrieved. It'd be great if we could find some other images."

Kate had no sooner uttered those words than Red made an excited sound.

"Whatcha got, Red?" Kate asked.

Red handed Kate a small stack of Polaroid pictures—five in all. Four of them were shots of just the plane. But one of them had a man in the foreground.

"I don't recognize him," she said, turning the picture over to see if there was writing on the back.

Red grabbed Robby, who was poking around several feet away, and led him by the arm to the pictures Kate was observing.

"We recognize that man," Robby said. "He was in a picture with the old lady—in one of her wedding pictures. Didn't she tell us that was her cousin?"

Red nodded.

"Boys," Kate said. "We've made some interesting discoveries today. But I need you to promise something for me. Do not, under any circumstance, ever discuss what we have found with another human being. Period. You need to forget you ever saw them. Too many people could get hurt if they are not handled in the proper way. Do you understand what I am telling you?"

Both boys nodded in agreement.

Kate then spread the pictures out on a nearby workbench, shot a close-up image of each of them with her cell phone, and sent them to Jack.

"See what you make of these," she texted. "We found them in a hangar on the old Breeze homestead, along with a vintage Cessna."

Chapter 97

I know that man!

Jack was having lunch with Allison Fulbright at a private club in Manhattan. He was describing to her the problems he had just experienced with the gang from Florida.

"They were the ones who killed Reg. They were after your gold."

"Doesn't surprise me one bit," she said. "I knew they were out there. And I knew they were trouble. Had Reg not cashed in some of that gold he *stole* from me, they would never have gone after him. He brought this on himself. It was not of my doing."

"I totally agree with you about that," Jack said. "But they just wouldn't give up. I don't know how much about this you've heard, but they kid-naped the boys, and one of their teenage friends. Had not Kate intervened at the last second, they would have killed all three of them."

"And I heard that Buddy was shot," Allison added. "By the same guys, I'd assume."

"I see you've been keeping yourself well informed."

"Of course I have," she replied. "That gold belongs to me—all one hundred million dollars of it. And I intend to get it back. In fact, I've fronted you with a considerable retainer to retrieve it for me.

"So, yes, I had operatives in the area keeping me briefed," she said. "I was more than a little concerned when you got shot. You might not have been aware of it, but I dispatched one of your old friends, Warren Cardfield, to make certain those fellows from Florida didn't get too close, just in case Reg had hidden the gold in that swamp."

"Really?" Jack retorted. "You actually sent old Tatts to check up on me?"

"Not to check up on you," Allison said. "I sent him up there to check up on my gold. I was concerned that it might have been buried in that swamp, and that the FBI would find it. Had that happened, I would never see a penny of it.

"Warren assured me that the gold your boys found had absolutely nothing to do with my gold."

"He should have looked me up," Jack said. "We could have had a beer together."

"He didn't want anything to do with you," Allison said with a smile. "He's scared shitless of you. In fact, he did not want to take this job. But I pretty much made him do it. I'll just say that he was very happy to see the Mackinac Bridge in his review mirror.

"He kept telling me that if he ran into you he knew you'd kill him."

"Well, that's probably an exaggeration," Jack said. "But I don't know. I had some people shooting at me, and I might have got a little nervous had I seen him in the shadows. I did take a bullet, you know—fairly serious, actually, as it turns out."

"I knew that," Allison said. "I was concerned that you might not be able to protect my gold, should it have come to that."

"You can rest assured that I will soon be delivering the gold to you."

"Well. I'll be damned. You've found it?"

"In a manner of speaking. I now know where it is."

"You do?" Allison asked. "Where?"

"In due time," Jack said. "I have to devise a plan to extricate it. When I do, I will see that it is delivered to you immediately."

"That's good news! Hell, that's the best news I've heard in a *very* long time. How'd you do it?"

"Reg's puzzle," Jack said. "The solution was in my pocket all the time. I just did not have the time or inclination to attack it properly. At least not until just recently."

"I had some of the top minds working on that puzzle—Alan Turing types. … Don't tell me it was that easy."

"It was exactly that easy," Jack said with a chuckle. "I popped it out of my pocket right before you walked in the club. I asked myself, *Just how would Reg think? Where would he hide it? And did he provide me a key to that puzzle?*"

"You're not going to tell me where it is, are you?"

"Absolutely not," Jack said. "But I will see that you get it back by the end of this summer, less my share."

"How confident are you about that?"

"Allison, need you ask?" Jack asked rhetorically.

His expression touched a nerve. And the fact that he had begun to read a text made Allison even more irritated.

"We're finished here," she said as she gathered up her things and stood. "I'll expect to see my property delivered within the month," she said as she tossed something in front of Jack.

"You might as well have this, Jack," she said. "It doesn't mean anything to me. Maybe it will to you."

Jack smiled and casually waved her off. He was more interested in what he was seeing on his cell phone, and he immediately called Kate.

"I recognize that guy!" Jack said loudly. "Actually, I don't recognize him, but the family resemblance is incontrovertible. That man has to be Zach Tanner's father!"

"Really?" Kate said. "The boys recalled Louise Breeze telling them that this man was her *cousin*. You and I both know what this has to mean."

"Don't discuss this with anyone," Jack told Kate. "We'll talk about it later. We need a game plan."

Jack sat there for several moments trying to digest the unsavory dessert Kate had just served him.

Finally, he picked up the little gift Allison had left him. The writing said, "Louise Breeze and Cousin—." There appeared to have originally been a name at the end, but it had been crossed off with a black permanent marker.

He turned it over.

It was a photograph of the same two people Kate had just sent him—Louise Breeze and a man. A man that Jack suspected to be the father of Zach Tanner.

"Tatts!" Jack said. "She got this from Tatts. How the hell did Tatts come by *this*?"

After a moment of deep thought, Jack leaned forward in his seat and ignited the image Allison had left for him with the flame of a floating centerpiece candle.

Chapter 98

Deviled eggs

That summer, Kate took her customary vacation time at the Sugar Island Resort. Everything had settled down considerably.

No longer did Jack have to be concerned about the Florida gang—the one responsible for Reg's murder. They were all dead—every last one of them. That was the state of existence Jack preferred for all his declared enemies.

He had not yet retrieved Allison's gold—that project he intended to get to after Labor Day, or mid-autumn at the latest. *She'll just have to be patient with me,* Jack reasoned. *After all, she has no other options.*

So, instead of engaging in work for any client, Jack had spent much of the summer taking care of personal business and doing things he really enjoyed. One of those things was cooking. Another one of his favorite pursuits was building and flying drones. The technology thrilled him. And the skill set he was developing seemed to fit his personality to a T.

"Could you help me out preparing for our celebration?" Kate asked her father.

She was planning to throw a major party. She had invited FBI Agent Thomas Snyder and his family; Millie Cox and her daughter; Sean and Stacy Bronson from Curtis; local historian, businessman, and Sugar Island resident, Lew Connelly and his wife Vanessa; Karin the Curtis librarian; and Sheriff Green, along with his entire Chippewa County Sheriff's Department. And, of course, the entire staff of the resort.

Sheriff Griffen did not make the list. Jack was not pleased that the sheriff had used him as the scapegoat to avoid the ire of SAC Dollar regarding the mishandling of the EMP weapon.

"What do you need me to do?" Jack asked, "Aside from preparing and cooking the whitefish?"

"I want to make a few dozen deviled eggs," Kate said. "And you're the only one who knows how to boil the eggs perfectly."

Jack thought about that for a moment and said, "Send Red and Robby in. I'll teach them how to do it."

Kate liked that idea, so she rounded them up and scooted them in.

"Okay, boys," Jack said. "I'm going to teach you something really fun today."

They immediately surmised that it would have something to do with building or flying drones, so they were excited.

"Today I am going to teach you how to make the perfect hard-boiled egg."

The boys looked at each other—their smiles disappeared.

"Don't be disappointed," Jack said, setting down the particularly large drone that he had been working on. "That's the way it is in life. Some days you eat the bear. And some days the bear eats you. This might not seem quite as intriguing as building a drone, but it's important information nonetheless."

The boys knew better than to protest too strongly. Besides, their experience taught them that "Uncle Jack" could make even the boiling of eggs an adventure. They were ready to learn.

"Take note," Jack said. "You must not miss one step, or you will have a mess on your hands. And Kate will not be happy.

"Are you ready?"

"Ready," Robby said.

"Okay, this is how you do it. First you take the raw eggs. In this case, I'd guess Kate wants about three dozen. So do four. You open all the cartons the night before and turn each egg over in the carton so that the fat end is up. If you haven't noticed, every egg has a fat end and a more pointed end. Fat ends up, on all the eggs.

"In some cases you cannot tell which end is the fat end. When that happens, place the egg in a bowl of water. You'll immediately see the more rounded end rise slightly.

"You dry the egg off, put it with the rest, and then slide all the cartons back in the refrigerator.

"The next day, you take a large safety pin and poke a good hole in the fat end of each egg. Poke it slightly less than three-eighths of an inch through the shell, and into the egg. That will allow the air sack to empty slowly as the egg heats up, instead of cracking the shell. ... Any deeper penetration and you will puncture the albumen—that's the part that becomes the white of the hard-boiled egg. It's not the end of the world if that happens, but it is not what you want, either.

"Now, you will need to heat up some water—quite a lot of water, for four dozen eggs. You should borrow two three-gallon coated stockpots from the kitchen. Fill each of them half full of water. Toss in maybe a teaspoon of salt—that is, unless all you have to work with is stainless steel. If that's the case, skip the salt.

"Bring the water to a good hard boil. Using a colander, carefully lower two dozen eggs into each. Try to slide them out of the colander all at the same time, so that they cook uniformly, and you don't break any shells prematurely.

"Keep the heat up so that they rapidly come back to a boil. Cook them for twelve minutes. At this elevation, and with the salt, if you boil them for thirteen, that's still okay.

"And then you pour the water and the eggs into a colander. Start spraying cold water on them immediately. Dump them back into the pot, still spraying them with cold water. Begin cracking the shells on the side of the pot until all the eggshells have been thoroughly fractured. Keep running cold water on them until the pot is two-thirds full.

"When I'm doing it, I will actually shake the eggs in the pot once I have removed the hot water, bouncing them off the sides of the pot. This will quickly crack the shells. Of course, you have to be applying cold water at the same time. And you do not want to shuffle them around too hard, or you will cause the hard-boiled eggs themselves to break open. You don't want that either.

"Peel the shells off while the eggs remain in the cold water, using the cold water in the pot to wash off clinging shards of eggshell. Put the cleaned eggs back in the colander to drain. Once all the eggs are peeled and in the colander, spray them one more time with cold water to wash them off. And then place them in a few one-gallon food storage bags, and stick them in the refrigerator until they've cooled enough to work with. Kate will determine when they are ready.

"If you do exactly as I have described, you will end up with forty-eight perfectly symmetrical, smooth eggs, ready for Kate to work her deviled-egg magic.

"If, however, you fail at any step along the way, the shells will stick to some of the eggs, or they will come out deformed, and she will have to mash them up for egg-salad sandwiches.

"One of the most critical steps is to hit the eggs with a lot of cold water *immediately* out of the boiling water and to see that all the shells are shattered immediately as well.

"Can you boys handle that?"

Red and Robby exchanged glances and smiled.

"Consider it done," Robby said. "We've watched you make them several times. We can handle it."

"Good!" Jack said. "Just what I wanted to hear. Once you've completed that project, come find me and we will play around with the drone I'm setting up."

That's really what the boys were interested in. They understood just how important it was to both Jack and Kate to have the eggs turn out perfectly. And they would definitely see to it that they performed their task properly. Because, if Kate was pleased with the eggs, Jack would be much more fun to be around than if Kate did not have a perfect product to work with.

Or, as Robby was fond of saying, "Ain't nobody happy if Kate ain't happy."

Chapter 99

The new drone

"How'd the eggs turn out?" Jack asked. He had already checked with Kate, so he knew in advance the answer to his question.

"Kate said they looked the same as when you did it," Robby said, exhibiting a bit of pride. "Except for one thing."

"Really?" Jack asked. "And what was that?"

"Kate said that when you prepare them, you eat a bunch before she gets them."

"And you guys restrained yourselves?"

"We thought about it. But we decided to wait until Kate was finished. They're much better then, anyway."

"I guess that makes you fellows our new official egg boilers."

"May we take a look at your new drone?" Robby said. "Kate's been telling us about it."

Jack led them back into his shop, which was located on the northern edge of the resort campus.

Once inside the shop, Jack unlocked a large wooden storage bin, slipped on a pair of latex gloves, and carefully lifted a huge, bright red drone out and set it on a workbench.

"Wow," Robby said. "That sure is beautiful. Looks like Ferrari Red. Have you flown it yet?"

"I've tested it a few times," Jack replied.

"It's larger than the one you had at Strangmoor," Robby said. "And not just a little larger—this one is huge by comparison. How big is it? It looks like maybe thirty-six inches across."

"It's forty-two inches," Jack said. "But it's the built-in electronics that makes it unique."

"Such as?" Robby asked.

"The cameras on this little gem will pan, tilt, and zoom," Jack said. "Plus, it can transmit real-time HD video images for up to two miles. The other drones I've used do not have cameras with those features.

"I can program it to reach a specified altitude up to three thousand feet, hover at whatever coordinates I tell it to, and it will hold that position to within inches. Provided, of course, those coordinates are not more than five miles away.

"It has a range of over five miles, but if I send it farther than that, there would be a chance it wouldn't make it back to me. So five miles would be its optimum retrieval performance.

"It is programmed to return to where it was launched if it believes that it is beginning to exceed its range, or run out of battery. That is, if my transmitter signal begins to grow weak. But that aspect could be overridden."

"You wouldn't want to do that, would you?" Robby asked. "You'd lose the drone."

"No, I wouldn't want that to happen."

"Cn we tst it?" Red showed his text to Jack.

"Of course," Jack said. "I thought you'd never ask."

For the next two hours, Angel, who with her mother was visiting at the resort, and the three "boys" put the drone through its paces, never exceeding an altitude of one thousand feet.

"We really have to be careful," Jack said. "Any higher and it could be a hazard to air traffic."

Robby, Red and Angel all took turns at the controls, while Jack's job was to switch out the battery every time it began to run low. Jack was insistent that all three teenagers, as well as himself, wear latex gloves while handling the drone.

"Well," Jack said, "we've exhausted all my charged batteries. I think it's time to put this puppy to bed."

"Thanks, Uncle Jack," Robby said. "That was a lot of fun."

"That goes for me too," Angel said. "I had an exquisitely fabulous time."

"Glad you enjoyed yourselves," Jack said. "I have to admit that I had a good time as well. You kids should see if Kate needs a hand. I'll clean up the chopper and get the batteries on the charger, and maybe we can do this again sometime."

"Cool," Robby said, "… Uncle Jack. Have you named it yet? You had a name for the drone that crashed in Strangmoor Bog. Do you have a name for this one?"

"I'm still thinking about that," Jack replied.

Chapter 100
The pilot

On the morning of the thirteenth day of the following September, Jack woke up early, even for him. It was a Sunday.

He went out to his shop, slipped on a pair of latex gloves, and applied a decal to the side of the big drone. It read, "Jack's Justice."

He checked to be certain that he had a fully charged battery—just one for this day. The drone's flight would be relatively short.

Lately, Jack took the two boys, and sometimes Angel, when he went out flying. Today was different. He was on a solo mission.

For a good number of days during the previous summer, Jack had arisen early and driven to a point on the east edge of Manistique Lake, north of Curtis. And there he fished.

But his activities were not limited to catching bluegills. There he also observed the construction and test flights of a Mercury STOL CH 750 taking place across the lake.

The Mercury STOL CH 750 is a two-seat light sport-utility kit plane. It is considered by bush pilots and other aeronautical enthusiasts to be a magnificent piece of flying equipment—especially considering that it is a kit plane. And when equipped with the amphibious float assembly, it becomes even more amazing.

The "STOL" part of the name means that it is designed for short take-offs and landings. Unlike some kit planes, the Mercury STOL CH 750 is a genuine bush plane. It is designed to thrive without benefit of airports.

Bush pilots are a special breed, best known for operating in the most inhospitable of environments, such as are found in northern Canada and Alaska. The planes they choose are smaller and lighter than what one would see in a hangar at a typical regional airport. Although many bush pilots do choose to store their planes in an airport facility, it's not necessary.

When not in the air, a plane such as the Mercury STOL CH 750 is equally at home in a large garage or a pole barn as it is in an airport hangar. And that was the way the object of Jack's attention was treated—it was housed in a pole barn on the shore of Manistique Lake.

The builder of the plane owned a nice piece of property on the west bank of the lake. He built an oversized pole barn close to the lake, with a nicely sloped approach to the water.

Initially, he used the barn to store his boats and a Monaco 44 SIG Premier. The boats he used in the summer time, and the motorhome he drove south for the winter.

Two years earlier, he had purchased a kit to build a Mercury plane with an amphibious float assembly. While his neighbors did not like the prospects of his continually using the lake as his own private "lake-based airport," they agreed to grant him a special dispensation for that one autumn to use the lake for testing on Sundays only, provided he operate within strict geographical limitations. He promised to relocate the plane after that time.

That would not be a problem for him, because he owned a small lake only a few miles west of Manistique Lake. It was just that his summer residence and facilities on the larger lake provided greater convenience during construction.

The pilot had begun testing his project in June. He would roll it to the water, float it, and run the engine, but he would not take off.

Beginning on the eleventh of July he flew the plane every Sunday morning. That date was not arbitrary—his agreement with the residents stipulated July eleventh as the earliest he would be allowed to take it up.

Because of the strict limitations placed on the pilot, he always adhered exactly to the same flight path until he reached an altitude greater than one thousand feet.

Once the pilot had satisfied himself with the success of the test flight, he would circle around and come back in for a landing—always using precisely the same flight path to touch down.

Also beginning in late June, Jack had chosen as his Sunday morning fishing spot a small public access pier directly across the lake from the pilot's pole barn. From there Jack could monitor the pilot's every move.

* * *

Jack had been quite busy as well, also putting the finishing touches on his flying machine—but special gear of a different sort.

Chapter 101
Jack's Justice

Jack looked across the lake, and then at his watch, "I've got twenty minutes," he said aloud. "Probably time to break out the bird."

He walked back to his Tahoe and drove to a secluded area nearby. He knew it would take him two minutes and twenty seconds to drive there because he had practiced the route a dozen times before. Once parked, he set the drone on top of his vehicle.

Jack had designed what could be described as a downrigger for his robotic wonder. This apparatus consisted of a high-quality, remotely activated spinning reel, which he had attached to the underside of the drone. It contained one hundred feet of thirty-pound fishing line.

He reeled out a few feet of the line and laid it on the hood.

He removed a Styrofoam cooler from the back of his Tahoe and set it on the hood as well.

* * *

Inside the barn on South Manistique Lake, two brothers were inspecting and logging the physical status of dozens of the component parts of their short takeoff and landing kit plane.

Whenever they found something not expected, they would correct the problem, and then enter the repair in their project logbook.

Early on, they had registered dozens of fixes—most were quite minor, but others could have posed serious problems had they been ignored. Lately, however, neither of them detected any issues whatsoever with the plane. That was a fact that, while it pleased the two men, did not lead them to grow careless. They were both experienced pilots, and they knew the importance of an abundance of caution.

Nevertheless, even though they continued to adhere to an enormous checklist before taking their plane up, their minds were beginning to look beyond the testing stage, to a time when their project could be put to practical use.

"How long before we can quit fiddling around with this bird and start getting serious with it?" the older brother asked.

"I still occasionally see Handler poking around in Curtis. I'm thinking he has a thing for that Slaughter woman—Karin Slaughter, the librarian. He seems to hang out a lot over there."

"And I've even seen him fishing in this lake," the older brother said. "I'll like it better when he decides to move along."

"Me too. I'm sick of having to pussyfoot around here, just trying to avoid that guy."

"Dad's starting to get a little antsy as well. Have you noticed?"

"I know he has, and it's pissing me off," the younger brother said. "It's not like he's contributing anything to the business anymore. He just lies in his hospital bed, flirts with his nurses, and bitches at us. Sometimes I just wish he'd die."

"That could certainly happen. Have you seen how he looks at that new nurse—Lilly? I think that's her first name. The poor old bastard's heart's gonna give out one of these days when she tucks the pillow under his head."

"We can hope. … Sometimes I'd like to take him up in a plane, and see just how well he can fly."

* * *

From inside the cooler that Jack had just set on the hood of his Tahoe, he carefully lifted out a round double-walled camo-painted ceramic device. The inner chamber contained eight ounces of C-4 explosive, with a battery-powered detonating device and a radio receiver.

The device's outer chamber contained approximately two hundred dime-to-quarter-sized pieces of glass. It was a bomb—one designed to shower everything within fifty feet with razor-sharp shrapnel made from shards of crushed blue whiskey bottles.

From an envelope stored in the cooler, Jack removed a twenty-foot length of one-hundred-pound test line. Connected to that piece of heavy-duty line every six inches was a 16/0 4 oz. weighted heavy-duty barbed treble hook. Earlier, Jack had used a diamond grinder to whet surgically sharp the point on each fishhook.

Jack then attached one end of the high-test line to the bomb, and the other end to the lighter-duty fishing line dangling from the reel that was affixed to the drone.

Using a pair of Leica Geovid 10x42 HD Binoculars, Jack took one long last look into the open door of the barn where the brothers stored their airplane.

"Well I'll be damned," he muttered when his eyes caught sight of a partially covered bright red drone. "Just as I suspected. That looks a lot like the one from the bog. … It won't be long now."

He looked at his watch again. *It's time,* he determined.

* * *

"I think your little buddy is just about ready to take his ride with us," the older brother said. "What do you think?"

"Bryce. You're referring to Bryce, I presume? Yeah, I think we've groomed him about as well as we have any of the others. He's totally hooked."

"What does that quitclaim deed you made him sign do for us exactly?"

the older brother asked.

"Not as much as I would like. But the nice thing is the 'first right of refusal' clause it contains. That puts us first in line to deal with little Bryce's soon-to-be widow for the rest of their property. And they're broke. He's gambled it all away.

"Once we pick up the rest of their land, we can develop our half-mile of lakefront. But we really need the access that only their property will provide. And we're only one plane ride away from getting our hands on it."

"Handler's our problem," the older brother chimed in. "Until he moves along, our hands are tied."

"I just wish I knew how much he knows about our little business," the younger brother said.

"I think he has his suspicions, but that's probably it. If he had any solid evidence, he'd have tried to nail us already."

"I'm not so sure about that. He's a cagey SOB. And he wants to protect the legacy of Dad's cousin. I think Handler knows that if he brings us down for those murders, the whole story about Dad and Amy Louise would come out, and that would tarnish the reputation of Millie and her daughter. Handler doesn't want to see them hurt. So, even if he thought he could make a case against us, he won't. We just have to wait him out."

"Yeah, you're probably right. I just hope he decides to crawl back in his hole and leave us alone … and soon."

* * *

Jack checked to be sure he had programmed the proper coordinates into the controller, and then double-checked to ensure that the GPS in the drone was working properly.

"Off you go," he said as he launched the forty-two-inch helicopter.

The large red drone, "Jack's Justice," at first climbed vertically. Once it had taken up the slack on the smaller line, it pulled the heavy line with the fishhooks along with it. And then, finally, the ceramic module lifted as well.

"Totally airborne," he said. "Time to get down to business."

He took the drone to a height of three hundred and thirty-seven feet—precisely ninety feet above the position he calculated the floatplane would reach at that exact point in its flight path. There he hovered the drone—waiting.

Using the onboard camera, Jack monitored the point on the shore where he anticipated the floatplane's takeoff. He was not disappointed.

Three minutes after the drone reached the appointed altitude the brothers began to rev up the engine of their plane. Jack checked his watch. He was still within the window of safety. If the plane delayed more than another ten minutes, Jack would choose to abort. But so far, everything was progressing according to plan.

Four minutes later, the plane began bouncing on the surface of the water. It appeared to be on the anticipated course.

Jack waited until the proper moment, and he activated the hydraulic arm, which released the fishing reel. If everything went according to his plan, the ceramic bomb would drop to a level ten to twelve feet below the height of the left wing of the floatplane.

The pilot was not expecting any surprises. The most dangerous parts of flying a floatplane, or any plane for that matter, are the takeoffs and landings. Once the floats lifted off the water, the pilot's major concern was in keeping the nose up and his speed increasing. On this Sunday morning, his only interest was in accomplishing those two things.

As a result, neither he nor his brother, who was riding beside him, even noticed the drone above or the gull-sized object directly ahead. So his wing clipped the hooked part of the line just as Jack had planned.

All that was needed was for one of the hooks to penetrate the relatively thin surface of the wing. However, three hooks dug into it, with the ceramic-covered bomb dangling only inches beneath.

And, just as Jack had anticipated, the thirty-pound test line broke almost immediately. He had been concerned that the shock of the wing striking the line might yank the drone out of the sky, but it did not.

Jack did notice that the view on the camera whipped around as the line broke, but the drone's electronics quickly righted the little chopper and returned it to the desired coordinates.

Because the bottom of the high wings were clearly visible from inside the plane, Jack assumed that the occupants of the plane would notice the dangling object, but he also knew that there was nothing they could do about it.

And since it would not dramatically affect the aerodynamics of the plane, he determined that they would simply adapt to it and continue to their intended altitude, turn around, and head back toward the lake.

As soon as Jack observed that the role of the drone was completed, he sent the signal for it to return to where he was waiting.

The course that the Mercury CH-750 took passed directly over where Jack was parked.

As it flew overhead, Jack visibly observed that the bomb had properly attached itself to the plane's wing.

Jack smiled as he read for one last time the words written on the rear of the fuselage—"Tanner's Folly."

Convinced all had gone as planned, Jack activated the detonator on the bomb.

The explosion took half of the left wing off, and ignited the ten-gallon fuel tank within it. The plane turned into a ball of fire as it spiraled to the earth.

When it hit, which was in the middle of a heavily wooded area less than a thousand yards from where Jack was parked, the fuel tank in the other wing also caught fire and exploded.

With thick black smoke rising above the tall pine trees, Jack's drone landed on his jacket, which he had placed on the ground beside his Tahoe. He packed it up and returned home to Sugar Island.

* * *

Isn't that the way it always is? Jack thought as he read the official NTSB report regarding the crash. *They attribute it to the "faulty construction of a kit plane." It never matters just how perfect a machine is, if it's a kit plane that crashes, it's always assumed that it was faulty equipment or improper assembly. But that's just fine with me. Let them keep thinking it was a mechanical failure. That way, they won't be tempted to investigate too deeply.*

* * *

Area news outlets reported the incident like this: "Zach Tanner, a forty-two-year-old lifelong resident of Curtis, and his forty-nine-year-old brother, Isaac Tanner Jr., were killed on September 13 in the crash of their homemade airplane. The kit plane broke apart and burst into flames above a wooded area just northwest of South Manistique Lake. The Tanner brothers are survived by their ailing ninety-two-year-old father, Isaac Tanner Sr., and their wives. Neither of the brothers left children."

Jack heard the report while having a cup of coffee with Lew Connolly in the back of Lew's bookstore. At his friend's request, Jack had delivered a framed picture of Red and Robby receiving their Geology Merit Badges. Lew wanted to hang the picture in his store as a conversation piece.

Jack could not help but smile at the news report regarding the death of the Tanner brothers. While no words escaped his mouth, one thought captivated his mind: *Now you can rest in peace, you restless souls of Strangmoor Bog.*

Chapter 102

All's well that ends well

After the deaths of Zach and Isaac Tanner Jr., Jack and Kate never again discussed the matter, or anything else having to do with Millie's mother or her illicit relationship with Isaac Tanner Sr., AKA "Cousin Joe."

Neither did they allow Robby and Red to broach the subject.

Millie and Angel continued to spend their summers at the Sugar Island Resort. Initially, Millie was inclined to buy property on the island, but Jack and Kate talked her out of it.

"Why would you want to do that?" they asked. "You've got a home right here with us and the boys whenever you want."

Millie did consult with Jack and Kate regarding establishing a foundation to help struggling families and businesses in the area, and she named them to head it up.

One of the first recipients of a grant from the Amy Louise Breeze Foundation was Sally Kinder, owner of Sally's Germfask Cafe. With the monies she was awarded she was able to pay off her mortgage, and no longer was she forced to do business at the whims of men like Zach Tanner.

Karin Slaughter received an Amy Louise Breeze grant to build a new wing on the library.

Jack and Kate sought out Andrea Cox, George Cox's widow, and from information she provided they tracked down Lesley Miller, the daughter of George and Andrea.

They found her living in Duluth with William Miller, her husband of twenty-five years, and their four young-adult and college-age children.

In the name of Amy Louise Breeze, they granted Lesley and her family five hundred thousand dollars.

Also, foundation money was used to airlift the tiny cabin that once belonged to Russell Cox and place it on a piece of property on M-77 just south of Germfask. There it was restored and endowed in perpetuity as a memorial to the brothers, Russell and George Cox.

As time progressed, many other deserving souls received grants in the name of the foundation. And while Millie never questioned Jack and Kate regarding those selected to receive the awards, she could not help but notice that a number of the recipients turned out to be the families of those whose lives were affected by the Strangmoor Bog murderers.

Oh, about the note that the old man placed in a cigar tube and tied around Buddy's neck. Between the water that soaked in when Buddy jumped in the lake on the way to Burnt Island, and the crushing of it by the bullet, the writing on the note was destroyed.

But most important of all, at least in the minds of Red and Robby, Buddy did make a full recovery.

* * *

And, in case you were wondering, greatly to ADA Beckett's chagrin, the case against Randall Croft was dropped. It seems that all of the witnesses against him had also dropped, in much the same manner as did Joe Tuco. Kate was disappointed at this turn of events, but not greatly surprised.

* * *

"Everything works out in the end. If it hasn't worked out yet, then it's not the end."

—Author Tracy McMillan (similar sentiments have been attributed to Steve Jobs)

Epilogue

The long-anticipated solution to the Inscrutable Puzzle

In *Jack and the New York Death Mask* (first book in the "Getting to Know Jack" series) Jack's close friend, Reginald (Reg) Black, left this bloody puzzle for Jack to find when he (Reg) was shot in a successful attempt to free Kate from her Eastern European abductors.

From the moment that Jack discovered it in Reg's blood-soaked trousers he knew it was significant, and that Reg had intended it for him to find. However, the first night that it was in his possession it was stolen from Jack's hotel room. The culprit: two of former First Lady Allison Fulbright's operatives.

Fortunately, Jack had copied the puzzle and taken an image of the original before the theft.

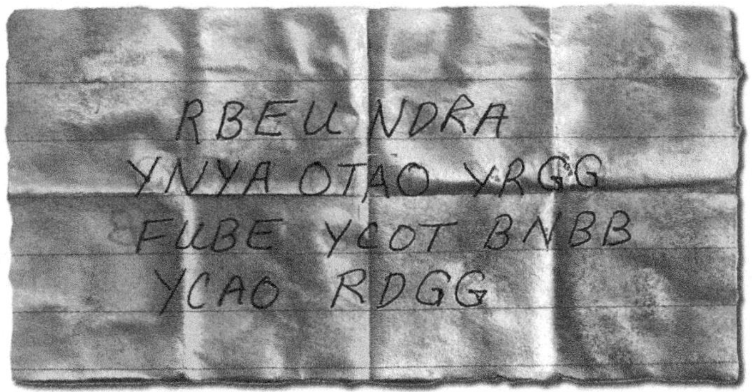

Both Jack and Allison were convinced that the puzzle, if correctly solved, would lead to the location where Reg had stashed the one hundred million dollars in gold that he had received from Allison as payment for the assassination of the sitting president, President Barry Butler.

However, instead of going through with the assassination, Reg worked with Jack to covertly thwart the attempt.

That left Allison without the fortune in gold that she had advanced Reg, a fact that did not sit well with her.

Simply put, she wanted her gold back.

Unfortunately (for her), Allison was unable to crack Reg's code and solve the puzzle.

Jack, on the other hand, had a better understanding of the way his friend thought, and eventually was able to solve the puzzle, retrieve the gold, and to return it to Allison.

That part of the story is explained in the chapters of this book. But the actual process Jack used to solve Reg's puzzle has been saved for the paragraphs of this epilogue.

First of all, Jack correctly assumed that his friend fully intended that the puzzle be solved. And not only that, Jack also believed that Reg had written the puzzle in such a way that its solution would elude the efforts of every attempt except for Jack's.

And, it turned out Reg was right.

Allison employed the best code crackers in the country, including the Alan Turing types, and even those who employed the most sophisticated software known to the CIA and Mossad. But none of these attempts was successful.

So difficult was the task of its solution that the puzzle quickly came to be known to Allison and her code crackers as the "Inscrutable Puzzle."

But Jack never regarded it as inscrutable. Jack knew that Reg would not have created a totally unsolvable puzzle. And so, when he finally decided to take a serious look at it, he found it quite simple to solve.

Because Jack was familiar with the way Reg thought, he assumed that the puzzle would be some form of a substitution puzzle—a cryptogram. Substitution puzzles are often regarded as simple cryptograms.

While he recognized that he might not be correct in that assumption, it at least afforded him a working hypothesis.

But, even though Jack suspected that it might be a cryptogram, his knowledge of the way Reg thought led him to assume two additional things about the puzzle: first, it would be based on some sort of readily available keyword, and two, that his friend would toss in one or more "monkey wrenches."

When it involves deciphering puzzles, cryptograms in particular, a monkey wrench could be anything that the puzzler might include that would discourage computer attempts, as well as those of a lesser Alan Turing.

Jack recalled that on the opposite side of the piece of paper upon which the original puzzle was written contained the words "Conrad Courtyard Hotel."

So, Jack suspected that there was a fair chance that the keyword for this puzzle was one of a few combinations:

CONRAD
CONRADCOURTYARD
CONRADCOURTYARDHOTEL

Obviously, the first is too short. And he didn't like the third possibility because it seemed too long.

That meant a good place to start would be CONRADCOURTYARD.

Eliminating the letters used more than once leaves CONRADUTY.

And then picking up with the alphabet after "Y" he came up with BEFGHIJKLMPQSVWXZ.

Of course, Jack realized that this approach might not be correct, but he had to start with something, and that seemed as logical a place as any other.

The original puzzle was RBEU NDRA YNYA OTAO YRGG FUBE YCOT BNBB YCAO RDGG

Immediately Jack observed that a large number of the letters in his proposed keyword were actually used in the puzzle. That suggested that he might have chosen the correct keyword.

However, when he started to plug letters in, it did not look right to him. The fact that so many of the letters in the cryptogram were repeated suggested that he was dealing with a series, or a multiple series, of numbers. Not letters.

So, working with that theory, he came up with the number 40 for the first two numbers of the series.

But then he was stuck, because the third character in the puzzle was an "E." Because there was no "E" in the keyword, and because there were only ten numbers with which to deal, therefore, the "E" must mean something else.

There must be some simple, logical reason for the "E" and also the "F", Jack concluded. *I must apply logic.*

"What are numbers used for?" Jack asked himself out loud. "Particularly such a large quantity of numbers?"

He concluded that since this puzzle was most likely some sort of treasure map, one logical working theory would be that Reg was communicating a set of GPS coordinates. While that approach might not prove correct, it seemed reasonable for Jack to chase the dog down that alley. So that's what he did.

Applying that keyword to a series of numbers (not letters), Jack created a schema that looked like this:

C 1
O 2
N 3
R 4
A 5
D 6
U 7
T 8
Y 9
B 0
E (.)
F (-)

All characters following "F" Jack wrote off as "Nulls." A null signifies nothing—it is nothing more than a place filler and can be added anywhere in a cryptogram.

This made total sense to Jack because he knew that coordinates would have a (.) and a (-) in them as well as numbers. So, "E" could be a (.), and "F" a (-). It could have been the other way around, but this order made more sense to him.

Applying CONRADUTYBEF as a working keyword to a series of numbers (not letters), and more specifically, coordinates, Jack came up with a preliminary solution that looked like this: 40.736459395285294(,)-70.91280300915246.

Jack would have liked to have had a symbol for the comma, but could appreciate Reg's choosing to end the first series with nulls, as opposed to the comma.

They looked pretty good to Jack as GPS coordinates—initially. But when he plugged them in he discovered that these coordinates did not exist.

The problem, Jack assumed, could have been anywhere. Perhaps these were not GPS coordinates, he thought. Or maybe Reg was not even dealing with numbers. Both were possibilities.

But, Jack still liked the direction he had chosen, so he proceeded to follow that line of thinking.

He then made another assumption. He guessed the greatest likelihood was that an experienced puzzle-maker such as Reg would want to make his puzzle reasonably simple to solve, but not necessarily easy.

To produce a higher level of difficulty, he would toss in an intentional problem—such as the before-mentioned monkey wrench.

The first set of numbers looked pretty good to Jack, so he turned his attention to the second. Jack thought that the "-70" appeared highly suspect, and, therefore, might have been the perfect place for Reg to have thrown in an anomaly.

But, Jack assumed that even in so doing, Reg would apply some logic—even with an intentional glitch. And, when he looked at it logically, the "0" seemed the perfect place to toss in that monkey wrench.

So, because the "0" is the third character in the second set of numbers (if viewed as coordinates), when Jack substituted a "3" for that "0" he came up with the following set:

40.736459395285294,-73.91280300915246

"Now, that looks more like it!" he said.

And when he Googled those coordinates, he came up with a gravesite in Calvary Cemetery—a plot right next to where Reg was buried!

"Eureka!" he nearly shouted.

Jack sat back in his seat and sighed deeply. He knew he had just solved Reg's puzzle.

A few months later Jack arranged to have the gravesite dug up. There he found and recovered the gold. Later he returned the treasure to Allison. ... And, of course, he collected the rest of his very substantial finder's fee.

* * *

Author's note: If you did not solve this puzzle, don't worry—no one else did either. There will be more puzzles in future Jack Handler books. Some of them will be easier. I fully intended to make this one very arduous, if not impossible. And it looks like I succeeded. Thanks for your efforts.

I hope to meet up with you again in future Jack Handler books.

Cast of Main Characters in the Getting to Know Jack Series

(Characters are listed in a quasi-chronological order.)

Jack:

Jack is a good man, in his way. While it is true that he occasionally kills people, it can be argued that most (if not all) of his targets needed killing. Occasionally a somewhat sympathetic figure comes between Jack and his goal. When that happens, Jack's goal comes first. I think the word that best sums up Jack's persona might be "expeditor." He is outcome driven—he makes things turn out the way he wants them to turn out.

For instance, if you were a single mom and a bully was stealing your kid's lunch money, you could send "Uncle Jack" to school with little Billy. Uncle Jack would have a *talk* with the teachers and the principal. With Jack's help, the problem would be solved. But I would not recommend that you ask him how he accomplished it. You might not like what he tells you—if he even responds.

Jack is faithful to his friends and a great father to his daughter. He is also a dangerous and tenacious adversary when situations require it.

Jack Handler began his career as a law enforcement officer. He married a beautiful woman (Beth) of Greek descent while working as a police officer in Chicago. She was a concert violinist and the love of his life. If you were to ask Jack about it, he would quickly tell you he married above himself. So, when she was killed by bullets intended for him, he admittedly grew bitter. Kate, their daughter, was just learning to walk when her mother was gunned down.

As a single father, Jack soon found that he needed to make more money than his job as a police officer paid. So he went back to college and obtained a degree in criminal justice. Soon he was promoted to the level of sergeant in the Chicago Police Homicide Division.

With the help of a friend, he then discovered that there was much more money to be earned in the private sector. At first he began moonlighting on private security jobs. Immediate success led him to take an early retirement and attain his private investigator license.

Because of his special talents (obtained as a former Army Ranger) and his intense dedication to problem solving, Jack's services became highly sought after. While he did take on some of the more sketchy clients, he never accepted a project simply on the basis of financial gain—he always sought out the moral high ground. Unfortunately, sometimes that moral high ground morphed into quicksand.

Jack is now pushing sixty (from the downward side) and he has all the physical ailments common to a man of that age. While it is true that he remains in amazing physical condition, of late he has begun to sense his limitations.

His biggest concern recently has been an impending IRS audit. While he isn't totally confident that it will turn out okay, he remains optimistic.

His problems stem from the purchase of half-interest in a bar in Chicago two decades earlier. His partner was one of his oldest and most trusted friends.

The principal reason he considered the investment in the first place was to create a cover for his private security business.

Many, if not most, of his clients insisted on paying him in cash or with some other untraceable commodity. At first he tried getting rid of the cash by paying all of his bills with it. But even though he meticulously avoided credit cards and checks, the cash continued to accumulate.

It wasn't that he was in any sense averse to paying his fair share of taxes. The problem was that if he did deposit the cash into a checking account, and subsequently included it in his filings, he would then at some point be required to explain where it had come from.

He needed an acceptable method of laundering, and his buddy's bar seemed perfect.

But it did not work out as planned. Four years ago the IRS decided to audit the bar, which consequently exposed his records into scrutiny.

Jack consulted with one of his old customers, a disbarred attorney/CPA, to see if this shady character could get the books straightened out enough for Jack to survive the audit and avoid federal prison.

The accountant knew exactly how Jack earned his money and that the sale of a few bottles of Jack Daniels had little to do with it.

Even though his business partner and the CPA talked a good game about legitimacy, Jack still agonized when thoughts of the audit stormed through his mind.

Kate:

Kate, Jack's daughter and a New York homicide detective, is introduced early and often in this series. Kate is beautiful. She has her mother's olive complexion and green eyes. Her trim five-foot-eight frame, with her long auburn hair falling nicely on her broad shoulders, would seem more at home on the runway than in an interrogation room. But Kate is a seasoned New York homicide detective. In fact, she is thought by many to be on the fast track to the top—thanks in part to the unwavering support of her soon-to-retire boss, Captain Spencer.

Of course, her career was not hindered by her background in law. Graduating Summa Cum Laude from Notre Dame at the age of twenty-one, she went on to Notre Dame Law School. She passed the Illinois Bar Exam immediately upon receiving her JD, and accepted a position at one of Chicago's most prestigious criminal law firms. While her future looked bright as a courtroom attorney, she hated defending "sleazebags."

One Saturday morning she called her father and invited him to meet her at what she knew to be the coffee house he most fancied. It was there, over a couple espressos, that she asked him what he thought about her taking a position with the New York Police Department. She was shocked when he immediately gave his blessing. "Kitty," he said, "you're a smart girl. I totally trust your judgment. You have to go where your heart leads. Just promise me one thing. Guarantee me that you will put me up whenever I want to visit. After all, you are my favorite daughter."

To this Kate replied with a chuckle, "Dad, I'm your only daughter. And you will always be welcome."

In *Murder on Sugar Island (Sugar)*, Jack and Kate team up to solve the murder of Alex Garos, Jack's brother-in-law. This book takes place on Sugar Island, which is located in the northern part of Michigan's Upper Peninsula (just east of Sault Ste. Marie, MI).

Because Kate was Garos' only blood relative living in the U.S., he named her in his will to inherit all of his estate. This included one of the most prestigious pieces of real estate on the island—the Sugar Island Resort.

Reg:

In *Jack and the New York Death Mask (Death Mask)* Jack is recruited by his best friend, Reg (Reginald Black), to do a job without either man having any knowledge as to what that job might entail. Jack, out of loyalty to his friend, accepted the offer. The contract was ostensibly to assassinate a sitting president. However, instead of assisting the plot, Jack and Reg worked to thwart it. Most of this story takes place in New York City, but there are scenes in DC, Chicago, and Upstate New York. Reg is frequently mentioned throughout the series, as are Pam Black, and Allison Fulbright. Pam Black is Reg's wife (he was shot at the end of *Death Mask*), and Allison is a former first lady. It was Allison who contracted Reg and Jack to assassinate the sitting president.

Allison:

Allison is a former first lady (with presidential aspirations of her own), and Jack's primary antagonist throughout the series. She fears him enough not to do him or his family physical harm, but she and Jack are not friends. She seems to poke her nose into Jack's business just enough to be a major annoyance.

Roger Minsk:

Roger is a member of the Secret Service, and a very good friend to Jack. Roger is also friendly with Bob Fulbright, Allison's husband, and a former president.

Red:

This main character is introduced in *Sugar.* Red is a redheaded thirteen-year-old boy who, besides being orphaned, cannot speak. It turned out that Red was actually the love child of Alex (Jack's brother-in-law) and his office manager. So, Alex not only leaves his Sugar Island resort to Kate, he also leaves his Sugar Island son for her to care for.

Red has a number of outstanding characteristics, first and foremost among them—his innate ability to take care of himself in all situations. When his mother and her husband were killed in a fire, Red chose to live on his own instead of submitting to placement in foster care. During the warmer months, he lived in a hut he had pieced together from parts of abandoned homes, barns, and cottages, and he worked at Garos' resort on Sugar Island. In the winter, he would take up residence in empty fishing cottages along the river.

Red's second outstanding characteristic is his loyalty. When put to the test, Red would rather sacrifice his life than see his friends hurt. In *Sugar*, Red works together with Jack and Kate to solve the mystery behind the killing of Jack's brother-in-law (and Red's biological father) Alex Garos.

The third thing about Red that makes him stand out is his inability to speak. As the result of a traumatic event in his life, his voice box was damaged, resulting in his disability. Before Jack and Kate entered his life, Red communicated only through an improvised sign system, and various grunts.

When Kate introduced him to a cell phone and texting, Red's life changed dramatically.

Robby:

Robby is Red's best friend. When his parents are murdered, Robby moves into the Handler home and becomes a "brother" to Red.

Buddy:

Buddy is Red's Golden Retriever.

Bill Green:

One other character of significance introduced in *Sugar* is Bill Green, the knowledgeable police officer who first appears in Joey's coffee shop. He also assumes a major role in subsequent books of the series, after he becomes sheriff of Chippewa County.

Captain Spencer:

Captain Spencer is Kate's boss in New York. The captain has been planning his retirement for a long time, but has not yet been able to pull the trigger. Kate is his protégé, and he almost seems to fear leaving the department until her career is fully developed.

Paul Martin and Jill Talbot:

Two new characters do emerge in *Sugar Island Girl, Missing in Paris (Missing).* They are Paul Martin and Jill Talbot. They do not appear in subsequent stories.

Legend:

Legend is one of the main characters in the sixth book of the series, *Wealthy Street Murders (Wealthy Street)*. In this story, Jack and Kate work with Red, Robby, and Legend to solve a series of murders.

Mrs. Fletcher:

Mrs. Fletcher, one of the caretakers at Kate's resort on Sugar Island, progressively plays a more prominent role as an occasional care-provider for the two boys. And, of course, she becomes embroiled in the intrigue.

Sheriff Griffen:

The sheriff first appears in *Murders in Strangmoor Bog (Strangmoor).* He is sheriff of Schoolcraft County, which includes Strangmoor Bog, and Seney Wildlife Preserve.

Angel and her mother Millie:

In *Strangmoor*, the seventh and last book in the "Getting to know Jack" series, two new main characters are introduced: Angel and Millie Cox.

Angel, a precocious fun-loving redhead (with a penchant for using big words), quickly melts the hearts of Red and Robby, and becomes an integral part of the Handler saga. There's a pretty good chance we will see Angel and Millie in the next series as well.

That new series is called "Jack's Justice."

Made in the USA
Columbia, SC
08 August 2018